Michael E. Lloyd

MISSING EMILIE

Originally published during 2012
in *Bewildering Stories* magazine
(www.bewilderingstories.com)

Cover design by the author

Other novels by Michael E. Lloyd:

Observation One: Singing of Promises
Observation Two: Standing Divided
Observation Three: Changing Hearts
Donna's Men

ISBN 978-1-326-47601-4

First Print Edition 2015

Acknowledgements

With thanks as always to my trusty first readers, to Jerry Wright and Don Webb of *Bewildering Stories* for their never-ending support, to the people and places of *la belle France*, and to all who made the Sixties what they were.

MEL
Cambridge, England

Book I

SELF ABOVE ALL

Something in the Air

Baumettes Prison, Marseilles, France

Monday 27 December 1965

<u>Weekly Report on Prisoner Arthur Narone</u>

Arthur Narone is still behaving well, though he continues to avoid almost all contact with other inmates.

He has once again earned no negative conduct points. I suggest that from 1 January 1966 his Library Time allowance could safely be increased by a further one hour per day, and that we should agree to his recent request for the use of one additional library pencil and notepad per week.

Narone persists in his habit of kneeling in the corner of his cell each Sunday evening and writing a new number on a low section of the wall. He still refuses to explain the significance of this increasing series, which yesterday rose to 348. As reported before, we have never pressed him hard on his strange ritual: we assume that it holds some positive, perhaps religious significance for him, and that it is best to allow it to continue.

R.B. (Senior Warder 42284, Team F), 27 Dec 1965

<u>Weekly Report on Prisoner Bertrand Irvoise</u>

The behaviour of Bertrand Irvoise has changed steadily over the past four weeks, as previously reported, and more dramatically during the recent days of Christmas. He has now withdrawn from almost all contact with his usual social circle. Today he asked to be granted a long period of private Chapel meditation each day, and he desires a meeting with the Padre at the earliest opportunity. These latest, thoughtfully made requests are definitely not in character for Irvoise, and this situation now clearly requires the attention of a Senior Warder.

P.F. (Warder 42771, Team D), 27 Dec 1965

* * *

'Allô!'

'Inspector Hardy?'

'Speaking.'

'This is Fabius Delacroix.'

'Ah, good morning, Governor. I trust you had a pleasant Christmas?'

'Pleasant enough, Inspector.'

'Good. So, you have some news for me?'

'I do. Narone is still acting quite normally. And Irvoise appears to have played his part to perfection.'

'Excellent! So will you now put the wheels in motion?'

'I will.'

'Thank you, Governor. And I wish you a very Happy New Year.'

'And the same to you, Inspector. *Au revoir.*'

Nice Little Earner

Marseilles

Six years earlier: Late September 1959

'Is that the Island Bar?'
   'Yeah.'
   'I need to speak to Paul Ruford.'
   'Don't know if he's in this evening ...'
   'He is.'
   'Who's calling?'
   'Tell him it's a cousin of his. I have some urgent family news.'
   'Hold on ....'

'*Allô!* Who is this? Robert or Georges?'
   'Neither. And I wouldn't fall for that old trick! I'm afraid I can't tell you my real name, Monsieur Ruford, but you may call me Xérus. And this is not about family. I do however have an *extremely* attractive proposition for you ...'
   'How did you know I was in here?'
   'I'm sorry, what did you say?'
   'How did you know I was in here??'
   'I followed you from your apartment. Look, can you get them to turn that music down?'
   'But it's *Mona Lisa.*'
   'So?'
   'So I like it. I'll just speak a bit louder. But why the hell should I listen to you anyway, whoever you are?'

'Because I have selected you very carefully, Paul, and I can help you make a lot of money very fast and very easily ...'

'Ah. OK, keep talking.'

'Right. Well, I lived in Marseilles some years ago, and I made a lot of very useful contacts there, if you know what I mean. So I knew all the rumours of your many talents and achievements, and I knew exactly what you looked like. And today it was easy enough to establish your home address, and of course I know that right now you're drinking in the Island Bar ...'

'Are you trying to intimidate me?'

'Not at all. As I said, I'm trying to help you make a lot of quick money. Now, I presently work in a bank in the centre of Nice. And I'd like you to take on the job of planning and leading a robbery there, on a date to be advised, in exactly the manner I shall prescribe.'

'What?? You must be out of ...'

Zoooom! Zoooooom! Zooooooooom!

'Bloody Vespas! Sorry, what were you about to say, Paul?'

'It doesn't matter. But where the hell *are* you?'

'In a public call box, not too far away.'

'OK. Get on with it, then ...'

'Thank you. So, you will be the lynchpin of the operation. Your team will earn approximately sixteen million Old Francs in used notes from the haul, and you'll be in charge of distributing it. So you'll be able to take a much bigger cut than the rest of them put together, won't you?'

'I'm still listening ...'

'Good. You will recruit the team yourself. Make it as small as you can. I don't want to know any of their names. Ever. And none of them should already know you in person – or each other. They should not meet up until the hour of the robbery. And you should split up as soon as possible afterwards, and make no further effort to contact each other. Ever.'

'That's all completely ridiculous!'

'No it isn't, Paul. Keep listening. If you stick with those ground rules, then if any of the others end up getting caught, they won't be able to reveal the identities of their team-mates, *or* of you and me. Our risks will be minimal.'

'Hah! How exactly do you plan to keep me interested in this stupid idea for at least another two minutes, Monsieur Xérus?'

'That's just what I expected you to ask, Paul. Your reputation is clearly well deserved.

'I will give you an immediate personal cash advance of an additional one million Old Francs, also in used notes, and a substantial further amount for your planning and operational expenses. And since you will actually be making off with the *entire* proceeds of the robbery, and then taking the share I have promised and only delivering the rest to me a little later, I'd say I was also giving you a great deal of my trust as well, wouldn't you?'

'Well, it certainly sounds that way ...'

'Good. Now, there is one more rule I need you to agree to. I shall control *all* future communications between us. You will never make any attempt to identify me or contact me directly, or the whole business will be abandoned and I shall then use some of the interesting information I have about you to make your life very difficult ...'

'I knew you were threatening me all along ...'

'Oh, please get real, young man. I'm not willing to deal with baby villains. Are you going to say "Yes" unconditionally, here and now, or do you want to think about it for a couple of hours?'

'I *have* been thinking about it. Do you seriously expect a team of people who've never even met each other to carry out a major armed robbery? With no rehearsals? It *is* ridiculous. And crazy.'

'Simple can be beautiful, Paul. And safest, *enfin*. And it would be your job to make it work. But perhaps you don't want the money or your liberty, in which case ...'

'Pah! OK, I can't believe I'm saying this, but maybe it's just crazy enough. I'll think about it. I'll need more than two hours, though ...'

'Too bad. That's all you're getting. I'll phone you at the call box on the corner of Rue Berlioz and Cours Lieutaud at exactly ten o'clock. Don't write that down. Never write anything down. And I'll want a definite "Yes" or "No" on the spot. If it's "No" – well, you'll suddenly have a lot of other things to start worrying about. But if it's "Yes" then we'll be sworn partners, I'll give you some more details, and you'll be able to pick up your cash advances this evening. Yes, this evening, Paul. So think about it very carefully. Until ten o'clock ...'

So who is this Xérus? Is he just stringing me along, or does he really work in a bank?

Well, maybe he does ...

Is he some junior clerk? He didn't sound very young. And he says he has over a million *balles* to hand out tonight!! Show me a bank clerk who can offer to do that! On the other hand, perhaps he has some rich friends pulling his own strings ...

'Hey Vic, can't you turn that bloody music down?'

'But it's *Mona Lisa*, Paul. I thought you'd like to hear it again ...'

'No, I wouldn't! Turn it down!'

'All right, all right ...'

Perhaps he's a security guard gone native? Pah! He'd have even less money to throw around in advances. No chance. And anyway he sounds far too well informed.

Or maybe he's the manager? Stinking rich and wants to get even richer. Hah! Can't see one of them wanting to go down in history as the guy whose precious bank got robbed. Stupid idea.

'Only sixteen, only sixteen ...'

Sixteen million *balles*??

Gotta get out of here.

'You OK, Paul? Bad news?'

'Not really, Vic. Just can't hear myself think. Going for a little walk. Seeya later.'

'Sure.'

Some guy in the middle ranks, then? Knows a bit about how things work. Hey, maybe he's even the boyfriend of some *woman* in the middle ranks! Nice idea, Paulie ...

Merde! What's the point of all this guessing? Xérus wouldn't tell me even if I asked him straight out.

You go where you gotta go, right?

So why should he trust me to play along and deliver? Apart from making those vague threats? They're empty threats anyway, 'cos he can't pin a thing on me from any of my previous little jobs.

Can he?

Suppose I just walked off with his advance? Or talked? Or dropped out halfway through, or exposed his bank out of spite, or whatever?

Suppose we disappeared with *all* the money after the job and he ended up with nothing? Hey, nice idea, actually ...

So is he plain stupid, or does he have some power base I don't know about yet?

Better assume he's not stupid. But I still don't feel there's any real pressure on me to keep my word if I do agree to do the job.

And he wants me to make a decision tonight! Do I actually have any choice?

Dammit!

Hang on. Maybe this is some sort of institutional trap to catch me and a few other guys red-handed? A clever new collaboration between the police and the banks. Well, it might be. But it might be *anything*, dammit!

Gotta take it at face value. Gotta just decide which answer is more risky ...

* * *

'*Allô!*'

'It's Xérus.'

'Where are you now?'

'Still not far away.'

'In another phone box?'

'No.'

'Can you see me?'

'How did you guess? But don't move or turn around – just keep talking normally, OK?'

'OK.'

'So, the answer's "Yes"?'

'I suppose so.'

'Good. You won't be changing your mind, Paul. And you'll receive your advance in a few minutes.'

'How?'

'I'll come to that. And by the way, just call me "X" in future, OK? Much more efficient.'

'OK.'

'Now, you and I are going to take advantage of the upcoming change from Old to New Francs.'

'Hah! A lot of people have been talking about the possibilities that presents.'

'But we're not just going to talk about it, Paul ...

'You will probably be carrying out the robbery in late November, a few weeks before the first public issue of the Henri IV 50 New Franc notes in January next year. We wouldn't want to leave it until after that, because then the haul might include lots of those brand new notes, and they could be much more easily noticed and traced.

'No, the proceeds will include *only* the three current types of 5000 Old Franc note – the *Terre et Mer* design from 1950, and last year's Henri IV design, and the Henri IV presently being over-printed as a 50 New Franc note.'

'I saw one of those surcharged notes for the first time last week.'

'Right. Now, it will be many years before those old high-value notes go out of currency. But the public always gets nervous about change, and people are starting to deposit more and more of them in their bank accounts – they've been keeping them in their traditional under-the-mattress savings! – in the run-up to the brand new issue in January. So there are likely to be very large amounts of extra cash floating around the banks at the close of certain days towards the end of this year.

'But there should be a lot of the much newer Henri IV notes in your haul, because people are far more likely to have acquired *them* recently than the old *Terre et Mer* ones, which many banks are no longer re-circulating. And this is good, Paul, because the lower the serial number on such a high-denomination old note, the greater its purchasing power was when it was first procured, so the more "dubious" it is, if you get my drift ...'

'You mean it would be riskier to try and use or exchange it today – especially after a robbery!'

'Exactly. But as I say, I don't expect many of those to turn up in the haul.'

'That sounds reasonable. So what do you expect me to do now?'

'I'm sorry, Paul, that big truck drowned you out ...'

'What do you expect me to do now?'

'I want you to make a broad plan and then build your team over the next three weeks. And you need only three more important bits of information from me, for now. First, you must obviously include a driver who knows the streets of central Nice very well indeed.

Second, you'll be entering through the front door, while the bank is still open, and you won't need to go beyond the main hall. That's where the cash will be held. And third, you'll need just one good-sized holdall. More on that later.'

'All right. But where *is* the bank?'

'I'm not going to tell you that yet. Just get yourselves organised so that you can pull off the job anywhere in the city. Then I'll need you to convince me your plan will work. When I'm satisfied, I'll tell you the exact location, and you can reconnoitre it fully and finalise all the details.'

'I don't like this, X. You're asking me to work almost completely blind here.'

'Quite so. That keeps us all as safe as possible for now.'

'Huh!'

'Anyway, I'm not giving you the option. You have my ground rules, and the information you need at this stage and no more. I'm leaving you to set everything up exactly as you wish. You'll have at least seven weeks from now until the day of the robbery, and maybe as many as ten or eleven. I shan't be letting you know the actual date until the evening before.'

'What!!'

'But that's all well into the future, Paul. For now, just get the team together and memorise your plan. And you must be back in Marseilles, at the call box at the junction of Rue de Rome and Rue Armeny, at eight o'clock on the evening of Sunday the eighteenth of October. Got that?'

'Yeah.'

'And if that phone isn't working, go straight to the box one block south at Boulevard Paul Peytral.'

'OK.'

'And remember ...'

'I know, I know. "Don't write any of that down." Correct?'

'Yes. It's very good to be dealing with another professional, Paul.'

'Hah! But now you just listen to me for a change, Monsieur Bloody X. You seem to know all about me, but I have no idea who you are, hiding behind your clever little nicknames. I don't think that's a good way for professionals to work together ...'

'Oh dear. I must seem either very stupid or very trusting. After all, what's to stop you double-crossing me in any number of ways, at any time?'

'Well, not a lot, I reckon ...'

'Ah. Well actually, Paul, I do seem to remember hearing a little whisper, long ago, that Ruford is not your real name ...'

'What?? Who the hell told you that?'

'Afraid it's completely slipped my mind. Now, do you really want to discuss the subject any further?'

'You little ...'

'Yes, Paul?'

'Nah, forget it.'

'Good. Because I'd much rather demonstrate my gratitude than argue with you like this or start talking to those who *might* want to take it further. You see the litter bin on the pavement, five metres up the street?'

'Yeah.'

'Right. There's nobody waiting to use your call box, so don't hang up. Go to the bin, lift up the newspaper, take out the envelope underneath it, and come straight back to the phone.'

'OK.'

'I'm back.'

'I know. Look inside the envelope.'

'OK ...'

'Satisfied?'

'Yeah. More than satisfied, X.'

'That's very good, partner. Now pocket it, put the phone down, get the hell out of there, and start doing some real thinking.'

* * *

'*Un express.*'

'*Oui, monsieur.*'

I wonder if Xérus followed me home last night?

Pah!

Keep it small, he said. And simple.

Huh! If the team isn't allowed to work together at all before the job, that's exactly how it'll have to be. And I'd better follow his rules to the letter, at least for now. He's probably still watching me like a hawk.

But he can't do that for long, of course, if he really does work in that bank. He'll need to get back to Nice tonight, ready for another bourgeois Monday morning.

Unless he's on holiday in Marseilles for who knows how long?

Oh, forget him, for heaven's sake! He's out of my control!

So, how many men will I need? Well, I'll do all the planning and provisioning myself, and I'll lead on the day. I'll need a driver, of course, and he can arrange the wheels. Should he go in with me? No, he must stay in the car with the engine running. Can't risk any problems there. So I'll also need a solid guy as the muscle watching my back.

Three men, minimum. That's a really small team! Very exposed to a single error or a bit of bad luck. But the more I bring in, the more complex the communications. Before, during and after, but especially before. And the more chance of springing leaks too.

No, three has to be just right.

'Voilà, monsieur.'

'Merci, garçon.'

Now, I'll need to disappear from here soon, with a simple cover story for Vic and the other guys. Unexpected family business, of course – Xérus already set that up for me in his first phone call! Very clever. And I'll need somewhere cheap and out-of-the-way to stay in Nice. There'll be a side benefit, of course. It'll be so good to get away from this bloody autumn Mistral for once. It's really been wearing me down this year.

I don't want anyone else from Marseilles involved. The driver has to know Nice very well anyway, as Xérus said, so I'll need to do some risky local digging for him later. But can I find the muscle guy without too much public fuss? I've only been to Nice a handful of times myself, and I never met anybody there I could use for this job. And anyway Xérus said I should not already know the people I recruit.

So, did I ever hear of someone suitable who has left Marseilles and moved to Nice?

Can't think of anybody off the top of my head. And I can't start asking around! Better go for a long walk. That always helps ....

That rasping Mistral is still tormenting me. And the cicadas sound as if they're trying to beat it at its own game today. Can't wait to get out of here now. Another smart move, Xérus!

But who the hell do I know of in Nice??

Hah! Been staring me in the face all along! But it *was* almost seven years ago ...

Gustin Aignant, of course. At least a dozen little shop robberies here in the early Fifties. Everyone in Marseilles knew it was him – except the stupid police. Then some Smart Alec sang for his supper, and Aignant vanished overnight. We all thought he'd been pulled in. But he never landed up in any cop shop. Must have had some very good contacts, though, 'cos the very next day that Smart Alec disappeared too! Never heard mention of any funeral.

And once that scum of a grass was lost to the world, the police were back where they'd started. But Aignant had already legged it. And all the rumours said he'd gone to sunny Nice! Of course, the *flics* there had nothing on him either. And three or four years ago, I swear I overheard someone saying he was back to his old tricks again.

Yes. Gustin Aignant.

I'll get hold of a good street map of Nice tomorrow. And a copy of the business directory. Wonder if they have a separate listing for "Lowlife Bars Near The Port"?

* * *

'Bar Marteau?'
   'Yeah.'
   'Has Gustin Aignant been in tonight?'
   'Who??'
   'Gustin Aignant.'
   'Never heard of him.'
   'OK.'

Oh well. Eight down, lots more to go ....

'Bar du Tronc?'
'Yeah.'
'Is Gustin there?'
'You mean Aignant?'
Bull's-eye!
'Yeah, course I do ...'
'Not yet. Usually comes in around nine.'
'Sure – just thought I might catch him a bit earlier tonight. I'll call back.'
'OK.'

So here we go. But I'll need to take a good look at the street map first.

* * *

'This is Aignant. You the creep that's been phoning round all the bars for me?'
'Yeah. Anyone wonders, just tell 'em it was your dad calling to wish you Happy Birthday.'
'It ain't my birthday.'
'Tell 'em he always remembers late.'
'What do you want, mister?'
'I want you to rob a bank with me in a few weeks' time. A bit of help with the planning, and five minutes on the job itself, and you'll get two-and-a-half million *balles* on the spot. Guaranteed.'
'What??'
'You heard me.'
'Hang on ... Hey, keep the noise down, you imbeciles!! ... OK, which bank?'
'I'll tell you later.'
'Huh! Why should I trust you? Maybe you're a cop. Or ...'
'I'm not. And I'll give you two hundred thousand up-front at our first little meeting in Nice, very soon. Just the two of us, OK? You can bring a gun with you if you want. But I won't be carrying one. Is that enough to trust me?'

'Depends if I believe a word you're saying ...'

'Sure it does. You want a fistful of quick cash, and a lot more to follow, you'll believe me and we'll meet up later this week. But if you're scared of me, Aignant, we'll forget the whole thing and I'll find ...'

'I ain't scared of nobody, mister! Where d'ya wanna meet?'

'First things first. I'll just call you "G" from now on, right?'

'OK ...'

'And you're going to choose the name of a flower for me. Any flower.'

'What??'

'You heard.'

'*Merde*. Don't know many flowers. OK – a rose.'

'Fine. So my name's "Luc Rose" – to you and you alone. Got that?'

'Yeah.'

'Good. Now, your bar's on Rue Bonaparte, near Place Garibaldi, right?'

'Yeah.'

'This Thursday evening, at exactly eight o'clock, you will walk straight past that bar on the other side of the street, heading towards Riquier, and keep walking until I introduce myself. And don't tell any of your "imbecile" pals about the big party, or our first little date, OK? 'Cos I'll spot 'em a mile off, believe me, and that'll be the end of it, and you won't be going home any richer.'

'OK.'

'And carry a pack of Gauloises clearly visible in your right hand.'

'But that's my gun hand. *Ah, merde!*'

'Hah! Don't worry, G. We're already the best of friends, right? And you can make it your left hand.'

'OK. I'll be there. With my gun.'

He'll be getting less than a tenth of his share up-front. And he sounds hungry for the rest. So I reckon I have at least a ten-to-one chance of staying alive on Thursday night.

I like those sorts of odds.

OK. Tomorrow I'll leave the next two months' rent with old Norbert, two days in advance. He's going to think I've lost my head! I'll give *him* the "urgent family business" story too.

Then I'll pack a big suitcase with all I need for a few weeks away and with room to spare!

And I'll clear the rest of my own stuff from the apartment and store it in the lock-up. Just in case. Three more suitcases should do it. And two separate taxis, one to the main bus station as a decoy, and one out to the garage. Then I can take a roundabout route back on foot. Mustn't leave any easy trails!

And I'd better call a few cheap boarding houses near the railway station in Nice, and book something up before I leave on Wednesday. Don't want anyone to remember me wandering the back-streets as soon as I arrive there ...

Rue Bonaparte, Nice

Thursday 1 October, 8 p.m.

Another tiny peek round the corner ...

Aha! That must be him. Right on time, and nobody behind him – yet.

And still fifty metres away. He can't possibly have noticed me. Count to ten ....

OK. Another quick peep.

Still no-one else with him. And he's carrying the Gauloises.

Right. The bait's in place. Back into the alcove now. Big hat on. Sunglasses on. Moustache still secure.

He'll get to the corner about five seconds from now. And as soon as he reaches the kerb ...

'Stop right there, G. This is Rose.'

He's stopped.

'And please don't look this way or come any closer. You don't need to get to know me that well. Stay just where you are, light up a cigarette, and admire the view up the street for a couple of minutes.'

'I don't have any matches.'

'Pretend you have. And listen hard. Then you'll get your cash advance.'

'OK.'

Dammit, there's a car stopping. Ah, it's just a taxi. But it could still mean trouble ...

No, it's only a woman getting out with a little dog.

'You still there, Rose?'

'Yeah. Just being careful. Right, I need you to find me the name of a very good car thief who knows the streets of Nice like the back of his hand. But the two of you must never have met before, and he must never get to know your name. And you don't make *any* contact with him yourself. Think you can do that?'

'Sure.'

'Certain?'

'I said so, didn't I, mister? Got a couple of ideas already ...'

'Good. And I'll need to know the name of *his* favourite bar, too. And when he likes to drink there. You have three days to sort it. And remember, no-one else gets to know about our little game, right?'

'Right.'

'Be at the call box at the junction of Rue Barla and Rue Ribotti at exactly six o'clock on Sunday evening, ready to give me the info. OK?'

'Yeah.'

'And check the phone's working as soon as you get there. If it isn't, go straight to the box two blocks up at Rue Arson.'

'Got it.'

'Now look down at the pavement, just round the corner of the wall ...'

'Another pack of Gauloises.'

'Right. You're gonna toss your own pack away, close to it. Nice and casual. Then have second thoughts and pick it up again, to see if there are still some smokes left. Except you'll pick up the other pack, right? Do it now.'

'OK ....'

'Happy?'

'Yeah.'

'Good. That's all. Now just carry on walking in the same direction.'

Nice

Sunday 4 October, 6 p.m.

'Allô!'

'Who's speaking?'

'G.'

'Rose here. OK, do you have that name for me?'

'Yeah. You need to talk to a guy called Bertrand Irvoise.'

'Have you ever met him?'

'No.'

'Or spoken to him?'

'No.'

'Know what he looks like?'

'I do now. Seen him a couple of times since you and I met on Thursday. Had to check out his drinking holes, didn't I? Don't worry, he never noticed me.'

'How will I recognise him?'

'Short and weedy, late twenties, balding early, droopy face, always looks like he's just heard bad news. Don't think he's too bright. Works in a scrapyard, part-time. That's where he learnt how to break into any model of car, fast. And drive it around Nice, fast as you like.'

'That's *very* helpful, G. Thank you. And where can I find him?'

'Bar Lépante seems to be his favourite place. But not before eight-thirty. And I only saw him there on Friday and Saturday, of course. Maybe he'll be in later tonight. Maybe not.'

'That's fine. OK, you and I won't need to talk again for a while. I'll leave you a phone message including the word "rose" at the Bar du Tronc, one afternoon when I'm ready to give you a final briefing. So from now on you'll need to drop in there to check for it early each evening, after seven o'clock. Just tell 'em you're expecting your dad to call again fairly soon. Got that?'

'Yeah.'

'And the day you get that message, be back at this phone box at nine o'clock in the evening. With the same backup plan.'

'OK.'

'But we'll also need a way to alert each other if there's ever a problem, right? So we must also both check for a special signal from the other one at six o'clock every evening. And if either of us *does* leave a signal, you're to go to this same phone box at nine that evening, just as for the final briefing, and I'll call you. Got it?'

'Yeah ...'

'And here's how we're going to leave our signals ....'

Rue de Lépante, Nice

Wednesday 7 October, 10 p.m.

Another whole evening wasted waiting for Irvoise to show his face! And they must be getting really fed up with me calling them to check. Maybe Aignant was right about him only coming here at weekends.

I'll give it another half-hour. Unless these drunks coming up the street decide to take an interest in me ....

It's him at last! Fits the description perfectly.

OK, let him settle for ten minutes ....

'Ici Bar Lépante.'

'Hi. Is Bertrand Irvoise there tonight, please?'

'Still after him, eh? What's he done to you, then?'

'Nothing. He's an old pal of mine. So, is he there or not?'

'Yeah. I'll get him ....'

'Who's this? I don't have any old friends ...'

'That's a good line, Monsieur Irvoise! And maybe you don't. But I'd really like to be your *new* friend ...'

'What does *that* mean?'

'They say you're pretty good at breaking into cars, Bertrand.'

'Are you the police?'

'Do you think I'd tell you if I was?'

'Er ... no.'

'Right. So maybe you'd better take the risk, because I'd like to pay you two million Old Francs, plus two hundred thousand up-front this evening, if you'll do a little job with me soon.'

'Sounds very interesting. Go on ...'

'I'll need you to steal a nice little motor, and meet me and another friend at a local bank, and then drive us away. If you get my drift.'

'You mean a robbery?'

'Yes, Bertrand. Very sharp of you ...'

'No violence, right?'

'I'm not planning any.'

'Good. So when do we do it? Tomorrow?'

'Whoa, slow down, Bertrand! No, it won't be for some weeks. You haven't even got your advance yet. And we still have a couple more things to talk about.'

'Oh. All right, then ...'

Phew. This is going to be very hard work!

'So, first off, I'm only going to call you "B" from now on. OK?'

'Sure. I think I can see why.'

'Right. And now please choose the name of an animal for me.'

'You want me to buy you a pet?'

'No, I don't, B. Please just think of an animal.'

'OK, I've done that.'

'Right. So, what is it?'

'You want me to tell you the answer?'

'Yes please, B.'

'It's a gazelle. I like gazelles.'

'That's very good. So from now on you will call me "Luc Gazelle", right? No-one else knows that name.'

'Do you look like a gazelle, Luc?'

'No, I don't. Now, do you want your money?'

'Oh, yes please.'

'Right. Hold on for about one minute ....'

'Still there, B?'

'Yes.'

'OK. As soon as we finish this call, go out of the bar, turn left, walk towards the phone box on the corner, and take an envelope out of the litter bin just before you reach it. Got that?'

'Yeah.'

'Good. But first, here's how we're going to make contact before our next call, or in an emergency ....'

Rue de Rome, Marseilles

Sunday 18 October, 8 p.m.

'*Allô!*'

'Who are you expecting?'

'Xérus.'

'And what was that song we were listening to the other day?'

'*Mona Lisa.*'

'Good evening, Paul. Is everything OK?'

'Yeah. I've been ready for ten days. As far as I've been able to go ...'

'Excellent. So, please tell me your broad plan.'

'All right. I've kept it as simple as I can, 'cos that's what you wanted, but it all feels a bit thin to me. And I still know nothing about which bank we're hitting, or what alarm systems it has, and so on. So I might have to make a few changes ...'

'OK, OK, Paul. Get on with it, please ...'

'Very well. There will be only three men in the team. Two of us will approach on foot and wait separately, one on each side of the entrance to the bank. When the car arrives, we'll both make sure it's parked in the right place, and then the two of us will join up and go straight in. Nobody outside will suspect anything is happening, and you'll need to make sure no-one inside hits any alarm buttons or makes any phone calls. As long as you can do that, there should be no big rush. We'll get out as soon as we've got what we came for. The driver knows the streets of Nice very well and he'll take us to a secluded split-up point within a few minutes. And that's it – so far.'

'Sounds reasonable. Happy with the guys you've recruited?'

'Sure.'

'And they've never met each other?'

'No!'

'Fine. So, here's what you need to know now. The bank always stays open late on Monday evenings, to take in extra deposits from the traders at the weekly Antiquities Market on Cours Saleya, which finishes at around five-thirty. In fact we sometimes have a special security van collection, well after the close of business at seven, if that day's cash intake is expected to be particularly high ...'

'All right. But ...'

'So you will be making your entrance after dark, at six-forty-five precisely. OK?'

'Got it, X. But *which* bank is it, *enfin?*'

'Banque Artisanale on Rue Alberti.'

'You must be joking!'

'No.'

'But the Sûreté headquarters is on Rue Alberti, at the junction with Rue Gioffredo!'

'Very pleased to see you've done your homework, Paul. Yes, it's only two blocks south of the bank. But there's no direct alarm link to any police service. They don't believe anyone would be stupid enough to try and stage a robbery right under the noses of the law.'

'Too right! I told you this sounded crazy at the start. Now I'm certain of it!'

'Calm down, Paul.'

'No, I will not! I can't risk a dozen squad cars screaming straight up Rue Alberti if someone manages to get a phone call into the *flics*. They'll either nab us on the spot or be on our tail all over the city!'

'I don't think that's likely to happen, if you carry out the job properly. I've done my planning too, remember. The local alarm bell hasn't been tested for months, and I can promise you it unfortunately won't be working at all that day. And there will be nobody in the back offices to call the police. The few staff remaining on late Monday evening duty will all be in the main hall, in full view. But if you're still not happy ...'

'Hah! How many banks have you robbed recently, Monsieur Bloody X? You use professionals, you leave it to them, OK?'

'OK ...'

'So now I know *exactly* how to do this. I always wanted to take two other guys in with me anyway. I'll find a second driver, and we'll use two cars. We can arrive in a big one and use it to block off Rue Alberti – it's not very wide. We'll have to move a lot faster inside the bank than I'd planned, 'cos that blockage will tell people something's going on. But the other car will be all ready and waiting for the getaway.'

'That's very quick thinking, Paul.'

'Oh, I've thought of a lot of options in the past three weeks, X. But at last I can make a proper plan, and you'd better agree to it, here and now.'

'Yes, I'm perfectly happy with it. I always assumed there would be at least four of you anyway ...'

'Oh, very clever. So what happens next?'

'I'll need to phone you again in precisely one week's time, to confirm your new plan is all in place. Are you based in Nice now?'

'Yeah. I had to come all the way back to Marseilles especially for this phone call! Didn't really want to show my face again here, so I've been staying well disguised today and I'm going straight back tonight on the last train.'

'OK. I'll give you a phone box rendezvous plan for Nice before we finish this evening. But first, let's talk about the cash you're going to steal.'

'Right!'

'Make sure your bag is big enough to hold one hundred wads of 5000 Old Franc notes. Because that's what you'll be demanding, OK? There will be one hundred notes in each wad. Work it out ...'

'Hang on ... that makes fifty million *balles*, right?'

'Dead right.'

'And you're only giving us sixteen million?'

'Plus your own big advance and expenses. Not bad for a few minutes' work, Paul. You can buy three or four brand new Rolls-Royces with that sort of money.'

'And *you* get to keep well over thirty million?'

'Well, this is *my* little project, not yours, isn't it? And don't forget it could be *you* keeping it all, if you decide to double-cross me and don't deliver the balance in the way I'm about to explain ...'

'You still sound far too trusting for my liking, X.'

'Well, I'm actually very comfortable, my friend. But if you *are* planning to double-cross me, please say so right now, and get ready for what will be hitting you very soon. That way you'll avoid an even worse outcome if you leave it till later ...'

'Look, let's just get on with it, can we?'

'That's better, Paul. So, here's exactly how I'll want you to deliver my share ....'

Reconfiguration

Nice

Monday 19 October

'Un express.'
   'Monsieur.'
So, one full week until I take the next call from Xérus.

I don't have to tell Gustin Aignant about which bank we're hitting. Or anything about Plan B. He didn't know much about Plan A anyway. So I won't need to contact him at all.

Bertrand Irvoise can drive the approach car. But I must get him to find us a second driver very soon. He should know his competition by reputation. So I'll leave him a special signal before seven o'clock, and talk to him tonight.

First things first, though. I need to do another full day's detailed research on the ground now, checking out all the approaches to Rue Alberti and the bank, deciding exactly where we're going to set up that road block, and foot-slogging the options for the getaway route.

And I must make sure I know just when it gets dark here in late November.

* * *

'Is that B?'
   'Of course it is, Luc! You signalled me today!'
   'Right. Remember my name?'
   'It's Luc! I already said it!'
   'The rest of it, I mean ...'

'Hang on – yeah, it's Gazelle, right?'

'OK. Happy with the money?'

'Yeah! So is there a problem?'

'Not a problem, my friend. Just a small change of plan. We're now going to use two cars. We'll be arriving at the bank in one of them, and you're going to be our first driver. We'll definitely need a big long station wagon for that job, OK?'

'OK.'

'And I'd like you to suggest who the new getaway driver could be. I'm sure you're aware of other car thieves in Nice who know the city streets really well ...'

'Of course I am.'

'But are there any you've never met before?'

'One or two ...'

'Good. So please have a very careful think about it, and be back at this call box again, at nine-fifteen on Wednesday evening, with a name for me. Remember, it must be someone you don't know at all. And he must be good. And able to keep a secret. OK?'

'OK, Luc.'

'And here's where you'll be picking me up, and where you'll then be taking us in that nice big car you're going to steal ...'

Wednesday 21 October, 9:15 p.m.

'This is B.'

'And this is Gazelle. So what do you have for me?'

'I've found the perfect guy for the getaway car, Luc. And I've never met him. We've just talked on the phone ...'

'What? You've spoken to him already?'

'Yeah, last night. But I didn't tell him my real name. And he wants to be known only as "Théo" – but that's not his real name either.'

'What the hell *did* you tell him?'

'Just that I knew someone who needed a driver for a nice little job ...'

'And that's all?'

'Yeah.'

'Hang on a minute, B. I need to think about this ...'

'Sure.'

Is it manageable? Probably. I can put a lot of pressure on this dim little weed if I get any problems with his shy Théo character.

And the clock's ticking away. Guess I'll have to live with it ...

'All right, B. But I'm holding you fully responsible for him, OK?'

'But ...'

'No buts. Now, get straight back to Théo and say I'll be calling him at nine-thirty tomorrow evening, and he can expect some cash then too. Here's the phone box location ...'

Thursday 22 October, 9:30 p.m.

'Théo?'

'Yeah.'

'*Bonsoir.* I understand you might like to earn some good money for borrowing a nippy little car and taking me and a couple of friends for a nice safe drive around the city one evening ...'

'What's it worth?'

'One million *balles* at the end of the trip, plus another hundred thousand up-front, here and now.'

'You're on. But if you don't deliver, I'll break your neck on the spot.'

'That seems fair, Théo. Care to pick up that old Gitanes pack from the floor of the call box?'

'OK .... Yeah, that's a very good start.'

'Right on the spot, I'd say.'

'Yeah.'

'And now you need a name for *me*, Théo. Think of a bird, please.'

'A pigeon.'

'Fine. I am now "Luc Pigeon" to you and you alone. And here's how you and I will be keeping in touch ....'

Sunday 25 October, 8 p.m.

'Good evening, Paul. I trust your revised plans are all in place?'

'Yes, X, they are. We'll be doing the job exactly as I suggested last week. I've reconnoitred the streets as fully as necessary, and the team now includes two drivers. I'll give everyone their final briefing after this call.'

'Very good. And I assume you've been using some sort of messaging system to signal the need for any unplanned telephone contact?'

'Of course.'

'So we must now establish one of our own.'

'I've been wondering when you would realise that ...'

'Ah, Paul, your lack of confidence continues to disappoint me. I have always had a little system in plan. *Mais naturellement, hein?* It is only now that I wish to deploy it.

'So, if you should ever feel it necessary to speak to me urgently, please go to the junction of Rue Lamartine and Rue Pertinax at exactly eight-thirty that evening, and chalk the number 88 on the pavement at the corner of the wall of the grocery shop. You must then walk straight up to Café Racine, two blocks to the north, and remain inside. At nine o'clock precisely the barman will receive a call for you under the name of Stéphane Garaune.

'And if I should desperately need to talk to you, I shall simply phone to speak to Monsieur Garaune at that time, at that café. So please ensure you are in there by nine o'clock every evening from now on, for at least fifteen minutes, ready for a possible call.'

'Fair enough.'

'But assuming we shall never need to use that special system, Paul, you must now await my final communication. You will be at the phone box at the junction of Rue Rossini and Rue Gounod at precisely eight o'clock every Sunday evening from the eighth of November onwards, and you will wait there for thirty minutes. If I do not call, you may relax for another full week. But if I *do* telephone, it will simply be to advise you that the robbery is to take place the following Monday evening, exactly as planned, and to give you any special new information.'

'Understood. But what about a backup call box, in case I find that phone is broken?'

'Indeed. Please go straight along to the one at Rue Hérold.'

'OK.'

'And I suggest that your team should also be waiting at individual phone boxes for your possible call to action, from eight-thirty on each of those Sunday evenings.'

'But of course.'

'Good. So do you have any further questions, Paul?'

'No.'

'Until we speak again, then ...'

Monday 26 October

OK. Today I'll need to leave the coded messages in each of the three bars. Then I can make the final briefing calls tonight.

And after that, we'll all be ready for Xérus' shout.

* * *

So, that's done. They'll all be waiting at their own phone boxes each Sunday evening.

Hmmm. Aignant had a lot more questions than I'd expected. He still seems very uncomfortable with taking orders. And he wanted to bring his own gun to the party. But at least he finally agreed not to, and promised to do the job exactly as I want it done. Glad I still haven't told him which bank it is!

Irvoise was a pushover, of course. He's never even *asked* for the name of the bank! He may be dim, but I'm certain I can rely on him.

I'm not very happy about Théo. When I asked him to repeat what I'd said about the plan, it took him a while, but it was almost word perfect. I hope he wasn't writing it down, despite my instructions. It sounded as if he'd had a lot to drink. And he said 'Yes' when I asked him if he had. Well, at least he's honest. And at least he promised to drink nothing on the day.

Thursday 29 October, 9:15 p.m.

'This is B.'

'And this is Gazelle. OK, I got *your* special signal today. What's the problem?'

'I just heard Théo broke his arm in a bar brawl two nights ago.'

'Oh, wonderful! How the hell is he going to drive the getaway car now?'

'Ah, I didn't expect you to ask me that, Luc. Well, I suppose he could ...'

'No, you idiot, it wasn't a serious question! You've really let me down, haven't you?'

'Well, I hope not, because ...'

'Oh yes you have! This thing could be happening in just a few days' time, and now we've lost our damned getaway driver!'

'But ...'

'I *told* you I don't want any buts! Théo was *your* idea and *your* responsibility, remember? So what are you going to do about it?'

'I keep trying to tell you, Luc! I've already found us a very good substitute ...'

'Ah. All right then, keep talking ...'

'His name's Arthur Narone. Only in his early twenties, but he's a bit of a legend around here already. I've never met him, I've just heard about what he often does with his nights ...'

'And what is that, exactly?'

'He steals the best cars off the street – always after midnight – and drives around the city and the hills like they were Monte Carlo. Then he delivers 'em back, one block away from where he took 'em, and strolls home while it's still dark. Probably wears a new pair of cheap gloves every time and dumps 'em straight in a litter bin. No-one ever knows their car's been lifted till they find it missing the next day. And when they call the police, they now get told to check out the surrounding streets for themselves. There's never any damage, just a lot less gas in the tank! The *flics* have never caught him red-handed – *their* cars just aren't fast enough! But the rumour is they've now stopped worrying about him. Harmless, they reckon. I'd say he's actually got a lot of their drivers' respect as well.'

'Sounds as if he has yours too, B. But you didn't suggest him to me before ...'

'Well, I figured he might be a bit young for you, and he's got no real jobs under his belt, if you know what I mean. But now that Théo's out of the picture ...'

'Yeah, yeah, yeah. OK, Narone does sound like a good bet. So where does he live?'

'Oh, I don't know that, Luc. Decided I'd better not go sniffing around this time, 'cos I could tell you weren't happy after I'd contacted Théo myself ...'

'No, I wasn't. So you've got no idea how I can find the kid?'

'Oh, sure I have. He works at old man Soron's little repair garage out on Rue Fontaine de la Ville. They say he lives near there too.'

'Aha! And where exactly is that?'

'North-east of the port. Pretty rough area. Take care if you go down there alone.'

'Thanks a lot ...'

'I mean it, Luc.'

'OK. Sorry, B. And ... well, I'm grateful for what you've done to try and sort this for me.'

'Oh, thank you!!'

'All right, all right, man! So, what does Narone look like?'

'Never seen him myself, Luc. But I've heard them say he's quite slim, with a big wave of hair and dark eyes.'

'OK, that'll do. Right – if you don't get any more signals from me, you can assume I've hired the guy and we're back on track. And you can call Théo now to tell him he's off the team. OK?'

'Sure. And ... well, good luck.'

'Thanks, B. Yeah, thanks a lot.'

I thought it was all going too smoothly.

Need to get stuck straight back into it. Hope the rain lets up soon. But at least there's not too much wind!

I don't think Xérus needs to know about this little hiccup. One getaway driver's much the same as another. But I'm going to have to take some bigger risks than usual. Time really is running out fast. Can't mess around with any more phone calls. No, I must make direct contact with this Arthur Narone as soon as I can. I'll check out the garage tomorrow, and when he finishes work I'll follow him for a few hours and develop my persuasion plan ...

Casa della Musica
Rue Benoît Bunico, Nice

Friday 30 October, 11 p.m.

'Move your bar stool, Arthur. I've still got a lot more sweeping up to do!'
'OK, Max, OK ...'
'It'll be time to go soon, son.'
'Yeah, I know ...'
'And please don't go doing anything more to upset Emilie. She's too precious to me!'
'What do you mean?'
'You know what I mean, Arthur.'
'No, I don't.'
'Well, I suggest you think about it.'
'Give me another beer, Max, and maybe I'll try ...'
'OK. But you've got ten minutes, no more.'
'It's a deal.'

Did she really have a headache? And why did she insist on going home on her own straight after the show?
It's getting worse, isn't it? But I don't know why.
Wish I wasn't so bloody poor! She's earning so much more than I am. Wish I could sing *or* play an instrument, let alone do both brilliantly like she does!
The *gros mec* and the *fine artiste*. Sounds like one of those silly old fables!
She really doesn't talk to me the way she used to. Or smile like she did most of the time on our little holiday in Italy. Can't believe that was only six weeks ago ...
I don't understand her.

But last night was just amazing! Managed to keep it up for over an hour! Nobody does it better. Maybe if she'd been with me she'd have understood the beauty of a Jaguar.

They'll never catch me.

I fancy a convertible tonight ...

'Time's up, Arthur. And you make sure she's smiling again when she gets here tomorrow evening.'

'Huh! G'night, Max.'

So, should I go straight up to Place Garibaldi and have a few more beers in the dive? Or get a couple of strong coffees inside me and then find a pretty little Merc to take for a ride?

'Arthur, please don't turn around, if you know what's good for you. Just move straight into the alley on the left ...'

Merde! I'm going to get mugged.

'That's fine. Stop there. And please don't worry. I have no intention of harming you. In fact I want to lend you a helping hand. How would you like half a million *balles* in your pocket by the end of November?'

'Hah! Who do I have to murder for that?'

'Nobody. You just have to steal a small, very ordinary car – not a snazzy fast one like you're used to taking ... yes, I know all about your little joyrides – and help me and a couple of friends make a sharp exit from a bank.'

'Where?'

'Here in the centre of Nice. I understand you know the streets very well indeed ...'

'Are you serious about this?'

'Yes. And I'll prove it. There's forty thousand in this paper bag. I'd guess that's about one month's wages for a junior mechanic like you. And you'll get another *year's* worth as soon as the job is done. So I'll just toss the bag down at your feet ... there you are ... and you can pick it up, and take a look, and keep it.'

'And what if I refuse?'

'Can you really afford not to?'

'Maybe ...'

'Well, in that case I'll make sure there's some solid evidence against you from every one of your future night-time escapades. And I might already have something on you from the last one.'

'You're not worrying me one little bit.'

'Are you sure about that? And then there's your precious Emilie, of course ...'

'How do you know about her??'

'I just watch and listen, Arthur. It's very easy.'

'You leave Emilie alone!'

'I certainly will, my friend. As long as you agree to help me with this job. So why don't you pick up the bag and do yourself a nice little favour?'

I don't think I have a choice. At least not for the moment ...

'All right ....'

'So, happy with that?'

'It's exactly what you said.'

'Yes, it is. Now, I'll be calling you just "A" from now on, and you can call me ... well, why don't you suggest a name? An aeroplane, perhaps?'

'The Comet?'

'Of course. Very modern. I'm now "Luc Comet" to you and you alone.'

'OK.'

'You will never try to identify me in any way. And you won't be saying a word of this to anybody, will you?'

'No.'

'Good. Now, you'll need to be waiting for us early one evening outside the Banque Artisanale on Rue Alberti, and then getting us smoothly up to the north-west, near the Gare du Sud. So I want you to make a full mental plan of all the possible routes and detours. Nothing written down. OK, partner?'

'OK.'

'And here's how you and I are going to contact each other, as and when we need to ...'

* * *

I don't believe this. Ten minutes ago everything was normal. Nothing in the world to worry about. Well, almost nothing. And now I've signed up to a bank robbery.

Pennies from heaven.

But maybe I should say 'No' when Comet telephones me, and give him back the money. And take the risk of getting shopped for the joyriding. And promise myself never to do any more of that.

But he dropped those nasty hints about Emilie too.

She'd go crazy if she heard about this. So I'd better not tell her.

Hmmm. I need to think it all through properly at work tomorrow. And if I do decide to go ahead with it, I can spend all day Sunday making the plan. Just as Luc suggested.

I'm not in the mood for that little Merc now. It'll have to be the beers instead.

Nice

Sunday 1 November

I really don't like the city so much in the autumn. Too many reminders that summer has gone. I love the summers. Especially this year's. Those wonderful afternoons trying to get comfortable on the stony old beach with Emilie! And our few days on *real* beaches in Italy. Pity about the little disagreements ...

It's going to rain again soon. Most of the people out on the streets haven't come prepared for that. They'll soon be scurrying!

The old *violoniste* isn't fretting about it, though. She's here in all weathers. But I've hardly ever seen anyone give her a *sou* ...

'Voici, madame ...'

'Ah, merci m'sieur! Si gentil!'

Look at those palm trees now! Even they seem fearful of what's around the corner.

And around the next corner ... I can hear him already ... yes, there's the accordionist as usual, singing his heart out. He makes a lot more money than the old lady. Probably 'cos he's a lot better looking than her. *C'est la vie.* And no wonder Emilie makes a small fortune in tips every week!

The cicadas are still singing too. But they'll be hungry soon. *Ah, la Bise, la Bise ...*

Fais bise, Emilie!!

* * *

So, into Rue Alberti. Luc said it's the bank up near the next junction.

Yes, there it is. Just keep strolling, don't look at all interested in it ...

OK. I'll lift a car near Place Garibaldi, with plenty of time to spare in case of problems. Then I'll come in via Avenue Félix Faure, and park up and wait right *here*. When it's time to go, we can quickly turn out of sight onto Rue Pastorelli, and wind our way through the streets up to Rue Marceau, and then head west towards the Gare du Sud.

I'll walk the whole route very carefully now, and then all the way back again.

* * *

Right, that'll work. It's time for some lunch, on my way back down. And after that I'll walk it all over again, and memorise the best detours at every corner. And check all of *them* for any big new road works. That's going to take me the rest of the afternoon.

* * *

OK. It's all completely clear in my mind now. But I'll borrow a bicycle late on Monday afternoon and check it out again, just after dark and after the rush hour. 'Cos that's exactly when Luc said it'll be happening, didn't he?

I deserve a beer and a long rest on the beach now!

* * *

Nearly time to go home. Only one thing left to check today ....

OK, I'm back at the bottom of Rue Alberti. Let's see – it's five-thirty now, and dusk is coming on fast. It'll be almost dark in about half an hour. So I'll borrow that bike at six tomorrow, straight after work.

But by the end of the month, it'll be dark about forty minutes earlier, of course.

Wow, the palm trees seem even more worried now, with that backdrop of heavy thunderclouds building over the sea! And ... oh, that huge mass up there in the south is like a great big human fist – with three or four separate fingers!

Merde! Can I never forget?

Sunday 22 November, 8 p.m.

Third weekend in a row waiting here for Xérus' call. And everyone else at the ready again too.

Very heavy clouds this evening. It's really dark now ... and getting cold. Only one more Sunday left in November. Surely this hasn't been a huge wind-up all along?

Mon Dieu, it's ringing!

'Allô!'

'Paul?'

'Yes. X?'

'Yes. Tomorrow evening, six-forty-five. Just as planned, no changes.'

'Right.'

'All OK with you?'

'Yes.'

'Good. Don't let me down.'

* * *

'Allô!'

'Is that A?'

'Is that Comet?'

'Be in place by six-thirty.'
'OK.'

'Allô!'
  'Is that B?'
  'Is that Gazelle?'
  'RV at six-thirty-five.'
  'OK.'

'Allô!'
  'Is that G?'
  'Is that Rose?'
  'RV at six-thirty-six.'
  'OK.'

A Good Job Spoiled

Central Police Station
Rue Gioffredo, Nice

Monday 23 November, 10:30 p.m.

'Right, Irvoise – here's a transcript of the first part of your statement on today's events. We're trying to turn the whole thing into something approaching readable French. You've been very co-operative, and that's good, but we need to know a lot more. And do you really still expect us to believe you'd never met any of the others before?'

'Yes, Inspector.'

'And you don't even know their names, apart from that "Luc Gazelle" nonsense?'

'Nah.'

'Well, we know you're none too bright, Bertrand, so we'll be helping you try much harder to remember them, I promise. And we'll keep asking your delightful friend too, the scum! But read this through first, and sign it. Then you just might get that cup of coffee ...'

> I borrowed the Renault Domaine at ten o'clock this morning, from a side street near Nice-Ville station. The owner had been wearing his smart business suit, as usual, and he'd caught an early train for Marseilles. He's been doing that every Monday morning for the last few weeks. And he never gets back before eight. Maybe he goes further, towards Paris.

But I had three other good alternatives to choose from if he hadn't actually turned up today.

I got into the heavy Renault easily and managed to start it straight away. Then I drove it to a car park and left it with dozens of others for the rest of the day. I went back for it well before six o'clock, as the rush hour was dying down, with plenty of time to sort out any new starting problems. But again I had no trouble, and I just sat there in the dark with it ticking over until six-thirty.

Then I put my big hat on and drove to the corner of Rue Gioffredo and Rue du Lycée to pick up Luc. As soon as I stopped and held up two fingers, just as I'd been told to, the passenger door opened and a guy got in holding a large empty holdall. He was wearing a long oversized coat, his collar was up, his own hat was down over his eyes, and he had a very bushy moustache which I'm sure was false. He seemed quite short, like me, but he was stocky, and when he spoke his voice was very high-pitched and Italian-sounding. I'm certain he was putting that on too. He'd seen me glance at him, and he said, very firmly, 'You just keep looking straight ahead, like I told you. Now drive carefully along to the next junction, turn left onto Rue Foncet, and stop at once to pick up G.'

I did what I was told. As I braked I saw Luc hold up three fingers, and the other guy got straight into the back seat behind him. I didn't look at him, but I already sensed he was a big lad. Nobody said a word. Luc just gave me the thumbs-up, and that meant I should now take the quickest route from there to the bank.

Two minutes later I was driving gently up Rue Alberti. The rush hour was over now, as we'd expected, and there were no queues up ahead, but it had started to rain again. I slowed down as we approached the red lights at the junction with Rue Pastorelli. There was a Fiat 1400 parked up half on the pavement, exactly as planned, just past the entrance to the bank. Out of the corner of my eye, I could see the driver had his own hat pulled down over his forehead, and his nose stuck in a newspaper. He wasn't moving a muscle. Luc said 'OK, he's all ready. And the lights are green now. Keep going ...'

I turned right, drove along to Rue Gubernatis, and turned right again. The traffic was still no problem. When we reached Rue de l'Hôtel des Postes, I took another right and that brought us back to the junction with Rue Alberti. One last turn and I was heading up towards the bank again. I pulled in behind the row of parked cars on the right, thirty metres short of the entrance and the little Fiat, just as Luc had told me to. And I waited for him to make the next move.

He reached into the holdall. It wasn't empty after all. He pulled out a handgun and passed it to the guy behind him, who just grunted as if he wasn't very impressed with it. Luc took out another one for himself, and I guessed we were ready to go. But then he stuck his left hand back in the bag, pulled out a third gun, and held it out to me.

'You never said I'd be carrying!' I protested. 'You never asked,' he said, pointing his own gun straight at me. 'You think I'm crazy or something? Put it in your coat pocket and don't argue.' I took it. I didn't argue.

'OK,' he said, adjusting the rear-view mirror. 'Nothing behind us for at least fifty metres. Get this car in place, now!'

I pulled the huge estate out and up onto the left-side pavement till it was scraping the wall, slewed it quickly toward the cars parked on the right, and backed it up on the turn, blocking the rest of the one-way street and most of the pavement. Then I stalled the engine and left it in first gear with the handbrake on. With its keys still somewhere on a train from Marseilles, that big baby wasn't going anywhere fast. And Luc was already shouting 'Out!'

As I pushed my own hat down over my eyes, Luc was easing through the narrow gap I'd left at the front. No room for even a motorbike to pass through that! He began walking calmly towards the bank, and I joined up alongside him, still looking straight ahead. I knew G would be coming round the back of the car and staying just a couple of metres behind us.

There weren't many people on that stretch of Rue Alberti, and those I did see just seemed confused about what was going on, or were trying to spot the movie cameras, or were carefully scurrying away. Just as Luc had said he expected.

A few seconds later we reached the bank. The entrance door was closed, but through the front windows I could see a few people inside, although nobody was looking at us, of course. No sign of the security guard from that side – as usual. I'd only ever seen him through the windows on the left, standing just inside the front door. So, I assumed, had the others during their own recces in the street.

'Pull your gun when I pull mine,' hissed Luc. Then, a bit more loudly, 'Sunglasses on!' And then 'OK, masks up, and go!'

We hoiked up the big neckerchiefs we were all wearing, and Luc boldly opened the front door and strode through with me at his shoulder. Before the dopey guard had time to react, G must have got a gun to his head, and I heard him saying 'Don't move, don't talk, stay alive, OK?' And Luc was drawing his own weapon and loudly announcing our arrival ...

Bertrand Irvoise, 23 November 1959

'So, before you sign it, Bertrand – do you agree that this is an acceptable transcription of your account of what happened up to that point?'

'Yes, Inspector.'

'Good. The Investigating Magistrate will be delighted. Please sign it at once.'

'Voilà.'

'You sound a little tired.'

'Yes, I am very tired.'

'Oh dear. Well, we shall need to review your statement of subsequent events a little later, when the typist has finished struggling with it. Meanwhile, you may have that cup of coffee – this is going to be a very long night. And while I'm away, Bertrand, I'd like you to think very hard about those names, OK? But don't waste any time on the gorilla who came into the bank behind you. He's sitting comfortably just down the corridor, and we know exactly who *he* is. No, please just try to remember a little more about your friend "Luc" and the other driver ...'

* * *

'So, Madame Padroux, you are perhaps feeling a little calmer now?'

'Yes, I think so, Inspector.'

'Good. A cup of fine tea and a short rest usually work wonders. Now, what you have managed to tell us so far has painted only a patchy picture of what occurred earlier today. So would you kindly start again from the beginning, and allow us to make a written record of it this time?'

'Very well.'

'Excellent. First then, your full job title, if you will ...'

'I am the Senior Counter Cashier at the Banque Artisanale du Midi.'

'Thank you. So, in your own time, *s'il vous plaît* ...'

> Three men marched in through the door. They were all wearing big brimmed hats, sunglasses, and masks like cowboys. The tall one stopped next to our security guard, Marco, and immediately hit him in the face with a gun and threatened to shoot him. The others came towards us. They were waving guns too, and then the one with a huge moustache started shouting at us in a high-pitched voice ...

'Everyone stand up. Now!'

We all did.

'Everyone move back from the desks. Now!'

We all did.

'Who's in charge?'

'I am,' said Monsieur Orceau, very calmly. He's the Deputy Manager. Poor man.

'Right,' said the leader, very clearly. 'You have sixty seconds to fill this bag with wads of 5000 franc notes. There's room for over one hundred of them. And don't argue – we know the money is in that safe. Just do it. NOW!'

And he threw the holdall at poor Charles-Pierre, and then pointed the gun straight at me ...

'You – help him! And you! And you!'

We all rushed to assist Charles-Pierre, who was opening the day safe as quickly as he could.

'If anyone else makes a move or says a word, the guard gets it first. Then it will be you and your customers ...'

There was complete silence, of course. Just the sound of Charles-Pierre stuffing the wads of notes into the bag on the counter as we passed them along to him.

'Pack it more carefully!' the little guy screeched. 'I want it full, not half-empty!'

Charles-Pierre gave him a dirty look. I think that was a bad mistake.

Moments later, the leader screamed 'Faster! Faster! You've got twenty seconds left!'

'OK, OK,' muttered Charles-Pierre.

A few moments later it was 'Faster! Faster!' again.

Charles-Pierre paused for a moment and glared at him. That did it. The awful man said 'I warned you,' and aimed his gun and shot him in the shoulder. Just like that! Charles-Pierre screamed and slumped to the ground. The holdall was quite full already, but I kept my head down and took over the job of stuffing more wads into it. Then the leader shouted 'OK, that's enough!' and ran forward and grabbed the heavy bag with both hands. Then he hurried to the entrance with the other little man at his heels.

The big guy pushed the door wide open to let them through, and then started to back out himself. That's when Marco decided to be a hero, the idiot! He threw himself at the robber, trying to grab his gun, and it went off – in Marco's chest, I think. He collapsed in a pool of blood, and the big bastard ran straight out, shouting 'Nobody try to follow me, or else!' and slamming the door behind him.

I knelt down to help Charles-Pierre, who was still conscious but obviously shocked and bleeding quite badly. I'm sure many others were doing what they could for poor Marco. And I heard two people phoning for the police and an ambulance.

It then seemed to take you all a very long time to get here, considering how close ....

But no! What is the point in saying that?

And this is all I can tell you.

'Thank you, *madame*. I understand how difficult that must have been for you. And yes, I regret that we were all delayed by a simple but very effective roadblock and its knock-on effects.'

'Ah, I see. I am glad I held my tongue, Inspector. So, do you have any news of Charles-Pierre and Marco?'

'Yes, we do. Monsieur Orceau's shoulder wound is not too serious. The doctors say he will need some of those remarkable new antibiotics and a good period of rest, but there is no major damage.

Monsieur Charnière's condition is a lot worse, but they tell me he is stable and they are expecting him to pull through. The bullet missed his heart by six centimetres.'

'Oh, this is so awful. But I did hear someone say you've already caught at least one of the robbers ...'

'I'm afraid it would be quite inappropriate for me to comment on that at this time, *madame*. And I have no reason to detain you any longer this evening. I shall order a car to drive you home at once – unless of course you wish to go instead to the hospital for any ... attention.'

'No, I would like to go straight home, thank you.'

'That is most reassuring, I think. I shall arrange for your statement to be prepared for signature at a convenient time tomorrow. *Bonne nuit, Madame Padroux* – and please try not to worry too much about your brave colleagues. They are in very good hands.'

Slight Change of Plan

Central Police Station
Rue Gioffredo, Nice

Monday 23 November, 11:30 p.m.

'So, Bertrand, let us move on to the point where you left the bank ...'

Luc and I walked out and hurried down to the waiting car. The engine was already running, of course. Luc took the front seat, as planned, and I got in behind the driver, who just kept looking straight ahead. I was surprised when G didn't pile in next to me at once, and Luc was already cursing him out loud. But as I turned round to do my last little job, he dived in and slammed the door, and Luc screamed 'OK, go, go, go!'

And we went. We were just twenty metres from the green light, and there was no queue because of our little road block, of course, and we turned right at once and headed east along Rue Pastorelli, and Luc said 'Well?' I knew he was talking to me.

'We're probably clear. Only fourteen seconds from reaching the car to turning the corner. And the lights have changed now. Could have been much worse ...'

We turned left into Rue Foncet.

'And ...?'

'Nobody came out of the bank. Only three passers-by stopped to watch. None of them seemed to be looking at the number plate. But one of them did start moving towards the bank. He won't have seen our faces, but he's probably giving them a description of the car by now, for what that's worth.'

'OK. Keep watching behind. And you – take it steady, no speeding, remember? But be ready to hit the gas if the police pick us up ...'

The driver just nodded. We were now heading west along Boulevard Dubouchage.

'And what was that noise inside the bank after we left?'

'I had to deal with the guard.'

'You fool! OK, weapons back now!'

But at that moment I spotted a police officer strolling along in the same direction as us, and I hissed *'Flic!'* and automatically looked away! As soon as we'd taken a sharp right into Ruelle des Prés we passed our guns forward to Luc, who stuck them in his coat pockets. Then he took four wads of notes from the bulging holdall on his lap and handed them across to me, as he'd promised. And he pulled out five more for G to grab from behind. But the guy wasn't happy ...

'I want more than this now, Luc, after having to sort out the guard. I'm gonna need a lot of protection ...'

'Tough.'

'Want me to show how tough I can be? I'm sitting right behind you, remember ...?'

Luc cursed again, passed two more wads back over his shoulder, then zipped up the bag. G grunted and started to say 'I'm still not ...'

We were running north up Rue Docteur Balestre, and approaching the junction with Rue Biscarra. There are no lights at that one, and everybody has to be careful and give way. But suddenly there was this big truck coming in from the left, just as we were about to shoot

across. Our driver swerved to the right and hit the
brakes, but the road was wet and we skidded into a
signpost on the corner of the kerb. We weren't going too
fast by then, but the Fiat wasn't built to handle even
that. The front wing just folded, Luc was thrown
forward onto the dashboard and the windscreen, with
the money bag up against his chest, and his door sprung
open.

The truck just kept going – the driver probably had no
idea there'd been an accident – but the car behind it
slowed down and stopped. Luc was obviously hurt, and
he was already shouting 'Everybody out and get away!'
But then he looked at our driver and said 'Wait ... not
you. You're helping me! Now!'

I didn't mess around. I jumped out and ran off up Rue
Biscarra. But I could hear people chasing me. I'm not as
fit as I should be, but I reckon I could have outrun them.
Then three guys up ahead of me saw what was going on,
and now I was trapped, and they all pounced on me and
that was that.

I don't know what happened to the others.

'Happy to sign that for me too, Bertrand?'
    'Yes, Inspector.'
    'Excellent. At this rate there won't be much left for the Magistrate
to investigate.'
    'Really?'
    'No, Bertrand – I was being just a little ironical. But I'll come back
to that in a minute ...
    'As for what happened to the others ... well, your back seat pal
didn't make it much farther either. He ran back down the street with
a few people after him too, lost his hat on the way, turned the corner
and bumped straight into the police officer you'd passed, who
recognised him at once. No contest. It was lucky for them both he'd
handed over his gun in the car, or we might have another attempted
murder on our hands. Because he had blood spattered all over his
coat, Bertrand, and we already have witnesses to say it was the tall

man who shot the security guard. And if the poor guy makes it through, I'm sure he'll be making a formal identification.

'But we know exactly how to handle our old friend G, as you call him, and he and I have already had another long and very persuasive discussion. And I'm now convinced he really doesn't know *any* of your names. Even inviting him to spend a few hours with the gentlemen at the Soviet consulate in Marseilles wouldn't drag much more out of him, I'm pretty sure.

'Whereas we haven't begun to question you in that way at all, have we, Bertrand? Because you've been so very co-operative already. And I don't *really* think you were the little guy with the moustache who shot the Deputy Manager. Although ...'

'No, no, no, Inspector, it wasn't me, I swear! I didn't want *any* violence!'

'But you know, Bertrand, I do feel you could tell me more than you've been willing to, so far. And I hope you've been thinking very carefully about that. It could do your case a lot of good, you know ...'

'I've told you already I don't know any names, Inspector.'

'And I still don't believe you. So please have another nice little think, OK ...?'

* * *

'I am very sorry to have kept you waiting, Monsieur Jareau. But at least I have some good news for you. We have found your car, and it is undamaged.'

'Ah, that *is* good news, Inspector.'

'Indeed. The bad news, of course, is that you won't be able to use it for a while. And then you'll be needing a new set of keys. Now, I'm listening ...'

> Well, as I drove across the junction, I saw a small Fiat had just crashed into a signpost. There were four people still inside, so I pulled over and stopped a little way past it. But by the time I was out of the car, the men in the back seats were running away, and the driver was helping a little guy with a stupid moustache out of the front door. That's when I realised why no-one else was

already helping them. The passenger had a gun and he was keeping everyone away. Then he looked straight at me and shouted 'Open your back door and start the car!' Well, you do what you're told when someone's pointing a gun at you, don't you?

The little guy was holding a heavy bag in his other hand, but he was wincing and was obviously injured. The young driver helped him make it into my car, then he got in too, and they slammed the doors. The little guy said 'Move it! Fast!' and I sped off down Rue Biscarra. Then he turned to his pal and said: 'Get him back onto our route, OK!' And then he started moaning gently to himself.

The young guy sent me left at the lights, then left again along Avenue du Maréchal Foch, and then right, which brought us onto Rue Hancy, just one block up from the crash. Then we went north for some time ... up into Rue Miron, and then into Rue Diderot. He wanted me to go west at Rue Marceau, but there was a traffic queue a bit farther along, so he made me carry on north for another block. We finally took a left at Avenue Mirabeau and crossed into Rue Vernier. Then the little guy suddenly took charge again, and said 'Turn left here! Now!'

I swung into the side street – I later found out it was Rue de Villeneuve – and drove down past the big closed doors of a furniture factory. Then the boss man said 'OK, stop here, get out, and stand well back in that alcove. Don't move for at least five minutes. I've got the car's number, and if we get caught in it, I'll find you and you'll pay, I swear!' The minute I was out, his mate was in the driving seat, and they shot off up to the lights and turned right into Rue Trachel. I stayed put for several minutes, just as I'd been told to, and then I found the nearest café and called the police.

Rue Trachel, Nice

Earlier that evening: Monday 23 November, 7 p.m.

'You need to get to a doctor, Luc ...'

'Don't be stupid. Shut your mouth and keep driving. Straight ahead until you reach Boulevard Gambetta. OK?'

'OK.'

This has all gone so wrong. At least there are no police cars behind us – yet. Maybe they're waiting up ahead. But what the hell's he going to do now? It's almost two kilometres back round to the planned stopping point. We should all have split up and disappeared by now! Instead of that I'm stuck in another hot car next to a bagful of hot cash and an injured bank robber. And did that other guy actually *shoot* someone in there ...??

'Hey, wake up, kid! This is Gambetta. Take a left, then go south as slowly as you can.'

'Left? Are you sure?'

'Yeah, left!'

Ah, he must be planning to get out. And I don't care if he forgets to pay me. I just want out of here myself. But – oh, he's unzipping the holdall again, and stuffing some of the money in his pockets ...

'OK – I promised you half a million. That's one of these wads. Well, here's two ... but you're going to earn them.'

'No, I ...'

'Take them and shut up. My chest and my shoulder are hurt. I've probably got a few broken ribs too. Aaaggh! And my head's just started killing me. I must have banged it on the door column. I can hardly lift the bag now, let alone carry it along the street or up any stairs. I've taken a few wads for myself, but I can't risk getting caught with too much on me. Aaaggh! So I'm leaving the bag on the back seat. You're going to have to look after it for a while.'

'But ...'

'No buts. Right, pull up now, under that big tree. It's even darker just there.'

'OK ...'

'And keep your head down. Now, you're going to dump the car as soon as you can, then take the money, stay in the shadows and hide it somewhere safe. But not at your own place! And listen – if you should get caught later, I KEPT THE BAG. Got that? I don't want anyone hounding you for it. So when I get out, I'll pretend I'm carrying something big under my coat, in case anyone sees me. And I'll be in touch when the heat is off. Don't leave town, and don't do anything stupid, or else. I know where you live and work, and a whole lot more – and don't forget I know about Emilie, too. So be a smart kid ... aaaggh! ... and do exactly what I've said.'

'All right, Luc ...'

'Good. Any action in the rear-view mirror?'

'No.'

'Anyone hanging around the car?'

'No.'

'OK, I'm getting out now. Aaaggh! Right, drive away nice and easy as soon as I close the door ....'

Merde! What did I do to deserve this? Well, I'm certainly not staying in this awful little rat-trap for long. I'll lose it in one of the dead-end streets further down on the right. Thank god it's really dark now ....

OK. Next right is Avenue Depoilly. That'll be perfect. Here we go ...

Now slowly along to Rue François Aune. Yes, there are several empty spaces beyond the junction, all the way up to the wall at the far end. And hardly any street lighting. It's particularly dark under those trees on the right. I'll pull into the first big gap and have another little think ....

OK, nobody's watching me. What now?

Think I'll back up a little, then shift across to the passenger seat and creep out into the shadow of the trees. No-one will spot me there ...

Now I'll grab the bag from the rear seat and shove it under the bumper of the Citroën behind me ...

Phew, it's heavier than I expected. No wonder Luc decided he couldn't carry it in his condition!

So, back inside and shift across again. Then wait and watch for a bit ....

Still nice and quiet. OK, I'll pull out now, drive along another fifty metres, and park up near the end of the avenue. If anyone sees me walking away from the car, they'll report that I wasn't carrying a thing, and Luc will be happy.

OK. Lock the other doors from the inside. Now get out, nice and nonchalant. Lock the driver's door. Cut behind the car onto the pavement and under the trees. Now stroll quietly back up the avenue ...

Still no-one around. And no sign of life in any of the windows opposite. Bend down to tie my shoelace when I reach the Citroën, and haul out the bag ...

... and now keep walking back towards Rue François Aune, and stop just around the corner.

So, what next?

The wind's getting up, and I think I can smell more rain in the air.

But first things first. This bag's too closely associated with the robbery, and there were plenty of witnesses to the accident. Where can I get a big suitcase at this time of day?

Up in the African bazaars right behind Nice-Ville station, that's where!

Hmmm. The people at the scene of the crash will also remember my shiny old suit. I'll need to do something to hide that too, and fast.

And this ridiculous hat is almost as incriminating. I'll stick it in the bag for now.

But these car keys will be going to the bottom of a litter bin very soon.

OK, I'll carry on north up Rue François Aune, cut over to Gambetta, cross under the railway lines, turn right into Rue de l'Abbé Grégoire, and then go around the square. I'll hold the bag close to the wall all the time, and use all my joyriding experience to make sure I'm not being followed.

Concentrate hard now, Arthur. It's time to make *your* run – at a walking pace.

Rue Reine Jeanne at last! But I'm *certain* there was never anyone behind me.

And it's finally starting to rain again. Just right!

Yes, lots of bazaars still open on the other side of the street. There's the one that always has a dozen suitcases lined up on the pavement. And I'm sure there's a men's clothing shop a bit further along ...

Yes, just where I remembered! That's perfect.

OK, it's worked once tonight, and it can work again. Up to the end of the block, cross the road and turn the corner ....

Nobody hanging around. Good. And lots of tightly parked cars here, as usual. Shove the bag under the rear bumper of this one. Then stroll back down to the bazaars ...

'Ah, bonsoir m'sieur ...'

'*Bonsoir*. I think we might get a real downpour soon. Do you have a full-length grey raincoat, please? Nice and cheap, eh!'

'Not so cheap, *m'sieur*, but very good quality. Let me help you try this one for size ... Ah, it is exactly right, *n'est-ce pas*?'

'Yes, it is. And I'd like a black beret too, please.'

'*Et voilà! Très chic, m'sieur*. What else may I get for you?'

'That's all I need. Here ...'

'And here is your change. *Merci bien, m'sieur, et au revoir.*'

And now for the suitcase ....

OK, all set. But if that's bag's been nicked, I'm on the first jet plane to Mars ....

It's still there. Don't know whether to laugh or cry.

Got it! Now into the first alcove I can find ...

Damn! It's too fat for the case. I'll have to pull out a few bundles and stuff them down the sides.

So this is what a fortune feels like!

But whose fortune? Not mine. Good fortune? Or ...?

Don't be tempted, Arthur.

There, it all fits now. Hah! I sound like Hercule Poirot. But I hate Agatha Christie. Why did Emilie make me read those stupid stories out loud to her on the beach?

Wake up, man! And carry on walking. You're just another dull visitor to Nice now, right?

Right.

But I'm only a couple of blocks down from where we dumped the driver of that car, for heaven's sake! He might still be hanging around. I need to get off the streets and well away from here ...

Got it! There's a main bus route only two blocks further along Rue Reine Jeanne ....

Nobody waiting at the stop. I'll stand a few metres away, back in the shadows ....

Here comes a bus. Don't move forward to stop it till the last moment ...

Perfect. No-one suddenly appeared and got on. So I'm still in the clear.

And we're going north, away from the city centre. Maybe I can relax for a few minutes ...

No, of course I can't! I need time and a safe space. There are far too many people on this bus! Have they heard about the robbery yet? Have they heard a description of any of us? Nobody's looking at me. Or are they just pretending not to?

But any one of them might remember me later. Reckon I'd better double back to the city centre and find somewhere nearer home where I can sit and think in the dark, without being watched or disturbed.

A secluded little public garden would be ideal. Plenty of those in Nice, but they all close at dusk, don't they?

Maybe I could just hole up on the Esplanade, right under the noses of the police on Rue Gioffredo? That's the last place anyone would look for a bank robber, less than two hours after the event. Especially now he's kitted out like a bourgeois Parisian.

OK. We're on Avenue Borriglione, and no-one else is about to get off the bus. I'll stop it at the next corner.

All clear again. I really can relax now. I'll wait here quietly for a bus back down to Masséna. Then I *will* just be that new kid in town.

Esplanade Charles de Gaulle, Nice

Monday 23 November, 8:45 p.m.

Made it! And it's not too busy. Still plenty of people around, though. And those unhappy palm trees, of course. But the cicadas have finally run out of voice, haven't they?

OK. I just need to find a small bench and plonk myself right in the middle of it ....

So what do I do now?

Give myself up? No need for that, surely? At least not yet – I'm still convinced I made a clean getaway.

Go on the run? But where to? With all the money in this big suitcase? Ridiculous idea! With just some of it, then? But what to do with the rest?

Or should I return it all anonymously? How? When? Well, it would be easy enough to dump it under another car, here and now, and make a quick call to the police, and then try and forget it had happened. But that wouldn't change things very much, would it? I'll still have been part of an armed robbery.

And Luc would *not* like any of those options, would he?

Or I could do exactly as he instructed, and hide the money, and carry on as normal.

As normal? Hah! Until he resurfaces, I mean ...

I don't have any real option. I can't risk turning him into an enemy. For Emilie's sake, if nothing else.

So, where can I hide it? Not in my own pokey apartment. There's nowhere I could store it out of sight there, even if I wanted to. But of course that would be a really stupid thing to do anyway. And Luc said that was the one place I should *not* hide it.

But there's nowhere else, is there? I don't have any real mates, and I wouldn't trust any of the guys at work, or the ones I've spoken to occasionally in the Old City bars. And it wouldn't be fair to drag any of them into this, anyway.

That only leaves Emilie's place ...

It's quite small, but it's a lot bigger than mine! And there'd be plenty of room for the suitcase under her bed, and it has a cover that goes down to the floor all the way round. And I'd probably only have to leave it there for a few days, till Luc contacts me and I'm able to get shot of it.

But then again it wouldn't be fair on Emilie either, would it? She'd certainly object. And she seems to have been in an even worse mood with me recently, so maybe she'd actually refuse. But I'd simply have to insist, wouldn't I? She'd just have to stand by her man. Because there really is no other option.

Why is that bloody statue pointing its finger at me? It deserves to have ...

But it's not pointing at me at all, is it? Just a trick of the light. Just my stupid imagination again, dammit!

OK. She's doing the early spot at the club again tonight, so she'll be finished soon. Hah! Then she'll be "Emilie Cigale."

She should get home by ten. I'd better sit tight here for a while. Then I'll grab a bus up to Place Garibaldi, and walk down towards her place like a visitor looking for cheap digs. I'll be a bit too close to home for comfort, but it'll be very dark and no-one will associate me with this old man's get-up!

Rue Bavastro, Nice

Monday 23 November, 10:30 p.m.

No-one has followed me. Front door's wide open, as usual. And the lobby's deserted.

OK, straight up to the first floor, then along to the far end ...

Glad there are no windows on the corridor. I can still be certain nobody's spotted me.

But there's no light showing under Emilie's door. Surely she's not still out? Must remember to knock very quietly – I don't want anyone else poking their nose into things tonight.

No answer. Damn! Knock a bit louder, but only once more ...

Still nothing. And the door's locked. She must still be at the club. Or maybe she got involved in a spot of *après-spectacle.*

If only she had a phone – but then she isn't in there to answer it, is she? Think harder, you idiot ...

That neighbour across the corridor! What was her name? Ah yes, Danielle – older woman, some sort of nursing assistant, works nights at the hospital. Found me standing here late one afternoon, waiting for Emilie to get back from the shops. Invited me into her apartment and sat me on a lumpy old sofa and made me drink that awful instant coffee while she spent thirty minutes telling me her life story.

But she *also* told me I could wait in there any time I needed to, didn't she? 'I'm always losing things, Arthur! So I daren't risk locking the door and then losing my key. I've got nothing in here that anyone would want to steal, and all the furniture belongs to the landlord ...'

The sofa! In a furnished apartment! So even if *she* were to move out in the near future, the sofa would stay put! And if I then had to break in to collect the money, well, too bad.

Right, I'll do it. Should I knock first? No, she's sure to be out at work by now. And I have her permission anyway!

Fingers crossed ...

It's not locked! OK, locate the light switch ... yes, same position as Emilie's ... but mustn't touch it till I'm inside with the door closed and I've checked out the window on the end wall ...

Can't see much, but there's the window ...

Not directly overlooked, of course. Just like Emilie's. I'll close the curtains. Then I can risk the light switch ...

Yes! The sofa's still in the same place, opposite the front door. What an awful shade of pink!

Right, let's get on with it. Tip it all the way forward. What do we have? Just a long run of thumbtacks all the way round, holding the bottom fabric onto the wooden base. No problem. Need to find a table knife and prise four of them off the back edge ...

There! Easy. Now I can post the wads of banknotes through the gap, one by one, and flick them out to the sides as much as I can. And I'd better count them as I go ...

Finished. Seventy-four in all. Wow! I'll work that out later – it's time to move now. Push the thumbtacks firmly back in again ... and give them each a very gentle tap with the knife for good measure. Done.

Now tilt the sofa back the other way, to spread the wads around a bit. That's it. Now upright again, and back in place. Perfect! It looks no different – just as lumpy, but the cash is all underneath the springs and the stuffing.

Right. Knife back in place. Holdall back in the suitcase. Light out. Curtains open again. Shut the door as quietly as I can behind me. And get out of here fast ....

Now, what am I going to do with the rest of this junk? Spread it around all over Nice? No, there's too much chance of one item being found.

Keep it all together, then? Shove my new raincoat and beret into the case with the empty bag and the silly hat, and take them all for a ride up into the hills, and lose them over a convenient cliff edge? That would give me an alibi, too – that pretty little Alfa-Romeo's been waiting patiently for me to steal her for the last three days. I'd rather get done for borrowing a car than for robbery with probable violence.

No, that's all far too complicated, and it'll take a long time and add loads of unnecessary risk. I need to cut and run fast now.

OK, I *will* stuff everything into the suitcase, but I'll add a dozen bricks from that demolition site over on Rue Cassini, and then I'll take a little stroll down one of the harbour walkways, and come back empty-handed ...

Rue Fontaine de la Ville, Nice

Monday 23 November, 11:30 p.m.

Right, that's the last anyone should see of that lot for a very long time. God, I'm tired. But I'll be home in a couple of minutes. Gotta get to bed!

Hang on. I've still got both of my own wads of cash on me. Might be a good idea to take a leaf out of Luc's book and split them up. Just in case ...

I have to go past the garage. Praise be to old Soron for letting me have a key! He only did it to encourage me to arrive early every morning and make the coffee. Well, now I get the payback. I'll leave one of the wads in there for a few days ...

But where the hell am I going to hide it so the other guys don't sniff it out? This isn't going to be easy ...

Got it! Wrap it up in a page of an old newspaper, and then in a scrap of rubber sheeting to protect it, and then use a bit of sticky tape to hold it together – and then push it under that huge old tool chest in the side bay. If it will fit. Better check that first ...

Yes! There's a gap of five centimetres between the bottom drawer and the floor. If I shove the package half-way back, no-one will spot it even when the drawer's well open. And the best thing is, I can push it out again from the side, any day I fancy! Good thinking, Arthur!

Job done! And the drawer moves in and out without disturbing it.
OK, lock up again, and I'll be home in less than a minute.

* * *

Made it!
Jeez, I'm starving, but I'm too exhausted to look for anything to eat. This is worse than being drunk!
What's the time now?
God, it's after midnight! Hey, maybe this has all just been a bad dream. But I don't think so.
I'm switching off the alarm clock. I'm not going in tomorrow morning. I'll tell them I got sick during the night.
But is that a good idea? Hell, I don't know ...
Concentrate, Arthur. Jacket off first, right? Then ...
Nah, can't be bothered with the rest.

The Birds in the Trees

Central Police Station, Nice

Tuesday 24 November, 1 a.m.

'All right, Inspector. I've been thinking about it. And I certainly don't want to make you angry. As long as you promise ...'

'I'll do my best, Bertrand.'

'Well, I swear I know nothing at all about Luc. But I do know just a little more about our getaway driver.'

'Go on ...'

'I think his name's Narone. Young guy. Works at Jean Soron's repair garage on Rue Fontaine de la Ville. He may live round there too, but I don't know where, and I don't want to know.'

'Description?'

'No idea, Inspector. He was wearing a big hat, and I was sitting right behind him in the escape car, remember? And after the crash I didn't stop to take a better look, if you know what I mean.'

'OK, Bertrand. I still don't think you've told me all you know, but it'll do. It may even get you another cup of coffee. Because we already have descriptions from several other witnesses. And we've heard a few rumours about Monsieur Narone ourselves ...'

Hmmm. He's probably still living on the same street. But we'll check that out first, so we don't hit the wrong apartment ...

* * *

'I'm sorry, sir. We still haven't found a home address or a phone number for Jean Soron.'

'This is crazy, Brigadier Lebrun. What is it?'

'Crazy, sir.'

'Too right. It's nearly three hours since Irvoise sang! OK, I'm going home to get some sleep. You can take a little nap right here. Because at six o'clock you'll be going down to that garage with one of the others to wait for Soron to arrive. Call me by seven at the very latest, or as soon as you confirm Narone's address. And then you can get that lazy Magistrate out of bed and tell him we need an arrest warrant at once ...'

Rue Fontaine de la Ville, Nice

Tuesday 24 November, 8:30 a.m.

What a dump this corner of town is! Just a few labourers walking to work, a couple of cheap run-down businesses, and some very rough-looking apartment blocks.

And that must be the garage up ahead on the left. Surprised I can deduce even that after only two hours' sleep. But the two waiting squad cars give it away ...

'Got the warrant, Lebrun?'

'Yes, sir.'

'Good. Checked it thoroughly?'

'Yes, sir!'

'Even better. Maybe we'll pay you this month.'

'Thank you, sir. And I reckon you should see the morning newspaper before we go in ...'

DARING RAID ON INSECURE CITY BANK!!!

Four armed men held up staff and customers of the Banque Artisanale in Nice at gunpoint yesterday evening and made off with a haul estimated at over 100 million Old Francs. The robbers appear to have known in advance that this huge sum of money was being stored in the main hall at that time.

Eyewitnesses report that several shots were fired at a dozen terrified customers. Thankfully they all missed their targets. But a senior manager was seriously wounded, and the bank's lone security guard was gunned down in cold blood and is in a critical condition at the city's Saint-Roch Hospital.

The robbers then crashed their getaway car during a reckless high-speed police chase through the busy rush-hour streets. Two of them managed to escape in a second hijacked car, after assaulting its unlucky owner. But after putting up violent struggles, the others were mercifully arrested at the scene by heroic members of the Nice citizenry.

Unidentifiable sources report that the two captured bank robbers were found to be in possession of a total of some eight million Old Francs. But where, we ask, is the ruthless gang leader, who apparently made off with the rest of the haul after he and his partner dumped the hijacked driver near Rue Trachel??

'How come they always seem to know a lot more than we do?'
    'Perhaps they make much of it up, sir, and double all the numbers as a matter of course.'
    'Yes, Lebrun. Perhaps they do. So, where is he?'
    'Just two hundred metres down the street, sir.'
    'And ...?'

'I kept all the uniforms back here and cased the building on my own, thirty minutes ago. It's a tacky old block set at a sharp angle to the street. Narone's apartment is on the second floor, third door to the right after the stairs. There's no lift. Fire escape's at the other end of the corridor, but I'll bet that door's locked anyway. If he jumps out of his only window he'll land on some very nasty-looking old iron. And that's it, sir. I suggest we cruise down in quiet convoy and pull up just past the building, out of sight of anyone inside. And maintain silence till we make our entry.'

'Good work, Brigadier. OK, let's go. I'll be right behind you all ...'

* * *

CRASH!

'What the hell ...??'

'Hands above your head! And don't move!'

'Still in bed and fully dressed, well after eight o'clock, Narone? A fit young man like you should be hard at work by now. Late night, perhaps?'

'I don't know what ...'

'OK, he's secure, sir.'

'Right. Check that jacket first, Lebrun ...'

'Yes, sir ... Jackpot, sir!'

'Well, well, well. This is a bit out of your league, isn't it, Narone? A nice fat wad of used 5000 Old Franc notes, answering perfectly to the description of a lot of others that went missing yesterday evening. You wouldn't happen to know where the rest of them are?'

'No!'

'Or the boss man with the silly voice?'

'What silly voice?'

'OK, Brigadier, you do the honours with Stirling Moss here. The rest of you can get started on a full search – it won't take very long in this pokey little mouse-hole. And I'll see *you* down at the station, Narone. After I've had some breakfast.'

Central Police Station, Nice

Tuesday 24 November, 12 noon

'Right, Arthur – you don't mind if I call you Arthur, do you? – I've had a good read through your statement again, and I'd like you to reconsider a few things before you sign it, OK?'

'Whatever. It's rather cold in here, isn't it, Inspector? Any chance of a nice cup of tea ...?'

'I also think you might do well to show a bit more interest in making me a much happier man, Arthur. I have this instinctive dislike of people who associate themselves with attempted murderers ...'

'What?'

'You heard me.'

'OK. I guess I'd better try a bit harder.'

'You'd better come to mean it eventually, my boy. Right, let's stick with that subject for starters. Did you know the others were all carrying guns?'

'No. Not until the guys in the back of the car handed theirs in to Luc, just before the crash.'

'Did they talk about what happened inside the bank?'

'No. Well, one of them did say he'd had to deal with a guard. But I didn't know what he meant by that.'

'He meant he'd nearly put him in a coffin, Arthur. And there's still a fair chance he has ...'

'Ah, merde!'

'Very apposite. And your pal "Luc" is also very handy with a gun ...'

'He's not my pal! ... What? Did he shoot somebody too?'

'Oh yes, Arthur. The Deputy Manager. Not a very pretty picture, is it? Not quite the same as borrowing a little MG for a quick run round the hills ...'

'No.'

'Going to be a little more helpful now? You know it makes sense ...'

'Yes, Inspector.'

'Good. So let's move on to Monsieur Luc Comet. Did you make that name up all on your own?'

'Well, half of it, yes.'

'Pah! So, when he got out of the car on Boulevard Gambetta, he took the money bag with him, right?'

'I've already told you that. If you'd met him yourself, you'd realise he wouldn't have let go of it in a hurry!'

'Unless ...'

'Unless what?'

'Unless he was hurt in the accident and couldn't carry it. The driver of the car you hijacked said he thought the boss man had been injured.'

'It was just a bump on the head. He told me he was fine as he left the car.'

'Hmmm. And where does he live, Arthur? Near where you dropped him off?'

'I've told you that too – I have no idea!'

'All right. Now ... remind me what time you got back last night.'

'A little after midnight.'

'Yes. So it took you nearly five hours to walk home after you dumped the car on Avenue Depoilly. Did you perhaps go via Cannes?'

'Very funny.'

'Where were you all evening, Arthur?'

'I was wandering around the city, trying to work out what to do for the best. You know – get out of town, or give myself up, or hope I'd got away with it and just go home. It took me all that time to decide to carry on as planned. I had the money Luc had promised me in my pocket, so I was happy enough. Of course, you've got it now.'

'That single wad of notes was your only payoff from that huge haul?'

'Yes. I don't know how much was in the bag altogether, but it looked like an awful lot.'

'Well, you certainly came cheap compared with the other two.'

'I don't care. I didn't actually rob a bank, did I? Or shoot anybody ... Hang on – how do you know how much *they* were paid?'

'Oh, we have them both tucked up nicely here already. And their pay packets.'

'*Merde!* Now I understand how ...'

'Don't jump to any reckless conclusions, Arthur. Just concentrate on making the best of things by helping us as much as possible in the hours and days to come, eh? So, you'd never seen any of them before?'

'No. And I hardly saw the other two on the day. They just jumped in the back seat outside the bank and then got out again fast after the crash. Luc had told me not to turn round and look at them, and I didn't.'

'What about "Luc" himself?'

'He press-ganged me in a dark alley in the Old City three weeks ago, and stayed out of sight behind me the whole time. And yesterday he was wearing a big old hat and sunglasses and a bushy false moustache. I wouldn't recognise him again, not even if ... no, you're actually a lot taller than him, Inspector.'

'Don't push me, Arthur. Now, you said in your statement that he had a sort of gruff Marseilles accent. That's strange, because I have witnesses from the bank who say he spoke in a high-pitched *Italian* accent ...'

'So what does a senior detective like you make of that?'

'I won't warn you again, Narone!'

'OK, OK.'

'Right, I've got three of you already, and before the week is out I'm going to find "Luc" and the insider who must have set him up. But I'm not convinced you've told me the whole story ...'

'Yes, I have.'

'Hmmm. We found three thousand *balles* in your trousers pocket when we arrested you, didn't we?'

'So what?'

'Well, I'm guessing that's all you have left over from last Friday's wages, after paying your rent and buying some food.'

'With insight like that, I suspect you'll make it to Chief Inspector very soon.'

'I'll take that as a "yes". So what's a poor church mouse like you doing with another *thirty-five* thousand in his bedside drawer?'

'That's none of your business. But I'll save you the effort of trying to find out. It's my savings.'

'Pah! You've managed to save a whole month's wages in the few years you've been out at work and probably earning a pittance? You must really think I'm stupid!'

'No comment.'

'Right, that'll do for now, Arthur. Unless – is there anyone you'd like to pay you a visit?'

'What? Oh ... No, I don't think so. Well, maybe ...'

'Yes?'

'No, forget it. Waste of time.'

'Let me know if you change your mind.'

'I shan't.'

'Fair enough. You can have that cup of tea now. And I'll be talking to you again soon, I'm sure.'

'I can't wait, Inspector.'

'So what do you think, Lebrun?'

'About Narone, sir?'

'No, about the origin of the universe.'

'I think he's being so bloody cocky because he's got nothing more to hide, so he has no fear of being caught out. I think we've learnt all we're going to learn from him.'

'And I think you're probably right. But I'm going to leave *him* to think he might be coming under a lot more pressure. So get yourself some lunch, then go back to the garage, talk to his workmates and see if there's anyone we can use to squeeze a bit more out of him ...'

'Yes, sir. And where will you be?'

'Interviewing the poor sods who got shot – if the doctors will let me. And then following my nose ...'

Saint-Roch Hospital, Nice

Tuesday 24 November, 2 p.m.

'And what happened then, Monsieur Orceau?'

'Well, I caught the bag he'd thrown at me, and left it on the counter, and opened the safe behind me, and grabbed a handful of wads, and took them back to the bag. My three nearest colleagues had rushed over to the safe by now, collecting more handfuls and passing them across to me. It had all gone very quiet. Then the leader started complaining we were going too slowly. I tried to concentrate on getting on with it as fast as I could. But maybe I gave him a bit of a dirty look at one point. Because he suddenly pointed the gun straight at me, and everything seemed to slow down, and then he shot me!'

'Madame Padroux has told us you made rather more objections than you've just suggested ...'

'Huh! Well maybe I did, Inspector. I was very angry. But it probably wasn't a good idea to show it.'

'Indeed. So, please continue.'

'Well, nobody came to help me at first. I think Christine took over filling the bag. Then I heard more shouting, then nothing for a while, and then another shot and people screaming. Then the door was slammed and Christine knelt down at my side. I don't remember much more after that – until I found the ambulance man kneeling beside me too, and talking to me ...'

'Thank you, Charles-Pierre. That was very helpful, and you have all my sympathy. What have the doctors told you?'

'They say my injury is not too serious. Two or three more days in here, then lots of bed-rest at home.'

'Yes, that's as I understand it too.'

'And they said Marco was *very* badly hurt, but he's stable ...'

'Indeed. We shan't be able to talk to him for some time, though. Now, have you seen the morning paper?'

'Yes, I have. A lot of lies and exaggerations, of course, but it did say that two of the robbers have already been caught. Well done, Inspector!'

'Thank you. And I'm pleased to say that early this morning we also apprehended the getaway driver.'

'Excellent!'

'Yes. But the leader is still missing, and we're pretty sure he has the money. Well, most of it, anyway – we've recovered the payoffs he made to the other lowlifes. We have witnesses who say he was carrying the bag when he was seen over on Rue Biscarra and later on Rue de Villeneuve, and when the getaway driver finally dropped him off he was apparently still holding on to it.'

'That's no surprise!'

'No, it's not. Now, please tell me again, for the record, Charles-Pierre – which of the robbers were carrying guns?'

'All three, for heaven's sake!'

'And once again – are you certain which one of them shot you?'

'The leader, of course! The one with the moustache and the squeaky voice.'

'Yes, that all ties up with what Madame Padroux told us. And it's what the other little guy said too. Now, about the Manager of your bank ...'

'Monsieur Tillier? He was away all day, at our Head Office in Marseilles.'

'Indeed. And he was halfway back to Nice by the time anyone thought about trying to telephone him there. So he only learnt about the robbery when his train arrived at eight-thirty and he found my brigadier waiting at the station with one of your staff to point him out.'

'He must have been shocked!'

'Yes, I believe so. But all the indications are that this was an inside job. So we are naturally obliged to question him about it, and we have already done that. He seems totally surprised by the whole affair, and very keen to understand who was behind it ...'

'But of course he is. And so am I! You don't *really* suspect Raoul, do you?'

'We always need to keep an open mind on these things, Charles-Pierre. But I must say we now have a more promising lead to follow ...'

'Really?'

'Yes. We have spoken again with Madame Padroux, and she has now remembered that your junior clerk Giuseppe Hauvert did not turn up yesterday morning. Are you able to confirm that for us?'

'Oh yes! I'm afraid I had completely forgotten too, but yes, we spoke about it briefly, and we concluded he was unwell and not able to telephone us. It is rare for him to be absent from work.'

'I see. Well, we have already visited his apartment, and he is not there. The concierge has told us that she received an urgent phone call for Hauvert at nine o'clock on Sunday evening, and had to go upstairs to get him to come and take it. As soon as he put down the receiver, he told her he would be going away for a while.

'And at eight o'clock on Monday morning, two of his neighbours bumped into him as he was locking his front door. He was carrying a suitcase, and when they asked if he was leaving, he said his grandmother was dangerously ill back in Genoa, and he was going to her at once.'

'I see. You do know his father is French, Inspector ...'

'Indeed. We're trying to locate him – and his wife. And we've asked the Italian police to help us check whether young Hauvert *has* crossed the border, and to establish his grandparents' address, and to pick him up if he ever arrives at their house. But I think it's more likely he'll just hole up in somewhere like Sanremo with that suitcase – it's probably empty – and wait for his share of the loot to be delivered, probably by the guy who made that alibi call for him. If he's very lucky ...'

'You suspect him that strongly?'

'Well, all the evidence points his way, doesn't it, Charles-Pierre?'

'Yes, it certainly seems to.'

'So, I'll be concentrating on him for the rest of the day. I'll keep in touch.'

'Thank you, Inspector.'

Taking Stock

Passage Grégoire, Nice

Tuesday 24 November, 3 p.m.

Twenty hours since it happened. Damn that truck! Narone did well to avoid it on that slippery road. But I told the kid to take it steady!

I'm certain nobody saw me struggling back here last night. It only took five minutes, and if anyone had, I'd have received a visit or two by now. So I'm probably in the clear – so far.

And I can't see any cuts, just a lot of bruises. Well, no *external* bleeding, at least. So I haven't left a trail.

But I'm feeling really weak now. Hardly slept a wink. Too many different injuries, and always the noise of another train going past, just as I think I'm drifting off.

My head's still killing me, but I know I'm thinking straight. And I'm sure I *have* broken a rib or two, but they'll heal in time. Hope they haven't punctured anything!

It's the chest pain that's worrying me most. Fifty million *balles* is a very solid object when you ram up against it at speed! Maybe one day they'll put those fancy new seat belts in *every* car. And my shoulder feels a lot worse too. It's not dislocated, but it's not good.

So I'm in poor shape, right? Dare I try and see a doctor? No, that's still a crazy idea. Well, certainly not in Nice, anyway. The news will be all over town by now. I tried not to make it too obvious, but those witnesses will have told the *flics* I was injured in the crash. All the hospitals and surgeries will have been alerted.

But I'm probably going to get worse if I don't get any treatment. The pain's bad enough, but who knows what else might be going on inside me?

Doctors, that's who.

And mothers, Paul-Philippe.

I don't know anyone else here who could help me out till I get a bit better. And even in Marseilles there's nobody I could trust. They'd ask too many questions, and then start shooting their mouths off or blackmailing me for a big share of all the cash they think I now have – hah! – in return for their silence and the services of some back-street quack ...

Well, I can't stay in this black hole any longer, that's for sure. That will give me no options for treatment or care if things get a lot worse. I'd better go straight back to Marseilles. I've got a week left before I need to pay another month's rent. A week to decide what to do next, with a bit of sunlight coming into my room again.

I'll need to dump the guns soon. Where? In Nice? Huh! No way am I strolling around *these* streets in this condition. It'll have to be Marseilles, dammit! So, I'll need to arrive there late this evening, pick up a cab near the station, and get it to stop a few minutes' walk away from the apartment. Then I can drop off my suitcase, take another cab down to the port, lose the guns one by one in the water, and get another cab back.

I'll need to wait till after dark before I leave here. So I'll catch the seven-thirty train. And I'll have to get changed into different clothes first, even though doing that's going to be very painful. Then I can safely walk the few metres up to Boulevard Gambetta and get a cab round to the station. It's not very far, but I can't go all that way on foot, with this case to carry. Even though it's a lot lighter than I'd planned.

And I daren't buy a sandwich here, even though I'm starving and feeling even weaker. I'll have to wait and pick up something in Marseilles, when I've finished the business at the port. And maybe even find a late-night bazaar and get in some food for the next few days. Then I'll be able to hole up while I think things through.

Can't really risk buying a newspaper here either. Perhaps I'll be able to take a peek at a front page at the station, or find one lying around on the train. I really do need to know what's been happening since the crash. And especially whether they caught Narone with the money ...

Elsewhere in Nice

Tuesday 24 November, 9 p.m.

So the evening paper has picked up a bit more information. I wonder how much of it has been confirmed? There's no news of any more cash being found. Or Ruford himself. Where the hell is he hiding? Maybe he's laying low in his digs in Nice. Or maybe he's decided to get out of town for a while – or longer.

Was he injured in the crash? And has he already managed to hide the rest of the money where we agreed, or has he kept it with him? It's impossible to know, right now. I'll have to be patient and keep my eyes and ears open ...

But what about the getaway driver they caught this morning? Arthur Narone. I shan't be able to get to him, of course, even if I wanted to take the risk of revealing myself – he'll be stuck in a police cell or up at the Maison d'Arrêt until he goes to trial. But the newspaper says his girlfriend's a singer in an Old City club. They obviously haven't managed to dredge up her name yet.

Well, I must give Ruford a bit of slack, in the circumstances. But if he doesn't make contact in the next couple of weeks, I may have to find some way of getting Narone's young lady friend to help me. But again, that could mean showing my face. And I really didn't want to have to do that. Ever.

This is not going to be easy.

Rue Marengo, Marseilles

Tuesday 24 November, 11:30 p.m.

Finished at last! Guns dumped in the harbour. Enough food and drink here for at least a week. No sign of Norbert and his deaf old wife – but they'll have been in bed for at least an hour, anyway. And no other inquisitive neighbours popping out to ask where I've been for the past eight weeks!

But I can't put up with the pain in my chest much longer. I'll take two more aspirin and hope I can get a bit of sleep tonight, without any damned trains to disturb me. Then tomorrow I'm going to have to make some big decisions.

'Cos it's all gone to pot now. Good job I found those newspapers on the train. I don't give a damn about Irvoise or Aignant. But Narone arrested as well, in his own apartment?? How the hell did he let that happen? There's no mention of the money, though. Just the single wad he was carrying. Not the *two* I gave him, just one ...

But if he managed to hide the other one, then he must have hidden the bag as well. Maybe in the same place. And somewhere other than his apartment, of course.

Unless someone stole it from *him*, or he gave it away to his mates, or the police have ...

Pah! I can't worry about all the things that *might* have happened to it! Stupid! I've got to assume he did just what I told him to, and *then* got careless. Or maybe the poor sod was shopped by Irvoise. That wouldn't surprise me.

But I can't contact Narone and recover the money now, can I? And maybe not for years. So much for emigrating with nearly twelve million *balles* – or a lot more if I'd decided not to share any of it with Xérus!

Merde! I'd almost forgotten about Xérus. He must be feeling really happy too. And he said he knows where I live, didn't he?

Oh boy.

I'd better look on the bright side. At least I took nine of the wads, and I still have some of his advance left. Best part of five million altogether. I just need to decide where I should go, pronto, to enjoy it in peace ... or maybe to pay some doctor a lot of money to keep his mouth shut and save my life.

Gotta try and sleep now ....

Wait a minute! The paper mentioned Narone's girlfriend. Surely he didn't leave the money bag with *her*?

Well, even if he did, it's going to be a while before I can get back to Nice and track her down to ask her myself.

Oh, why the hell can't I get to sleep? I need some more aspirin ...

Back Down the Rabbit Holes

Central Police Station, Nice

Wednesday 25 November, 9 a.m.

'Ah, good morning, sir. I trust you've had a good night's sleep after your little trip to the border ...'

'Only what I need and deserve, Brigadier. If the Italians had actually given us a bit more co-operation on the phone, I would not have had to waste my time chasing them up in person.'

'And may I assume we have not yet unearthed Giuseppe Hauvert ...?'

'You may. But we shall, believe me, as soon as they decide to give him some real attention. Now, what about young Narone's pals?'

'Well, he doesn't really seem to have any, sir. His workmates at the garage are nothing more than that. They told us he used to hang around with an old school friend when he first started work there, but he hasn't mentioned him for years. We did pick up something about a girlfriend, though. So did the writer of the article about Narone in the evening paper, of course ...'

'I didn't see anything about *her* in it!'

'That part only made the final edition, sir – on the streets at five o'clock. If you'd been here yesterday evening ...'

'I *knew* he had a girlfriend! *Cherchez la femme ...*'

'That's exactly what we have been doing, sir. We visited the club where she works – turns out she's a very popular singer – and got a name. Emilie Courbier.'

'I've heard of her. In fact I've seen her show! Was it the Casa della Musica?'

'Indeed, sir. The owner gave us her address after a bit of persuasion, but he said she wasn't likely to be at home on such a nice afternoon. He was right. We got there at three – no reply. Tried again at six, but she was still not there. So I decided to visit the club at seven-thirty – she was due in by then, to do an early evening spot – and I waited for over an hour, but she never arrived. The owner was very surprised and extremely annoyed. So at nine o'clock the lads and I went back to her apartment and got the concierge to open up.'

'And ...?'

* * *

'Is there anything more you'd like to tell me now, Arthur?'

'No, Inspector. I told you everything yesterday.'

'Very well. But you'll remember I asked if there was anyone you'd like to see?'

'Yeah.'

'And you almost mentioned your pretty little girlfriend, didn't you?'

'What? How did you know that?'

'I must have been using some of that senior detective's intuition ...'

'And how did you find out about her, anyway?'

'By spending the taxpayers' money on making a few enquiries. It's what we do around here, most days. But I'm sorry to say we've drawn a blank. Your precious Mademoiselle Courbier disappeared before we could even make her acquaintance. So of course I'm forced to wonder why ...'

'You mean you went to her apartment and she just wasn't there at the time ...?'

'Nothing so simple, I regret. On our third attempt we invited the concierge to unlock her door for us. Nothing left but the furniture. She's gone, Arthur.'

'What? Why would she suddenly do that?'

'Why indeed? Carry on thinking like that and we'll make a senior detective out of you too. And to answer your question, *I'm* thinking that maybe it was actually *you* who made off with the money after dumping the injured "Luc". And maybe you took it to Emilie's place and left it with her before you finally went home on Monday night ...'

'What???'

'It's a perfectly good theory. We even have a statement from a neighbour who lives on the same floor as Emilie, saying she thinks she heard knocking on one of the front doors late that evening.'

'Pah! So what? I think it's a ridiculous theory. But ... maybe someone else believes it too, Inspector.'

'Well, there *was* a passing reference to her in the evening paper ...'

'What? You shouldn't have told the press about her! Maybe she's been attacked or even kidnapped!'

'I've told them nothing, Arthur. And the paper didn't even mention her name. I don't think anyone has got to her. Another neighbour told us later that he'd seen her leaving with a large suitcase around eight o'clock yesterday evening. And I've just spoken to the manager of the club where she works. Used to work. She called him at nine-thirty last night to say she wasn't coming in and wasn't coming back. He was not amused, but she wouldn't explain why. No, Emilie must have seen that press report and simply walked out on him and you and everybody else. Probably all because of what you did on Monday ...'

'But she just wouldn't! Someone *must* have put her under pressure! How do you know she made that call of her own free will? You *have* to start a proper search for her at once! Please!'

'I can't waste my resources like that. She's a big girl now.'

'She's nineteen, Inspector!'

'Exactly. Almost twenty, in fact. A lot of Frenchwomen of her age have been married for nearly five years.'

'But you believe she's holding the money from the robbery!!'

'Oh no, I never really thought that, Arthur. And you have now convinced me I was right. *Merci beaucoup.*'

'What? Oh, damn you and your devious methods!'

'That's a rather poor line to take, young man. But then you're not too skilled at holding onto those who actually care about you, are you ...?'

'What do you mean by that?'

'I'll leave you to work it out. And by the way – I don't really think "Luc" left you to look after the money bag. We now have a statement from someone who lives at the far end of Avenue Depoilly. She reports seeing you from her window – emerging from the car, locking it, and walking back up towards the crossroads. She soon lost you in the shadows, but she swears you weren't carrying anything. She thought nothing more of it at the time, apart from mild annoyance that you'd parked in her exclusive cul-de-sac. But a few hours later she saw us examining the car, and she came forward.'

'Well thank you very much for telling me, at last!'

'But I didn't have to, did I, Arthur? It's just by way of illustrating what I was saying about nurturing your friends ...'

Saint-Roch Hospital, Nice

Wednesday 25 November, 7 p.m.

'It is very good to see you again, Charles-Pierre. And the reports of your colleagues are clearly accurate ... you are looking a lot stronger than you were on my first visit!'

'Ah, thank you, Monsieur Tillier. I am fortunate to have received so much kind attention and concern. And yes, I am indeed feeling much better today. But if only ...'

'If only what?'

'If only they knew how to serve hard-boiled eggs properly here.'

'*Mon Dieu!* What is the problem, my friend?'

'They should always be of moderate dimensions and served at the correct temperature, sir. Too small and warm, and they are like *tagliatelle* on fire; too large and cold, and they are like rubbery, tepid ice-cream. But when heated and presented *comme il faut*, a hard-boiled egg of the ideal size – bitten, not sliced, *naturellement* – is a match for a spoonful of the finest Russian caviar or a perfect Martini, and should be consumed within the space of ten seconds. With no salt or pepper, of course.'

'Ah, the life of the gourmet has regrettably never been mine, Charles-Pierre.'

'No, sir. But I suppose I should not really expect it in this place. I have experienced perfectly-served eggs only four times in my life –

in Turin, Edinburgh, Paris, and would you believe it, Aix-en-Provence!'

'Such is life.'

'Indeed. But thankfully I expect to be discharged tomorrow.'

'Ah, that is excellent news! But it does nothing to alleviate my discomfort and embarrassment for what happened to you on Monday, my friend.'

'Sir, you must not feel in any way responsible ...'

'However, I'm very happy to be able to tell you that the Head Office people have now confirmed that we will cover all your hospital costs, and allow you as much sick leave as you need to fully regain your strength.'

'Oh, thank you, sir!'

'And I'm also discussing an appropriate *ex gratia* payment as compensation for everything you have bravely suffered in the line of duty.'

'That's very kind of you, sir, but I really don't expect ...'

'Hush, Charles-Pierre! And don't let me hear you say that in front of any of *them*! Just leave it to me, all right?'

'Very well. And – oh dear, how can I put this, sir? – have the police and the Marseilles people been giving *you* a hard time? Because the Inspector did tell me he would need ...'

'No, not really. Of course they've all asked me a lot of loaded questions, but such inquisitions are never difficult to handle when you're telling the truth, are they?'

'Of course not, sir.'

'And how about you?'

'Oh, the Head Office people just wanted to hear my account of events for themselves, of course. And Inspector Hardy has been a real gentleman. He's visited me twice a day, and kept me up to date with all the developments – well, I assume he's told me all of them! – and he seems pretty confident they'll pick up Hauvert soon, one way or another ...'

'You know, I'm not at all convinced that Giuseppe was the insider. He always seemed such a good lad, and I can't see how he could have gathered enough information to be able to get it all set up ...'

'Yes, I agree it's hard to credit, sir. And maybe everyone *is* jumping to the wrong conclusions about him. But who else *could* it have been?'

'Well, if they're willing to believe it was him, then it could have been *anybody* working in the branch, no? Anybody. Or someone from another branch. Or even an employee of the security van company. Or maybe even Marco Charnière ...'

'What? You don't seriously think he organised all of this and then got shot in the chest for his pains?'

'No, I don't, Charles-Pierre! I have every sympathy for our faithful servant and his family. And we shall be looking after them appropriately too, I can assure you. No, I was simply making a point about how difficult this sort of investigation must be for the police and the bank.'

'Indeed, sir. Yes, indeed ...'

'So – I shall leave you to relax again now. Enjoy your bed-rest at home as much as you can! Ensure your eggs are boiled to warm and perfect hardness! And take plenty of gentle exercise once you're up and about, before you even think about coming back to work.'

'I shall, Monsieur Tillier. And thank you once again for all your kindness and support.'

'Ah, it is nothing, Charles-Pierre. No more than a hero deserves at this sorry time!'

Rue Marengo, Marseilles

Wednesday 25 November, 8 p.m.

The pain's getting worse by the hour. It *must* be internal bleeding or something just as nasty. But what do I know?

Nothing, that's what.

If it carries on like this, I shan't even be able to walk down the stairs, let alone do any more shopping or even have another bath. And this place stinks enough already!

Why the hell won't those birds stop singing? What have they got to be so happy about?

They're free, I suppose. Like most people in France. Like me.

But I reckon I only have forty-eight hours left to do something. And that means moving away and getting help. If I don't, I'll be stuck here till my food runs out, or Xérus comes knocking at the door demanding his money.

So ... I could try to find another apartment, in a different part of the city. *If* I still have the strength. It'd need to be even cheaper than this one! And then I'd have to take the risk of asking around straight away for the name of a local doctor who wouldn't ask any questions about my little car accident. And pray he'd never associate me with something that happened in Nice several days ago ...

I'd have enough clean cash left to pay him off for a while, and get food and other stuff delivered to my door. But what happens when it's gone? I can't start throwing these high-value banknotes around like confetti. I always knew I'd have to manage them very carefully – but now I won't be able to do that myself till I'm a lot fitter.

Merde! I don't have any option, do I? I'm going to have to find someone to look after me, organise visits from discreet doctors and nurses, do my shopping and housework, launder the money, *and* keep the secret as well! 'Cos they'd soon work it out, even if I tried not to tell them. Who can I trust to do all that? No-one!

> There is someone, Paul-Philippe. Did you *completely* forget me when you left Toulon and changed your name?

And even if I could manage to look after myself without any help ... do I really want to live in secrecy and seclusion for months or even years? With nobody to talk to about the challenges? That's not the life I've been planning since I said 'Yes' to Xérus.

> I will help you, my son. I will forgive you for discarding me all those years ago. Yes, I will help you now. Come home, Paul-Philippe.

Mother! Of course! It's ideal! She's still only – how old, actually? – yeah, about fifty-two, and she was perfectly fit when I last saw her. She would never betray me, and she can give me all the help I need. She probably won't argue, especially if I turn up on her doorstep in this sorry state. And if she *does* object, too bad. I'll just have to persuade her.

That's it, then. I'll leave here first thing in the morning, before Norbert's even awake, and get an early train to Toulon. I can worry about the stuff in the lock-up later. And I must go back to using my birth name and papers. Xérus hinted at the start that he thought I might have changed my identity, but he never suggested he actually knew my real name – or where I'd come from when I arrived in Marseilles. Nobody can possibly know any of that! So I've got nothing to lose. Once I'm back home with *maman*, I'll be Paul-Philippe Carne again, and there should be no way for him to track me down.

She'd better still be living there. She'd better still be alive! But I can't mess around trying to find out in advance. And if she's *not* there, well at least I'll be out of *here* ...

Central Police Station, Nice

Wednesday 25 November, 9 p.m.

'I've just received a phone call, Brigadier. We have Giuseppe Hauvert!'

'Excellent, sir! And *was* he holed up in Sanremo with a big empty suitcase?'

'No. He was on a train back to Nice with a small case full of his own clothes.'

'Ah. And ...?'

'They're bringing him in.'

* * *

'So what exactly did the caller say to you, Hauvert?'

'Very little. He simply told me I needed to get out of France at once, and stay out – for my own good.'

'Why?'

'I have no idea! I asked him the same question, but he ignored it. He just said that if anyone saw me going, I should tell them my grandmother was very ill. And then he put the phone down!'

'So *did* you visit your grandmother?'

'Of course not, Inspector. She's in fine health. That's just what the Sicilian *told* me to say.'

'Sicilian?'

'Yes. He spoke good French, but with a strong Sicilian accent.'

'I see. But only thirty-six hours after you left for Italy, we found you on your way back with a ticket for Nice in your pocket. Why the change of mind?'

'Well, I did get out of France first thing on Monday morning, because I was feeling really scared. But I stopped in Ventimiglia and spent all of yesterday and today thinking about it. I don't know why that guy told me to leave, but I've done nothing wrong and I decided I just wasn't willing to be intimidated like that. And when I saw the reports of the robbery ...'

'Ah, you know about it, then?'

'Of course. It's all over the Italian papers. That's when I knew I had to come back to see poor Monsieur Orceau and Marco, and in case anyone thought I was somehow involved. Because I keep getting the feeling the two things are related ...'

'Well, I suggest you let *us* do the detective work, Hauvert, and you just worry about the mess you're in.'

'I'm not in any mess, Inspector. I've told you exactly what happened. And as soon as I can, I'd like to get home for some sleep, and then visit my colleagues in the hospital ...'

* * *

'Well, Lebrun?'

'Always after my opinion first, sir?'

'Just consider it as advanced training, Brigadier. Yours, that is. So ...?'

'Hmmm. Either he's a young man of surprising moral fibre, or he's lying through his teeth and has already collected his share of the money from "Luc" and maybe even delivered the rest of it to a fence in France or Italy.'

'And which of those do you think is more likely?'

'You mean France or Italy, sir?'

'No, Brigadier. Fundamental innocence or guilt?'

'Well, now that we've met him, and heard him say everything he said without blinking ... I'd say the former, without any doubt.'

'I can see I'm going to have to watch my heels carefully in the months to come, Lebrun. Yes, release him without charge. But I want a tight tail on him for forty-eight hours, and then we'll review the situation.'

Thursday 26 November, 2 p.m.

'I assume the Investigating Magistrate has told you that you will be transferred to the Maison d'Arrêt later today, Arthur?'

'Yes.'

'Well, unless there are any further developments, or there's something more you wish to tell me, I shall see you in court ...'

'Fine.'

'Very well. But ... I really should not be telling you this, you know, but two independent witnesses to the car crash have sworn that you were carrying a gun.'

'What?? They're lying!'

'Well, I cannot prove that, of course. But I do suspect their memories or their motives to be flawed.'

'So what are you doing about that??'

'Still so angry with me?'

'What do you think? You've put Emilie in huge danger, but you're doing nothing about that *either*!'

'Hmmm. I really wish you could try harder to trust me, Arthur. And you're about to have a lot of time on your hands to work on that.'

Thursday 26 November, 4 p.m.

'So what has Hauvert been doing today?'

'Job-hunting, sir.'

'What??'

'Yes. After visiting Orceau and Charnière in hospital this morning, he went straight to the bank looking very distressed. Half an hour later he came back out looking even more unhappy, downed a couple of beers in the nearest bar, and then bought a newspaper and started studying the Vacancies page. And I'm absolutely certain he wasn't play-acting for the benefit of anyone who might be watching him.'

'That's really bad, Lebrun. When I called Raoul Tillier last night to tell him the lad had come back to Nice of his own volition, he never said he was planning to sack him on the spot.'

'Maybe Charles-Pierre Orceau phoned Tillier from the hospital and pushed him into doing it, sir. As a sort of surrogate punishment for both the guy who shot him and the real insider.'

'You're been reading Freud again, haven't you, Brigadier?'

'Well ...'

Marking Time

Toulon, France

Six weeks later: January 1960

Still no news of the money being found.

And I'm the only one who knows that Arthur Narone took the bag. Unless he was spotted with it after he abandoned the car. Unlikely – it was dark, he's a bright lad and he's used to evasion on the streets of Nice.

So I must carry on assuming that he managed to hide it. And that he didn't double-cross me in any way. 'Cos there's still no benefit in wondering if he did. Unless I'm going to give up on it completely – and I'm not doing that. But I'll only know for certain when the opportunity to contact him eventually arises.

And I definitely can't attempt that yet.

For one thing, he's still in the Nice jailhouse awaiting trial, and even if he were out on bail it would be madness to let myself be associated with him in any way, at this time. And I can't try to get anyone else to approach him on my behalf either. Anybody watching him – and a lot of people will be watching him for a long time, won't they? – would spot what was happening at once, and start wondering if he really did make off with the money. No, I must always keep that secret to *maman* and myself alone, and accept I am going to have to play a long, deep game.

And apart from that, I'm in even worse shape than I was on the day I came home. *Maman* is doing all she can, and without any argument, so I guess I should be grateful for small mercies. But I'm not convinced her so-called doctor friend knows what *he's* doing. I might have to persuade her to find another one. But that would just double the risk of exposure again!

If only I'd been able to get some proper treatment in those first few hours! But it just wasn't on, was it?

Thank god I'm out of Xérus' reach now, and maybe forever. Until the day I make a move on Narone, of course. That might put him straight back in business. And who the hell is Xérus, anyway? Must be the manager, Raoul Tillier. What a cheek to set it up like that, and then the luck of getting away with it – 'cos the newspapers say he's still in charge of the bank! But he never got his huge cut, did he? He never got anything. Yeah, give him a glimmer of a chance and he'll be coming after me someday, somehow, somewhere, on a count of gross betrayal. And without that bagful of cash, I'll have nothing to bargain with. That's why Narone will always be crucial ...

And Tillier is only part of the problem. That deputy manager – Orceau – will have been after my blood ever since he went back to work just before Christmas with his arm in a sling and all that sickly press attention. I've turned him into a bloody celebrity, but he won't be looking for me just to express his gratitude ...

No, I'm not about to make any more stupid moves. Head down, and keep it down.

Nice

Four weeks later: February 1960

No-one to talk to properly about the whole damned mess, of course.

This is when I miss Sarah the most. And little Colin. He'd have been twenty-one next month!

But it's hypocritical even to think like that. I set the whole thing up to try and forget them, and start some sort of new life at last, and have a bit of fun after all the years of mourning and emptiness.

So it's a good thing I'm not even pretending to talk to them about it.

Anyway ....

Ruford never did hide my money where we agreed he would.

So did the bastard hold onto it all for himself? Or did he keep his word on the contingency plan, and hide it somewhere else "to be advised"?

He hasn't answered any of my prearranged calls. Maybe he was there waiting for the ones I didn't make in the shambles of the early days, and then he stopped bothering. Or maybe he never went to any of the phone boxes at all.

But there's no point in banging my head against that brick wall any more.

And there's been no message left in the dead letter boxes either.

The other three losers will go to trial sooner or later, and they're sure to end up with long sentences. And I wouldn't like to be in the big monkey's shoes, in particular, with Charnière's family and friends baying for his blood ... in prison or not.

But Ruford is out there somewhere, with *my* money. Is he still in Nice? Or did he go back to Marseilles? Or somewhere else? And has he got it all with him? Or just some of it? Or none at all?

I can't risk making any enquiries about him. Or trying to contact any of the others. I must keep myself completely disassociated from the whole gang.

He swore he would keep his side of the deal, and he hasn't, even though he managed to get away from that utter screw-up. So my new life of ease will have to stay on hold till he surfaces and I can settle the score, in spades – and finally get my hands on the money.

That could take a very long time, of course. And require a great deal of effort on my part. Especially if I were to just let things follow their natural course. But those Old Franc notes won't be valid currency forever. So perhaps I *will* eventually have to help things along a bit instead, and find some way of flushing Ruford out. But how, and when?

Well, I'm going to have to bide my time, at least until the trial is over and probably well beyond that, and just keep watching and listening very carefully.

But when I *do* catch up with him, I'm going to want my thirty-four million, no messing. And I'm going to get as much of *his* cut as I can as well, to pay him back for all of this.

And Arthur Narone is still my only real route to Ruford, isn't he? Because by the time I started looking for his little girlfriend, she was long gone ...

Nice

Four months later: June 1960

LONG JAIL SENTENCES FOR THE ROBBERS!

Today, at the Palais de Justice in Nice, sentences were finally passed on the three ruthless villains who in late November stole almost fifty million Old Francs from a city bank and seriously injured two of our upstanding, heroic citizens.

Gustin Aignant will go to prison for twenty years for armed robbery and attempted murder, Bertrand Irvoise was given sixteen years for armed robbery, and Arthur Narone, the gang's getaway driver, will serve ten years for armed robbery. They will all pay their penalty to society in the Baumettes Prison in Marseilles.

The fourth member of the gang, believed to be known only as "Luc" by his associates, is also expected to face charges of attempted murder once apprehended. This newspaper maintains full confidence in our city's illustrious police force, and looks forward to the early arrest of this enemy of the Republic and the recovery of the large sum of money still believed to be missing.

The initial presumptions of the existence of a fifth member of the gang, rumoured at once to be an employee of the bank itself, have slowly evaporated over the past six months as the police have steadily eliminated all possible suspects from their enquiries.

Five out of Ten but Improving

Baumettes Prison, Marseilles

Five years later: May 1965

Still no letter from Emilie.

Hah! I've said that to myself every day for nearly five years.

She must know I'm here – it was in all the newspapers on the day the trial ended. If she ever read them, that is. If she was still in France. If she was still alive ...

Always the same stupid thoughts!

If I really wanted a letter from somebody, I suppose I could have tried to contact my mother at any time. I still have the address they gave me when I left the orphanage. But if she was happy to dump me there all those years ago, she's hardly likely to want the world to know her unwanted son turned into a jailbird.

Ah, merde! How many times am I going to think those useless thoughts too?

And damn that stupid pattern in the ceiling plaster! How many times am I going to look up at it? How many times am I going to see that palm and those three fingers??

I'd have gone crazy in this awful place years ago, if it weren't for the library and my writing. What an irony! Your body must lose its freedom before your mind can be liberated!

Well, mine had to, anyway. And that's actually a rather good line. Maybe someone already said it. Maybe even Rousseau! But I can use it anyway. Ignorance is bliss. "Innocent of plagiarism until proven guilty!"

And I *have* had a few letters. Mainly rejections, of course! But I shall treasure the acceptances for ever!

OK, it's nine o'clock. They're all playing cards and baiting each other. Diary review time ...

Hah! It's exactly three years and eight months since my last beating.

And flipping back from that entry ... oh, it's really weird ... almost the same words every time:

> 'So, who WAS Luc?'
>
> 'I have no idea! Aaaggh!'
>
> 'Where did he go?'
>
> 'I don't know! I just dropped him off on Gambetta! Aaaggh!'
>
> 'How much was in the bag?'
>
> 'No idea! I was just the driver, remember? Aaaggh! He gave me one measly wad of cash before he got out of the car, and the police took that back off me the very next day! Didn't you read the papers? Aaaggh!'

Those days were the worst of my life.

And look at this entry! The only time I ever got asked *that* question. But I was ready for it. I'd rehearsed my awful reply for months:

> 'Did you actually run off with the money bag yourself?'
>
> 'No! Didn't you read that witness statement? Perhaps you're illiterate. Or maybe your mother was born really stupid. Which is it, eh??'

Of course, he took a big swing at me. But I ducked and head-butted him! The only time I ever fought back. And it worked. That particular ape never bothered me again. But we both got a lot of negative behaviour points, and my request to use the library more fully was then denied for another six months.

Ah, memories ....

I don't think Irvoise or Aignant were behind any of those beatings. Neither of them has any idea that Luc *did* give me the money bag, so they can't be holding any grudges against me. Unless they believe I could have handled things better at the moment of the crash! But they surely wouldn't think that. They know I avoided a front-on collision with that lorry and probably saved their lives. And they heard my full story during the trial. It never changed. I'm a very good liar. Fine qualifications for a writer!

The pressures on them for information about Luc finally dried up too, of course. If the rumours are to be believed. And they always are. But I'm still hearing word that Aignant's face keeps getting rearranged, even though he's in the high-security block. That poor bank guard must have a lot of influential friends. Thank god I was just the driver!

OK, diary review time over. Back to Anais Nin and *Cities of the Interior* ...

A Helping Hand

Toulon

Three months later: Late August 1965

Nearly six years since it happened. And those banknotes will only be legal tender until April 1968. All three issues, dammit! So there's less than three years left to get my hands on them. I'm going to have to do *something* – and sooner rather than later.

But I couldn't have done anything till now, could I? It was two years before I could even sit up properly in bed, and another year till I could try and walk again. Then it took months to get my leg muscles even half-working. I'm still convinced that quack had no idea how to treat me. But I suppose my internal injuries must have been pretty bad, so I shouldn't put all the blame on him.

'I'm alive, I'm alive, I'm alive ...'

Damn this new British pop music! What's wrong with the good old French songs?

'Turn it off, *maman*!'

Where's she gone now?

'Maman!!'

At least I'm getting through most days with hardly any pain. Except when I try to get out of this chair! And it's no big deal to walk down the stairs anymore. Getting back up them is still an effort. But it's been good to get some fresh air recently – not much of a Mistral out there, thank god! – and see a few of the old neighbours again. Old is certainly the word for most of them!

It's not just the fact that the notes will expire in 1968. The cash I did manage to get away with is running out fast, but I can't see myself being able to do any sort of paid work for years yet – if ever. Not that I would want to anyway. And I'll still be needing that doctor and the drugs for a long time. His charges keep going up, too, and I can guess why. He'd better not push it too far ...

'I can't get no satisfaction ...'

Damn that radio!

But how can I break through and make contact with Narone? Nothing has changed. Or maybe it has. Maybe he was put under pressure in jail and spilled the beans about where he stashed the money bag. Maybe it's all long gone.

No. I've got to keep assuming it's still safely hidden away.

'Help! I need somebody ...'

Damn!

But I still can't afford to try and send in someone to talk to him, or find a way to bribe one of the other inmates to do it. Far too risky, and I'd lose the little control I have left. Control? Hah! And why should he co-operate anyway? Well, he could be encouraged to, of course. But I'm not going to get the chance to try.

And I keep wondering whether I could somehow persuade Irvoise to talk to Narone and get something out of him. Birds of a feather. But it always comes back to the same problem. I simply cannot take the risk of showing my face or using a go-between to set up anything like that.

'Make it easy on yourself ...'

'Maman!!'

No, I'm just going to have to carry on being very patient, and pray for something to change in time for me to take advantage of it before those notes become completely worthless.

'*Maman!* Is that you at last? Where's my dinner?'

Nice

Two months later: Sunday 31 October

The time has come to make a move. I've watched and waited six long years, but none of my very discreet enquires have got me any further. And the banknotes will go out of validity in 1968. I must try to flush Paul Ruford out of hiding soon – wherever he is – and get my hands on what's left of the cash while I can still do something with it.

And there's still only one route to Ruford and that money. I'm going to have to arrange my own special Private Investigator ...

Nice

Monday 8 November, 10 a.m.

'Inspector Hardy?'

'Speaking.'

'*Bonjour*. This is Raoul Tillier at the Banque Artisanale.'

'Ah, good morning, sir. And how are you?'

'I am very well, thank you.'

'And looking forward to next January, I'm sure!'

'Ah, you have clearly heard of my impending retirement.'

'Indeed. I wish you a very happy new life, *monsieur*.'

'Thank you again. Now, I assume there have been no further developments since we last spoke?'

'I regret not, Monsieur Tillier.'

'Well, I have been talking recently with Charles-Pierre Orceau, and we have come up with an idea for your consideration.'

'Yes ...?'

'Ah, we think this would be most effectively discussed in person, Inspector. And for obvious reasons of continuity we feel it would be best if Charles-Pierre were to pursue it with you. So may I suggest a very discreet meeting between the two of you in the near future? Perhaps later today ...'

Somewhere in Nice

Monday 8 November, 2 p.m.

'So, Inspector, on the assumption that "Luc" and the money are still hidden away somewhere, and hopefully still in France, we have devised a little scheme to try and draw him to the surface.'

'I am intrigued, Monsieur Orceau. Pray continue ...'

'We believe that Arthur Narone is the key to uncovering "Luc". So we propose that you visit the governor of Baumettes Prison and ask him to co-operate in arranging for Narone's early release.'

'But on what grounds, *monsieur*?'

'On the basis of a new statement by the other driver, Bertrand Irvoise.'

'He has made a new statement??'

'Not yet. But we should like you to help him do so.'

'This already sounds well out of order, Charles-Pierre.'

'I do not deny it, Inspector. So perhaps you would prefer it if we dropped the idea at once ...'

'No, sir. I should very much like to hear what you have to say. Off the record, of course ...'

Avenue du Prado, Marseilles

Sunday 14 November, 9 p.m.

'Good evening, Governor Delacroix. I am Inspector Simon Hardy, and may I present Monsieur Charles-Pierre Orceau?'

'Good evening, gentlemen. Please come through to the lounge and take a seat ...'

'Thank you, Governor. And we are most grateful to you for agreeing to meet us in your own home. But I am confident you will soon understand the reason behind our desire for such discretion.'

'I am waiting to be convinced, Inspector.'

'And I thank you for your indulgence too, sir. So, in a nutshell, we believe it is still highly desirable, and in the public interest of course, for the fourth member of the Nice robbery gang, known of course only as "Luc", to be apprehended and the rest of the stolen money recovered, if possible. And we feel that if the young getaway driver Arthur Narone were to find himself back in the outside world again, as soon as it is feasible, there is a good chance that "Luc" might be tempted to surface at last, to deal with the new situation.'

'And why might he conceivably do that, after all this time?'

'For a number of reasons, Governor, any one of which would suffice. "Luc" might fear that Narone could then be approached by every villain in Nice and beyond, and pressed into giving a fuller description of him. Or even that Narone might reveal something he knows about his whereabouts or that of the money. Or maybe "Luc" was somehow implicated in the disappearance of Narone's girlfriend at the time, and has some motive for making contact with him about it. Or maybe Narone was supposed to receive a much bigger share than the single wad of notes he ended up with after the crash, and "Luc" will want to pay him off before the kid goes sour and starts his own search for him. And there are many other possibilities ...'

'Hmmm. And how, pray, do you imagine this "Luc" character would actually become aware that Narone had been freed?'

'Oh, the underworld has rapid and effective communication channels, Governor – as I'm sure you are well aware. But just in case "Luc" is living a very isolated life, perhaps in another city, I would also anticipate a couple of small and rather careless leaks to the local and national press, several days before Narone's eventual release back in Nice.'

'You do realise, Inspector, that you are proposing to set this unfortunate young man up as a defenceless bait for many ruthless sharks ...'

'I feel that is a matter of perspective, sir. We shall be keeping very close to him, I can assure you, and you might perhaps regard him less as bait and more as our own rather special agent. And I come back to the matter of the public good. So, since time is increasingly of the essence here, as the date approaches when those banknotes will cease to be legal tender, we feel that a little oiling of the wheels may perhaps be justified.'

'Hmmm ...'

'And we therefore propose, Governor, that I arrange for one of my junior officers – one not previously known to any of the robbers, and suitably "disguised" – to visit the prison for a short meeting with the gang's other driver, Bertrand Irvoise. That meeting, which will of course quickly become common knowledge throughout the prison, should have as its pretext that the visitor is a distant relative bearing some important news of his family.'

'I am already very unsure about this, Inspector.'

'Our motive is but the securing of natural justice, Governor. So please hear us out before you come to a judgment.'

'Very well ...'

'Once my man is firmly behind closed doors with Irvoise, and Irvoise alone – such *complete* security would of course be your responsibility, sir – he will tell the prisoner that he has come for a very different reason, and will suggest that nobody knows why he is *actually* there. And he will hint at some tangible future benefits for Irvoise if he agrees to give his full co-operation.'

'He will then "reveal" that he has been secretly commissioned by "Luc" to visit Irvoise, and he will tell him the story we have devised. Which is as follows ...'

'His partner "Luc" has regrettably not been able to contact his old friend Bertrand until now, for various reasons – his ill-health after the car crash, the obvious security exposures, and so on. But he *has* been safely laying low with all the money remaining after paying off his "sponsors" fully.

'And he is well aware – it was of course reported in all the newspapers – that both Irvoise and Aignant sadly lost their personal shares of the haul when they were arrested. So he has always been extremely keen to ensure that they will both receive the same amounts again when they are finally freed. And since the gang actually made off with a lot more cash than he had actually hoped for, their sponsors kindly allowed him to keep back enough for those duplicate payoffs.'

'I think I can already spot a lot of fabrication in this "story" ...'

'Indeed. And more is necessary, Governor, to complete the deception.

'Irvoise will then be told that "Luc" wishes to go still further than that, because he has now had a major, guilt-driven change of heart with regard to Arthur Narone. He is feeling deep remorse that the young man received such a long jail sentence after being co-opted rather unwillingly for a very simple role, and considering he bore no real moral blame for even the robbery, let alone the wounding of the Deputy Manager and the security guard.'

'I trust you are now fully recovered from that awful experience, Monsieur Orceau?'

'Largely, thank you, Governor. My shoulder will never be back to normal, but I am otherwise fine.'

'*Bravo!* Well, Inspector ...'

'I have not quite finished, sir.

'And so – the story will go – "Luc" now wishes to make amends to Narone by trying to get him a reduced sentence and an early release, and giving him some extra cash as well – because he only received a very small payment, and the police immediately recovered that too.

'And "Luc" suspects that Irvoise may have been pressed into identifying Narone to the police. Perhaps my man will ask him: "Is that actually what happened, Bertrand?" And the answer will probably be a sheepish "Yes" – because that's exactly what did happen, of course. And then: "So maybe *you* feel a bit of remorse too ...?"

'*Et voilà!* The dim-witted Irvoise will then be persuaded to make a full new statement about Narone's very limited role in the robbery – for example, how he was only called in at the last moment, which I do believe to be true ... that he was never carrying a gun, which is also probably true ... that he did not know the other robbers would be armed, which may well be true ... that he was pressured to do the job with any number of possible threats against him and his girlfriend ... and so on.

'And that statement can be made in the context of a dramatic, almost religious conversion to be undergone by Irvoise this coming Christmas, causing him to "want to do the right thing after all this time." In exchange for this, "Luc" promises to *double* the amount of Bertrand's future second payoff, using a big lump of his own proceeds. And he is also convinced that this admirable act of

Christian charity towards Narone will hasten his old friend's own eventual release on the grounds of good behaviour and new-found moral rectitude.'

'But this is a quite astonishing proposition, Inspector!'

'I cannot agree more, Governor. But will you support it? That is the question.'

Turning the Key

Baumettes Prison, Marseilles

Friday 14 January 1966

'You may sit down, Narone.'

'I was told I must remain standing, Governor Delacroix.'

'Just sit down, Arthur.'

'Yes, sir.'

'Now, in the light of new information received, and your continued good behaviour, the police and I have been reviewing your position. And I believe there is a strong possibility that you could be released at some time in the next few months.'

'Oh! Thank you! But ... I mean ... Oh dear, this has come as quite a shock, sir!'

'Yes, of course.'

'But does that mean there will have to be a re-trial?'

'I think not. We have various ways and means within the system to arrange for early probationary release at our own discretion.'

'I really don't know what to say ...'

'Then say very little, Arthur. That is often a good policy. And now ...'

'But can you tell me what new information you have received, sir?'

'There – you are already disregarding my advice!'

'I'm sorry, sir.'

'So, I suggest you begin to think about how you will handle your new-found liberty. And since it appears I need to be more specific, I recommend you do not discuss the situation with any of the other inmates. Not that you seem to spend any appreciable time with them ...'

'I do prefer my own company, sir. Especially in this place, if you know what I mean ...'

'Yes, yes, yes. Anyway, that is all I can tell you for now, young man.'

'Thank you, sir ...'

'No, don't get up yet, Arthur – I have one small question for *you* first.'

'Yes, sir ...?'

'We are all baffled by the numbers that you write on your wall every Sunday evening. If you will let me into your little secret, I will promise to keep my own silence on it ...'

'Are you serious, sir?'

'I do not often have the time or the mood for joking in this job, Arthur. So, will you tell me, or not?'

'Of course I will, sir. It is merely a count of the number of books I have read since I was brought here. I have always been extremely grateful for the existence of the prison library, modest as it is, and for the special efforts that have often been made to provide me with books from other libraries and a good supply of writing materials.'

'We try to seize opportunities for reform and improvement whenever we can reasonably do so, Arthur.'

'Yes ... or at least to enable them, sir. And I believe you have been successful in my case. I hadn't read more than a dozen books in my life before I came here, and I now recognise that most of those were rubbish. But last Sunday my count reached three hundred and fifty!'

'More than one a week! Bravo! So, what types of book have you been reading?'

'Oh, all sorts, sir. I've tried to focus on the great classic stories and plays, including lots in translation, but I've read many modern novels too, and studied a good number of historical and scientific works. I certainly know a lot more about the world than when I arrived here! And I've had plenty of bright ideas and formed a lot of new opinions too.'

'Some of which you have turned into your own creations, I understand ...'

'Oh, you mean my short stories! I've written five or six, and I've sent them all off to pulp magazines. Thank you for allowing me to do that too. A couple have actually been published! But they were really just early exercises, I think. I'd like to be able to produce something far more substantial. Perhaps I'd better get on with that straight away now, while I still have the time to finish it!'

'Very witty, Arthur. And that spirit should help to see you through the challenges to come. So, we shall talk again once I have some firmer information to give you.'

'Thank you, sir. Yes, thank you so much.'

Three months later: Tuesday 12 April

'So here you are again, Monsieur Narone.'

'Good morning, Governor. And to you, Frère Octavio.'

'Good morning, Arthur.'

'Well, young man, the process has taken a little longer than I had hoped, but I am very pleased to inform you that you will finally be released from detention by the Republic in three months' time, specifically on the fifth of July. However, as is the normal practice, you will be transferred back to the Maison d'Arrêt in Nice tomorrow morning to complete your sentence and prepare for your rehabilitation.'

'Ah, thank you, Governor! And it will be very good to meet Frère Gauthier Calou again after all these years – assuming he is still there, of course ...'

'He is indeed, Arthur, and he is very much looking forward to seeing you again too.'

'Ah, that is excellent news, Padre!'

'So, may God be with you in the days to come, my son.'

'Well, I'm not sure .... Hmmm. May I ask you a small question?'

'Of course you may.'

'You see, I've been thinking a lot about Bertrand Irvoise's dramatic epiphany over Christmas-time, and wondering what ...'

'Ah. Frankly, Arthur, I feel that is a subject strictly between ...'

'Yes, the Padre is quite right, Arthur. You seem once again to have forgotten my advice about keeping your silence unless you have good reason to speak.'

'Very well, sir. I'm sorry, and I shall not pursue the matter.'

'Good. So I shall now say *"Adieu"* and hope never to see you here again!'

'*Adieu*, Governor. *Adieu, Frère Octavio.* And thank you for everything you have all done for me.'

Maison d'Arrêt, Nice

Sunday 17 April

'A thousand welcomes, my son! How good to see you again, and heading in the right direction this time!'

'Hello, Frère Gauthier! Ah, your sense of humour has not been forgotten, I can assure you.'

'And *your* reputation has preceded you back here, Arthur.'

'Oh dear. I tried so hard to be well behaved in Marseilles ...'

'Ha-ha-ha! An equally good sense of humour too! No, I mean your success as an exciting new author!'

'You've heard about my writing?'

'But of course! I am deeply interested in it, for many reasons.'

'I'm stunned! But I've really only written a few little stories ...'

'Two of which have been published! Both of which I have read and enjoyed. I'm very impressed, Arthur.'

'Wow! Well, thank you, Padre. Actually, I've been thinking about trying something a little different, but it's been hard to concentrate recently, with my release on the horizon ...'

'*Naturellement.* But perhaps the rather lighter regime of this place will be a little more conducive to that.'

'I hope so!'

'And I shall do all I can, Arthur, to ready you for your re-entry into the fast-changing world outside ...'

Toulon

Two months later: Wednesday 22 June, 9 a.m.

'Heaven be praised, *maman*! Look at this, in the morning paper –
Narone's back in the Maison d'Arrêt in Nice, and they're releasing
him in July!'

'*Enfin, Paul-Philippe!*'

'But it doesn't say exactly when.'

'That's understandable.'

'And who knows? ... they might even let him out earlier. OK, I've
waited long enough for this. I can't afford to miss him now. I must
get straight back to Nice and find a way to watch over the jail until
he walks through that door.'

'Do you still think he'll stay in the city after he's released?'

'Yeah. It's his home, isn't it? And maybe that girl's still waiting
for him! Or perhaps he'll decide to collect the cash from wherever he
hid it, and then try to get out of town. So we'll need to tail him for a
while, and maybe it will all be very easy. But if he shows no signs of
going for the money, I'll have to find a way of encouraging him.'

'So when do you plan to leave?'

'As soon as we've packed my case! And I'll call you at the phone
box on the corner at eight o'clock tonight.'

Rue de la Gendarmerie, Nice

Wednesday 22 June, 8 p.m.

'It's me, *maman*.'

'*Bonsoir, Paul-Philippe*. So, you have a plan already?'

'Yes, I do! There are several very scruffy apartment blocks all the
way along the street opposite the front wall of the jail. I'm phoning
from a call box outside the one at the top end. And there are "To Let"
notices on the windows of three separate apartments, up on the third
and fourth floors. It's perfect. I'll be able to see the jailhouse gate

from any of them, and both ends of the street with a pair of binoculars.'

'OK ...'

'I've got myself a room downtown, just for tonight. And early in the morning I'll have to take the risk of watching the jail entrance discreetly from this end of the street, just in case they let Narone out then!'

'Very discreetly ...'

'Of course. Now, *you* must pack a case for a long stay, get the early train over here tomorrow, rent one of those apartments in your name, and move straight in. Then you'll need to buy a cheap old car and a pair of walkie-talkies.

'At seven tomorrow evening, I'll call you at the box I'm phoning from now, to check that everything's gone OK. Then later on, well after dark, I can join you in whichever apartment you've chosen.

'And the next day we'll start the observation. Each morning you can go out to the bakery just before the hour at which they release people from the jail – whenever that turns out to be. We'll then make contact on the walkie-talkies, while you're actually waiting in the car just round the corner, and I'll watch the gate of the jail from behind the curtains. If Narone appears, we'll be in business and we'll play it by ear from there. Otherwise you can just go ahead and buy the day's bread and milk as usual, and we'll kick our heels for another twenty-four hours. *D'accord?*'

'It sounds as if it might work, Paul-Philippe ...'

'Do you have any better ideas, *maman*? And do we have anything much to lose?'

'Probably not. OK, I'll start packing. Until tomorrow evening ...'

Maison d'Arrêt, Nice

Sunday 3 July

'So, my friend – only two days to go!'

'Yes, Frère Gauthier. It's almost impossible to believe ...'

'Well, I think you are now as ready as you are going to be. And have you finally made any progress with your grand authorial plans?'

'Well, yes I have. I'm actually thinking of writing a story about my own new life after I'm released. However it turns out. Not in the form of a personal journal, though. Everyone does that these days ... Sartre, Camus, everyone – hah! But as an ordinary novel.'

'That sounds much more like Roquentin than Meursault.'

'You know about them, Padre?'

'Oh yes.'

'Wow! Well, I think you're right. I'd much rather try a fresh start than just shrug my shoulders and not bother about anything. I've never felt much like Meursault, or really understood him.'

'That's no surprise. It's funny though, Arthur ... tell me, have you ever seen the Livre de Poche edition of *L'Etranger*?'

'No. I worked with a hardback edition in the prison.'

'Hmmm. Well, I just happen to have a copy of it on my bookshelf ...'

'You've actually read *L'Etranger*?'

'But of course. One should understand a thing very well before attempting to judge or criticise it. And sometimes one discovers a work that modifies rather than simply reinforces one's own faith. Anyway ... take a look at the front cover illustration of young Meursault standing on the beach.'

'*Mon Dieu!* It's me, Padre – or at least it's just what I looked like in 1959! Right down to my cheap shiny Italian suit. I'll be wearing that again when I walk out of here!'

'Indeed. Uncanny, isn't it? But I agree that is where the resemblance ends. I don't get the impression you'll be keeping *your* hands stuck in your pockets like the young man in that painting. So, you're planning a Roquentin-style renaissance?'

'Yes. I'm going to try and stay away from any criminals, and get back on the straight and narrow, and make amends where I can. There are some loose ends I'll need to tie up – and there's a girl who may still ....'

'Yes?'

'Oh, I just don't know, Padre.'

'Well, I wish you all the luck in the world, my son.'

'Thank you. And I'm planning to call my story *Reparations*. How does that sound to you?'

'I think it's a fine title. And I'm sure you'll be able to make its message come to pass. I realise it won't be a diary, but are you planning to write it day-by-day, a bit like a sailor's log book?'

'Oh, no. I wouldn't try to write a novel if I didn't know how it was going to end!'

'This one could take you a very long time then, Arthur. In fact, it might never be completed ...'

'Hah! No, I just mean I'll take lots of notes as I go along, and then when I think I've come to some real resolution of things, I'll put it all together. And that will simply take as long as it takes.'

'Bravo!'

'Thank you!'

'Now, I didn't ask to speak with you today merely to hear about your latest plans – although I'm absolutely delighted with what you've told me. It makes what I have to say even more pertinent ...'

'What do you mean, Frère Gauthier?'

'I'd like to trust you with a little secret, and a lot more.'

'My goodness! Well, of course you may trust me, Padre. You are my only real friend, you know – if I may be so bold as to consider you as one ...'

'Of course you may, Arthur. So – a young lady by the name of Pureza Seles lives not far from here, near the centre of the New Town. She owns a small bookshop and the apartment above it.'

'That doesn't sound like much of a secret!'

'No, Arthur. The secret is that she is my daughter.'

'*Mon Dieu!* Ah, excuse me, Padre. But surely you are not married?'

'No indeed. And I never have been. But Pureza was born nearly thirty years ago, long before I considered entering the Church.'

'So "Seles" is her maiden name? And actually her mother's?'

'Precisely. I had gone to Spain in 1936, in a rush of political fervour at the very start of the Civil War. I met Rosita Carmen in Barcelona, and we fell in love, and the inevitable happened. But Rosita was not ready for marriage, and there were all sorts of barriers to our remaining together. We parted, still very good friends, a few weeks before the baby was due. But we kept closely in touch, and over the years I managed to see Pureza on several occasions as she was growing up.'

'Did Rosita choose the baby's name?'

'No. We both came up with it, quite independently, after she was born. How sentimental, *non*?'

'Not sentimental, Padre. It sounds heartfelt and immaculately fitting.'

'The writer speaks! Yes, fitting indeed, Arthur. And four years ago – some time after you had gone to prison in Marseilles – Pureza decided she wanted to break free of the oppressive atmosphere in Spain, and also get to know me much better. Rosita had no objections, and between the three of us we managed to pull together enough money for a deposit on the purchase of the bookshop. Pureza has a steady income from it, and she is slowly paying off the loan. And by the way, she too has read those short stories of yours ...'

'Oh, this is fascinating, Frère Gauthier, and I would love to hear a lot more about it. But why on earth are you telling me?'

'Well, I assume you have only the modest amount of cash that was in your possession when you were arrested in 1959.'

'A very fair assumption, Padre. And that's worth even less now, of course. I don't expect it will be enough for a month's rent in advance, let alone any other living costs.'

'Indeed. So, Pureza proposes to meet up with you on the day of your release, and you may then stay in her spare room for a few days or weeks, while you find yourself a job and some other accommodation.'

'Oh, that is extremely generous of you both! Do you do this for every ex-con who passes through here?'

'No, Arthur. This is the first time we have even considered it. We both feel a strong need to protect, support and encourage you.'

'Mon Dieu!'

'Yes, I suspect He is behind our thinking, my friend. But of course you don't have to take *any* of us up on this offer. You're a free man – well almost, and I know Rousseau would completely disagree! – but to be frank, I think you would be a complete fool if you didn't.'

'If you've read Rousseau too, Padre, how can I possibly disregard your advice?'

'Hah! That's the spirit, Arthur! So, it's all settled.'

Stepping Out

Rue de la Gendarmerie, Nice

Tuesday 5 July, 8:50 a.m.

'Are you receiving me, *maman*?'

'Loud and clear, Paul-Philippe – as usual.'

'OK. It's nearly nine o'clock. Maybe today's the day.'

'Maybe. Or maybe not. There's always tomorrow. *Patience, enfin!*'

'Yeah. OK, stand by ...'

'Allô!'

'Pureza?'

'Yes, I'm ready, *papa*. And the taxi's waiting right outside the call box.'

'Good. Everything's running on time, as usual. I've said my goodbyes to Arthur, and he should be coming through the gate in a couple of minutes. Let's hope there will be no problems for either of you ...'

'I'll be OK, *papa*. And anyway, you said you would ask the guard to keep an eye on him till he's safely in the car.'

'Yes, and I've done that. So now we must simply put our trust in ... Aha, he's on his way already! Off you go at once, my child, and may God be with you both.'

'Merci, papa.'

'My god, it's him, *maman*! Narone's coming through the gate, right now!! Get ready to move ...'

'Take it easy, Paul-Philippe, and just tell me what I need to do ...'

'OK. Well, there's nobody to meet him on the pavement. If he walks your way you can just leave the car and follow him. If he goes the other way, you can track him in the car for a while and then on foot. I can't see inside any of the cars parked up in front of the apartments, but he does seem to be waiting for someone ...'

'Aha ... a taxi has just gone past me and turned into Rue de la Gendarmerie. I've got its number. There's a young woman in the back seat.'

'Yes, I can see it now! Narone's spotted it too ... and it's slowing down for him. OK, start the car, *maman*, but don't move off just yet.'

'The engine's already running, Paul-Philippe.'

'All set, Lebrun?'

'All set, Hardy.'

'OK. We're staying in the cars, of course. The action's from left to right, so I'll need to go first – any moment now. Join up as soon as we pass you ...'

'Roger.'

'He's in the taxi now, *maman*, and it's moving off towards the river. You can get going ... no, wait, something else is happening! Another car's pulled out behind the taxi. It's dark blue and there are two men in it. *Merde!* – I'll swear they're police. OK, you'll have to follow that one instead, *maman* – but very carefully! Go!'

'I'm already moving, Paul-Philippe. Just turning the corner. Yes, I can see the blue car – I'm keeping my distance, and ... hang on, there's *another* one pulling out behind it! This one's silver ...'

'Yes, I see it too, right below me. And those two guys look like *flics* as well! Oh, wonderful!'

'Calm down ...'

'OK. So, you're following three cars now, *maman*. Good luck – and if there's any hint they've spotted you, wipe that walkie-talkie clean and chuck it out the window fast!'

'I'll do my best, son. You just make sure you're waiting in the call box, on the hour every hour for the rest of the day, till I can phone you ...'

'I'll be there!'

'So, Lebrun – maybe "Luc" and that young woman have commandeered a taxi, or maybe she's doing the job for him ...'

'Or maybe something else.'

'Of course. But do you *see* anything else?'

'Yes. There's an old Renault not far behind me. Been there ever since we got going ...'

'Which was only sixty seconds ago.'

'That's true. Driver's a peroxide blonde in her fifties. Big sunglasses. Seems to be singing along to the radio and checking her hair in the mirror.'

'Clearly a bastion of the Nice underworld, then.'

'Maybe, Hardy. But probably not. More likely going downtown for some early low-price shopping.'

'Glad we agree. OK, let's concentrate on the taxi. As soon as it stops we'll make a new plan ...'

Quai Saint-Jean-Baptiste, Nice

Tuesday 5 July, 9:10 a.m.

'It's stopping, Lebrun – outside a small bookshop. I'll go on past it and pull up thirty metres down the street. You park right where you are.'

'OK, I'm braking ...'

'So what's happening now?'

'They're paying and getting out. We're both ready to walk ...'

'So are we ...'

'Ah, no need, Hardy. The woman's gone straight to the front door of the shop and she's unlocking it.'

'Yes, I see her in my side mirror ...'

'And the old bird in the Renault has just driven past me.'

'Are you still fretting about her?'

'Well ...'

'Well, don't.'

'OK. So, Narone and the woman are now inside the bookshop.'

'Excellent. I'm guessing the taxi's clean. I'll get it checked out, of course, but it looks like the woman's our mark. We'll share the surveillance for the rest of the day. And ... thanks for your help, Lebrun.'

'No problem, Hardy. Nothing better to do with my time ... yet.'

Turn at the second right. Then right again, and find somewhere to park ... here!

Wig off. Sunglasses off. Different jacket. Change into walking shoes. And hide it all away.

There ... a new woman!

It's nine-fifteen. Two minutes till I'm in place on the embankment, and I'll call Paul-Philippe on the hour. Just have to hope they didn't come straight back out again ...

Tuesday 5 July, 10 a.m.

'*Allô!*'

'It's me, Paul-Philippe. Mission accomplished.'

'Wonderful! Where are they?'

'At *Le Bouquineur* bookshop on Quai Saint-Jean-Baptiste, near Rue Defly. I can see the front door from this phone box. I had to lose them for a few minutes, 'cos of the *flics* and getting changed, and hope they weren't just picking up the latest James Bond and moving on. But the police cars are still parked where they stopped, with both men in each one, so Narone and the woman must still be inside. I'm guessing she owns the place and he's going to stay there for a while. Maybe she's an old flame ...'

'Ah, well done, *maman*! So, will *you* stick with him for the rest of the day?'

'Of course. No way should we let the *flics* spot a *man* sniffing around after him, at least for today. And I'm sure they haven't noticed me ... when I left the car I walked up two blocks and came back onto the embankment well behind them, and crossed the road at the lights with several other people. They can't even see me in their mirrors. I've got a copy of Paris-Match to read, and there's a café nearby. I can sit inside, out of sight, and still watch the door of the shop. But hopefully Narone will go out for a stroll before anyone starts getting suspicious of me. And that may also give me a chance to get a proper look at any of the policemen who follow him ...'

'Great. OK, good luck, and watch your back.'

'Thanks. Are *you* staying in all day?'

'No. I'll go downtown myself later, in disguise, and completely update my list of public call boxes and their numbers. And I'll expect you home when you've seen Narone safely into bed tonight.'

'Home? Hah! I'm looking forward to getting back to my own bed in Toulon. I really hate this awful old mattress!'

'I know, I know, *maman*. But at least we're halfway towards a result! You'll need to pick up on Narone again early tomorrow morning, of course, and set him up for my first contact as soon as you can. And once he's back under my thumb, we can *both* get the hell out of Nice and do the rest of it by phone ...'

Three hours later

'Is that Charles-Pierre Orceau?'

'Speaking.'

'Simon Hardy here. Narone was met outside the jail by a young woman in a taxi, and we now have them both under observation in a bookshop on the embankment.'

'Congratulations, Inspector!'

'And let us hope she proves to be working with "Luc" ...'

'Yes, indeed. So, please keep me closely in the loop.'

'But of course, Charles-Pierre. We are both in this together. I shall report my progress to you on a weekly basis.'

'Thank you, Inspector. You may be assured of my deepest gratitude if and when we achieve our long-sought aims.'

'Lebrun to Hardy ...'

'Go ahead.'

'Very glad to see you're back with us, Simon. And I do hope you enjoyed your little stroll. Now, I've been thinking ...'

'And ...?'

'Well, if that attractive young bookshop owner is some sort of front for "Luc" then I'm the Emperor of Japan.'

'Yes, I've been thinking the very same thing myself.'

'OK. So should I send Brigadier Tauron off to get me some sushi for lunch?'

'Probably not. I suspect you're right, for once. But we must keep watching and following them until I decide otherwise. As long as you're still happy with that ...'

'But of course, *mon ami*. Your goal is my goal, until I am perhaps called away to attend to something even more pressing, like the next gangland murder.'

'Thank you, Ricard. And ... wait ... hey, they're coming out of the shop!'

'Check.'

'And the woman's locking up. Time for *everyone* to stretch their legs. No lunch for you today ...'

Book II

REPARATIONS

Foreword (*De Profundis*)

In the summer of 1966, when I left this place for the second time – and for "freedom" at last – I grandly told the prison padre that I was thinking of writing a novel some day. A story about picking up my life again. But I also said I would only attempt that when I felt I had reached a significant point in my efforts at reparation for the mistakes of the past.

From the start, things went very differently from what I had planned or expected. But although only fifteen months have passed since my release, I feel I am – ironically – now safe again at last, and I believe it is time to start to tell that little story.

It is dedicated, of course, to Emilie.

Arthur Narone
Nice Prison
October 1967

Postscript: And now my story is completed, and my third departure from these depths is imminent. May I find true freedom this time.

AN, April 1968

Watching the Detectives

The small graffiti-covered gate of Nice Prison closed quietly behind Arthur Narone as he watched a white taxi approach and slow to a halt in front of him.

In the back sat a dark-haired woman in her late twenties. His own age now, he reminded himself. She was smiling broadly and winding down the window.

'Arthur, I assume?'

'Señorita Seles?'

'Yes. But please call me Pureza. Right, in you get, quick as you can ...'

She slid smoothly across the seat and Narone clambered in beside her, perching his battered old suitcase on his knees.

'OK, Thomas, let's go!'

'Oui, mam'selle.'

Narone had wondered for some days about what he would say next. But now, in his first moments of freedom for more than six years, nothing would come. And Pureza Seles was clearly allowing him plenty of space. By the time they reached the end of the street and turned right to run alongside the river towards the city centre, there had been only cautious smiles on each side and no further conversation.

It was the taxi driver who broke the uncomfortable silence.

'We are being followed, *mam'selle.*'

'Are you certain, Thomas?'

'For sure. Two cars, two men in each. They were waiting in the parking spaces opposite the jail. And they are *flics*, mark my word.'

'The police? Well, I suppose it could be worse. Did you expect this, Arthur?'

'No. But I guess it's no great surprise.'

'That's a very sanguine attitude ...'

'I don't see much point in worrying about it. I'm a free man now, and if those idiots want to waste their time watching my back, well, good luck to them!'

Pureza smiled broadly again, sat back, and waited.

'Oh, look, they've knocked down that awful old warehouse on the corner ... and this long row of shops is brand new, isn't it! And there seems to be a lot more construction work on both sides of the river up ahead ...'

'Yes, Arthur. Nice is changing fast. We're more than halfway through the Sixties now! And it's not just the buildings ...'

'Too true! I just saw my first real mini-skirt!'

'And what did you think?'

'I daren't tell you!'

Pureza roared with laughter. 'I think you're already adapting quite well, *mon ami*.'

Narone turned his head to look directly at her. 'You already consider me your friend?'

'But of course.'

He fell silent again for some time, and then remembered there was a lot he really ought to be saying.

'So where are we going now, Pureza?'

'Well, I told Thomas to drive straight back to my place. Do you think we should do something different?'

'No, I don't. If we're being followed, they can track us on foot just as easily as by car. And you have to go home eventually. So why waste everybody's time?'

'Arthur, you are a very refreshing spirit! OK, we carry on as planned!'

As they swung onto Avenue Pauliani, Pureza was looking straight ahead again with an expression of contented anticipation, while Narone pretended a new fascination with the latest commercial development projects on their right. But he was actually studying the full profile of his attractive new companion. The smooth, dark skin of that delicate little face – a half-Spanish face, he knew that of course, but with something of the East about it too; her black, slightly wavy hair, falling loose and natural and free in a style so different from those over-architected coiffures of the late Fifties; and her dress, the simplest of shifts in a warm mixture of ambers and browns like the costume of a young American Indian, very modest at the neckline but riding unabashed above those pretty little knees ...

And now they were stopping, on Quai Saint-Jean-Baptiste. At least this particular stretch had not changed very much. And there was the promised little bookshop!

'The police cars are parking too, *mam'selle* – the dark blue one in front of us and the silver one behind. Please take good care ...'

'Don't worry, Thomas, we shall. And thank you for all your help, my friend. I know we can rely on your discretion.'

'But of course. Good luck to you both.'

Narone mumbled his own words of gratitude to the driver as he followed Pureza out of the nearside door. They entered the relative safety of the bookshop, and she locked up again at once.

They walked straight through the small shop and into a tiny kitchen at the back. Pureza stopped to light the gas under a kettle of water, then led Narone up the narrow stairs and onto the landing.

'There's the bathroom, Arthur. This is my bedroom. And down here at the front is the living room. But it has a sofa bed, see? ... so it's *your* room for as long as you wish. We'll share it in the evenings, of course, for music or TV or reading ...'

'Are you quite sure about all of this, Pureza?'

'Of course I am. It will be wonderful to have some company again.'

He briefly wondered what that "again" meant, but quickly forgot about it. Pureza was contemplating his very small suitcase.

'There's no wardrobe, I'm afraid, but it doesn't look as if you need much space just yet! There's plenty of room in those drawers. And there's a front door key for you in that ashtray. So, make yourself at home, and I'll get us some coffee ...'

He mumbled his thanks as she glided away, then walked over to the window to gaze at the stream of traffic making its steady way down to the city. And he was soon shaking his head in disbelief and frustration. He used to know every make and model of motor car on the streets of Nice – *and* how to break into them all – but he'd lost all interest in them after the robbery, and most of those passing by were completely new to him.

He was still lost in those thoughts when Pureza reappeared, holding two big, strangely stubby, brightly patterned mugs.

'It's only Nescafé today, I'm afraid. I need to open the shop as soon as I can now. We can talk properly at lunchtime. Which reminds me ...' She was eyeing his suitcase again, and her serene smile had become a devilish little grin. 'Do you have *any* other clothes in there, Arthur? Because you really can't stay wearing that sad old suit and narrow little tie for one minute longer, or you'll get yourself arrested again ...'

Narone laughed out loud for the first time since leaving jail.

'Your guess is as good as mine, Pureza! Open, Sesame!'

But the catches were corroded, and he had to struggle to force up the lid.

'Hmmm. Well, I only have these old work clothes – one pair of blue jeans and a couple of rough cotton shirts. But they're clean enough, see? Not many oil stains or whatever, 'cos I always had very good overalls to wear. And they've obviously been washed in at least one prison laundry!'

Pureza took a quick look. 'Hmmm. I think you and I will need to go shopping quite soon! But they'll do for today – in the right sort of café and the right part of town!'

'What, out beyond the port, where I used to live and work?'

'Oh no, Arthur! In the hippy new Old City! Now, I really must get on. Come back down any time you like ...'

His tatty little old suitcase. Bought second-hand for the week's summer holiday with Emilie in 1959, then jammed under the bed in his crummy apartment. The *flics* would have thrown all his possessions into it on the day they arrested him. It must have followed him from the police station to the Maison d'Arrêt, and on to Marseilles Prison, and then back to Nice. He'd seen it again this morning for the first time in nearly seven years.

Those shirts and the blue jeans. A few socks and some bits of underwear. One more pair of shoes, in even worse shape than those he was wearing. *Articles de toilette* – hah! And his cheap old watch. He'd be needing that again now. Still working? Yes!

A few old personal papers and a couple of pathetic popular novels. They could all go straight in the bin.

Then there was his cash. The three thousand *balles* remaining from his final wage packet in 1959. That wouldn't be worth much now!

But there was also around thirty-five thousand left over from Luc's advance. The police had never been able to prove it wasn't his life savings, as he had claimed, so it was still here, and it was still his. That made about three hundred and eighty New Francs altogether. Should be enough for several weeks' living expenses, if he was careful.

And the key-ring with the Jaguar motif. Empty now. His apartment key had no doubt been returned to the landlord. And old man Soron would have demanded back the spare key to his garage. Of course the police would then have searched the place at once, presuming that Narone could have hidden the bag of cash there if he *had* actually run off with it. Hopefully no-one had ever found his "own" second wad of notes under the big old tool bench. He could soon be needing that too.

It was very thoughtful of the police not to have included the open bottle of milk and the lump of cheese he would have had for breakfast that morning.

That was all that remained of his old life. And then there was the stuff he had amassed over the past six years and handed over to the warder for packing last night. Amassed? That was a very big word for a small pile of research notes and draft texts, a few items of correspondence with low-grade publishers, and his occasional diary. But they were all important. Even if he never worked with them again, they represented his stepping stones to a proper future life.

There was no personal correspondence from his years in prison, because there had never been any.

He shrugged his shoulders and stored everything away in a single drawer. Then he changed into the blue shirt and the over-tight jeans, and went to look in the bathroom mirror as he combed his hair. His signature Elvis Presley wave and the short tidiness of the back and the sides already felt strangely wrong.

He descended the stairs to the little kitchen and walked cautiously through into the bookshop.

Pureza was busy dealing with a customer, and there were three others browsing or waiting for her attention. She looked up briefly, gave Narone another big smile and an encouraging tilt of the head, and then went straight back to her work. Confident that he now had a green light, he began a quiet and haphazard tour of the little shop, his admiration for its contents growing with every minute that passed. And on several occasions he noticed, quite by chance, that she was watching him out of the corner of her eye, clearly delighted with what she was observing.

On the rare occasions over the next two or three hours when there was momentarily nobody else in the shop, he wondered whether he should try to start up another conversation. But Pureza clearly had many other things to do in those precious spare minutes, and he resolved to continue his exploration, and his random dipping into interesting-looking volumes, without disturbing her at all. And he could see from her occasional wry smiles that she was appreciating that too.

Finally, just before one o'clock, she escorted her latest satisfied customer to the door and then turned the hanging sign around to show "Closed".

'Well, Arthur, I have done some very good business this morning – you must have brought me a lot of luck! – and now it is time for a very special lunch! *¡Vamos!*'

Studiously ignoring the men in the unmarked blue police car as they strolled past it in the bright summer sunshine, they crossed the Esplanade, penetrated into the relative gloom of the Old City, and found a trendy little restaurant tucked away just off Rue du Malonat.

Throughout their short walk, Narone had been wondering where those policemen were right now. All four of them! *And* anyone else who might still be interested in him. But he had not been able to concentrate on spotting any of them, with Pureza chatting merrily away at his side – no doubt to discourage him from doing exactly that.

And then they sat down at a brightly-laid corner table, and he drank his first glass of beer for almost seven years. And then another.

And then he ate a wonderful three course meal, with good red wine.

Pureza, who had chosen only a very light lunch for herself, continued to talk almost non-stop while he ate, but he only nodded or gave very cursory replies to her occasional little questions, and he realised later that he could hardly remember a word of what she had said. His head had been too full of the other sights and sounds of freedom, the invisible but undoubted presence of all the detectives, and the unaccustomed alcohol.

And then he drank real coffee. Three large cups of it, by the end of the meal. And now Pureza was clearly expecting fuller and better answers to her obviously honest and caring questions.

So he began to try a little harder, and he finally rose to the challenge when she asked him about his writing, brushing aside her mentions of his earlier work and revealing instead his plan to eventually produce some sort of story about these early days of freedom.

'An excellent idea!' she declared with ceremony (but it was evident to him that she was already well aware of it). 'And whenever you need to do any research, especially on everything you've missed over the past few years, you must feel free to use the bookshop as a library and a workplace!'

He mumbled his thanks yet again. And then, of course, she hit upon the biggest question of them all.

'So what are you planning to do with the rest of your life?'

He met it with an answer to match.

'To be perfectly frank, I'm torn between wanting to enjoy it to the full and devoting myself to searching for Emilie.'

'Your old girlfriend?'

'Yes.' He noticed an immediate change in Pureza's previously eager countenance, and something – maybe the spirit of Anais Nin – was suggesting it was a well-controlled reflection of a much greater emotional reaction to his reply. 'So I'll probably end up trying to do both.'

'I perceive a bit of a conflict there ...'

'Of course. And I think I'll come down mostly in favour of Emilie, until I can discover what became of her, and hopefully track her down and persuade her we should try again.'

'After nearly seven years?'

'Oh yes. And I *had* been hoping for no further involvement with anyone associated with the robbery. But the police – and maybe others – are obviously already at my heels ...'

'Well,' said Pureza, her face now a picture of selfless resignation, 'I shall live in the hope of a wonderful future for us all. And whatever you decide to do, I promise to help you achieve your goals, and to try to keep you out of trouble or danger.'

'Look, I really don't expect ...'

'Now, Arthur, if either of us is challenged about how I came to know about your release today, I think we should pretend that we first met many years ago on one of my brief early visits to Nice, and that you were simply permitted to write to "your old friend" to ask her to collect you from the jail. And that we then just took it from there. OK?'

'As you wish, of course. And I swear I will keep my own promise never to reveal the secrets of your family in anything I write.'

'Thank you. Now, I'm sure we would have known each other's birthdays in those good old days, wouldn't we? Mine is the twentieth of October, so you have plenty of time to save up for a little *bagatelle*! And when is yours?'

'The fifth of September.'

'Oh, that's far too long to wait to give you what you really need! We shall go shopping for your new clothes at the weekend! And now I must get back to work!'

'I'd like to stay downtown for a while, if that's OK.'

'Of course it is! You have a lot to rediscover! But please be in by seven o'clock tonight. I have a little surprise for you ...'

Narone had vaguely planned to take a gentle stroll around the Old City and then perhaps along the Promenade and the beach. But by the time he reached the Place du Palais the beers and the wine and the heat of the day were having their natural effect, and he spent much of the afternoon stretched out on a bench, drifting in and out of sleep. But he repeatedly perked up as he spotted the approach of one exciting new dress fashion after another, especially those of the opposite sex, often accompanied by the bouncy pop sounds emerging from the amazing new transistor radios carried around by Nice's richest kids and young American grand-tourists.

'This is music to watch girls by!' he said to himself at one point. 'Someone ought to write a pop song about *that*!'

As the rush hour and the temperature both wound down, he abandoned all further ideas of the beach for that day and set off for a favourite bar in one of the farthest corners of the Old City.

And as he passed the huge, familiar wooden door of No. 1, Rue Barillerie he could not prevent his eyes from wandering, as they always used to, to its small bronze knocker in the shape of a delicately costumed wrist and a hand with all its fingers still intact. He shook his head vigorously in a vain attempt to erase the awful persistent memory, then hurried on, dived into Les Murailles and ordered a small beer.

But when the bill arrived he decided that, until further notice, most of his future beers would need to be shop-bought. Except when he really fancied one in another favourite old bar, of course ...

Hmmm. The cost of living in 1966 was going to prove much higher than he'd expected. But his cash should still last him about three or four weeks, so long as he continued to get free board and lodging at dear Pureza's place and only had to pay for his lunch and incidentals. So he would lay low with what he had, for now, and not yet risk going to collect the wad of big notes he'd hidden at the garage.

And he would try to completely forget about the huge sum he had stored for Luc in Danielle Orvine's old sofa.

Around seven o'clock he started to wend his weary way back to the bookshop, very careful not to indicate that he now believed he *was* indeed being watched. He already had his suspicions about a keen-looking young man who was probably still "with him" and might well be a baby policeman, and he'd also noticed a cheaply-dressed, middle-aged woman walking or relaxing not far away on three separate occasions.

Pureza had prepared a special Niçois dinner in her tiny kitchen, and the mildly scolding look in her eyes reminded him that he was at least fifteen minutes late.

'I'm sorry. My old watch seems to have stopped again. It's not spoiled, is it?'

'No, Arthur. Not yet. But please wash your hands and sit down at once.'

Maybe this was an example of that domestic bliss he had occasionally heard about.

They ate in near silence. Initially Pureza had been keen to know all about Narone's first afternoon back in the city, but he felt equally keen not to talk and to concentrate again on enjoying another delicious meal. She got the message quickly, and let him be. But later, as she was making coffee – 'Real coffee, this time, *amigo*!' – she broached the subject that had often occupied his own thoughts that day.

'So how are your finances?' Her ironic grin said it all.

'I'll be all right for a while. And I'll start looking for a job soon, of course.'

'Arthur, I really think you should take a little time to find your feet before getting stuck back into work. I want you to know I trust you completely and I'm willing to lend you some cash. And there will be no hurry to pay it back.'

'That's very kind of you, Pureza. But not now, eh? Maybe a little later, if I run into problems ...'

'All right. But you *must* stay here for free until you have more than enough income to pay me, OK?'

'OK. And thank you for all your kindness towards me.'

'It is my pleasure, Arthur.'

The smile on her face at that moment reminded him of Emilie's – in their early days. And suddenly he felt very full and very tired, and he said so.

'I'm not surprised, my friend. You've had a busy, demanding day and lots of good food for a change! I'll help you make up the bed straight away, and I'll do the washing-up later ...'

* * *

He awoke early, of course, purely from habit, and then drifted in and out of sleep again for several hours, luxuriating in the absence of any pressure to get up and get on. By the time he dragged himself downstairs, Pureza was already hard at work in the bookshop. He decided against causing a minor disturbance in the kitchen, all for the sake of one free cup of instant coffee, and walked briskly through the shop with a cheery *'Au revoir!'*

She looked across at him, nodded her smiling encouragement once more, and turned back to her customer.

He looked at his still fully operational watch. There was not much of the morning left, and he was not feeling very hungry. He was certainly going to follow Pureza's advice to forget any ideas of job-hunting, at least for today, and despite his resolutions of the previous evening he was determined to splash out on a nice but fairly modest restaurant lunch – his first meal out and about on his own as a free man again!

So he would just grab a quick breakfast nearby, then buy himself a newspaper and a proper writer's notebook, find a shady bench on the Esplanade, and spend an hour or two reading and capturing the moods and the events of the previous day, his first beautiful day of freedom.

After discovering the crazy price of coffee and a croissant in even the lowliest of Nice's embankment cafés, he concluded he would definitely need to take advantage of Pureza's morning offerings too!

One after another the city's church bells were singing out the noonday hour, and he had made all the notes he needed to, for now. And so far he had been completely undisturbed. But he was sure there had been a different detective following him today, and although Narone had not yet been able to see the man's face properly, his demeanour was remarkably familiar. Time would tell.

And if that ageing beach-girl was also still around, he thought, she must be wearing very different clothes today, and keeping her head well down.

But who else might be out there, dammit? Luc himself? Or the "genius" who set it all up in the first place? Or any number of lowlifes who fancied their chances with the getaway driver who just might know where all that cash had been hidden?

So why had none of those possible "watchers" simply snatched him already and driven him off into the hills for a full interrogation? Or at least approached him in a backstreet and tried to pressure him into revealing where the money – or even Luc himself – was hidden?

Well, that had happened a few times in jail, hadn't it? And he had always claimed no knowledge of the whereabouts of the cash, and tried to remind those animals – in between the punches and the kicks and the fighting-back – about that high-class resident of Nice who had sworn in court that she'd seen him leave the second car with nothing in his hands. Hmmm. Maybe the message had finally got out, and he wouldn't be molested again. Or maybe he would. Well, he was ready for them if they came ...

He was absorbed in his appreciation of a fine escalope of veal in a friendly restaurant on Rue du Marché when the waiter reappeared beside him with an opened wine bottle on his tray and a small piece of folded paper lying neatly beside it.

'This note appears to be for you, *monsieur*. It was left on my tray while I was busy at this end of the bar.'

Narone looked at it rather warily. It was inscribed: "For A, at the table by the stairs. And another glass of wine." He quickly plucked it off the tray and held it tightly in his fist.

'Yes, it is definitely for me. Thank you. And ... one moment ... here, please take ...'

'*Merci, monsieur*, but that will not be necessary. Whoever left this for you also left me a very good tip.'

The waiter was generously topping up Narone's glass.

'Oh! So did you notice who it was?'

'I regret not. You can see how crowded the place is today. Could have been anybody. Looks like a woman's writing to me. Maybe it was the one in the big straw hat ...'

'You, I noticed her come in. Where is she now?'

'She has already departed. But then perhaps it was one of those rich *young* things over there. They have all been eyeing you up, and more! *Alors, bonne chance, monsieur ...*'

The waiter winked and hurried away. Narone quickly pocketed the message, and tried hard to ignore the glances of the girls at the bar while he enjoyed the rest of his lunch. Then he left the exact payment on the table, walked out into the narrow street, and pretended to be consulting his newspaper as he carefully retrieved and unfolded the note. It read: "Be at your very last call box at four this afternoon. Or else. And talk to nobody between now and then. I shall know if you have. COMET."

So Luc *was* still around. And Narone had just two hours to decide whether to obey the man's stark commands, or start running again.

He'd always feared this would happen, of course. Maybe straight away, like this, or maybe not for a while. But anyway ...

He was not concerned for himself. He could put up a good fight if necessary. Like he had in jail. Or maybe Luc would play it really dirty. Too bad if he did.

No, the problem was still Emilie. "Or else," the message said. Poor innocent Emilie. If Luc really *did* still have any knowledge of where she was. And now there was Pureza too. Luc must know all about *her*, of course. At least she was in this voluntarily. But that didn't make her any safer either ...

Maybe he should just accept that he'd have to agree to collect the money and return it to Luc. That must be all the guy wanted, surely? Should be easy enough, if it was still there in the sofa. And that would be an end of it, at last.

Yes, of course he must play ball. Otherwise he would share the responsibility for anything Luc then decided to do. And this was supposed to be a time of reparation, not of further damage. He was a man now, not a silly selfish kid. Probably.

He'd have to think on his feet on the phone, of course. But he was good at that, and he actually had plenty of time this afternoon to wander around and prepare for it. And yes, he well remembered exactly where he'd waited, three Sundays in a row, for that final call to arms in November 1959 ...

* * *

He sauntered up to the phone box, picked up the receiver and put it to his ear, pretended to dial a few numbers, then discreetly pressed the hook back down, and waited. Ninety seconds later the bell rang, and he quickly opened the line again.

'Hello, Arthur. So, do you remember *my* first name too?'

'It was "Luc" seven years ago.'

'Right. Let's get straight on with this, then. All I want is those banknotes. I want you to hand them over in complete secrecy, and then I want to get out of this country for good. Got it?'

'Yes ...'

'So did you hide them somewhere safe?'

'Of course I did.'

'OK. Now listen carefully. I do *not* want to know where the money is stashed. That way I can't be tempted to try and find it myself – that would be far too risky for me. And I won't be able to reveal its whereabouts if I'm ever "pressed" by anyone – if you see what I mean.'

'Yes, I do.'

'So don't *ever* tell me where it's hidden, Arthur. But ... is it still there?'

'How can I possibly know that? I only got out yesterday!'

'Just wondering if you actually stashed it at your new girlfriend's bookshop.'

'I thought you didn't want to know where it was! And do you really think I'd have gone straight back there ...?'

'No, I don't. But did you ever tell *anybody* where you hid it?'

'No.'

'Good. So ideally you would go and collect it for me at once ...'

'But ...?'

'Well, that may not be the best thing, for now.'

'Because I'm being watched?'

'Maybe. So you will carry on just as you have been doing, for a while. You will not leave Nice. And you *will* collect the money for me very soon, once I'm happy that people have stopped taking an interest in you.'

'What people would that be, Luc?'

'Just people.'

'But surely those "people" need to be convinced that I know nothing about where the cash is hidden and have no plans to collect it. Because until they're persuaded of that, Luc, they're going to stick to me like glue, aren't they?'

'Yes, you're probably right about that ...'

'So I'd better be seen to be devoting myself to something completely different. Perhaps I should pretend to be looking for my friend Emilie. She may still be living at her old place, but after more than six years I doubt it! Or maybe you decided I'd left the money with her, and tried to beat it out of her when you discovered I was beyond your reach in a police cell ...'

'No, I didn't do that, Arthur. But there's always time ...'

'Want me to pretend I still care?'

'Maybe you do.'

'And maybe I don't. Anyway, do you happen to know if she's still living there? 'Cos if she is, I'll need to find something else to seem to be preoccupying me ...'

'I have no idea. But I'm sure you'll soon find out. And ... wait a minute ... anyone watching you might equally well assume you're looking for her because she *does* have the money, or at least knows where it's hidden. And maybe she actually does ...'

'No, Luc. She had absolutely no idea, I swear. I have never spoken to her, or seen her, or left her any messages since we did the robbery. I don't know why she left me to rot in jail, and frankly I don't care!'

'Hmmm. But if that *is* the case, I could always put a little pressure on your latest "old friend" at the bookshop ...'

'Look, can we stop this stupid game of cat and mouse? Either you trust me to sort things out for you as fast as I safely can, or you don't – in which case, get out of my life for ever!'

'I'm the one calling the shots here, Arthur. So there's no point in trying to give *me* orders. But I *am* willing to run with your suggestion. You can spend a few weeks "hunting for Emilie" and keeping a good eye out for anybody tailing you.'

'OK. And once I think I'm in the clear, I can leave you a signal and ...'

'No. No signals this time, at least for now – it's too complicated. I'll drive all the communications. I'll call you again at noon on the first day of August, at the box at the top end of Rue Pierre Devoluy. And if we ever fail to make a phone rendezvous, Arthur – if the planned call box is out of order, or whatever – you need to be at *this* one at noon the following day and every day after that, until we're back in touch.'

'All right. And meanwhile you – or maybe that lady of a certain age ... I guess she's a good friend of yours – will be tracking me all the time as well, eh?'

'I don't know what you're talking about.'

'You must be joking. Anyway, I'll soon know when you've stopped wasting your efforts.'

'Don't be too confident about that. And by the way – what are you doing for money?'

'I'll be OK for a while. I still have a bit of your advance left, and maybe I'll get myself a little job later.'

'What about those two wads of cash I gave you in the car?'

'I hid one of them the same evening – in a completely different place from the rest of the money. The police found the other one in my pocket when they arrested me.'

'Maybe you also took some more from the bag ...'

'No, I didn't.'

'We shall see. And perhaps there *will* be a bit more for you – when you deliver. Meanwhile, when you decide to pick up your hidden wad, be *very* careful how you spend it. One bill at a time, different places ...'

'Yeah, yeah, Luc. I'm not stupid.'

'Good.'

'And I hope this is obvious, Arthur – you do *not* talk to the police, OK?'

'Of course I won't, man! Think I want any more trouble?'

'No. Very sensible.'

'So have we finished now?'

'When I say so, Arthur. And – yes, we've finished. Until the first of August.'

Narone found the nearest bar, sat down in the window seat, planted an enforced grin on his face for the benefit of any possible watchers, and ordered a large beer.

So, he would have to hope and pray that the money was still where he'd left it. He'd bought himself four weeks, at least, and although he was desperate to focus on what had happened to Emilie, he now had another job to do – which of course could help him in that quest. And he must also try to get his hands on Luc himself, to remove this new pressure *and* any threat the man might actually pose to Emilie. And maybe he could even learn something about her whereabouts from Luc, before turning him in, or whatever ...

But how to ferret him out? He had no idea. That woman who kept popping up really must have something to do with it, and he would keep a good eye out for her in the next few days and maybe follow her if he got the chance. Apart from that, right now he could only hope for a lucky break.

The life of relative ease he had been happily anticipating was already vaporising before his eyes. He sustained his pretended grin, drained his glass, and went for another long but this time rather anxious walk of re-familiarisation with the evening sights and sounds of his city.

* * *

The next morning he had a simple diplomatic breakfast with Pureza and spent a couple of hours politely browsing in the bookshop, quietly observing everything going on but still preoccupied with Luc's disarming phone call.

Then, sensing a lull in business and an imminent coffee break, he made his excuses and escaped into the clear air of another Riviera summer's day.

The one thing he really did not want to consider right now was any sort of paid work, despite what he'd said on the phone to Luc. But in case he *was* still being watched, he publicly exorcised that demon at once by checking half-heartedly on the employment prospects in the first half-dozen cafés he passed. The only offer he received was a two-hour late evening dishwashing job at an extremely low rate of pay. So he was quickly able to give up the idea "for now" and felt confident that Pureza would applaud his good sense in following her advice to remain *décontracté* for as long as he could afford to.

Wow! Every sort of sound emerging from those transistor radios! Great rock 'n' roll classics, and boring old Country and Western, and that exciting British beat music he'd missed out on completely, and the much richer pop songs now coming out of America. Not much French stuff, though. But that was no bad thing, especially when the best they could offer was still good old Johnny Hallyday ...

Pop-art and op-art and who-knows-what-art everywhere, on prints and posters and advertisements and magazine and book covers. This was surely the decade of the image rather than the word! And he wanted to be a writer?

Even a television set perched up above the bar in one of those cafés, giving everyone the latest news uninvited. Television would have reported the Paris massacre in 1961, wouldn't it? And the Sputniks, and the first topless swimsuit, and the death of Kennedy, and Beatlemania, and *everything* he had missed. And someone had said there would be colour TV in France next year!

And the fashions, of course! The fascination of them! The girls!

The girls. He would really have to work on breaking down his fear of approaching them. He'd managed it properly once, with a lot of effort, and it had paid off. But that was nearly eight years ago ...

After lunch he forgot about the girls, sought out the public library and spent the entire afternoon reading the daily newspapers. He had not been at all interested in doing that while he was in jail, and now he was wondering why. It might have been a lot more useful than writing those silly stories!

On the other hand, he would always *much* rather be making things than just lying around or watching what others were doing with their lives. Or perhaps, to be more specific, he quite liked watching people and *then* writing about them.

Or was all that pure nonsense? Was he actually very lazy at heart, but always trying to disguise it? Writing was hard work, for him. And did he really enjoy the *doing* of it, or just the pleasure of finally finishing something? He could think of many far more enjoyable things! But they were never on offer to somebody like him ...

How could he know any of the answers? And why should he be worrying about this anyway? That was what his fictional anti-heroes did! Surely nobody in the real world wasted their time and talents thinking about things like that? Wasn't everybody else far too busy making friends and having fun?

It was half-past five. Pureza would be closing the bookshop soon. And this morning she had again made no mention of dinner plans. He was already certain she would love to cook for him every day, and he really could not afford to ignore *any* opportunity for a free meal. But that first evening with her had clearly demonstrated that he was not yet ready for the intimacy of such situations. With anybody – slim and pretty, or not.

So he would spend another evening on his own, and eat a nice cheap meal just whenever and wherever he fancied it.

At ten-thirty, after dropping into several cafés for hop-flavoured aperitifs, he teetered out of a *very* cheap snack-bar in the depths of the Old City and began to wend his way through the ill-lit, narrow alleys leading back up to Boulevard Jean Jaurès. And as he turned into Rue de la Loge, he had a sudden throwback to the night Luc had accosted him at that very spot, nearly seven years before, and press-ganged him into service as a getaway driver.

Maybe it would be Luc's lady friend this time, he was thinking to himself. That might be a bit more entertaining! Although he had to admit he hadn't caught a single glimpse of her all day ...

'Good evening, Narone.'

'Who the hell ...?? Oh, it's bloody Inspector Clouseau!!'

'Care to linger in this doorway for a few moments, my friend? No-one knows we're here.'

'I know that better than you! And I'm no friend of yours, Hardy!'

'Fair enough. But *I'm* one of the few *you* still have, Narone. And you'll finally come to realise that, one of these days.'

'Oh, just go away!'

'I'm afraid I won't do that, just yet. I'd much prefer to talk about you.'

'Why should you give a damn about *me*?'

'Well for one thing, you're a famous writer now ...'

'That's utter nonsense, and you know it! Just a couple of stories in a pulp magazine. And how did you hear about them anyway?'

'I get reports, Narone. I get reports ...'

'Huh! Detection by armchair. Still *Inspector* Hardy, is it?'

'Yes.'

'Still not Chief Inspector?'

'No.'

'And how's your nice young Brigadier Lebrun?'

'He's Inspector Lebrun now.'

'I see! You must be delighted for him. Please pass on my heartiest congratulations.'

'I shall ...'

'So now you have another fine sergeant helping you to stalk me!'

'Louis is still only a *gardien*, Narone, but he holds great promise.'

'Oh, I'm even more impressed at your new power base, Inspector! And please give "Louis" my deepest condolences.'

'Finished yet?'

'Maybe – for now.'

'So, I presume your new girlfriend is working for "Luc" ...'

'Of course not!'

'Hmmm. So she just happened to be passing the jail as they let you out, and fancied what she saw?'

'If you like. The women were certainly falling all over me in prison ...'

'And the two of you are living as a couple already?'

'No comment.'

'How do you *know* "Luc" isn't driving her, Narone?'

'This is ridiculous! Can we please get on with it, Chief ...? Oh, I *am* sorry, I mean *Inspector* Clouseau.'

'Now you just ...'

'No, *you* just listen to *me*, big man. Señorita Pureza Seles – that's her name, by the way, in case you haven't managed to detect it yet – has nothing at all to do with the robbery. She's just an old friend. They let me write to her from prison to ask her to pick me up and give me somewhere to stay for a few days. OK?'

'OK, Arthur. For now.'

'Oooh, back to first name terms now, Inspector? You must want something very badly. If only I knew yours ...'

'Lying again, Arthur? It was in all the newspapers at the time.'

'Then I must have felt it was not worth remembering.'

'Right, that's enough! Now, we've had you under surveillance ever since you were released ...'

'I know that. Eyes in the back of my head. Two cars, four cops on Day One. And reducing ...'

'Ah. Fair enough. I suppose I'm not surprised. And it probably bodes well for the future, actually ...'

'Why?'

'We'll come to that. Meanwhile, we watched you make – or take – a phone call at four o'clock yesterday afternoon ...'

'Yeah. I was phoning my bookie.'

'It was a very animated conversation!'

'It concerned a very animated horse.'

'Oh dear. Arthur, can we please stop playing these games? I'm really still on your side, you know.'

'Hah! You didn't believe me when I said I never had the money bag.'

'Yes, I did. And there was a witness who confirmed it – remember?'

'You still never believed me.'

'Yes, I did. Anyway, we're having this little meeting very privately because if any of the many scumbags who are no doubt still interested in you discover that you've been talking to me, they'll immediately assume you are informing on them and you'll then be in extremely deep ordure. And of course I could choose to abandon my charitable discretion on the subject at any time. With me so far?'

'Yes ....'

'Good. So, you can get on with telling everyone you're busy writing some fancy new fairy tales, or maybe just searching for your long-lost little girlfriend – aha, that struck a chord, didn't it, Arthur! – but what you'll really be doing is working for me.'

'I see ...'

'We want "Luc" and we want the money, wherever he's hiding it.'

'We??'

'Well ... me, at least.'

'Why so impassioned about it, big man?'

'Because it is a job not finished. I want to see "Luc" in jail, where he belongs, for a very long time. I want justice for the injury to Charles-Pierre Orceau. And I want the money – or whatever's left of it – returned to the bank.'

'A fine crusade, Inspector. And seemingly most unselfish. So, is that all?'

'No. I also want any clues "Luc" can give me to the identity of the man who masterminded it.'

'If there ever was one ...'

'I'm still convinced there was. There *had* to be! And he was probably an insider.'

'So, no great changes to your strategy since 1959, then?'

'No, Arthur. And you are going to help me realise it. We didn't get you released from jail early out of sympathy.'

'What?? You mean I've been set up as bait? That's bloody ...'

'Forget the righteous protests, Arthur. Think of yourself more as Probationary Agent Narone. The faster your release helps me find everything I'm looking for, the more grateful I shall be – if you get my drift. And I'm talking carrots *and* sticks here. The longer it takes, the less carrot and the more stick.'

'Why the big rush, Simon?'

'Ah, you've suddenly got your memory back! How amicable! And I haven't mentioned any timescales yet, have I? But if our "Luc" *is* still hovering in the background and hears you've been released – or maybe he knows about it already, one way or another – and wants to make contact with you for some reason, he'll need to make his move fairly soon. Those old-issue banknotes will be worthless in about twenty months' time.'

'What?'

'Oh, please don't pretend you didn't know that either!'

'OK. So since *you're* talking of carrots and sticks, should I assume that elusive promotion to Chief Inspector has passed you by forever, or it there still an outside chance of scraping it?'

'You really are pushing your luck yet again, Narone ...'

'Yes, I am, *Inspector*. But no wonder you're so keen to have me help you search for the end of the rainbow ...'

'Oh, just shut up for once and listen, man! As I was saying, you need to put it about that you're looking for Emilie ...'

'That's just what I'm intending to do anyway!'

'Excellent. Get people thinking you suspect she was scared off by someone who thought she was holding the cash or at least knew something about it or "Luc" or whatever. But as and when you get the chance, sniff around to try and pick up anything you can about what actually happened to *him*.'

'And what if I discover nothing?'

'You keep trying. As I said, the sooner you get a result, the better. But I don't want you forcing things and blowing any chance of finding him. And I realise I may need to be patient. He might not emerge until a lot closer to the deadline of April 1968, but then there will be far less time for him to dispose of the money. So he'll have to make a calculated decision on the timing of his move. We need to be right on the ball when that happens.'

'You're still assuming he's held on to most of the cash, and not spent it or fenced it. And that he's probably still here in Nice. And that he'll discover I'm out of jail and want to talk to me. And ...'

'I have to assume all those things and more, Arthur. There's no other chance of catching him or getting the money back.'

'So you really *do* need me, don't you?'

'Yes, I do. But remember the sticks I promised if you decide not to play along. I could nab you for the slightest misdemeanour and get you thrown straight back in jail. And I could even conjure up some new witnesses who would swear you *were* carrying the bag of cash when you left the hijacked car. I could make the rest of your life hell, Arthur, if I chose to ...'

'But you *still* really need me, Inspector ...'

'OK, smartarse, cut the talking and get on with the job. Here – you will phone me on this number with your progress reports, every Monday morning at nine o'clock, without fail. You will not leave the city without my permission. If you ever *do* fail to call me, I will assume you've broken this trust, and by the next day there will be a "Wanted" poster in every police station and border point in France.'

'OK ...'

'And I'll be watching you anyway.'

'You'll have the manpower to tail me twenty-four hours a day?? You must be joking!'

'Only a bit, Arthur. Only a bit. Best assume you'll always be under observation ...'

'So you saw me drinking at Le Tonellier late last night?'

'Yes.'

'That's remarkable, Inspector. 'Cos I've never been near the place in my life. Sorry about that. Let's try something else. What did the waiter bring me halfway through my lunch at the Astérix yesterday?'

'A top-up of red wine.'

'Well done!! And ...?

'Nothing else.'

'Bravo! So you're watching me *occasionally*. And I guess I should find that partially reassuring. Now, I believe you mentioned carrots a couple of times ...'

'The carrot is that I will keep off your back while you get on with the job.'

'Oh, that's marvellous! And there I was thinking you'd be helping me out with my finances.'

'Not just yet. But there is a rather attractive police reward outstanding, for information leading to the arrest of "Luc". And another nice little one from the bank for the recovery of their money.'

'I can't wait. Literally.'

'Well, you did have thirty thousand *balles* in "savings" when we picked you up in 1959! That should last you a good week or two these days, especially if you're not paying any rent to your new girlfriend. And I suggest you get yourself a little part-time job, to give you something to do when you're not hunting for Emilie.'

'Oh, thanks a bunch. And as it happens, I'm already looking at local opportunities for smart young executives. Tell me, did you ever have any teenage children?'

'Why?'

'Don't worry, Simon. I'm not planning to go after them. Not my style, and you know it. I'm just interested in what sorts of casual work they might have picked up in their vacations ...'

'I'll take that at face value, Arthur, but don't push your luck *any* further, OK?'

'And ...'

'I had three very expensive daughters. They didn't work in the vacations, and my costs were never-ending. But I couldn't take any of them to watch a football match!'

'No *wonder* you want to be friends with me ...'

'Hah! So, who *did* you talk to on the phone yesterday afternoon?'

'I was calling Pureza to say I would be staying out all evening, and not to bother to cook me dinner after all.'

'Ah, no *wonder* she was animated! On your way, Arthur.'

Balancing Act

Narone spent the next two days in a very strange mood, trying hard to re-acclimatise himself in his constantly stimulating new world but regularly falling back into bemused, protracted ponderings.

All through the conversation with Inspector Hardy, he'd been wondering whether to mention that Luc had already been in touch. And he'd continually held back from doing so. Cards close to his chest for now. He had absolutely no feel for which way this was going to break, and if that hard-nosed villain were to pick up the slightest hint that he'd been talking to the police, let alone mentioning he was actually in contact with Luc, well ...

And there had still been no further sign of the woman who'd been following him during those first two days. Luc's woman, without a doubt. Although from the little he recalled of the man from those two brief encounters seven years before, he was surely a good deal younger than her. Maybe he just preferred much older girlfriends – or had married one. Or perhaps she was his big sister. A family affair. Hah! She was practically old enough to be his mother!

Anyway, the two of them had almost certainly stopped watching him. It would probably be a complete waste of their time now, of course. And they might not even still be in Nice. Why risk it, after all?

But of course the woman's disappearance had removed Narone's brief half-chance of quickly getting a fix on the man himself.

On both mornings he made an effort to be as friendly as he could with Pureza during their brief clashing encounters at the bathroom door and their hurried shared breakfasts. Well, *she* was always hurrying. *She* had a real job to do.

But the moment she opened the bookshop to her customers and immersed herself in her work, he felt a wonderful sense of release and scurried through as fast as he decently could, calling out his usual 'See you later!' without actually involving himself in any backwards glance or smile.

He knew Pureza was a saint, and he already adored her for that. But he also knew he only needed saints for a few minutes per day, and that they should not be over-encouraged.

So he spent the rest of that summery week largely in his own quiet company, luxuriating in the leaf-green public gardens or fantasising on the flesh-carpeted stony beach, walking around the city and observing more and more of the changes that had been taking place, watching the beautiful people strolling hand-in-hand all around him, and always carefully considering how best to manage his two closely related tasks. Luc and the Inspector had both given him a good deal of freedom, and although they each had very different aims, there were many overlaps in what they wanted him to do. And he would exploit those overlaps as fully as he could.

But he reminded himself on one of those afternoons (or was it Anais Nin whispering in his ear again?) that he really should make the effort to go back to the bookshop that evening and spend a little time with Pureza, since that was what she really seemed to want. And he *would* get another free dinner out of it, which was certainly not to be sneezed at.

* * *

On the Sunday, as promised, she took him for some extended window shopping for his early birthday presents. And the following morning they went back downtown together to purchase all the clothes she had selected for him – oh, he really had no idea, she had declared, and he completely agreed – and she ended up opening the bookshop almost two hours later than usual.

That excursion gave him a very good excuse for the long delay in making his first "nothing to report" Monday morning call from Pureza's living room to an obviously concerned and annoyed Simon Hardy. But Narone did at least then unveil his initial strategy for finding Emilie. For the time being, he told the Inspector, he felt he should risk making only *very* low-profile enquiries about her disappearance. For example, it would be crazy to go sniffing around her old apartment straight away. Anyone watching him would be sure to think he was trying to retrieve the cash!

Hardy concurred, and Narone enjoyed the irony.

* * *

He began his investigations that very evening – at the Casa della Musica, of course. But as he approached it he was dismayed to see its name had been changed to the Happy Hallyday – in English! – and its facade had been freshly painted in bright oranges and limes. And inside it was now a very different sort of place. Good old Max was long gone, he soon discovered, and despite its pathetic trendy "pop-rock" name there was no longer any live music, and of course all the barmen and waiters were new. So its institutional memory had been totally lost, and Emilie Courbier, the thrilling, young avant-garde artiste who seven years earlier had turned that humble dive into one of the Old City's most popular night spots, was remembered only as a dated myth in a small framed photograph, retained – probably through the new owners' pure oversight – high up in the corner of the wall above the bar.

Narone walked out of the place in utter disgust. He sensed, there and then, that despite his continuing ardour for Emilie – or at least its embers – it could be days or even weeks before he summoned up the will to continue his search. But if challenged, there and then, he could not have explained why.

He spent the next three days trying once more, but largely failing again, to immerse himself in the carefree society of his new Nice.

He was still seeing beautiful young women everywhere, of course, many of them strolling or sunbathing alone. But he always passed them by. They had chosen to be out and about on their own, they obviously wanted their privacy, and he must not disturb it or do anything to alarm them.

So he continued to watch and wait for something to prod him back into some sort of action.

And as he wandered home on Thursday evening, he turned a corner and suddenly noticed the heavy clouds that were coming quickly in from behind the setting sun, and he saw again the freak formation that had perturbed him so much a few weeks before the robbery: the image of a huge and almost stationary fist with several long and puffy fingers moving steadily away from it ...

He ran in a cold sweat all the way back to the bookshop.

* * *

The next morning he awoke early with a new sense of purpose. He was out of the bathroom even before Pureza's alarm clock had sounded, and by seven-thirty he had left her a little *"Ciao!"* note and was hurrying down towards the port, with a plan to spend the morning visiting every single café within five hundred metres of Rue Bavastro and having a nice little chat with each of their owners – particularly the older, long-established ones.

It did not take him long to confirm, from four separate, gossipy sources, exactly what he had always suspected. And it tied up pretty well with those uncaring taunts of Inspector Hardy soon after his arrest. Emilie Courbier had undoubtedly abandoned her beloved apartment within a few hours of the mention of "Narone's show-business girlfriend" in the evening newspaper. And as far as each of his informants was concerned, she had then disappeared off the face of the earth.

But an elderly fish-wife, sipping her late-morning *express* through toothless gums, could not help overhearing Narone's casual enquiry to the venerable *patronne* of La Grande Lune, and broke in before he had finished speaking ...

'*La petite clarinettiste?* Poor child. They chased her away! The bastards!'

'Ah! Who were they, *madame*?'

'No idea. No-one has. But she was too smart for them, *enfin* ...'

'What do you mean?'

'Everyone thought she'd got straight out of town. And one of her neighbours said she'd mentioned Marseilles as she was leaving, the clever little minx. But my grandson saw her two days later, after dark, on the corner of the stretch of Rue de la Croix behind the church.'

'But that's the nastiest little street in the Old City!'

'Better nasty than sorry.'

'Was he sure it was her?'

'Oh, yes. He never forgets a body.'

'You don't mean ...'

'*Mais non!* She was just coming back with a little shopping. Must have cut and dyed her own hair in a hurry, he said. Made a poor job of it.'

'Did he see which block she went into?'

'No. He just watched her turn into the street from Rue Rossetti. He decided it was best to completely ignore her. Good lad. He never told anyone but me, and it's probably the only secret I ever kept in my life – hah! But it's been a long time, and you have honest eyes, *monsieur*.'

'And ...?'

'That's all. He never saw her again. So, how long *has* it been?'

'Six or seven years.'

'Yes. Pah! Only God knows where she is now, *la pauvre petite clarinettiste!*'

Narone rewarded the tired old woman well for her information and consideration towards him, but he left the place with his depression redoubled. And by the time he had drawn a blank in all the other nearby cafés and bars, his spirits had reached an even lower low.

The trouble was, he kept reminding himself, he could never be sure if that well-intentioned grandson had been right. If Emilie had left Nice on the day after the robbery, as she'd hinted to her old neighbours, it was very unlikely that the injured Luc had been in any sort of position to watch her and tail her to the four winds. But if she *had* stayed in the Old City, and moved straight to Rue de la Croix, then she might well have been recognised there by any number of other lowlifes, and the news could easily have got back to his oppressor.

No, he could never be sure. But for Emilie's sake, he had better still run with the assumption that Luc really might know where she was living now, even after all these years. So he must probably continue with his plan to pursue the man as doggedly as he could.

But he would need to take some more time out to think this through quite carefully. And a beer or two would definitely speed that process along.

* * *

The following Monday, after a hazy, best-forgotten weekend and another fact-free chat with the Inspector – and still without a firm plan for locating Luc – Narone had a haircut himself. Purely out of habit. And he was surprised at how little the barber chose to cut off. But he did not complain, even as he was paying up at the end. He already suspected it would be his last haircut for a very long time, and not just because of his financial position.

But that was indeed already looking weak. Less than a fortnight since his release, and more than half of his cash already gone. But he was not keen to try and recover the hidden wad from the garage yet. Let anyone still watching him continue to think he had only Emilie and the novelty of the Sixties on his mind.

So he must now take up Pureza's offer of a loan. And he would tell her he was completely broke already, and could do with about two hundred New Francs at once. That would give him a little extra leeway. And a saint would always forgive a sinner.

She actually lent him three hundred on the spot that afternoon, insisting it came without term or condition and that she would never remind him about it.

With his conscience pricking him lightly but perceptibly enough, Narone at once resolved to try and spend several evenings "at home" over the coming weeks, continuing to enjoy Pureza's delicious free dinners and making a real effort at meaningful conversation. He gently floated the idea to her, and she agreed with relish.

And with that small commitment made and implemented the very same day – he even helped her with the washing-up this time – he decided as he drifted off to sleep that he could now afford to ignore all the other pressures for a while and carry on with his new life of daytime ease. He deserved it, after all this time. No point in opening any more of Pandora's boxes until he really needed to ...

* * *

On their fourth full evening together he finally felt he should ask Pureza, out of simple *politesse*, if she would care to tell him a little more about her family. And after promising once again that he would never write a single word about what she said, he quickly learnt a great deal more than he was expecting about her childhood and her teenage years in the north of Spain.

When she had finished speaking, they were both very quiet for a minute or two. And then, of course, it was her turn to enquire.

'But what about *your* parents, Arthur?'

'Ah. Well, my situation was a little similar to yours. But also very different, I think.

'I was born in Contes, up in the hills above Nice. Hah! ... I must have been destined to be a writer!

'I only have vague memories of my father. He disappeared when I was three or four years old. Who knows why? It was war-time ...

'Anyway, my mother presumably couldn't cope after that, for whatever reasons, because one day when I was nearly five – it was at the height of the German-Italian occupation of the Midi – she dressed me up in my warmest clothes and packed a small bag with a few other bits and pieces, and we got on the rickety old bus and it took us all the way down to Nice. Then she led me through the grubby streets of the Old City and into the lobby of the Palais du Sénat, and kissed me on the cheek and told me to wait there. And then she went back out onto the little square and never returned.

'When someone finally took pity on me and looked in my little bag, he found my birth certificate and a note asking them to take me in.

'I came to understand much later that a part of the old Senate building was now being used as a makeshift boys' orphanage. And I lived there for the next nine years. Well, nearly twelve, actually. I moved into the adult wing when I was fourteen, and I had to go out and get a job to pay for my room. I found one as a street cleaner.'

'Oh, you poor boy. Did you have any brothers or sisters?'

'None that I was aware of.'

'What was your mother's name?'

'I must have read it a thousand times, Pureza. "Marie-Louise Narone, née Evraux." That's exactly what it said.'

'And your father's?'

'I can't remember.'

'So you don't still have the certificate?'

'Oh yes, I do.'

'Ah. And have you ever tried to find them again?'

'No. I was working for seven years – I was lucky enough to pick up a job as an apprentice car mechanic when I was sixteen – and then I went to jail, and then I came here. And now I think it's my turn to stop talking. Let's do the washing-up, eh?'

* * *

On Monday the twenty-fifth of July, Narone phoned Simon Hardy straight after breakfast as usual.

'I still haven't got anywhere with my general enquiries, Inspector. So I'll probably be taking the plunge and visiting Emilie's old apartment fairly soon. Happy with that?'

'Sounds like a good move. But remember – don't force it, OK? Anything else to report?'

'No.'

* * *

Throughout that week, Pureza's fine dinners were always on offer and Narone's appetite for them was not yet wilting. And late on the Thursday evening, as they sat drinking coffee on the sofa in his room, Pureza steered the subject round to his latest situation.

'I'm delighted to see you're still busy doing next to nothing, Arthur. You deserve it, after all those years in jail. But are you getting anywhere with your searches?'

'For Emilie, you mean?'

'Well, yes ...'

'Afraid not. I've picked up a tiny clue or two, but nothing I can really follow up yet. It's possible she stayed on Rue de la Croix for a while before moving on. But I can't be sure. And I haven't said anything more to you about it because I felt ... well, you may not really want to discuss her.'

'But of course I do, Arthur. She means a great deal to you, so I care about her too. Were you able to talk about her with anyone in prison?'

'Hah! As if anybody there was interested in *her*! No, most of them only wanted to find out what I might know about the stolen money or the guy who got away. And a few of them were just interested in me, if you know what I mean. Good job I was in the low-security wing with the other petty criminals rather than the really nasty pieces of work! I managed to keep my ... well, to look after myself on that front. But only just.'

'Poor Arthur! Look, would you like to talk about Emilie with *me*? It might help, in more ways than one.'

'Oh, I'm not sure. It hurts even just to think about her ...'

'Why don't you try? Shall I make us another pot of coffee first? Or would you prefer something a little stronger? I have a bottle of Cointreau which I keep for special occasions ...'

Narone sighed, as much with relief as with resignation.

'All right, Pureza. I'll help you out with the Cointreau, and I'll tell you a little about her.'

'Good! But you must stop if it gets too painful ...'

'Emilie actually told me a lot about herself during our year together.

'She was born in December 1939, in an expensive corner of Nice up at the top of the Boulevard de Cimiez, or whatever it was called in those days. Her parents were devout Catholics – unlike mine, or the people running my orphanage! – and she was educated in a private convent day-school. The war ended only a few months after she started there. And she made plenty of good friends in her early years. All girls, of course.

'For a long time she was completely accepting of everything she was taught at that school. But then the discipline began to harden, and the punishments and humiliations and threats of eternal damnation steadily increased.

'Have you read James Joyce's *Portrait of the Artist as a Young Man*?'

'Oh yes, Arthur.'

'So you'll understand. And Emilie came to realise that she could not reconcile any of this with the concept of "charity" which was –

shamelessly, she felt – being recommended in parallel to her and her innocent and – she also felt – rather naive young schoolmates.

'From the age of thirteen she became ever more disillusioned with this hypocrisy, and she later toyed with the idea of "active" rebellion. But she quickly reasoned that she had no power base at that time, and taking any "action" would only bring about a focused persecution and a huge increase in her unhappiness. So she just grinned and bore it – for many years. And she slowly recognised that she was not alone in her combined despair and cowardice. But still none of her schoolmates would dare to let their voices be heard.'

Narone paused and smiled wryly to Pureza as he proffered his glass for another large measure of the heart-warming liqueur. And then he sat back and frowned more deeply than she had ever seen him frown.

'Emilie's home environment was also a very enclosed one. She had one younger sister and no brothers, and her convent-dominated world meant she had hardly any contact with the opposite sex throughout her childhood. Just the occasional visit to or from a couple of childish boy cousins, who often taunted her cruelly for reasons she just did not understand.

'And her parents did nothing to encourage any involvement with boys as she got older and entered her teenage years. But she found herself becoming prettier and prettier – everyone at school kept telling her so, and several of the older and more assertive girls made repeated advances to her and sometimes went a good deal further.

'And so her disillusion and revulsion with her world continued to increase. And she was experiencing no positive "real" experiences to offset all of this – apart from her enjoyment of music and her love of playing the recorder, which was the only instrument she was allowed. But her school only tolerated very limited, facile group performances of sacred pieces, and even those were considered a sop to the "rather too modern" music teacher – Pureza, have you read *The Prime of Miss Jean Brodie*? – and largely a waste of precious, real learning opportunities. Even brief and informal break-time ensemble experiments were heavily discouraged.

'By the time she was sixteen Emilie had had enough, and in March 1956 she walked out of that school – the first of her class to conceive the idea, and the first to actually see it through. You can imagine her parents' reaction. But she had spent years preparing for this moment, and she was not going to cave in now. Even when they took her key and ordered her out of the house.'

'No!'

'Oh, yes.'

'The poor girl! And having to leave her little sister! How did she cope with that?'

'I don't know, Pureza. I never asked.'

'Men!'

'Anyway, the peaceful revolutionary in her now emerged unfettered. She packed a suitcase and came straight downtown. She was at once attracted to the developing "beat" scene, and in the poorest part of the Old City she found a large communal house in which fine principles appeared to reign over the desire for power or money. She was warmly welcomed there and given a small corner of the floor in one of the overcrowded rooms, with mat and sleeping bag to be supplied at the guest's discretion and no attempt at segregation of the sexes.

'But she coped. Anything was better than that school or her heartless home. And of course she really wanted to make more music, and also learn to sing. But the only instrument she could play – and she knew she played it very well – was her little descant recorder, and that would not do at all! So she resolved to get her hands on a cheap clarinet. She knew that the fingering and the blowing and all that stuff was rather different, but she'd loved its sound on the few occasions she'd heard it on her parents' radio, and she felt it was the right step to take. And she also quickly learnt she would soon have to start making a financial contribution to the operating costs of her lodgings, or the guys running it would be inviting her to make payments in other ways. So for both of those reasons she needed to find herself a well-paid job.

'She started off by waitressing in a New Town café, which was certainly not well paid in itself, but she somehow managed to do very nicely in tips. Beauty always wins over brains in this world, doesn't it, Pureza? Later on she moved to a more up-market restaurant, where the tips were better still, and then she got a serving job in an Old City music club and was soon promoted to head barmaid. And now she was finally able to afford her second-hand clarinet.

'A year after that, in September 1957 – she was almost eighteen now – she'd cultivated her playing and her singing to the point where

the management was willing to let her do a "spot" and see how it
went. And it went very well. So she was given a regular weekly slot,
and two per week soon afterwards. Six months later, following a
huge increase in custom during the Carnival Weeks, they reshaped
the whole place around Emilie and her performances, which were
quite unique ...'

'In what way, Arthur?'

'She had taken old Thirties and Forties jazz standards from all over
Europe and the States, and formal nineteenth century songs,
especially German ones, and the latest Fifties folk songs from
America, and traditional French folk songs too, and more, and given
them all a completely new feel ... sometimes in unaccompanied song,
sometimes just on the clarinet, and often in a fascinating combination
involving the sudden, unexpected "insertion" of one of those modes
into the thread of the other! It was absolutely captivating!

'And her *entrée* was always equally remarkable. There would be a
sudden trill on her clarinet from the darkest corner of the room, to
grab everyone's attention. A bit like the start of Gershwin's
Rhapsody in Blue! Then she would emerge from the shadows and
walk ever so slowly into centre stage dragging a small round table
behind her, as a pale spotlight picked her up and steadily increased in
intensity. Then she would breathe a husky *"Bonsoir!"* into the
hanging microphone, hop up onto the table as light as a feather –
dramatically crossing her lovely legs to send her soft, black knee-
length skirts flowing loosely all over its surface – then look
charmingly but pointedly at any customers who needed shutting up
completely, and begin to sing.

'And the magic never failed, Pureza. It never failed.

'The management of the Casa della Musica knew a good thing
when they saw one, and they made handsome increases to her
performance payments with every month that passed. So by early
summer she was able to afford some nice new clothes, and she later
moved into a private apartment down by the port, although that
apparently ate up every bit of her new earnings straight away. And at
last – she even told me *this*, Pureza – she was able to entertain her
occasional boyfriends in the privacy of her own home.

'The management had often offered her even more lucrative long-
term deals, of course. But she was a canny young woman, and she
always insisted on a simple week-by-week unwritten promise on

both sides. Which is probably why she felt able to walk out on
everybody the day after the robbery ....'

'Arthur? Are you OK?'

'Yes, I am. Sorry – just feeling a bit sad again, right now. May I
have one more little top-up, please?'

'Certainly – if you really want it.'

'Thanks.'

'So was it around that time that you met her?'

'Yes, it was. But perhaps we could stop there for now, Pureza. I'll
tell you more another evening, OK?'

'Of course, *mi amigo*. Of course.'

Narone woke up several times during the night, as those three large
glasses of rich sweet liqueur repeatedly made their presence
uncomfortably felt. So he was in no mood to drag himself out of bed
when the noise of the Friday morning traffic finally roused him from
sleep again. Instead, he just lay there feeling nauseous and only
achieving the occasional burst of lucid thinking.

He was probably beginning to enjoy – no, that was too strong a
word for it – to appreciate the time he was spending with Pureza.
And she *was* very pretty, and that made it all the more pleasant ...

But he was sure his initial thoughts about her on the day of his
release, as he'd sat by her side and admired her full profile in the
back of that taxi, were simply those of a young man who had been
nowhere near a woman for almost seven years, and certainly not
those of someone about to fall in love.

No, he definitely saw her more as a kindly big sister. Or even as an
always-there-for-you mother ...

But if Pureza held little romantic attraction for him, he couldn't
escape the nagging realisation that for the past two weeks he had
done absolutely nothing more in the search for his long-lost Emilie.
And he probably should be trying harder. So he would need to buy
himself a lot more time from his cash-hungry taskmaster.

* * *

At noon on Monday the first of August, following another empty
checkpoint chat with the Inspector, Narone was at the phone box on

Rue Pierre Devoluy to receive Luc's promised monthly call, reminding himself to give absolutely no hint of his ongoing dialogue with Simon Hardy.

'*Allô!* Is that Comet?'

'Hello, Arthur. So, shall I assume the police are tailing you and monitoring this call and trying to trace it as we speak?'

'Of course not! No-one even knows you've made contact with me!'

'That's the right answer. But ... hey guys, in case you *are* listening in – do you like my funny voice? And even if you *do* trace any of my calls, it will be a waste of time. I'll by moving all over the place to make them, OK?'

'Listen, Luc, you really don't need to go to all that trouble. I told you, nobody knows ...'

'Hmmm. So, any news of your precious little showgirl?'

'No.'

'As if you really cared, eh? Right, assuming you're no longer being watched, I think it's time for you to pick up the cash.'

'I'm afraid that's not a very good idea. I'm pretty sure I *am* still being followed. Certainly not by you or your own lady friend, of course. But maybe by the *flics*, maybe by others ...'

'Damn!'

So he didn't disagree, thought Narone. That settled it, then. Wherever the two of them were now, they were almost certainly not watching him. So he would keep the initiative ...

'So I really shouldn't go and collect the money straight away. But I might try later in the month, if the heat's died down by then. OK?'

Luc sighed and paused, obviously gathering his own thoughts.

'All right. That's probably best, in the circumstances, so I won't argue for now. We'll let it run until I call you on the first of September, usual time. But I wanna hear about some real progress then, OK? Here's the location of your next phone box ...'

Good! Another whole month ahead, without very much pressure on him. He still had no further leads on Emilie to follow, but maybe later in the month he *would* feel happy to start checking out her old apartment block and going in to collect the cash hidden in Danielle's sofa. And while he was there he might also pick up something more about Emilie's disappearance.

So he now made a positive decision to hang loose – he really liked that trendy new American phrase – and get around (there was another one!) in the town and on the beach for most of the day, over the next few weeks. But he would spend his mornings in the bookshop for the foreseeable future, doing some of the catch-up reading that Pureza had sensibly suggested on their first day together. And he would report "no progress" to the Inspector every Monday for as long as he felt he could get away with it.

He started his current affairs research the following morning. And after a few attempts at light conversation, which all became one-sided very quickly, Pureza once again got the message about the writer in his private bubble, and let him be.

He might well have been hanging very loose during the days that followed, especially in the afternoons and most of the evenings, but he soon began to realise his life was settling into a bit of a pattern. He would probably have to do something about that.

* * *

At one o'clock every day Pureza would close up for lunch. Sometimes Narone could be persuaded to pop out with her for a beer and a baguette. But most days he preferred to finish what he was reading while she hurried down to the New Town shops, and then go out on his own just before she returned.

At lunchtime on the sixteenth of August, six weeks after his release from prison, he was immersed in Julianne's *History of Gaul* when the telephone rang. He sighed deeply at the disturbance, contemplated ignoring it, and then realised it just might be Pureza calling him with a problem.

He walked over to her desk and picked up the receiver.

'Arthur Narone?'

'Yes ...'

'Welcome back to Nice. You do not know me, but I arranged our little robbery in 1959, and I'd now like you to finish the job for me.'

Narone swallowed hard and wondered how to play for time.

'Ah. Well ... hey, why should I believe any of that?'

'No special reason. But it's true. You surely never thought your little "leader" planned and funded it all by himself?'

'No, I guess not.'

'Did he ever mention his sponsor?'

'Maybe, maybe not.'

'Very canny, Narone. Well, just in case he did, I'll tell you the name I gave him. It was Xérus. Does that ring a bell?'

'Maybe, maybe not.'

'Fair enough. But do you really think I'd have risked inventing that name here and now, and telling you about it, if it wasn't exactly the one I had used with him? Because if I am a fake, and he actually mentioned someone completely different, I would now have blown it completely and that would be the end of this phone call, wouldn't it ...'

'Yes, I suppose so ...'

'Indeed. And I'd hate to have to put pressure on your old girlfriend, *and* your new one, to try to convince you further.'

'You know where Emilie is??'

'Maybe, maybe not, Narone. Two can play at that game. Best to believe I do, eh? Now may we proceed?'

'Yes.'

'So, all the evidence was that boss-man made off with most of the cash, right?'

'That's exactly what happened.'

'Unless *you* have it, of course ...'

'No, I don't!! How many times do I have to tell people that?'

'Calm down, Narone. I believe you. Trouble is, boss-man never got back to me, and he failed to deliver my share of the proceeds. But I'm a trusting sort of guy, and I'm sure there must have been a very good reason. Maybe he simply lost my number, or something perfectly understandable like that. So I've been very patient, and I'm confident he's still holding it all safely for me. By the way, what did he call himself?'

'I won't say.'

'Very well. Just give me something I can use with you.'

'Hmmm. Let's call him "L", shall we?'

'Remarkable. And you can call me "X", Narone. So, I should deeply appreciate the pleasure of Monsieur L's company once again, for a number of reasons, and I also want every single wad of notes that was left in that bag when you last saw him. Now, I don't suppose he's been in touch since you got out of jail ...?'

'No.'

'Right. So your job now is to prise him *and* the cash out of the woodwork, one way or another. Loud and clear?'

'Yes. But it sounds impossible.'

'You must make it possible. I want the money as quickly as you can get it to me, and by the end of March at the very latest. That gives you more than seven months to find it, and will allow me at least twelve months to dispose of it before it ceases to be legal tender. But try not to make it take that long, OK?'

'What happens if I don't play ball?'

'I'll be watching you, and I'll know. And you and your girlfriends will soon start regretting it, on a daily basis.'

'So how exactly do I go about this impossible task? Perhaps you'd like to start by telling me everything you knew about L at the time ...'

'No, I won't do that, Narone. Or not yet, at least. If the police see you making a sudden beeline for his old haunts or whatever, they might guess I've been in touch with you. And I do *not* want them to know that, OK?'

'OK ....'

'No, I think you should make it look as if you're hunting for L for your own good reasons. The Nice underworld knows who you are, and how you ended up with nothing to show for your efforts and over six years in jail. So don't be shy. Maybe start to put it about in the bars around the port that you're trying to find the man to demand a bigger share of the cash he must still be hoarding.'

'I'm not very comfortable with that idea, X. And I really don't know anything about the Nice underworld!'

'Well, the more people who get to hear what you're trying to do, the less likely you are to get pressured by those who may still be thinking you ran off with the money yourself.'

'Oh, that's extremely thoughtful of you.'

'Don't get cheeky with me, Narone. Now, I'm not going to dictate *how* you go about it. And I'm not going to get in your way either – I can't risk that. But in two weeks' time I want to hear exactly what you've decided to do.'

'So are you going to pay me in full, up-front, for this exclusive service?'

'Shut it, OK? You seem to be all right for cash, so you'll have plenty of spare time to start asking around. Just get on with it. I'll call you again at noon on the thirty-first of August, at the following phone box ...'

Narone did not wait for Pureza to return, but locked up the bookshop and made for the nearest bar to take stock of his new situation over a largely liquid lunch.

So now there was somebody else potentially threatening Emilie! And he would have to trust that this Xérus character *was* the robbery's mastermind. This was all getting rather too hot.

He really must snap out his demob languor at once, and get back to his search for Emilie – while making Luc believe he was still focused on collecting the cash, and at the same time making Xérus *and* the Inspector believe he was hunting for Luc!

But of course he also needed to get his own hands on Luc, and now on this Xérus guy as well – to put them both out of action one way or another, with or without the help of the police. They really *could* still be in a position to harm Emilie, as each of them had intimated. Not to mention poor Pureza. And either of them could hold a clue to each other's whereabouts – or Emilie's.

Six more days till his next scheduled call to Hardy. Should he mention this approach from Xérus then, despite being warned not to? Or leave it for a while? Perhaps he should phone the Inspector at once? Or maybe never tell him about it?

Hmmm. Reporting it to the police would take *some* of the weight off his shoulders, but it would prove that the insider – if that *was* what Xérus was – really did exist and was still around. And that might greatly change the complexion of the mission Hardy had given him. Did he really need that? He was managing to keep the Inspector well at bay, for now. Why invite more work and more hassle? Always remember Pandora.

Of course, the police still knew nothing about his ongoing contact with Luc either – or so he had to assume. Should he now reveal anything about *that*?

No. He would play this *his* way. He would probably collect the stolen money as soon as he could, then maybe use it to bargain with Luc for information on Emilie. And if that led to the man overplaying his hand and surfacing in some way, Narone could spill the beans to Xérus, and maybe he'd get careless too. And then Hardy's Cavalry could come charging in from all corners and clear up the whole stupid mess.

Or something like that.

But chasing after those pathetic criminals was not uppermost in his mind right now. If there was a chance of uncovering Emilie's tracks the easy way, and picking up the hidden cash in passing, why take the hard way first? Yes, he had put the next little job off for too long already.

He left the bar and strolled down to the beach to build his plan. And he was determined to kick it off the very next day.

* * *

Confident that neither Luc, nor his lady friend, nor Inspector Hardy, nor even Xérus or any other lowlife was likely to be following him, but still taking absolutely no chances, Narone left the bookshop straight after breakfast and devoted more than two hours to a complex circumnavigation of the New Town, his eyes in the back of his head as usual. Finally, after ducking and weaving his way through the narrowest streets of the Old City, he emerged into the southern environs of Place Garibaldi in the absolute certainty that he was still unaccompanied.

Now he could at last change gear. He sauntered chirpily around the square, then along Rue Bonaparte and down Rue Bavastro until he reached Emilie's old apartment block. He had not been there for almost seven years, and it had clearly benefited from a bit of a facelift. But the front door was still wide open, and it was soon obvious that the facelift was purely cosmetic.

He climbed the grimy stairs and walked to the end of the corridor. His plan was crystal clear. He would knock politely at Emilie's door, and simply tell the new occupants that he had been out of town for a few years and was not aware that she had moved away. And maybe he would be lucky enough to pick up another hint of where she might have gone.

But nobody answered. Fair enough. Now he would knock at Danielle's door. If there was no reply, he would try the handle and see if it was unlocked, as it always used to be. But that was not very likely – she too had probably moved away long, long before. And if somebody *did* answer ... well, if it turned out to be Danielle, they could chat about the old days, and he could ask after Emilie, and so on. And if it was someone else, he would just play it by ear, as usual. Either way, he should easily be able to check that the old pink sofa was still there on the opposite wall.

But again there was no reply. He could not risk going in here and now, even if the door was unlocked – there might well be somebody inside who would make a very loud fuss about that. But he *could* very gently try the handle, just to see ...

Locked! So Danielle too had almost certainly moved away. And now he must mount a proper observation of his own.

* * *

For the rest of that day, and throughout the following long evening – after a similarly careful cross-city approach – Narone watched that apartment block like an hawk, either from an outdoor table of the café-cum-boulangerie fifty metres down the street at the junction with Rue Fodéré, or sitting on the low wall opposite, shrouded in the afternoon shadows of the huge mass of the church of Notre Dame du Port.

On four occasions, different people serving in the café were eventually tempted to enquire about his vigil. Each time, he simply said 'I'm waiting for my girl to come home,' and they just laughed or winked, brought him another cup of coffee, and carried on with their lives.

But he got the result he needed. He saw two women passing separately through the front door at regular times on each of those days, with the lights in the two apartments he was watching going off or coming on in the late evening to coincide perfectly with their individual departures and arrivals. So he now knew for certain who was living in Emilie's old place, and he had to assume that Danielle had also gone for good. But what about that sofa?

Of course, he had now established probable safe times for breaking into Danielle's old apartment and recovering the money. But if the sofa was not there, where would he stand? Guilty of a silly little crime, and no better informed! Much better, surely, to make contact with the new occupant without running any real risks, and keep his options open ...

* * *

Soon after nine o'clock on the third evening he watched one of the women going out to work as usual. And half an hour later, the other one came home. As usual.

It was finally time to make his move.

He strode up Rue Bavastro, into the building, up to the first floor, and along the corridor, knocking loudly at Emilie's old door as soon as he reached it.

There was no reply, of course. Then he moved across to the other door and knocked with equal vigour. Its new occupant did not take long to answer.

'Ah, good evening, *madame*. I'm very sorry to disturb you. My name is Roland, and I'm an old friend of Emilie and Danielle. There was no reply when I tried both their doors the other day, and nothing again just now at Emilie's over there. I was hoping to find Danielle in, but obviously ...'

'I regret I have never heard of an Emilie living next door, *monsieur*. And the previous occupant of this apartment was an elderly gentleman, so I know nothing of a Danielle either. I fear I cannot help you at all.'

As the woman was speaking, Narone peeped surreptitiously over her shoulder and was dismayed to see a very different, very new sofa in the old one's familiar place. He breathed deeply and let her finish her apologia while he re-rehearsed his next strategic move.

'Oh well, that's life, eh? Never mind, *madame*. I guess I'll just have to ... Oh, my goodness – I see the awful old pink sofa has finally gone!'

'Yes!' The woman was nodding vigorously, clearly very pleased to hear that this nice young man shared her poor opinion of the monstrosity. 'It was here when I moved in last year. I told the landlord I really would prefer to buy a new one and take it with me when I leave. I was most surprised when he agreed at once, but then he told me his conditions. I had to pay for him to remove the old one.'

'Yes, Emilie told me Jacques was a mean old sot!'

'Jacques? You mean Roger!'

'Yes, of course I do! Stupid me! So Roger was finally able to haul that lumpy old eyesore to the dump!'

'Oh, no. He said he had a *completely* broken one in another apartment block, and that was the only reason he was willing to let me bring a new one in!'

'Hah! Landlords! What a joke!' Narone gritted his teeth. How far could he drag out this charade? 'Well, I think this one is absolutely beautiful, Madame ... ah, *pardonnez-moi*, but I do not know your name.'

'It is Edith Foraud, *monsieur*. And we obviously have the same good taste!'

'Indeed. Might I ask where you bought it?'

'At Vos Meubles in the New Town.'

'Hmmm. I'm tempted to get one for myself. Do they deliver and collect?'

'Oh, yes. And they actually took the old one away for nothing, so I was very happy! One up on grumpy old Roger for a change!'

He decided he had better not push it any further.

'That sounds wonderful. I'll definitely have to visit their showroom! Anyway, may I say once again how sorry I am to have disturbed you, Madame Foraud ...'

'It was no problem, *monsieur*. In fact it was a great pleasure to meet you!'

On his way out of the building, he stopped to speak to the new concierge. He was interested in renting an apartment if one should become available, he told her, so could he possibly have Roger's surname and phone number? And she reeled the information off without even looking up from her knitting. He scribbled it on a scrap of paper, thanked her, and slipped quickly away. But he did not plan to make contact with the crusty old man just yet.

* * *

Narone's occasional dinners with Pureza were continuing to prove very satisfying. Even if, as on the following Saturday evening, they usually carried with them the obligation to engage in another friendly little chat.

'You did promise to tell me how you and Emilie got together, Arthur. There's still some Cointreau left, if you're willing to talk about it tonight!'

'I think I'll pass on the Cointreau this time. But I guess I don't mind finishing the story, if you really want me to. I can see I'm going to have to do so one day or another!'

'Thank you! So, I'm all ears ...'

'Well, Emilie was never made to be a "star", Pureza. She told me soon after we met that her aspirations were really very ordinary. She simply wanted to live a "normal" life, if she could ever discover what that was, in the France that was still very much post-war in its personality but was slowly being coloured by social changes she could see starting to take place all around her – changes mainly influenced from abroad, of course, especially from Italy and the USA, and later from England.

'She said she desperately wanted this normality as an antidote to what she saw as the completely abnormal nature of her life up to then ... that awful convent schooling, and then singing solo for her living – though she loved it, of course, and she knew how lucky she was to be one of the few able to do it! – and then the inevitable one-night stands and the well-off but inconsiderate men. But she knew she was probably as much to blame as those guys for the inadequacy of her relationships. She'd had precious little help from anybody in relating to boys of any age, and now, after the "nothing sacred" openness of that communal house, she was living on her own – rather than with a bunch of "normal" teenage college girls, for example – and having to keep her defences up all the time.

'Of course, she reflected all her discomfort and vulnerability in her musical performances, both intentionally – it was a very powerful "mood" for someone to be in all the time, believe me! – and subconsciously; her shows had an intensity which was often way beyond both what she intended *and* how she assumed or believed she was coming across to her audience. She only became fully aware of this in August 1958, when one of the visitors to the club got the manager's permission to film her performance, and then chatted about it with her afterwards, and later invited her to visit his home to watch the little movie together. She was stunned by what she saw, and her new and trustworthy friend said simply "And now, *ma petite*, you at last understand why they all adore you."

'By late October, despite having lots of admirers and dates, some of them apparently quite uninhibited but short-lived and with no true passion, she had still had no steady relationships. And then I went to the Casa della Musica for the first time, after reading about her in the paper and hearing what people were saying all over the Old City. I stood up near her "stage" area on my own, and I could not take my eyes off her when she appeared. She told me later that she couldn't take hers off *my* "beautiful grey smokies" either, and she instinctively inserted an impassioned verse of *Jeepers Creepers* into the second song of her act. I'll never forget that moment, Pureza.'

'I'm not surprised!'

'I went back to the club regularly after that, and on my fourth visit, when she was sitting up at the bar on her own – for once! – after her show, I plucked up the courage to offer to buy her a drink.'

'It really took you that long, Arthur? You might have lost her completely with all that delay!'

'Yes, it took me that long. But she said she'd be very happy for me to join her, and whispered that she'd been waiting patiently for this to happen since my very first visit. And a little later she took my hand and looked me straight in the eyes and told me her *Jeepers Creepers* story!

'By December I was visiting the club most evenings, and we would sometimes go out to another bar together after her show. The drinks were always on her – I was permanently broke! – and she always took a taxi straight home, for safety's sake. But after a while she offered me a lift with her, one evening – I actually lived only a little way beyond her apartment block – and that then became the norm.

'Emilie was nineteen on the tenth of December, and she did not have to work that evening, so we were able to go out for a special dinner together. It was wonderful. And we went back to the same restaurant at Christmas-time. That was when she finally told me the story of her life.

'One starry night in January there were no taxis around after our usual little nightcap, and we were getting very cold just standing there, so I asked if I could walk her home. And she said she'd been wondering how much longer it would take me!'

'The manners of a fine Fifties gentleman, Arthur!'

'And of a fairly respectable Fifties lady, Pureza!'

'It sounds as though you were actually turning her respectable again!'

'Hah! Well, as it happens, I continued to behave impeccably – mainly because I really did not dare to say or do anything that might break the spell – so it was Emilie who finally took the next initiative in February, one evening during the Carnival Weeks, and encouraged me to stay the night when we reached her front door long after midnight.'

'Enfin!'

'Yes! And when the days got longer, we started to go out to the beach or on little trips in our free time. It was great – Emilie was available whenever I was keen on doing something with her, and she was always very giving. It was a really special springtime for me.

'We wanted to have a short holiday together in July or August, but I couldn't take one then because of the demand for the garage's services from the influx of tourists' cars – lots of people ended up with engine problems after the long drive down from Paris! And I think she would have had trouble asking for time out from the club too, in the height of the summer season. But I finally got a week off in early September, and we took a bus along the coast and stayed in Italy to celebrate my twenty-first birthday. Those were the happiest few days of my life, Pureza, and ... well, we never stopped enjoying ourselves, if you know what I mean.

'But it was over all too soon and we both went back to work and picked up the patterns we'd had before. Everything was going fine. Except I was still completely broke! And Emilie did seem to be a bit unhappy about something ...

'And then a guy stopped me in the back streets of the Old City and invited me to help him with a robbery he was planning. He knew I had some experience of stealing cars and driving them around Nice, and he offered me a lot of cash to be his getaway driver, and a lot of vague threats too if I refused to co-operate. And you know the rest, of course ...

'Well, I was rather preoccupied with that over the next few weeks, and I didn't see as much of Emilie as usual. When I did make an effort to visit the club or her apartment, she definitely didn't seem as happy as she usually was. Maybe she'd spotted something was worrying me. But she never said anything, and I didn't want to have to talk about it with her, so I stopped going to see her. And she wasn't dropping in at the garage or my apartment any more, and she missed a couple of our dates. So that November we ended up not spending very much time together at all. But I knew it would be OK once the bank job was out of the way and I could give her all my attention again ...

'And I *did* go to her apartment late on the evening of the robbery. I really expected her to be back there by the time I arrived. But she was still out. She must have stayed on at the club after her show. But she hadn't done that for over a year. Well, certainly not up till the end of October, anyway.

'So I went off home to bed, and the very next morning I was arrested, and that was that.

'I never saw Emilie again, Pureza. Never even heard from her. I know she left her apartment in a big hurry later that day. But I have no idea why, or what happened to her. She might have been ...'

'Hey, maybe it was nothing bad, *chico*. Maybe she was just confused and upset about what you had been doing – and not doing – and felt she simply had to get away for a while.'

'Maybe, Pureza. I don't think I understand women very well. I just know I really want her back.'

'But you're hardly putting every spare minute into hunting for her, are you, Arthur? And I'm not at all surprised at that, by the way, so please don't think I'm being unkind. But perhaps it means your devotion to her, or to the *idea* of having her back, is not as absolute as you may think ...'

'You may be right. I certainly know how hard it is to cope with the desire to find her and the frustration of the almost complete lack of information or leads. And of course I've just come back from outer space into a bright, exciting new world, and I do have a lot of natural urges to ... well, to catch up on all the pleasures I've missed out on for so long. And apart from all of that, I've got ... oh, never mind. I've already done far too much talking tonight!'

His gentle inquisitor sighed and let him be, and they ate the rest of their meal in silence.

Uncertain Recovery

Narone then spent a very uncomfortable Sunday on Nice's stony beach, only rarely allowing himself to be distracted by the sight of the untroubled, beautiful people lazily promoting their finest features all around him. Most of the time his poor mind was in turmoil.

Should he drive on with his straightforward hunt for the sofa and the money, and hope it would generate a lucky lead about Emilie in passing? Or start putting a lot more attention into searching exclusively for her, as Pureza had almost mockingly suggested he should? And how much time should he be devoting to satisfying the demands of all his different taskmasters – including himself – by trying much harder to flush out both Luc and Xérus?

If only he had someone he could talk to about it all! Someone willing to listen to his problems and maybe even give him a bit of advice. Pureza, of course, was the obvious "someone" – in fact she was the *only* one! But he couldn't possibly burden her with it. It would be utterly unfair to make her a party to this awful mess, even if he were to give her just the simplest picture of what was going on.

Wouldn't it?

Well, he certainly couldn't tell her anything about his contact with Luc. Because *he* was only on Narone's back because of the hidden cash, and he must never tell her or anybody else that he really did make off with it that night!

Maybe he could share the burden of the pressure he was now under from the mastermind Xérus who was hounding him to find Luc and the money? Pureza must already know a lot of the history of the robbery, one way or another, and she would probably be really sympathetic to his situation and redouble her charity towards him in every possible way!

But perhaps he should not go that far with involving her either.

She *did* however know that the police had been following them on the day of his release. So if he really felt the need to talk to her, one of these days, maybe that would be the safest place to start.

But not yet.

Hmmm. Every single *man* he was associated with right now was a menacing threat lurking somewhere in the jungle surrounding him. On the other hand, the only *woman* he had any sort of relationship with, in this complicated new world, was completely open and trustworthy, and seemed to care a lot about him. If only he could find a few more of those! But he was painfully aware of how gauche he had been in his teens when it came to making any sort of approach to a girl. And the free and easy Sixties atmosphere now surrounding him had so far done nothing to help him conquer those inhibitions. But maybe that was just because he was so preoccupied with all these problems right now.

And there he was again, back exactly where he'd started every time he'd tried to think this whole thing through!

After covering three identical circuits of this seemingly closed loop, he cursed silently, wandered up to the nearest beach café and bought himself a beer, casting a series of furtive sideways glances at a pair of pretty girls who were standing at the bar and looking very bored. They perked up and smiled when they noticed he was looking at them, and then he went straight back down to the risk-free company of his unwashed white towel.

* * *

'Good morning, Inspector.'

'Late again, Arthur.'

'I had a bad night's sleep. Anyway, I have something to report at last.'

'Tell me ...'

'I've spoken to a lot of people living near Emilie's old apartment. But they know nothing, apart from some vague rumour that she might have left Nice and travelled west. And I haven't picked up anything about Luc either.'

'What sort of a report is that?'

'A truthful one. Want me to carry on?'

'You have even more sweet nothings to tell me?'

'No, I mean carry on with my enquiries.'

'Yes, of course I do. And perhaps you could work a bit harder at it, eh?'

'But not force it, right? You're a hard taskmaster, Simon. I'll do my best. Don't hold your breath.'

He was getting low on money again, and in ten days or so he would be broke. So it was finally time to take another big risk and try to retrieve the wad of cash he had hidden at the garage. Luc would be assuming he'd already done that anyway.

He left the bookshop, crossed the river, and strolled into Place Garibaldi, stopping at the first free telephone box.

'*Allô!* This is Port Motor Repairs.'

'Oh, I am sorry. I was trying to call Soron's Garage.'

'It's OK, you've got the right number. I bought the place from the old boy three years ago. How can I help?'

'Afraid you can't. I need to speak to him personally. I'll call him at home. *Merci, au revoir.*'

Perfect! Straight on to step two of his plan. Via a stationery store ...

'Anyone about?'

'Only me, right now. Under the Peugeot ...'

He spotted a pair of feet sticking out from beneath a battered old van.

'Oh, hello there! I used to work here a few years ago. Just thought I'd drop in to see if any of my old mates were still around.'

'I recognise that voice. It's young Narone, isn't it?'

'Yeah! Who's that?'

'Maurice. Heard you were back in town. Hang on, I'm coming out ...'

Narone endured at least two minutes of leg-pulling and jokes about how he probably still had all that money stashed away somewhere really safe. Then he decided it was time to play his next card.

'Hey, Maurice – remember how it was always *me* who had to make the coffee?'

'Yeah. My turn now, right?'

'Thanks. And is it OK if I have a little wander around, for old times' sake?'

'Sure. Boss won't be back for ages.'

Once his old workmate had wiped his hands and was busy at the sink in the far corner, Narone strolled over into the side room and was relieved to see the ancient old tool chest was still in place. He whipped out the chrome-plated presentation pointer he had just purchased, extended it fully, stuck it under the right-hand side of the unit and – *Eureka!* – eased the small rubber-sheeting package forwards until it appeared at the front. Twenty seconds later it was safely in his jacket pocket and he was back in the main section of the garage, commenting loudly to Maurice on the sorry condition of the battered old van.

After the uncomfortable excitement of that little escapade, Narone was not keen to hurry quickly on with his search for the bigger crock of gold. Instead, he secreted the wad of one hundred stolen banknotes at the bottom of his clothes drawer, and merged back into the anonymity of the city. Over the next few days, in widely separated shops, he disposed of six old 5000 franc bills, purchasing a couple of cheap essentials each time and building up a small working fund of completely clean money.

* * *

The following Saturday, Pureza prepared another fine dinner, and this time she did not wait until it was over to move the conversation back to the subject of himself.

'You know, Arthur, you seem to have become more and more preoccupied with things ever since your first couple of carefree days out of jail. Is there something you want to tell me? Or anything I can do to help? I said at the very start that I would always be here for you, didn't I? And a problem shared ...'

'Hmmm. Yes, you're right, of course. I have had a lot of things on my mind. But I really don't want to bother you with them.'

'Please do, my friend. It helped to talk about Emilie, didn't it?'

'Well ...'

'So if there's something else ...'

'OK, Pureza. Yes, there is. Two days after my release, the detective who led all the original enquiries made contact with me. He said they wanted me to help them smoke out the guy who led the robbery – the one who got away with most of the cash. They're dangling some nice rewards in front of me if I help them find their man and the money – and they've made it very clear that I must co-operate fully or I'll be back in jail at a stroke.'

'I see ...'

'Oh! You don't sound very surprised!'

'That's because I half knew about it already. I picked up the bookshop phone to make a call and heard you talking to the policeman. On two separate occasions. And I listened in for a short while each time – not to pry or to spy on you, I swear, but because I actually felt very concerned. And I've been wondering when you would get around to telling me about it ...'

'Ah. Well, now I have. And I thought I was ...'

'Please don't get huffy about it, Arthur. My overhearing you was unintentional, and I've continued to respect your privacy on it, haven't I? So, *would* you like me to do anything to help?'

'No thanks, Pureza. I think I'll handle it myself after all. Just let me carry on making my weekly phone calls, please. And ... maybe still cook me a nice dinner from time to time?'

'Oh, Arthur!'

* * *

On the twenty-ninth of August, Narone bluntly told Inspector Hardy he had nothing to report, and put the receiver straight back down.

He then spent most of the next two days working on what he was going to say to Xérus in *his* second telephone contact. And on the last day of the month he received that man's call with rather more deference.

'So, what progress, Narone?'

'Not much, I'm afraid. I'm pretending to look for my old girlfriend, as we agreed, and I'm doing all I can on the side to pick up anything about what became of Luc after the robbery. Trouble is, I'm still not happy about talking openly about myself in the way you suggested. Frankly, I don't fancy any more kickings. So now I'm working on a different plan of my own, to get a lot closer to some of the villains of Nice or the other cities along the coast *without* them knowing who I am – to start with, at least.'

'Right ....'

'But that's all going to take time. And you've given me that time, X. So will you please let me push on with this for you, and not put me under too much extra pressure?'

'Huh! You'd better tell me exactly how you intend to go about it.'

'No firm ideas yet. But I may decide to leave the city for a while and come back in a different guise.'

'Soon?'

'Oh, no. I reckon I'll need another month here, to make it look as if I'm almost back to normal ...'

'In that case, I'll speak to you on the last day of September. And I expect to hear precisely what you'll be doing next.'

'OK, that's ....'

'Sorry, Narone, say that again – there must have been a big lorry going past.'

'Yes, there was. And I just said that was OK.'

'Right. Now, what about money?'

'I'm managing all right. I've had a small loan from an old friend.'

'Perhaps you should bank some of it for now. Keep it nice and safe ...'

'Very funny. So, is that it?'

'Yes. But don't do anything silly – you know what I mean. Until noon on the thirtieth. Here's the location of your next phone box ...'

* * *

The following day, Narone readied himself for the latest call from Luc. And this would need to be a very different status report. Should he say anything about the contacts from Xérus? Surely doing that would panic Luc and put Narone under much more urgent pressures, and probably blow any chance of discovering what Luc might know of Emilie's whereabouts?

No, he would make his update as vague as possible, and keep all his options open.

'*Allô!*'

'Right, what have you got for me, Arthur?'

'Good news and bad news.'

'Give me the bad news.'

'I hid the cash in ... something that seemed quite safe. But I've just discovered it was recently moved on.'

'*Merde!* So how can there be any good news?'

'I have a lead on where it may have gone. And there's every reason to suppose the money's still in it.'

'So what are you waiting for?'

'I only said I had a *lead*. I've still got a lot more careful sniffing around to do.'

'Pah!'

'I'm doing my best for you, Luc.'

'You've lost my money for me!'

'Rubbish! Listen, do you want me to keep at this, or shall I just drop the whole thing and stop worrying about you?'

'You're forgetting about the young ladies, Arthur.'

'Perhaps I really don't care about either of them. Perhaps I'd just like that little bonus you promised me in July. So, are you going to be patient or not?'

'Yes, I am – for a bit longer. Are you still being followed by the police?'

'Maybe. But not all the time.'

'Anyone else?'

'Possibly. That's why I'm going to have to be very careful.'

'Got any cash left?'

'Yes. I managed to recover the second wad of notes you gave me. I expect you were watching me when I went to collect it ...'

'Perhaps I was.'

'Like to tell me where it was hidden, then?'

'Don't play games with me, Arthur.'

He doesn't know, thought Narone. So they almost certainly weren't following him at all now. They might well not even be living in Nice – as he'd already suspected.

'Whatever you say, Luc.'

'OK, I'll phone you on the first of October, usual time, at the call box at the bottom of Avenue Pauliani. You've got *your* money now. Get on with finding *mine*!'

* * *

'Allô!'

'It's me, Inspector.'

'Aha! Happy Birthday, Arthur!'

'Thanks a lot, Simon. So do I get a nice little present from the Sûreté?'

'Yes – the promise of a small glass of beer when this is all over. Are we any closer to that?'

'Not much. But I'm working on a fine new plan. I'll keep you posted.'

'Very well. And ... enjoy your special day.'

'I shall – as soon as I put this phone down.'

Pureza too had remembered his birthday, of course, and at eight o'clock that morning she had presented him with another set of rather expensive, rather too trendy clothes, in exactly the right sizes. And he had protested, of course, for all sorts of good and polite reasons, but she still continued to insist that business had been booming since he'd come to stay. Her only condition was that she must be allowed to prepare another *cuisine niçoise* meal for them that evening. And he had agreed, of course, and given his best new friend a big hug of gratitude, and then come dangerously close to being kissed fully on the lips.

But Pureza would be hard at work for the next few hours, and he was now off Hardy's radar for another whole week, and he would not be hearing from Luc or Xérus again till the very end of the month. And it was his birthday, dammit! – his first one as a free man since celebrating his twenty-first on that wonderful little Italian holiday with Emilie in 1959 ...

He took the easiest and most undemanding option for the rest of the day, lazing in the early September sun on the stony beach – why on earth couldn't they just haul a few thousand tons of sand down here instead? – occasionally reading a page or two of his Camus novel, and most of the time admiring the ebb and (mainly) flow of carefully designed topless swimsuits. But he never plucked up the courage to wander over and inquire about any of their owners' plans for the rest of the day.

Even though she had shut up shop ahead of her normal time, Pureza was still busy with her dinner preparations when he finally turned up at a quarter to eight. She made him open a bottle of fine Champagne at once, and they shared most of it in the kitchen while she spent another hour putting the finishing touches to her special surprises.

So by the time they had lingered over the superb three course meal *and* the large slices of home-made birthday cake that followed, it was almost ten o'clock as they took the last dishes back out into the kitchen. And then Pureza stifled a small yawn and smiled and squeezed his arm and suggested they leave the washing-up till the morning.

'It's been a long day for both of us, Arthur, and I'd really like to go to bed now.'

'Oh, that's fine,' said Narone. 'I've decided to give myself another little treat. I'm going to visit the Casino for the first time in my life! But don't worry, I shan't be gambling very much, and I'll try not to disturb you when I get back.'

Pureza gave him an extremely dirty look, but said nothing and walked straight out of the kitchen and up the stairs. Narone wondered for a moment why she seemed so disapproving of his final little birthday fling, but then decided it must be because she thought he would be playing with *her* money.

He had only been inside the Casino for twenty minutes, having made certain to take nothing but his "new" currency notes out with him, when he spotted the tall blonde croupier working one of the *Vingt-et-un* tables.

He was all smiles at once – he simply could not disguise them, even when she caught him looking at her – but he could not bring himself to approach her. So he turned away, consoling himself with the thought that conversation with the customers was probably prohibited anyway.

He then played the tables carefully, but with no experience or any real skill, for an hour or so until he realised it was past midnight and his birthday was finally over. He'd lost a little money, but so what? It had cost him no more than a good meal for two. A very nice little birthday treat to himself. And he'd glanced across at the blonde croupier's table several times, but she had vanished at about eleven-thirty and had not reappeared. So, time for bed.

He nodded politely to the doorman as he left, and then found Françoise Guart waiting patiently outside, smoking a long menthol cigarette and greeting him with a smiling 'I thought you'd forgotten all about me, *mon petit*! So shall we go dancing, or shall we go straight home?'

Narone wondered several times over the next couple of days whether he should say anything to Pureza about his night out (and in) with Françoise. But when he realised he had no real idea *why* he was wondering that, he immediately dropped the stupid thought and went back to enjoying the excuse of another extended cooling-off period on the beach before continuing his pursuit of Danielle's old sofa.

And he never returned to the Casino.

But a little later he did implement his latest ongoing financial management programme. Roughly twice a week from now on, he would again be carefully purchasing a useful little item of clothing or toiletry or whatever, each time using one of his still very warm 5000 Old Franc bills to generate a fistful of very clean, smaller New Franc notes and coins.

* * *

On the twelfth of September, Narone called Inspector Hardy and told him he once again had nothing to report. And the next morning he went to another phone box, touched as much wood as he could see, and called the Vos Meubles furniture store.

'Can I help you?'

'I do hope so! You delivered a new sofa to my aunt's place in Rue Bavastro a few months ago, and you took the old pink one away to another of Roger Collard's apartments ...'

'Ah yes, *monsieur*, I remember it well. A very heavy old sofa!'

'Yes, indeed! Well, my aunt has mislaid a treasured little brooch. It's quite worthless, but it has great sentimental value for her, and she's rather distressed about it. She's searched everywhere, and she's now wondering if it perhaps got stuck down behind one of the seat cushions.'

'That sort of thing happens all the time!'

'Of course. So, could you possibly tell me where you took it for Monsieur Collard? Then she and I could perhaps visit the occupants and ask them politely if we could take a quick look for the brooch.'

'I don't see why not, *monsieur*. May I ask your aunt's name?'

'It's Madame Foraud.'

'OK. I'll check the records and make sure I give you the exact name and address. One moment, please ...'

That afternoon, Narone visited a second-hand bookstore in the New Town, negotiated a very special price on a job lot of two hundred old paperback novels, and filled three large cardboard boxes to overflowing. He then hailed a taxi to take him straight to Pureza's bookshop. After making quite a show of unloading each heavy box and leaving them on the pavement outside while he breezed in and loudly announced his commercial triumph to Pureza and four mildly disapproving customers, he then carried them one by one up to his room, stored them in the corner next to the chest of drawers, and stayed there for almost four hours until she called him down for dinner.

She had obviously spotted several of the book titles as he was coming in and out with the boxes.

'Did you really need to waste your precious money – my money, probably – on that load of rubbish, Arthur?'

'Oh, they really were a bargain, Pureza! And it's high time I read a bit of low-brow literature for a change. I've finished one of them already, and they'll last me for months and months!'

She rolled her eyes in undiluted disgust and changed the subject. Narone, who actually had no intention of ever reading *any* of those awful books, and now felt confident that Pureza would never go near the sullied boxes herself, was happy to follow her lead and talk about whatever she chose for the rest of the evening.

The next morning he repeated his lengthy perambulations around the streets of Nice until he was totally satisfied that he was still not being followed, and ended his tour at the Old City address given to him by the owner of the furniture shop. The building on Rue Droite was more run-down than the recently "improved" property on Rue

Bavastro, but its front door too was wide open – was probably never closed, he guessed – and this one showed no sign of having a concierge.

He climbed the stairs, found the door to apartment 19, and quickly worked out which window he would need to watch from the street. Then he left the building and looked around for the ideal observation point. But this time there was no easy option of a nice bench or a comfortable café. He would have to put up with loafing about, or just sitting on the pavement with his back to the wall and playing the penniless sleepy hippy. He chose the second option, took a large felt hat from his jacket pocket, pulled it down over his eyes, and made himself as comfortable as possible. He could see the shutters on the window of apartment 19 were wide open.

People entered and left the building throughout the afternoon. But just after three o'clock, an elderly woman appeared at that window and closed the shutters. A few long minutes later, she and her husband emerged onto the street. He was hobbling along with the help of a cane, and she was carrying an empty, worn-out shopping bag.

They did not look as if they had recently come into almost forty million Old Francs extracted from a "very heavy old sofa".

And it was well over an hour before they returned, now moving even more slowly than before. They went into the building with their meagre items of shopping, and eventually the shutters were opened and the woman was visible again, turning briefly to speak to her husband before moving back into the shadows of their dingy room.

Narone stood up and got away while the going was good, and spent the rest of the day refining his plan of action.

He was back in the Old City by two o'clock the following afternoon, differently dressed, again confident he had not been followed, and now armed with a few simple tools and a soft holdall of the same size as the one Luc had used for the robbery nearly seven years earlier.

He strolled casually down Rue Droite and past the apartment block, noting that the shutters of number 19 were fully open, as before. Then he moved into the wider adjacent Rue Rossetti and hovered there for over an hour, initially browsing the window displays of the only three shops nearby, then later taking up his dozy hippy position in a very different place this time, but always keeping one eye on the street corner.

And at three-fifteen the aged couple appeared again, right on cue, and shuffled off for – hopefully – another hour-long trip to the cheapest shops in town.

Narone did not hang around. As he approached the building, he was glad to see the shutters of number 19 were now closed. He would simply have to trust there was nobody left inside.

For a man long-skilled in making off with some of the world's most luxurious automobiles, breaking into that sorry apartment presented no problem. He even managed to do it without damaging either the cheap lock or the tatty woodwork. So nobody would ever know he had been there.

He opened the door and peeped in. Yes, there it was! He darted inside, closed the door behind him and got to work, quietly upending the sofa to reveal the bottom fabric and prising off not only the four thumbtacks he had carefully removed and repositioned all those years before, but a lot more besides. And now the first of the wads of cash was suddenly visible!

His heart was pounding as he counted them out of the sofa and into his bag. Thirty ... forty ... fifty ... sixty ... sixty-five. Those had been easy! But there were still nine left to find – he had never forgotten the number he'd posted through the little gap he'd originally made. So now he began delving more deeply into the farthest corners of the springs and the upholstery, and one by one the remaining wads succumbed to his grasping hand. Seventy-two ... seventy-three ... seventy-four!

He zipped up the holdall with a triumphant flourish. He had recovered all thirty-seven million *balles*!

He quickly pressed a few of the thumbtacks back into the wooden frame to ensure the material would not flop out to one side, stored the rest of them in his pocket, righted the sofa, and repositioned it exactly where it had previously been. Then, after checking there was no-one around in the corridor, he tiptoed out of the apartment, gently pulled the door closed behind him, and hurried down the stairs. He was back on Rue Droite less than ten minutes after he had entered the building, with no potential pursuers in sight. And three minutes later, he and his very ordinary travel bag had zigzagged unobserved through the rabbit warren of the Old City alleys and were now enveloped in the bustling crowds of the Cours Saleya market.

He spent the rest of the day on the buses – which of course took him back to that similarly anxious time immediately following the robbery – travelling the length and breadth of the city repeatedly for nearly seven hours before descending for the last time at the ill-lit central bus station and cautiously making his way up Quai Saint-Jean-Baptiste. Nobody had been following him all day.

And he'd had a lot of time to think, since collecting the cash. Maybe he should hang on to a few of those wads for himself, as Luc had so helpfully "suggested" a few weeks before. Surely the man could not possibly know exactly how much the gang had grabbed in the rush and confusion of that bodged robbery? So surely there would be no comebacks if he did help himself to the cut he deserved after doing all this extra work for Luc?

It was now well past eleven o'clock, and all the lights were out above Pureza's bookshop. He unlocked and re-locked the front door and made his way up to his room, exactly as he had done many times before.

And after using the bathroom as noisily as usual, he shut his own door again and got to work as noiselessly as he could. Five minutes later, fifty of his tatty old paperbacks were sitting in his new zip-up bag, four wads of banknotes had been tucked into his jacket pockets awaiting their next temporary home, and thirty-five million Old Francs were evenly spread out in brown paper bags at the bottom of three very large boxes of books.

The next day, while Pureza was out for lunch, he would walk down to Rue du Lycée and donate his bagful of unwanted novels to another second-hand shop. Then he would buy himself a cheap little rucksack, roll his four wads of cash up in a spare shirt and stuff them in along with an old pullover, and deposit it at the railway station left-luggage office for as long as they would allow.

Then he would spend the entire weekend deciding what he was going to say about the money to Luc, and to Xérus, and to the police.

If anything.

As he struggled to get off to sleep in the intimate company of such a fortune, he reflected on how he would have liked to give that poor old couple a bit of cash to make their lives a little easier for a while. But he could certainly not have afforded to leave any trace of his visit there today. Maybe he would find a way to do something for them, some other day ...

* * *

Narone's next Monday morning chat with the Inspector was completely information-free, and presumably none of the stress and anxiety of recovering the cash the previous Thursday came across in his voice, because Hardy seemed content – if that was really the right word – to let him carry on as usual for another week. And after making that call, he took an even longer breather, continuing his researches in the bookshop in the mornings and relaxing every afternoon in the steadily reducing temperatures of late summer.

But on the Thursday he at last felt motivated to make yet another effort to pick up Emilie's long-faded tracks. He would take the risk of contacting her stingy old landlord. He found an empty phone box, dug out the note he had scribbled in the concierge's office, and dialled the number she had dictated.

'*Hein?*'

'Monsieur Collard?'

'Who wants to know?'

'I'm an old friend of Emilie Courbier and Danielle Orvine. They used to live in your building on Rue Bavastro, but I'm just back in town after several years abroad and I've found they've both moved away. Do you happen to know where either of them is living now, please?'

'No.'

'Did you have any forwarding addresses at the time they moved?'

'The Courbier girl just disappeared. Pah! I had the bloody police on my back about her for days.'

'What about Danielle?'

'Mademoiselle Orvine? She was a nurse, wasn't she? Very conscientious. Yes, she left me an address.'

'Oh, that's great! May I have it please?'

'It'll cost you.'

'Ah.'

In the end they agreed a price. And that evening Narone took a taxi to Roger Collard's luxurious home up in the hills of Cimiez, rang the doorbell, handed over a lot of his own notes, and received a single handwritten note in exchange. The taxi then took him straight on to Danielle's new apartment block. But there was no reply at her door. Probably still working nights at the hospital, of course.

The next day he went back in the late afternoon. And there she was, very pleased to see him again, and my goodness he was looking so different now, and wasn't it a shame that Emilie had rushed off like that, and no, she had been out at work that evening, of course, so she hadn't seen her leave, and all she knew from her neighbours was that Emilie had apparently mentioned moving to Marseilles, and what the poor little flower was doing now she hated to think, and ...

Narone interrupted Danielle with a respectful little hug of thanks, and hurried away to his waiting taxi before she could get around to inviting him in for another cup of awful coffee and episode two of her own exciting life story.

* * *

At nine o'clock on the morning of the twenty-sixth of September, Narone picked up the phone and called Simon Hardy. He would still be neglecting to mention that he had now recovered all the stolen money.

'So, have you got anything on what happened to "Luc" yet?'

'No, Inspector. But I've been thinking. I assume you checked out all the obvious places that evening, like the hospitals and the bus and railway stations and so on?'

'Of course we did!'

'OK. I'll have to think a bit harder then.'

'That's just what you're here for, man! But you seem to be living a very free and easy life instead.'

'Still watching me, eh?'

'Quite often, Arthur. Quite often. Where are you getting your money from? You haven't done a single day's work since you got out, but you're not being nearly as careful as you were back in July and August.'

'It's really none of your business, Simon, but as it happens I've had a nice big loan from Pureza Seles. And you keep her out of this! Anyway, I'm still working on finding Emilie. I tracked down one of her old neighbours recently, but still no real progress. Just the hint that she may have gone to Marseilles ...'

'Look, I really don't give a damn about Emilie Courbier, and you know it! Pull your finger out and get on with finding me something on "Luc" instead.'

'But I'm not supposed to be forcing it.'

'It's time to start, Narone. Gently. Stop being witty and start using your wits.'

'OK, *Inspector*, I'll do exactly that. Till next week, then ...'

* * *

Narone took Pureza completely by surprise two days later by suggesting a quick café lunch together. She abandoned her shopping plans at once and happily accepted his invitation.

But when he actually offered to pay the bill at the end of another almost wordless meal, her surprise turned to a mixture of concern and fascination.

'Is there something you've been wanting to say, Arthur?'

'Yes, there is.'

'Spit it out, then, *amigo*. I need to get back to work!'

'Well, I may have to leave Nice for a while, quite soon. So I just felt I should let you know in advance.'

'Ah. OK. Something to do with the police, I suppose?'

'Partly.'

'Right. Well, I hope you won't be away for long. And ... is this also about your search for Emilie?'

'No, it's not. I'm afraid I've completely run out of ideas on that front. I don't suppose *you* ...'

'Hmmm. I'll have a think about it, Arthur. But please don't hold your breath.'

'Thank you.'

'And ... look, I've noticed you seem to be doing quite well for money, even though you've still not tried to get a job. And now you're offering to pay for lunch ...'

'Well spotted, Pureza! Yes, I had a nice stroke of luck at the Casino on my birthday. So I'll be returning your loan as soon as I feel I can. And I shouldn't need to borrow any more. So *now* will you let me pay the bill?'

* * *

As Narone stood in the phone box awaiting Xérus' month-end call, he repeated over and over again to himself that he must give absolutely *no* hint that he had already found the stolen cash.

And when the call came, he maintained his control.

No, he told Xérus, he had regrettably still not picked up any clues in Nice about the whereabouts of "L" or the money. Because he still had so little to go on, right? So now he was definitely planning to change his image and go "underground" in his search for the man. His cover would probably be that of a freelance left-wing journalist investigating the phenomenon of growing worker and student unrest in the country's biggest cities. And he would pretend to be very sympathetic to the principle of robbing the rich to pay the poor, "just like that guy who got away with it in Nice back in '59. A guy he'd really love to interview in secret ..."

But it would be some time before he could begin to play that game here, he insisted. He would need several more weeks to let his hair continue to grow and to cultivate a hippy moustache and so on. And that must all be done out of sight of any prying eyes. So he would be spending the whole of October, and maybe longer, well away from the city.

'Tell me where,' demanded Xérus.

'I haven't decided.'

'I'm not happy about that.'

'Just as I expected. So maybe you could now give me a hint or two about where L might be based, in case he wasn't living here back in those good old days. Then I could try to kill two birds with one stone ...'

'No, Narone. If I did point you at a particular place, you could waste a huge amount of time focused on it and maybe getting nowhere in the end. And that's time we just don't have. But I do agree he may not be living in Nice, and it's probably wise to spread your net more widely, probably out to the west.'

'Fair enough. My thoughts exactly, as it happens. So I'll just follow my nose. And on another subject, I've almost used up my small loan, and I'm doing all of this *just* for you. Like to give me some financial support yourself now?'

'No.'

'In that case I might be forced to carry out a little robbery of my own in the near future. I have a lot of ground to cover.'

'I did say you must do it your way.'

'Fine. It's your risk as much as mine.'

'Just get on with finding L for me, Narone – as fast as you can. Now, when can you be sure you'll be back in Nice?'

'No idea. But not until November at the earliest.'

'Say that again, please – must have been another big truck passing.'

'Not until November at the earliest.'

'All right. I'll give you to the very *end* of that month to get back in touch. If I have not spoken to you by then, Pureza Seles will be making a big claim on her fire insurance. Got it?'

'Yes. But how can we re-open contact? Want to give me your own number?'

'Hah! No, you will put a vase of pink flowers in the bookshop window by one o'clock on the afternoon in November when you're ready to take my call. And at nine that evening, and every evening afterwards until we're back in touch, you will wait at the following phone box ...'

So, Narone concluded as he put down the receiver, the slightly hard-of-hearing Monsieur X was definitely living somewhere in Nice, and Luc almost certainly was not. Well, that was progress, of a sort. And he'd bought himself another good chunk of time from one of his oppressors.

* * *

A little before noon on the first of October, Narone wandered out onto the embankment and along to Avenue Pauliani to receive the next phone call from Luc.

The longer the man believed the money was still missing, Narone had reasoned, the longer he would need him around, so the more time there would be to track down Emilie and both of the villains. Conversely, and even more significantly, the minute Narone handed over the cash he would become highly disposable.

So he would continue to play all his cards very close to his chest – with *everyone* who was hounding him. And he had his latest little story all ready.

'Arthur?'

'Hello, Luc.'

'Have you found my money yet?'

'No.'

'Talk to me ...'

'Well, I'd actually hidden it in some specialist car parts boxes at the garage where I was working at the time. I'd wrapped the wads up in several old plastic sheets and stored them at the bottom of three of the boxes. I knew I'd easily be able to collect them another day or night and deliver them to you – or find an even better hiding place when I had more time to think about it.

'Of course someone must have tipped off the police about me that night, 'cos I was arrested the very next day. I'm certain they never discovered the money there, which is very good, but I've now learnt that all the boxes were sold on quite recently to some spare parts re-distribution company. I'm still working on tracking them down.'

'*Merde!* Are you getting anywhere?'

'Not very far, yet. Care to join me? Might speed things up ...'

'Don't be crazy!'

'Then please leave me to get on with it for you.'

'What are you planning to do next?'

'I have an idea the boxes may have gone to one of the big cities over to the west, where there's more demand for the parts.'

'Hah! Or maybe someone's already opened them and taken all the cash!'

'Maybe, Luc. Want me to assume that and drop the whole business?'

'No. I already told you – we ... you must keep at it until you find the money.'

'And you *also* told me I must not leave Nice. Well, too bad. I'll probably need to go to Marseilles – although I'd rather not have to, in case I'm recognised by some other ex-con! I guess I'll check out Aix later. And I'll probably start in Toulon.'

'Why Toulon?'

'It's the first big town on the railway line, of course!'

'Yeah. Makes sense. OK, you'd better get on with it. You've got your own fat wad of money now. But you must use those big old notes very carefully in ... wherever you're going.'

'You already gave me that advice, Luc.'

'Right. So, are you going to be back in Nice for my next call on the first of November?'

'I can't be certain, but you can try. If I don't reply, phone again on the fifteenth. I'll make sure I'm here by then.'

'You'd better make sure you've found out where the money's gone, too. OK, here's your next call box location ...'

As he strolled back towards the bookshop, Narone was wondering why Luc seemed so sensitive about his mention of Toulon. Hmmm. He only needed to go to *one* of those cities to complete his change of image. So perhaps he should follow this latest instinct, depart for Toulon the very next day, and keep his eyes out for Luc's unstylish lady friend as soon as he arrived – just in case the two of them *were* living there and already conspiring to follow him! Because if she *did* actually creep out of the woodwork, that would give him a half-chance of turning the tables and pursuing *her* back to their hidey-hole.

But that was all highly unlikely, of course! Just silly wishful thinking. But the mere possibility of it had boosted his spirits *and* would give him some fresh new crumbs to feed to Inspector Simon Hardy on Monday morning ...

As soon as he was back in his room, he closed up the three boxes of old paperback books and sealed them roughly with a few strips of sticky tape. Then he removed his now somewhat depleted wad of stolen notes from his drawer and tucked it into his jacket pocket.

* * *

'Hello, Simon!'

'Right on time again, Arthur. And very bright and breezy for a change! So ...?'

'Well, I'm still in Nice.'

'And ...?'

'Actually, *Detective Inspector*, I'm not in Nice. But I'm very glad to hear you've stopped tailing me.'

'I ordered you to stay in the city!'

'And you also told me to use my wits. So now I'm acting like a proper *gardien* and following my nose. Don't worry, your loose leash is still a pretty strong one ...'

'Get on with it, Arthur.'

'OK. I've picked up a hint of where Luc may be living. I'm there already.'

'What sort of hint? And where precisely are you?'

'Oh, I don't think there's any point in overloading you with information, Simon.'

'Dammit, you can't ...'

'So I'll just get on with my job, OK? And perhaps we could cut my status reports down to once every three weeks, as of now. I don't want to take any more risks than necessary while I'm out in the cold ...'

'Who the hell do you think is running this show, Narone?'

'Right now, *Hardy*, I'd say it's me. I'll call you on the twenty-fourth. Trust me. *Ciao!*'

Plus ça change ...

Pureza had been very decent about it, of course, although his sudden announcement late on Saturday that he would be leaving first thing in the morning did seem to come as something of a shock to her. And she had looked very sad when he said he might need to move straight into some other lodgings when he returned.

But she had not pressed him for his reasons. And she had promised that his room would be waiting for him whenever he chose to return to it – and yes, since he'd asked so nicely, she would not throw out his boxes of crummy novels.

And she had insisted on making him a special big Sunday breakfast, and packing his old suitcase to the brim with all his trendy new clothes, and lending him several "real" second-hand books and lots of other bits and pieces, and paying for his taxi to the railway station.

Yes, Pureza really was a saint. And she had not even asked where he was going. Which had saved him the embarrassment of refusing to tell her.

So now he was safely installed in a pleasant-enough apartment in an anonymous corner of Toulon. Even if someone had followed the taxi from Pureza's and then sneaked onto that train – and he felt sure nobody had – he knew he had not been tailed when he got off and went searching for a room. So what if someone knew he was somewhere in Toulon?

His hair had been growing well since those brief minutes spent in the barber's chair at least ten weeks earlier. But now it was time to change the style from poor man's Presley to a "really heavy" centre parting. And his sideburns and moustache could be left to flourish too. He wasn't sure about a beard, yet. That somehow felt a bit too "deep-hippy" – but on the other hand it would strengthen his transformation, and it might make him really look the part of the angry left-wing journalist, if he ever did actually come to play that particular role. So he would let that grow too, and decide later whether to keep it when he eventually returned to Nice.

* * *

He spent most of the next few weeks in a combination of quiet reading, easy walking, solitary eating and drinking, strategic planning, and buying a little something most days with one of his many remaining 5000 Old Franc bills. He finally ditched his tatty little seven-year-old suitcase and purchased a much larger second-hand one. And he steadily sold off a lot of his trendy new birthday present clothes and used the cash to buy clean used items that matched better with the "perennial student" image he was determined to cultivate.

And then there was a mild diversion.

He decided on his third Saturday in Toulon to have a change from the two cheap local restaurants he had been frequenting since his arrival, and wandered downtown looking for a slightly more welcoming place for his evening meal. And as he was studying the menu on the wall of the Orchidée d'Or, suddenly there was Ursule, serving the customers at the front window table but giving *him* all her attention and a smile that could not be ignored.

He did not actually learn her name until she announced it when she brought him his dessert and could spare a few moments to chat. Or rather, to flirt unashamedly, as far as he was concerned. And she had already asked *his* name at the end of the main course. He had pulled "Roland" out of the hat, just as he had at Madame Foraud's apartment. Ursule seemed to like it. But she would probably have been just as happy with "Attila".

Ursule Hazan. Eyes as bright as his own, and a matching centre parting too! Half-African, half-European in her genes and her looks and her personality. Not a penny to spare each week and not a care in the world. Still limiting herself to big smiles and delicious chit-chat as she came and went past his table to serve her remaining customers and see them on their way tonight as fast as she decently could, but bubbling over into irrepressible laughter with everything they talked about as they strolled slowly back to her tiny, spotless apartment.

Ursule Hazan, *sa jolie Algérienne*. Wanting only to give and to take pleasure in equal measure. His first real spirit of the Sixties.

* * *

'Allô!'

'Hi, Pureza. It's me.'

'Arthur! How lovely to hear from you at last!'

'Listen, Pureza, I'm very sorry I forgot to call you on your birthday last week. I've been rather preoccupied. And I didn't send you a card or a present because the postmark would have revealed ...'

'Never mind, Arthur. It doesn't really matter. Want to tell me where you are over the phone instead?'

'I'd rather not, my friend. Just in case. But I expect to be back in Nice fairly soon, and I'll meet up with you whenever I feel I can.'

'OK. But are you in any further trouble?'

'Oh, no. Just working on the next steps in my hunt for Emilie and the bank robber.'

'Please take great care, Arthur.'

'I shall. And ... may I ask for a little word of advice?'

'Of course.'

'Well, I met a fascinating girl the other day and I'm a bit torn about what to do next. You know, what with Emilie and ... well, you know ...'

'What's her name?'

'Ursule.'

'Have you fallen deeply in love with her?'

'Oh, I don't think so.'

'That means you haven't. Is she in love with you?'

'I doubt it! It's more ...'

'Then I suggest, Arthur, that you get on with your search for someone who *is*!'

'Pureza? Hello? Pureza, are you still there ...?'

'Allô!'

'Arthur Narone here, Inspector.'

'So I win my bet.'

'Who with?'

'Myself.'

'What were you betting?'

'That you had not flown the coop for ever, and that you would phone me today as promised.'

'You're a very confident man.'

'That's because I think you're clever enough to know what's best for you, *enfin*. So, have you rounded up "Luc" and all the money now?'

'Yes, and I'm feeding the five thousand for lunch later today. Look, Simon, I suggest you take a few months' vacation and ask me that again in the New Year.'

'So what *have* you achieved, smartarse?'

'Not a lot. There's no sign of him so far, but I'm going to stick it out here for a bit longer.'

'And just *where* are you, Arthur?'

'That's still on a need-to-know basis, I'm afraid. Gotta go now. Big new plans to be made. I'll call you on the fourteenth.'

He had seen no sign of Luc's companion either, whoever she was. Which either meant they simply weren't in Toulon at all – which was by far the most likely conclusion, of course – or they had not been watching for him when he arrived, or they were just being very, very shy.

* * *

By Saturday the twelfth of November, Narone's hair was nearly four months long, and his beard, moustache and sideburns were all well established. But he felt he now looked more like a ragged nineteenth-century sailor with a "full set" than a sophisticated political commentator. That was fine for this particular day's plan of action, however – he had plenty of flexibility of disguise now, and he would need to stick with that unflattering beard for at least the next few hours. He had been steadily and carefully "exchanging" hot money for cold in the shops of Toulon, but he now required a rather more substantial injection of cash.

The afternoon brought the first solid bout of rain he had experienced since leaving jail. He shrugged his shoulders, tucked all his hair up into his big felt hat, purchased a long, button-up plastic mackintosh in the shop on the corner, and spent three hours walking all around the city, using a further twelve 5000 Old Franc notes to buy small essentials in each of twelve different stores. None of those big old bills would be individually banked until the following Monday at the earliest, but well before any particularly abnormal spate of their appearance in the city might possibly be noted, his long hair would be flowing again, his unflattering beard would be largely or even completely gone, the awful plastic mac would have been dumped in a rubbish bin, and he would already be off in a very different world.

He bought scissors, a razor and a tube of shaving cream in the final shop he visited, using some nice clean New Franc coins. He then spent that evening and the whole of the next day in his room – working on his beard, packing, reading, eating light and staying well away from prying eyes. And very early on the Monday morning he left his Toulon apartment, walked calmly to the station, and boarded the second eastbound train of the day.

He was going back to his hometown. And by staying away from Pureza's world, he would hopefully be relieving his kindly benefactor of any unwanted attention she might have been receiving.

And he was determined to gain himself a lot more living space – both literally and figuratively. So he would probably need to take on a new name, for the time being. "Roland" had come easily enough on two prior occasions, and that would do him fine – and he actually preferred the persona of a French folk hero to an English one. Now he just needed to think of a simple surname.

But best of all, unless his streetwise skills had suddenly become very rusty, he was certain that absolutely no-one in the world knew where he was at that moment – or what he looked like. He was free again, at last.

For now.

The phone boxes immediately outside Nice-Ville station were both in use, and Narone had to walk for several minutes up Avenue Malausséna to find an empty one.

'It's me, Inspector.'

'You're half an hour late.'

'Ever so sorry.'

'Still off in no-man's-land?'

'Depends where you think that is, General. But I expect to be back in Nice quite soon. And you needn't bother to keep your occasional eye on Pureza's shop. I'll be living somewhere else, and trying to delve a bit deeper into the underworld to get a handle on Luc for you.'

'So you got nowhere in ... ah, where was it, now?'

'I've already forgotten. And yes – I'm afraid I drew a blank there.'

'Well, we're going to need some real results soon, Arthur. And I shall want to know your new address.'

'Hmmm. It may be much better and safer for me if there's no chance of you or your buddies skulking around for a few weeks.'

'I'll be the judge of that.'

'Maybe, maybe not. You're driving a desk, Simon. I'm going down a mine.'

'But ...'

'I'll phone again in three weeks. If it's convenient.'

This time around he would be able to afford something much better than the dingy old room down by the port that he'd been living in at the time of the robbery. And anyway he would now need to be much closer to the world of the workers and the students. So he continued to walk north, away from the city centre, passing the Gare du Sud, crossing Liberation Square, and beginning his search for a modest writer's apartment in the streets around the Church of Saint Joan of Arc.

By lunchtime he had already identified three perfectly acceptable places. One of them had a suite of three small rooms and was only a bit more expensive than the maximum he had set himself. But then he discovered the landlord was insisting on seeing all his papers. He made the excuse that he wasn't carrying them that morning, and got out at once, saying he would return later if he was still interested. Another cheap but very small apartment came with the same conditions. But then, in the quiet, narrow Ruelle Michel-Ange he found a pleasant two-room set at a very attractive monthly rent, and his gentle enquiry about identification produced an assurance from the owner that no documentation would be necessary, as long as he paid up-front on a weekly basis – at forty percent above the rate he had just been quoted. He swallowed hard, accepted the terms, and several spotlessly clean banknotes later Monsieur Roland Manouet was comfortably installed in his latest new home.

He was well aware that he would soon need to re-start his habit of regular careful money laundering to cover the cost of this rather extravagant little folly. And fairly soon, at this rate, that reducing wad of one hundred big notes would be gone completely.

* * *

He was waiting for Luc's latest call. Should he tell the man he was not living at the bookshop now? Luc and his lady were almost certainly not in Nice, so why open another can of worms? That could create an even bigger risk of trouble for Pureza.

No, he would keep his secrets to himself for as long as he could.

The phone was ringing.

'Hello, Luc.'

'Where were you on the first of the month?'

'Toulon, if I remember rightly. Where were you?'

'Just shut up, OK?'

'But I've been back here for some time. As I'm sure you know ...'

'Found the money now?'

'No. But I've picked up another little lead, so I'm off to Marseilles soon.'

'You haven't been there yet??'

'No. So when do you want to call me again?'

'First of December, of course. Same time, same phone box.'

'That's only two weeks from now! I'll probably still be away.'

'Tough. You'll just have to take a few hours off. Be there!'

* * *

Narone had resolved to play his "official" cover game – or rather, a significant variant of it – in the afternoons and evenings, and devote the mornings to his private searches for Xérus and Luc. But he could not decide which of the villains to begin with, so he tossed a coin and it came down in favour of Luc.

And now that he was completely free of other things to think about, he began to appreciate how difficult this was going to be. He had so little to go on. He still felt sure that Xérus must know a good deal more about his old lieutenant. But until he was willing to give out a couple of little hints ...

Narone had never seen Luc's face during that first encounter in the Old City, and throughout the farce of their getaway drives the little man had been wearing his own heavy disguise. Obviously his name was not really Luc. And even if he wasn't from Nice, and conceivably lived in Toulon, how did that really help? Well, if he *had* been brought in from outside, he must have needed to do some local research in order to identify Narone as a getaway driver. Maybe the other driver, Bertrand Irvoise, had suggested him? But Irvoise was still in jail in Marseilles, so trying to get a lead on Luc from *him* was obviously out of the question. And Gustin Aignant was very unlikely to have known about Narone – not that he would be trying to eke out any information from *that* crazy thug, even if he weren't also tightly locked away.

No, he could do nothing with any of those unsubstantial scraps of information. He would just have to run with what he was sure of, and follow his nose in Nice for a while. And that meant starting with the simple fact that, almost seven years ago to the day, an injured bank robber had emerged from a hijacked car in the evening shadows of Boulevard Gambetta, not far from Nice-Ville station ...

He did not bother contacting the city hospital or any other clinics. The police were sure to have done that, as Hardy had confirmed. The Saint-Roch emergency ward staff of November 1959 would all be long gone, anyway. And why should any of those places allow him access to their incident records?

And there was no point in asking around at the railway station after all these years!

But he did proceed to wander all the nearby backstreets for several long mornings, looking in on any places advertising themselves as lodging houses – and plenty of others that weren't – enquiring first about a possible vacancy for himself ('Ah, sorry, I'm afraid I can't afford that much ...') and then more tentatively about any "no-questions-asked" doctors operating in the local area ('Because a pal of mine needed one urgently around here a few years ago, and I think he struck lucky, and I need one myself now ...'). But no-one fortuitously recalled that "pal" of his as a long-forgotten lodger, or came up with anything else, and most of them told him in no uncertain terms to push off at once.

Within eight days he had exhausted all the possibilities. Luc had probably just jumped on the first westbound train without anyone spotting him, and gone heaven knows where. So that was that.

And now it was the twenty-third of November, and he would need to get back in touch with Xérus very soon. So he called Pureza that afternoon, for the first time in over four weeks.

'It's me again.'

'Oh Arthur, I've been so concerned!'

'Everything's fine. Please don't worry. And how are you?'

'I'm all right. Just missing you a lot. Where are you now?'

'Don't ask. Hey, are my awful old books still safe and sound?'

'Of course they are, you idiot! But I've moved the boxes down to the cupboard under the stairs. They were cluttering up my living room!'

'OK, thanks. Now, there will be some carnations arriving by special delivery early tomorrow morning.'

'Oh, how sweet of you!'

'And I have a special favour to ask. It's all to do with the stuff I'm working on ... you know ... but I promise it won't cause you any problems ...'

'Well ...'

'I need you to arrange the flowers in the front window of the bookshop, straight away, and leave them there until further notice, OK?'

'So they're *not* a present for me after all!'

'But of course they are!'

'Oh, Arthur!!'

'Will you please do this for me, Pureza?'

'It doesn't sound as if I have much choice.'

'Thank you. And I'll be in touch again soon. *Ciao!*'

* * *

Narone took a bus ride past the shop at lunchtime the following day, and was relieved to see the vase of bright pink carnations clearly on display. So that evening he would go to receive the next call from Xérus. And he would let the man assume he was staying at the bookshop again, now that he was back in Nice. Because if Xérus should ever ask him why he had stopped coming and going there, then that would confirm that he was actively monitoring him in the city. Not very likely. But if it did happen, he would just play it by ear.

'Allô!'

'So you're finally back, Narone!'

'I told you I could get very busy, X, and I was right. I managed to steal enough cash to keep me going for several months, and I've been sniffing around in lots of towns and cities over to the west, trying to find sympathizers to the cause of our own little Robin Hood.'

'And what have you discovered?'

'Nothing, yet. So now I'm going to try that line here.'

'There's no evidence that L is living in Nice, is there?'

'No. But what else can I do? Unless you're willing to give me some other clues about him at last ...'

'No. Still too risky. You just keep at it. And signal me when you're ready to talk again. Same method, same timings, same call box, but *yellow* flowers, OK? Any time in January, but definitely by the end of the month. And Pureza Seles had better not forget to renew her fire insurance. Got it?'

'Got it. And ... Merry Christmas, X.'

'Just work on making it a Happy New Year for us all, Narone.'

So he would now switch his personal morning researches to the subject of Xérus. But what did he really know about the man?

Well, he was clearly a bit deaf in *both* ears! Narone had twice needed to repeat his words when a loud vehicle was going past, and surely Xérus would use his good ear for telephoning, if he were only deaf on one side? And his accent was strange ... it had the twang of the Midi, but as far as Narone was concerned, Xérus spoke a lot like those educated northerners he'd often heard on Pureza's radio. So maybe the guy came south a long time ago, and never looked back. A lot of Parisians would love to do that!

And if he *was* Luc's sponsor, and had funded the whole thing and supplied generous advance payments for everyone, he must have been very well off at that time, and possibly still was. Which meant he probably now lived in a very nice house, almost certainly here in the city or close by. And he didn't sound really old, so he was probably still at work. Maybe in the banking world. Maybe in *that* bank ...

The next day, during the busy midday hour, a not-so-young hippy sporting a pair of very dark John Lennon sunglasses and a string of colourful beads waited patiently in the longest queue of the Banque Artisanale du Midi. But when it was almost his turn to be served, he ducked out of the line and stood off to one side, facing away from the counters and fumbling around in his pockets and his shoulder bag for something he had obviously mislaid. Then he just shrugged and joined the end of another long queue.

When his turn finally came around again, he explained to the young cashier that he had been hoping to open an account with the twenty francs he'd received as a birthday present from his mother, but had unfortunately left his identity card back at the squat. She confirmed his suspicion that no bank account could be opened without some form of identification, and he shrugged his shoulders again, thanked her politely, wandered back outside, and made his way to a small café on Rue Pastorelli for lunch and a good little think.

Narone had managed a very solid piece of observation during those precious minutes spent inside the building. The security guard was in his early twenties – obviously not the reckless hero who had been seriously wounded seven years before and was still laid up in hospital at the time of the trial. Most of the clerks were also quite young, and two of them were girls. He had spotted a woman seated at her desk in the large office labelled "Deputy Manager" and immediately recognised her as the senior cashier who had testified at the trial. Christine somebody, he recalled. Modern times – lucky lady. And then, after Narone had joined the second queue, a tall well-dressed man in his fifties had come quickly through the corner door and gone straight into an even bigger office. And his face was equally memorable from those days in court. Charles-Pierre Orceau, the poor guy who had briefly related how he'd been shot in the shoulder by the stocky little man with the high-pitched voice and the silly moustache. Well, at least that awful experience hadn't got in the way of *his* eventual promotion either.

There was just one other guy at work in there, hurrying red-faced back and forth behind the counters. Early forties, probably, and little more than a messenger boy. He looked as if he earned a very low wage and would not hurt a fly. Even more relevant, his voice sounded nothing at all like that of Xérus.

And that was it. Dead-end street at the bank, and no other usable leads, right now.

But it was Friday afternoon, for heaven's sake, and this beer was tasting very good. Maybe he should stop thinking about Xérus *and* Luc for a little while, and plan a nice relaxing weekend with some of his great new student friends ...

Because while he'd been directly seeking his oppressors in his own particular fashion, Narone had also continued to give the appearance, for the benefit of the Nice-based mastermind who might conceivably be observing him back here, that he was busily slaving away at *his* particular cause. But he had decided even before his return to Nice that he would not be sticking with the cover story he'd originally sold to Xérus – the one in which he was a journalist investigating the gentle murmurs of worker and student unrest that were beginning to make themselves heard in various parts of the country.

No, he'd thought very carefully about that idea during his long, empty days in Toulon, and had recognised that there were probably not many real, oppressed workers to talk to in this pretty little rich-man's town ... apart from himself, of course! And how many of them were likely to know anything about the organisers of a bank robbery seven years ago?

And as for the students at the newly reconstituted University of Nice ... well, they might not take too kindly to being "investigated" if they really *were* politically active behind the scenes. But they should be much more amenable to the approaches of a budding young writer who was busy researching the rebellious, carefree *social* lives of typical Sixties Students for his next action-packed novel!

And his revised strategy had proved very successful – socially. He had met a lot of *very* interesting young people in the afternoons and evenings of the past ten days, and this evening he would be spoilt for choice on which of several all-night parties to attend.

Those parties – and he ended up enjoying every aspect of each one – continued through the weekend and, in rather more informal ways, into the following week. And since he presently had no more leads to follow in his mornings, that did not seem to matter very much at all.

So it was more by luck than judgement that he remembered on the evening of the thirtieth of November that he really should be in position for Luc's next phone call at noon the following day.

* * *

'Yeah ...?'

'Is that you, Arthur?'

'Yeah ...'

'You sound awful. Got a hangover or something?'

'Nah. I think it's the 'flu. Feeling really weak. Took me hours to drag myself back here from Marseilles this morning. The things we do for love ...'

'Stop fooling around!'

'I'm not, Luc! Gimme a break for once.'

'OK. So what have you got for me?'

'Nothing yet. But I still have a lot more places to check out. I'm going straight back to Marseilles this afternoon, and I'll get on with the job when I've recovered my strength. Are you willing to give me some help with it now?'

'No. You're still on your own. And make sure you're back in Nice on the first of January. I'll phone you at noon. Call box at the bottom of Rue des Ponchettes.'

'Whatever you say, Luc. Can I please go back to bed now?'

'Yeah. And get better fast!'

Narone congratulated himself on another fine performance as he wandered lazily back up to the student quarter, looking forward to rolling another joint with his pals and taking it nice and easy again for the rest of the day. If, of course, he could actually remember where he'd slept the previous night ...

* * *

He woke late the next morning and spent fifteen minutes persuading himself that he was *compos mentis* again. Then he spent another fifteen minutes deciding he should definitely review his situation. A little later he began to do just that.

It was highly likely that Emilie *had* left the city at once, rather than moving to Rue de la Croix, wasn't it? And even if the old woman's grandson had been right about that, there was little chance that Luc or Xérus actually had discovered Emilie there, right?

So they couldn't really know where she was now, could they? So neither of them posed any threat at all to her, did they?

So when he felt like looking for her again, one of these days, he would just follow his own trusty nose, wouldn't he? And *that* meant he didn't have to do any more searching around for Luc and Xérus themselves, to put them out of action, right? He just needed to keep out of their way as much as he could, and maybe put the hidden money up for auction to the highest bidder when they both decided time was running out.

So that was all settled. He would still have to take their phone calls and do whatever stuff they wanted him to, because he certainly didn't want them to get heavy with him ... or Pureza. But she could probably look after herself, couldn't she? And January was a whole month away, and he had seven years of catching up to do. It was time for some *real* end-of-term partying!

Now, what day was it? Ah, yes, Friday. Long time till Monday. Back to sleep ...

* * *

'Hello Inspector.'

'Late again, Arthur? And let me guess. Nothing to report, right?'

'Nothing firm. But ... I assume you've been watching to see if large numbers of old 5000 *balles* notes began turning up in a particular corner of Nice during the past seven years?'

'Of course we have. They've been coming steadily into the banks as the validity deadline gets closer. But there are still hundreds of thousands of them in circulation. And we've never seen *any* obvious hot-spots of activity.'

'The other big cities, then? Marseilles, for example ...'

'We've been watching there too. And Lyons and Toulouse.'

'And the smaller towns? How about Cannes?'

'Cannes, yes. But that place is almost impossible to monitor!'

'And Toulon?'

'Why Toulon?'

'Just a hunch ...'

'Is *that* where you've been for the last few weeks?'

'I've been everywhere, man. Well?'

'I don't know. I'll look into it.'

'Good. It's nice to know I can call on the police for support when I really need them. But there's no rush for the answer. I'm going back underground. I'll call you in four weeks' time.'

'But ....'

* * *

A few days later Narone had a pang of conscience and telephoned Pureza to tell her all was still well. And he at once received an invitation to spend the whole of the festive season with her.

That was definitely *not* what he would be doing, he explained, and for lots of very good reasons. But, OK, unless something really prevented it, and as long as he could work out how to arrive and depart without anybody spotting him and observing his new image, yes, he would come over to her place for a few hours on Christmas Day itself.

* * *

On Friday the sixteenth of December, he suddenly felt like a change from the indolence of drug-softened days and nights spent largely in the company of his over-intellectual pals, with the occasional diversion of a long game of strip poker when there were a few girls around for the evening. So he went back to his rooms in Ruelle Michel-Ange for the first time in many days, changed into the smartest clothes he had left in his wardrobe, checked the small ads for the city's latest night-time scene, and went out to the up-market-looking Nice La Belle disco bar. And there, show-dancing behind the over-talkative DJ and his turntables, were the heavily advertised Natalie Parras and Colette Lenovine.

They told him later that evening that they had been the closest of friends since the age of twelve. They were both nineteen now and studying hard at the University of Nice, sharing a modest New Town apartment but still unable to cope on the minimal contributions their low-paid fathers could make to their living costs. So, like many but by no means all of their fellow students, they needed to resort to part-time jobs to keep their heads above water.

And since they had for many years been devoted dance partners at their little school up in the foothills of the French Alps, and had later won several small awards for their innovative Beatles-backed *pas de deux* – which in the view of some observers went a good way beyond the early Sixties' norms of provincial public decency, particularly since the sixteen-year-olds had by then developed into a perfectly matched pair of slim, silky-haired and very well-proportioned young women – they had known long before starting out on their first university term exactly what sort of evening work *they* they would be seeking when they finally hit the bright lights of Nice.

They also told Narone, much later still, of their symbiotic, unspoken reactions to him the minute he'd walked into the place and sat down at an empty table near the dance floor.

'We've always done everything together,' purred Natalie, five minutes after the end of their set, as she handed him a long glass of beer while Colette carefully placed their own cocktails on his table and sat herself down next to him. 'So, what's your name, bright-eyes?'

'Look,' Narone protested, 'you're both really pretty, and I loved watching you dance, but ...'

'We noticed,' grinned Colette. 'You've been glued to your seat!'

'Yes! But I promise you I didn't know this was ... well, that sort of place. I'm sure I won't be able to afford your drinks. And I really don't ...'

'Hush,' cooed Natalie. 'It isn't. And we're paying, OK? My name's Natalie, and this is Colette. And we'd both just love to see you dance. With both of us, *and* one after the other, if you see what I mean ...'

'Oh! Well, that sounds great. Thank you! And you must let me buy you each a drink later, if the prices really are ... well, normal.'

'Only if you tell us your name!' Colette insisted.

'It's ... OK, it's Roland.'

'Come on then, Roly-poly! All together now!'

When the three of them left the club at one o'clock the following morning, the girls made no secret of their wish for "Roland" to came and stay with them, rent-free, over the coming vacation. Starting that night.

And after discovering how pleasantly long the nights could be when you were really having a good time, and soon afterwards phoning to cancel his earlier promise to spend Christmas Day with Pureza – 'I'm really sorry, but I have to be out of town again for a few weeks ...' – Narone was still in no hurry, as New Year's Eve approached, to abandon his exhaustive research into the delightful and rarely cerebral company of his two lovely dancing queens.

Discontent? What Discontent?

After a boisterous all night happening with Colette, Natalie and a lot of their closest friends, Narone had to make a very big effort to be at the call box on Rue des Ponchettes at noon to receive Luc's New Year's Day message.

'Got over the 'flu now?'

'Yeah. Bit of a hangover from last night, though.'

'Lucky you. So what have you achieved when you've not been busy going to Christmas parties?'

'I couldn't find out anything about the boxes of spares in Marseilles.'

'Dammit, Arthur, this has been dragging on for far too long! Those banknotes will be withdrawn from circulation in fifteen months' time!'

'Really? So are you ready to give me a bit of help with it at last?'

'No, of course not. Much too risky.'

'OK, I'll just keep at it, then. I'm going to sniff around in Aix next. Might stop off in Toulon while I'm passing – met a little lady there last time, if you know what I mean ...'

'You shouldn't be wasting your bloody time in Toulon again! Or messing around with women. You've got a job to do and I'm getting more and more fed up with your excuses!'

'Keep your hair on, Luc. I'll do all I can for you this month. Where's the next call box ...?'

Good. Luc was starting to get quite riled and impatient. Just what Narone wanted. The man had now hinted once again at his discomfort with the mention of Toulon. Perhaps one of these days he would make a more significant slip.

But Narone had no plans whatsoever to travel to Aix-en-Provence, nor to pay a return visit to the vivacious Ursule at the Orchidée d'Or.

He had plenty to amuse himself with right here in Nice, and still nothing specific he could be doing in his hunt for Emilie or those who just might know where she was.

He would need to call the Inspector as promised the next day, though. And maybe something would come of that. But hopefully not too much. It was rather cold outside.

Meanwhile, 1967 was beckoning. *Good Vibrations!* Back to the party!

* * *

'Where are you now, Arthur?'

'You really don't need to know, Simon. So, any joy with checking whether lots of those big bills ever started turning up in Toulon?'

'We've done our best. Nothing obvious. There were a good few more than usual deposited in a couple of districts in the months just after the robbery, but that's exactly when the first New Franc notes were being issued, and the banks have always said there were a lot of untypical depositing patterns at the time.'

'Nothing else more recently?'

'Just a steady stream, no hotspots. Apart from a small blip last November, spread over several banks. Just when you were away on your travels, as it happens ...'

'What a coincidence, Simon! Hey, you don't think Pureza Seles has been lending me hot money to spend in the hotspots of Toulon, do you?'

'No, Arthur, I don't. But has she actually been lending you lots of 5000 Old Franc notes?'

'Only one or two. And she does have a very healthy cash turnover.'

'All right, all right. So, are *you* getting anywhere in your hunt for "Luc"?'

'Not yet. But I'll be carrying on with my intensive enquiries, rest assured. Oh, hang on ... you don't happen to have any juicy little leads on the mastermind of the robbery, do you? Just in case I find myself with plenty of spare time on my hands, you know ...'

'I'll think about it ...'

'Fair enough. I'll call you in three weeks, Inspector.'

So there was still very little Narone could do right now, on any front. *And* it was even colder today. He would go back to partying once again.

* * *

But the following Saturday, the party was over as quickly as it had begun. Natalie and Colette came to the sudden realisation – within minutes of each other – that their new university term was starting on the Monday, and decided they had better shape up and get back to some serious study again. And that prompted Narone to wake up to his own cold reality and make a week-late New Year's Resolution of his own. He really must start trying much harder to lay his hands on Luc – for his own sake and Emilie's, and of course to satisfy both Xérus and the Inspector.

So he would spend a lot more time around the university buildings from the very start of the term, and get talking with some of the more outspoken students he'd briefly encountered in December. He would stick with his present "novelist" cover story to begin with. But as and when he judged it safe to do so, he could perhaps quietly mention what he would call his "real" mission as a sympathetic investigative journalist. And maybe, just maybe, he could achieve what he had theorised in the story he had originally sold to Xérus – some sort of access through those people to a few "activist" workers who might themselves provide him with an entrée into the criminal underworld of Nice.

And whether or not he then picked up any trace of Luc's whereabouts, he might just learn something about Emilie's.

Yes, he really should try to do this, and for *her* sake more than anybody else's. Not that he actually held out very much hope for the whole risky strategy ...

So on Sunday the eighth of January he returned to his base camp near the Gare du Sud, and began his bolder forays into the university campus. And over the next couple of weeks he did meet up with a few of the more "active" students. But he was rather surprised to discover that, in stark contrast to the dramatic and politically charged demonstrations on American campuses in recent years, the actions of the students in Nice appeared to extend little further than attempting to flaunt the university's regulations on the strict segregation of the boys and girls in different accommodation blocks.

* * *

Towards the middle of the month, Narone suddenly realised he was out of clean working cash. And then he discovered there was almost nothing left of the original wad of Old Franc notes that Luc had paid him in 1959 and that he had been steadily exchanging for New Francs since recovering them from the garage the previous August.

Damn! He must have lost a bit of control over the past few weeks. Well, he was not earning any money at the moment, and had no intention of doing so in the foreseeable future. So he would simply have to retrieve one of the four extra wads he had been keeping in a rucksack and regularly moving from one Riviera left-luggage office to another. Where exactly was it right now? He searched his wallet for the latest ticket. Ah yes, here in Nice at the Gare du Sud. So he would probably re-deposit it next back at the main Nice-Ville station.

He would carry on "exchanging" several of the notes from that second wad in the shops each week. And if Luc or the Inspector or anybody else should ever challenge him on his remarkably sustained "wealth" ... well, he would continue to insist that his entire income came solely from the selfless charity of dear Pureza.

* * *

After drawing a blank in his hunt, among the largely docile university students, for possible leads into the criminal underworld, Narone turned his attention to the workers of the city. With few large factories in this Riviera playground – and nothing like the Dassault complex in Bordeaux which had seen highly publicised strike action a few weeks before – there were no obvious focal points at which to begin his research. But he cautiously sniffed around here and there in the lower echelons of the service industries, and over the weeks to come he did encounter a number of rather disgruntled employees.

But most of the people he met were very glad to have a job at all, in the present climate of the last Stabilisation Plan and the slack labour market it had brought about. The famous Days of Action that had begun in France the previous May, with millions of workers walking out or sitting-in on limited-duration strikes, had certainly dragged employment issues much more fully into the public eye, and those protests had continued into 1967. But they had, as yet, brought about little or no change. The unions were still un-united, and the government was proceeding undeterred with its controversial employment reform policies.

So he had made no further headway, in his search for a lead on Luc, when the day arrived for his next phone call to the Inspector.

* * *

'Good morning, Simon.'

'Hello, Arthur. Listen, before we go any further – I've been thinking this whole thing through very carefully again, and I am still assuming you'd have told me if "Luc" had made *any* contact with you since your release ...'

'But of course.'

'OK. So what's new?'

'I feel I'm making a bit of headway in the world of the more militant students and the workers.'

'Care to elaborate?'

'Not really. I'm also beginning to feel rather exposed, so I don't want to take any more risks than necessary.'

'Hmmm. I'm not convinced you're ...'

'You've got some better ideas, then?'

'Well, no ...'

'Fine. Now, did you have that *other* little think for me? Is there *anything* you can tell me about our mastermind-cum-insider?'

'I wish there were, Arthur. I'm pretty sure "Luc" was the only one he ever dealt with. He's either left the stage for good or he's playing a very deep game.'

'OK. I'll get back to my own deep game, then. I'll call you on the thirteenth. *Ciao!*'

While he was in that phone box, Narone decided he would talk to Pureza again. Primarily because the end of January deadline for his next contact with Xérus was fast approaching, and she was once again key to making that happen.

And maybe she had now come up with a suggestion or two about how he could continue his hunt for Emilie more directly, rather than mostly hoping that something would turn up from his searches for Luc and Xérus.

Because it had been ... *merde*, it had been four whole months since his last specific effort to pick up her tracks, at Danielle's new place back in September! Hmmm. He certainly wouldn't be admitting that to Pureza ...

'It's Arthur.'

'Oh, how good of you to remember me.'

'Afraid I've been very preoccupied again, Pureza. But I do need another quick word ...'

'Hah! It will have to be very quick, Arthur. It's always busy here on Monday mornings. You know that!'

'OK. Well, I haven't had much more inspiration in my search for Emilie. Did you manage to get any ideas for me?'

'No, I didn't.'

'OK. I suppose I'll just ...'

'Look, Arthur – are you planning to come back and stay with me any time soon?'

'I don't know. Maybe.'

'Perhaps *you* could have a good think about *that*, eh? And ...'

'Yes?'

'Well, it will be Carnival time soon, won't it? I *had* been wondering if we could possibly spend a little time enjoying it together ...'

'Hmmm. Yes, that might be nice, but I think it would be too risky. I must make sure I don't blow my cover. I'm certain you wouldn't recognise me at the moment, and I want to keep it that way for now!'

'But isn't the Carnival the perfect opportunity to dress up in some other disguise?'

'Oh! Yes, I suppose it is.'

'So will you think about that too?'

'OK. And ...'

'I really have to go now, Arthur!'

'Hang on, Pureza! There will be some more flowers delivered on Friday morning. Please make sure they're out on display in the window by twelve noon.'

'Well, thanks a lot!'

'Don't mention it. And I *shall* be in touch with a decision about the Carnival. See you!'

* * *

It was Friday evening, and Narone was ready and waiting for Xérus' next call. He had checked early that afternoon that Pureza's new yellow carnations were clearly visible, and since then he had been thinking hard about how to try and draw something useful out of the man, this time ...

The phone rang.

'Hello, X.'

'Found L for me yet, Narone?'

'No. But please be patient. I've spent most of December and January getting more and more involved with the workers here, so there's still a chance of picking up some information, if there's any to be had ...'

'Huh!'

'And I've also been taking a different tack recently. I've started asking around to see if anyone wants to sell me any large denomination Old Franc notes at a special price. No luck so far, though.'

'That sounds very risky ...'

'Well, I'm having to be inventive, aren't I? But I'm starting to get nervous. Sooner or later someone's going to wonder why a reputable journalist is trying his hand at money laundering ...'

'Exactly! No, I really don't think you should be doing that. *Or* wasting your time in Nice at all.'

'But you've *still* not given me any specific clues about L or where to look for him, have you?'

'No.'

'So will you give me something now? I'm still undercover and in disguise, but I'm not certain I can keep it up for much longer. So surely the time is right ...'

'Well, I *have* been thinking about it. And the clock *is* ticking very fast. So maybe I *will* take the risk.'

'Go on ...'

'Very well. You need to go to Marseilles and find the Island Bar down by the port. Ask discreetly in there about a guy called Paul Ruford. Say you're a long-lost nephew or something like that, and see if you can pick up anything about where he's living now.'

'Right ...'

'And there's one other thing – but don't tell anyone you suspect it. "Paul Ruford" may well be a false name. So his real one might also just pop out of the woodwork.'

'Anything else?'

'Not for now. See what you can do with that. And stop messing around with your money-touting nonsense!'

'OK. But I can't go to Marseilles at once. I have other ... engagements. So, the usual signalling plan when I'm ready to report?'

'No, not this month. I'll phone you at noon on the last day of February. Here's your next call box ...'

At last! Narone could put a halt, for the time being at least, to his fruitless campaign to engage the workers of the city in his hunt for Luc. He now had something real to work with. So he would have a proper little rest this weekend, and make his forward plans, and choose some fancy dress for the Carnival.

* * *

On the first day of February, Narone took the latest call from "Paul Ruford" or whatever the man's name really was.

'Hello, Luc.'

'Well?'

'No success in Aix, I'm afraid. A bit more in Toulon!'

'What do you mean??'

'With that girl I mentioned!'

'Ah. Well, I'm delighted for you both. But what next?'

'I now have a promising new lead, and I'm going up to Avignon in the morning.'

'What sort of lead?'

'A hint from one of the dealers in Aix that a big repair shop there is expanding and buying up lots of unwanted spares.'

'That sounds a bit thin.'

'Every lead I get is thin, Luc. But I'm still following them all for you.'

'Yeah. OK, be back in Nice by the first of March. I'll phone you at noon at the following call box ...'

* * *

A week later, Narone and his ever-patient benefactor secretly enjoyed the closing days of the Carnival together. He had hired an attractive eighteenth century dandy's costume, and he noticed an admiring, almost peckish look in Pureza's eyes on more than one occasion. But he always managed to safely avoid engaging with it, and for his own part remained completely unmoved by her own surprisingly extravagant and very revealing transformation into a Hawaiian beach girl.

On the final evening, once the Mardi Gras festivities had begun to wind down, they sought out a quiet backstreet bar, both still in full carnival costume and make-up.

'Have you been enjoying yourself, Arthur?'

'Oh yes. I've been in a rather dodgy situation for the last few months, and it's great to feel as "free" as I do tonight. But it does take me back to ....'

'What's the matter?'

'Oh, I guess I'm still torn between searching for Emilie and having a good time before I hit thirty next year!'

'Hmmm. You've asked me on several occasions if I have any ideas on what else you might do to find out what happened to her, haven't you?'

'Yes.'

'Well, you're a writer, Arthur. Why haven't you been coming up with credible plot ideas of your own, for a story about someone's mysterious disappearance? And then following up those ideas, just in case something like that actually happened to her?'

'I have done a bit of thinking along those lines, Pureza. But there's been so much else going on in my head ...'

'I understand that, *chico*. All right – how about the plots of books you've *read*?'

'I've never read any of that sort of stuff. Before I went to jail I read very little, and it was pure rubbish! Since then I've done the opposite and concentrated on the classics and history and so on. Not many ideas from any of those.'

'And those awful paperbacks you bought last year? They're still taking up space under my stairs ...'

'Ah. Well, I hadn't got round to reading many of *them* before I had to go away.'

'Hah! Well, I *have* had one other thought. You could try getting some ideas from real fiction authors themselves. I've met quite a few at various literary events over the years, and I could probably put you in touch with some of them.'

'Oh, that might be interesting – and it could actually be very useful for ... But not right now, of course. Maybe later, when things are easier, eh?'

'What's your highest priority here, Arthur?'

'I told you five minutes ago, Pureza. I really don't know ...'

* * *

Narone's carnival break was over, and on Saturday the eleventh of February he took the midday train to Marseilles.

As soon as he arrived he got hold of a copy of the city telephone directory and checked it for "Ruford, P." Nothing. What a surprise. Then he walked down to the port and soon located the rather insalubrious Island Bar.

The bespectacled and clearly travel-weary hippy's initial enquiries after "Uncle Paul Ruford" in there, late that afternoon, met with some suspicion but no malice from the young waiter and the few equally young customers in the place at that hour. But they also met with no success. Narone decided to be patient, and thirty minutes later, as he was enjoying his second small beer, a much older man walked in and went straight behind the bar. The waiter spoke quietly with him at once, and then the owner – well, Narone presumed he was the owner – came over to his table and sat unceremoniously down.

'I'm Vic. You're looking for Paul Ruford?'

'Yes. He's my step-uncle. I know he used to live in Marseilles, somewhere near the port I think, but I never had his actual address. I'm bumming all over Europe right now, and I've just landed up here, so I was hoping I could sleep on his floor for a couple of nights, if he's still around. But I can't get hold of my parents today to ask them where he lives. This is the fifth bar I've tried, and I'd just about given up! But maybe I *have* struck lucky ...'

'Don't think you'll be staying with him tonight! He used to live up on Rue Marengo, but we haven't seen him in years. Late '59, it was, when he left. He told me there were some problems with his family just before he disappeared. But everyone used to joke that he must have done that big bank robbery in Nice and then scarpered abroad with all the money ...'

'Ha-ha-ha! Well, maybe he gave my parents his new address and they just forgot to tell me. You don't know which block he lived in, do you?'

'No.'

'Never mind – it was always a long shot. Thanks for your help, Vic.'

'Still looking for a room, then? We've got one free for tonight ...'

'I won't take it, at least for now – my heavy old rucksack's back at the station left-luggage office, so I'll probably look for something much nearer there.'

'OK. Good luck.'

'Thanks again!'

Narone drained his glass, waved his goodbyes to all his new acquaintances, and got well away from the place as casually and as quickly as he could. Then he looked at his street plan of the city. Rue Marengo. A very long street indeed. And a dead-end street as far as this little exercise was concerned. He would not even bother to visit it. He would go straight back to Nice on the eight o'clock train.

* * *

Another early Monday morning telephone appointment to get up for!

So, should he tell Inspector Hardy about "Paul Ruford" late of Rue Marengo, Marseilles? Surely not? If that information were in some miraculous way to allow the police to identify and arrest the most wanted Monsieur Luc, then Narone would lose any possible chance of pressuring the man in person for a lead or two on Emilie's whereabouts. And Luc would obviously tell them that it was actually Narone who made off with all the cash. And then there would be a whole lot of new demands from dear Simon. And Xérus would still be hovering somewhere above him, still angry and still *completely* unsatisfied.

No, he resolved as he walked to another remote call box, he would say nothing about "Paul" to his self-proclaimed best friend.

'Good morning, Inspector.'

'Still having a lovely time down there, Orpheus?'

'No, actually I'm not. It's getting increasingly hot out here in the cold.'

'Very funny. So, don't tell me ...'

'Your insight remains impeccable, Simon. But can I ask again if *you* have any clues that might help me identify or locate the *insider*?'

'I'm still thinking about that.'

'All right. So I'll just keep at it too. But you know, Simon, I'm really not cut out for this sort of thing ...'

'Then try cutting yourself another new shape, Arthur.'

'Well thanks a lot for that fine advice. I'll call you on the sixth of March.'

During the final days of February, Narone made a series of further half-hearted attempts to pick up something, anything, about Luc from the lowest-paid workers of the city. He had read *Animal Farm*, of course, and he had already formulated his own simple theory of society. "Opportunities are limited only by money. Money makes the world go around. Money is power. Money is pleasure. Money is health. Money is freedom. All Frenchmen have equal liberty, equality and fraternity, but a wealthy few have them rather more equally than others." So he had been hoping the country's latest industrial action – inaction! – that month at the Saint-Nazaire shipyard might have stimulated a little more anger among the more vociferous workers of Nice, and maybe some slightly looser talk. But nothing more was forthcoming.

He concluded that the few outspoken people he *had* met possessed a strong political drive, and were still inspired by the beginnings of the French Revolution nearly two centuries before. And maybe one day they would turn again to civil disobedience, or worse, in the name of their cause. But they were largely "honest" men and women, with few links to the criminal underworld, and *enfin* they were proving of no value to his search for Luc, let alone for Xérus. And he was occasionally finding some of them to be positively unhappy to have him around ...

So he now decided to give up his undercover quest, and take Pureza's hint, and go back to stay with her. A quick telephone call would seal it, in lieu of a kiss. And living there would save him a lot of money each month, so he would not have to be "exchanging" his stolen bills quite as frequently in the various shops of Nice. And perhaps, in fact, in only one of them ...

* * *

It was the last day of the month, and Narone was packed and ready to move out that afternoon. But first he had to take Xérus' latest call.

'So what's new?'

'Well, I've been across to Marseilles as you suggested.'

'And ...'

'Nothing. I spent three whole days asking around after Paul Ruford. Nobody recognised his name, not even in the Island Bar.'

'I knew it probably wouldn't do us any good. Might even have done some harm!'

'How?'

'Never you mind. What else have you managed to get nowhere with?'

'Well, as it happens, I think my attempts at buying Old Franc notes in bulk have got me noticed by the wrong sorts of people. I don't like that at all, and I may well have to come in from the cold very soon.'

'I told you it was risky! So what the hell are you going to do next?'

'I'm going to keep working on our little challenge, X. And any further useful clues from you will be mighty welcome.'

'Just get on with it, Narone. I'm really losing patience now. Next call on the thirty-first of March, at the phone box you used in January. And I want some results!'

At four that afternoon, Roland Manouet vacated his rooms on Ruelle Michel-Ange. Beneath his usual scruffy winter coat he was wearing the few relatively smart clothes he had retained during his time undercover. And once he was well away from that area, in a quiet backstreet between the two railway stations, he took off his old coat, stored it in his new large suitcase, and walked up towards Avenue Malausséna and the nearest barber's shop. After a substantial shave and trim that removed most of his shaggy sideburns and left his hair and moustache still fashionably long but a great deal neater, he emerged looking much as he had when he'd left Pureza's place for Toulon exactly four months earlier.

He found a nearby bar that he had never frequented, sat inside with a very welcome beer until well after dark, and then hailed a taxi to take him discreetly "home" again at last.

Pureza had prepared a very special dinner, of course, and Narone consumed it with gusto. He then scratched around in his head for a gesture he might make in return.

'I can repay that three hundred francs loan now, if you'd like me to ...'

'I still don't understand where all your money has been coming from, Arthur.'

'Oh, I've been doing all right. This and that, here and there, you know ...'

'Hmmm. I suggest you hang onto it until you're certain you don't need it.'

'OK, then.'

* * *

At noon the following day, Narone took Luc's next call. He was determined to try a little more bear-baiting.

'False alarm in Avignon, I'm afraid. The big outfit I'd heard about is only servicing German and Scandinavian cars now. So I'll be checking out Nîmes and Montpellier next. I would have gone across there directly if I hadn't had to come back here for this damned phone call!'

'You do what you're told!'

'Yes, I do. But I may need more than a few weeks this time. Can we leave the next call to the fifteenth of April?'

'No! You can make sure it takes you a month and no more! I'll call you on the *first*. Same time and place as today.'

'What's the matter, Luc? You sound a bit frustrated ...'

'What do you expect? Those banknotes only have another thirteen months' validity left.'

'I'm feeling pretty frustrated too. And my legs are working harder than yours.'

'Maybe they'd like to work a lot harder, eh! Listen – you get the money to me by the end of June, and I'll give you five extra wads instead of two.'

'I'll drink to that.'

* * *

Two days later Narone made a special effort of diplomacy – he wasn't at all sure why – and remained in the bookshop after breakfast rather than hurrying straight out as he usually did. Pureza did not conceal her pleasure, of course, but she also took advantage of the first short lapse in business to suggest that maybe he really should now try to find *himself* a nice little job.

He did his best to stall on this, and had still made no commitment whatsoever on the subject when two customers entered the shop in rapid succession, and Pureza's attention was immediately diverted away from him once again. And while she was busy researching something for the first of them, the second one approached him with two brand-new, expensive histories of eighteenth century France in his hands and asked for a personal recommendation as to which one to select. Narone, who had read neither of them in any depth but *had* skimmed through them both in one of his long browsing sessions there the previous summer, instinctively pointed out several great merits of *each* of the works, declaring that he had found neither to be badly executed in any respect, and that taken together they formed a fine, comprehensive and complementary study of their subject. The customer pursed his lips, then nodded sagely, bit the bullet and purchased both volumes for cash.

Pureza was delighted.

'I always hoped something like this would happen, Arthur! So, why don't you start working here with me for a few hours each day, in exchange for your room and breakfast, and dinner whenever you want it, plus a bit of pocket money and a small commission on all your sales?'

'Ah. I don't know about that, Pureza ... I don't really want to feel obliged to ...'

'And if you decide to move away again later, I'll also pay you enough to cover your rent and an evening meal!'

He could sense another of those patterns looming. No, already loomed. No, already almost in place. But he could also already see some benefits, and not just the obvious ones.

'OK, I'm willing to try it, Pureza, but only when I choose to, on a day-by-day basis – to give myself the time and the flexibility I need for ... well, for all my unfinished business. And I'll accept the commission, thank you, but I can manage without the pocket money.'

'You strike a hard bargain, my fellow merchant. But it's a deal. And since you started work at nine o'clock this morning, you've earned your first commission already!'

When Pureza closed the shop that evening she proposed another special dinner to celebrate their new business partnership, and Narone was delighted to accept. But, he said, he really fancied a short walk around the Old City on his own first, after spending the whole day inside and hard at work.

She chuckled at his little joke, and told him to be back by eight and not a minute later.

But when he returned, and ahead of time too, she was surprised to see a real change in his mood. She waited for him to say something, but to no avail. So halfway through the meal she simply had to ask if there was some new problem.

'Oh, no, *chica*. I'm just feeling a bit ... oh, I don't know, emotional, I suppose ...'

'Purely after taking a nice little stroll back in the comfort of your real world?'

'Actually, yes.'

He was even more sombre now.

'Want to talk about it?'

He sighed deeply and put down his fork.

'I told you I was brought up at the orphanage in the old Senate House, didn't I?'

'Yes.'

'Well, there were several families living in very poor apartments in the surrounding buildings on Rue du Saint-Suaire and Rue Barillerie. And I often used to look out of a window and watch the boys playing in the square right in front of me. There were rarely any girls with them – I don't know why.

'But when I was nine I did start to notice one. She was about fourteen, and she was out there occasionally in the early evening. But she wasn't playing with sticks and stones in the gutters with the other urchins. She was leaning on the lamp-post and smoking and chatting and laughing with the bigger boys. I was fascinated by everything about her – girls simply did not form part of my world. And I was stuck inside, so all I could ever do was watch them all enjoying themselves. Well, I assumed that's what they were doing.

'And I guess I must have become very jealous of those older boys. Because a few months later, I did something to get my own back. I never planned it, Pureza, but ...'

Narone broke off with a lump in his throat and his eyes suddenly very moist.

'My goodness, Arthur! Whatever did you do?'

He shook his head and could not, would not continue.

'Oh, I've never seen you like this before! Come here, you poor thing ...'

She leaned over and embraced him. It was the biggest and most loving hug he had ever experienced. But it did nothing to relieve his pain.

'What did you do to those boys, Arthur?'

He shook his head again. 'I never went near any of the boys.'

'Oh! The girl, then ...'

He nodded, brushing at his eyes with the back of his hand, his face red with the embarrassment of his tears.

'Won't you tell me a little more? For *your* sake, my friend?'

'I'm sorry, Pureza. I can't. I'm sorry.'

'At least tell me her name, Arthur.'

'I didn't actually learn it till a lot later.'

'And ...?'

'It was Thérèse. Thérèse Vonier.'

'And ...?'

'No, Pureza. I can't. I just can't.'

Are You Being Served?

'I'm back in the real world again, Inspector.'

'Back in Nice, you mean?'

'Probably.'

'At Pureza's place?'

'You tell me.'

'All right, I will. You've been there since the second of March – maybe even the first. And you've found yourself a new vocation. But I'm not convinced your latest hairstyle was a good move for a salesman.'

'Well done! Does anything ever escape your beady eye?'

'So you managed to avoid the slings and arrows of Nice's angry young men and women?'

'Yes. But it was a close call.'

'Pah! Anything on Luc and the money yet?'

'No. But I'm already pursuing other interesting lines of enquiry. Meanwhile, have *you* come up with any ideas about identifying the mastermind? Maybe something related to the bank?'

'I'm still thinking about it.'

'OK. I realise that must be quite demanding, so I think I'll leave it another three weeks before I call again. As long as that's convenient for you, of course. Our aim is to please.'

'Arthur, please just keep on trying to find "Luc" for us. That's really all I've ever asked, you know.'

'A votre service, monsieur!'

* * *

For Arthur Narone the month of March then passed heavily patterned and extraordinarily incident-free. He was continuously aware that this must be a lull before one or more very heavy storms, but he was determined to hang loose once again and do absolutely nothing to stimulate their onset. Luc believed he was busy out in Nîmes and all points west, Xérus had accepted that he was gently warming up again after his many months out in the cold, and Simon Hardy had been a very easy sell, as usual. And as for his hunt for Emilie – well, he was happy to allow his subconscious to continue to work that little challenge through in its own good time.

But he did take the opportunity to deploy the little scheme that had crossed his mind when he decided to come back to Pureza's place and had crystallised as soon as she invited him to work alongside her in the bookshop. On each of the first four days when she left him in charge at lunchtime, he opened the cash till and checked carefully for any recently taken 5000 Old Franc notes. And they seemed to crop up quite regularly. He had even accepted a couple in payment himself. So he would now proceed, over the coming weeks, to steadily exchange a good number of his own hot old bills for their nice cool 50 New Franc equivalents, with no harm done to anybody.

* * *

Narone telephoned Inspector Hardy from Pureza's living room early on the twenty-seventh of March, as promised.

'Well, I've been working very hard at my honest new trade, Simon. So I'm afraid I've picked up nothing more on Luc for you. But do *you* finally have any ideas for me on the subject of our mastermind?'

'Yes, Arthur, it might surprise you to hear that I do.'

'I'm stunned!'

'I think you may be able to help us extract a little more information from a gentleman by the name of Giuseppe Hauvert – if you can manage to locate him.'

'Who the hell is he?'

'He was a junior clerk in the bank at the time of the robbery, and he had disappeared earlier that day, en route to Italy – so of course he was a prime suspect from the very start. We quickly put a lot of pressure on the Italian police to help us find him, but then he turned up again in France after a couple of days, actually on his way back to

Nice! And all the evidence suggested he had absolutely nothing to do with the crime. But he had received a phone call the night before the robbery – from a French-speaking Sicilian, he guessed – sending him scurrying back to his family home. Presumably the caller was the real mastermind, setting young Hauvert up for us *and* creating a diversion. Which all worked very well, I must admit.'

'Three out of ten for achievement, then, Inspector ...'

'Be quiet, Arthur, and listen. To be perfectly honest with you, I've often felt we didn't ask Hauvert quite enough about that caller before letting him go without charge. He visited his injured colleagues in hospital the following day, very concerned for them. Then he went straight back to the bank, but he was given the sack on the spot! We then lost all interest in him for a while. But when we later tried to contact him at his parents' house in Lyons, to ask him a few more questions, they said he'd gone off to live with his mother's family in Genoa very soon after it had all happened, disgusted with the way he had been treated in France. And we decided not to bother to pursue him and aggravate the Italian police for a second time!

'So maybe you really could do a bit of specific detective work for us now. Ideally without mentioning the police, of course ...'

'And where exactly should I pretend my information came from ...?'

'Hmmm. I'll think about that. And in the end you may have to say you've spoken to us. But make it sound like your own private affair.'

'Sounds like a huge bag of laughs, Simon. I trust you'll be making it worth my while.'

'Standard rules, Arthur. Just agree to do it, please.'

'All right. But I'll need time to fit it into my busy social diary.'

'And I obviously need some time to think it through and prepare a full verbal briefing for you. Are you able to go to Genoa in mid-April?'

'Yes.'

'Then call me at nine o'clock on the tenth.'

* * *

That evening, Narone dined in style with Pureza and his own agenda.

'You remember you told me you've met quite a lot of novelists?'

'Of course.'

'Any Italians?'

'Three or four, yes.'

'Do any of them live up in the north, not too far from here?'

'Only Sergio Rozzino. He's from Milan.'

'You know Rozzino!'

'Not particularly well. But well enough to give you an introduction, if that's what you're thinking. He'll probably be here for the convention again in June.'

'Actually, I was thinking of something rather different, Pureza. You see, I need to go to Italy quite soon, to ... well, to help the police with their enquiries. And I thought it might be an idea to try out your little notion while I was there. To make the trip worthwhile, if you like – to see if I can pick up any ideas about ... well, for Emilie's sake, basically. And I've never been to Milan!'

'Are you *sure* you would be doing it for Emilie's sake?'

'Oh yes. So are you willing to try and contact Rozzino?'

'I said I would always do whatever I could for you, Arthur. And if that's what you really want, then I will. By the way, have you read any of his novels?'

'Actually, no.'

'Well, there are several on the shelves of the bookshop. If I'm going to arrange a meeting with him, I think that's the least you should do in preparation ...'

'Of course I will. And thank you yet again, *mon amie* ...'

'No problem, Arthur. Now, would you like to know how much commission you've earned so far?'

'No thanks! Because it's just like income tax! I never want to see it! Please deduct it from my outstanding debt to you every month, and tell me when I've cleared that completely!'

* * *

It was the end of the month once again. Time to take Xérus' latest call and sell him yet another line.

'Narone?'

'Yes, it's me. And I have some real news for you this time! I've just picked up a rumour that a lot of large denomination Old Franc notes surfaced in 1960 and 1961 in Sanremo and several other towns further to the east. So I'll be going across to Italy fairly soon, to see if the name "Paul Ruford" means anything to anyone over there.'

'But that was five years ago, Narone ...'

'And he might still be living there. Got to follow up all my leads, haven't I? So I'll signal you again once I'm back. Can't be sure how long it will take, so can we make it sometime in May?'

'Very well. Same rules and times, and this phone box again, but *red* flowers next. And ... good luck.'

* * *

For April Fool's Day, Narone had devised a nice little touch to add to his ongoing charade with the so-called Paul Ruford.

'Well?'

'No luck out in Nîmes or Montpellier, Luc. But I think I'm getting warmer now. Did I ever mention the spare parts were all for old Fiat models?'

'No, you didn't.'

'Well, they were. The previous owner of the garage in Nice – before my boss took it over twenty years ago – was a Fiat repair specialist and had obviously bought a huge job lot before the war. So I suddenly thought it might be worth trying back across the border. Plenty of Fiat servicing outfits in Italy!'

'Why didn't you think of that before?'

'Why is the sky blue? But even if I had, I don't think I'd have tried to go there yet. The police might have been watching me, for all I knew, and they might have thought I was fleeing the country.'

'So what makes you think it's OK to go now?'

'Because we're running out of time, aren't we? And I also have a solid lead at last! I've managed to discover that lots of unused spares were being bought up quite recently by a specialist renovation operation in Imperia.'

'You're kidding!'

'No, I'm not. And if I *do* get questioned at the border, I'll just tell them I'm taking a little holiday in Ventimiglia or wherever, and show them my hotel reservation and my return ticket. I think it's worth taking the risk now, Luc.'

'All right. Good luck. I'll phone you on the first of May. Here's your next call box location ...'

* * *

Narone spent the whole of the first week of the month in the bookshop, working at clearing his debt to Pureza as quickly as possible and speed-reading three short Rozzino novels from cover to cover in his spare moments.

Then on the tenth of April he called the Inspector as planned, and confirmed he was all ready to leave for Italy. Hardy gave him the promised full briefing about Giuseppe Hauvert, including the last known address of his grandparents, and Narone agreed to phone again on the first Monday after his return to France.

Two days later he boarded an eastbound train at Nice-Ville station. Luc believed he was going spare parts hunting in Imperia with the alibi of a Ventimiglia hotel booking, and Xérus thought he was off to Sanremo and beyond in search of a fictional spendthrift. But he would pass straight through all those delightful coastal resorts and restrict his researches in Italy to the cities of Genoa and Milan.

* * *

Narone was quite prepared for a dead-end at the home of Hauvert's grandparents. Even if they turned out to be alive and well, and even if the ex-bank clerk was still living with them, he suspected he might receive very short shrift from a man whose career had presumably been ruined by the actions of four or five despicable villains, one of whom was now standing on his doorstep more than eight years on and offering his hand in a gesture of peace.

So he was pleasantly surprised when Giuseppe, who was clearly only a couple of years older than him, nodded ruefully in recognition of the getaway driver's face – 'From all the newspapers, of course!' – and invited him in out of pure curiosity.

Narone kept it as simple as he could. He was back out of jail, and for justice's sake he was determined to find both the man who had set up the robbery and the gang leader who had escaped. He had discussed this briefly with the Nice police, and they had trusted him with this address – they would be as pleased as everybody else if Narone could somehow track down the mastermind. And surely Giuseppe's reputation was worth reinstating, if that were at all possible?

Hauvert played along – 'After all, what do I have to lose?' – and answered all the questions his visitor then threw at him.

But by the end of their conversation, Narone had established very little new information. Giuseppe's recollection of what the caller had briefly said to him on the phone, the evening before the robbery, tied up well with what Hardy had already told him. So did the report of his Sicilian accent. And it turned out that *everyone* at the bank had had access to Hauvert's apartment block address and phone number: the personal details of all members of staff were kept in an easily accessed notebook for use by anybody in an emergency.

And Hauvert could still not believe that any of his old colleagues had been involved.

'I've always hated Tillier for giving me the sack. But the old boy was no bank robber. Orceau was a nice guy, always helpful when I was doing my training, and very grateful for my hospital visit after he was shot. There were five younger clerks – one of them a woman – but I can't see any of them having the time or the contacts to arrange something like that. Pauron the messenger was a real softie, and he couldn't have planned a tea-party, let alone a robbery. And Charnière was just a regular security guard. If he was the insider, he made a real mess of it, poor sod. But of course he wasn't!'

'I'm sure you're right about him, Giuseppe. Actually, I had been wondering whether to pay him a visit too ...'

'Don't. If you go anywhere near him, and he discovers you were one of the gang, he'll break your neck on the spot.'

'OK!'

There was nothing left on Narone's list of questions. But as they parted with another friendly handshake, Giuseppe Hauvert proffered his grandparents' telephone number, just in case the amateur investigator later remembered something else he needed to ask.

* * *

Narone discovered that what he'd imagined as Sergio Rozzino's chic Milan apartment was actually a tiny attic in a run-down block in one of the grubbiest quarters of the city. And though he knew all about the poverty of writers over the ages, he found it hard to accept that a well-known author was still obliged to live in such cramped and uninviting conditions. But he decided it would be best not to mention that.

Rozzino was polite enough in his welcome, and his French was very good, but he looked as if he had been hard at work and was not too happy with the disturbance. Their conversation would clearly be lasting the length of just one small cup of coffee.

So Narone decided to begin with Emilie, and keep his introduction brief and quite vague. A young friend of his, he explained, had apparently needed to get out of Nice in a hurry, many years before, but had left no word for him on where she had gone, or why. And since then he had tried everything he could think of to uncover her tracks.

'And I really respect your work, *signore*. So do *you* have any bright ideas on how such a character in one of your stories might have acted in that situation?'

Rozzino sipped his coffee, drew on his cigarette, and stared out of the window for thirty seconds. Then he turned back to Narone.

'Was she living with her family?'

'No.'

'Would she have gone home to them?'

'Absolutely not!'

'*Bene*. So, money makes the world go around. Did she have any?'

'Well, she was earning good pay, part-time. But she was spending most of it every week on clothes, and bangles, and her apartment ... and me.'

'Did she have a skilled job she could go straight into, some place else?'

'No. Her work was specialised. Artistic. She'd have to search around hard for opportunities.'

'So she would have needed to pay for travel and accommodation and food and everything else for the foreseeable future, and she may have had very little cash in her purse to start with, right?'

'Right.'

'Did she have anything of value?'

'Oh! No, I don't think so. She abandoned most of her possessions when she left home. And anyway, they were only teenager's stuff. So ... wait a minute – there *was* her grandmother's old cameo ring. But she told me it was unique and that she would never dream of parting with it. She wore it all the time.'

'So you would recognise it again?'

'Of course!'

'Well, it's a long shot, Monsieur Narone, but there's your plot idea. I think you should pay a visit to every pawnbroker in Nice. And now I regret I must get back to my own work.'

Narone realised, as he descended the narrow staircase down to the fourth floor, that he had not asked the imaginative novelist for any ideas on how to smoke out either Luc or Xérus. But there had been no time for that. And anyway, Emilie was probably far more important.

* * *

Having dragged out his absence abroad for a full week, Narone arrived back at Nice-Ville station quite late on Wednesday the nineteenth. But he made a special effort to get up at a reasonable hour the following morning, and joined Pureza in the bookshop not long after she had opened up for the day.

And when there was a momentary lull in trade, he told her of his brief interview with Sergio Rozzino, asked her what she thought of the author's off-the-wall idea that Emilie might have sold or pawned some item of value, and mentioned his own recollection of her treasured antique ring.

'I think it's an absolutely brilliant idea, Arthur. You have nothing to lose by following it up as he suggested. And after all, you don't have anything else to do with your time.'

'OK, then. I'll probably give it a try after I've spoken to the Inspector on Monday.'

But he did then spend the next two hours deeply pondering each of the three conclusions Pureza had just drawn, trying to figure out how sincere, or conversely how ironic, her message had been in each case.

* * *

On the twenty-fourth, Narone called to tell Simon Hardy he had gleaned nothing new or of any value about the robbery's mastermind from his recent meeting with Giuseppe Hauvert. So he would now get back to his very loose pursuit of Luc, and phone again in a further three weeks. Unless, of course, Simon had any other bright ideas ...

He had none. Which of course made two of them.

Narone knew there were many pawnbrokers in Nice, and plenty of gold and money exchanges too. But if he really *was* going to try out Rozzino's idea, he had better do it methodically rather than relying on memory or the telephone book.

So as soon as his call to Hardy was over, he primed his wallet with the rest of the latest wad of big hot banknotes hidden in his drawer, left Pureza to manage the shop on her own once again, and purchased a brand new city map at the nearest corner store. Then he took a cab down to the Promenade and along the Quai des Etats-Unis to the Castle Hill elevator entrance. From there, at the top of Rue des Ponchettes, it was going to take him a long time to cover every street on foot, even though he planned only to browse in the windows to start with. But he would make a little list of any places that seemed worth a return visit for a further look inside and a conversation with their owners.

He found nothing on display in any of the pawn shops of the Old City, where that old woman's grandson had reportedly spotted Emilie going into Rue de la Croix. But one or two of them would merit later investigation. Then after a quick lunch he moved over to the area around Place Garibaldi and north of the port, where he and Emilie had both previously lived. He wrote the addresses of several more candidates in his notebook, as he criss-crossed the more modern grid of streets, but he saw no sign of the ring in any of their windows. Not that he held out any hope of finding it anyway.

At five o'clock that afternoon he reached the end of Rue Scaliero, decided to call it a day, and drew a line on his map.

The following morning, under cloudy skies, he picked up where he had left off and covered all the streets further to the north, right up to Boulevard Pierre Sola and Nice-Riquier station. Then he wandered back down to Pont Barla, had another quick lunch not far from the bookshop, and started on the streets of the New Town, heading south on the embankment and then steadily working his way up from Avenue Félix Faure, keeping to the east of Avenue de la Victoire.

And one hour later, just two blocks along from the Police HQ on Rue Gioffredo, he found the unmistakable ring of Emilie Courbier's grandmother glaring angrily at him from the window display of Versanne et Fils: Dépôt-Vente.

He stood glued to the pavement for a full three minutes, composing himself, and then breezed confidently through the door and approached the well-dressed man standing behind the counter, who clearly was already in the mood for business.

'*Bon après-midi, monsieur. Qu'est-ce que vous-désirez?*'

'Good afternoon. Well, I was wondering if you could possibly help me. I'm certain I recognise one of the items in your window, and I'd really like to know who left it with you, please.'

'Kindly show me the piece you are interested in, sir,' said the shopkeeper, escorting Narone to the back of the display and drawing open its curtains. They peered together into the glistening cornucopia, and Narone pointed it out.

'Aha! Yes, a very fine cameo ring, in immaculate condition. Early nineteenth century, in eighteen-carat gold and agate. The elegant lady wears a pearl necklace and earrings, with the delightful shades of her dark and light brown curls set against the white background of her bonnet and face.'

'And ...?'

'Oh, it had been sitting there for years when a rich American hippy purchased it from us last summer. She said it would be "cool" to have something old-fashioned while everyone else was only interested in modern things. But she brought it back a week later, when she realised she was running out of money for the rest of her grand tour of Europe, and Daddy had refused to wire her any more. I made a nice little profit on that transaction. It's a very valuable piece, *monsieur*.'

'OK – so I'm really lucky it came back and it's still here. But who sold it to you in the first place?'

'Oh, I'm afraid I can't remember much about that. It was my mother who purchased it, while I was away. So I shall have to ask her. One moment, please ...'

He plucked the ring from its perch, closed the curtains, returned to the door behind the counter and called down the passage: 'Valérie, please watch the shop for a moment while I go and get *mémé.*'

'*Oui Papa.*'

A girl of twelve or thirteen appeared and hovered, smiling shyly, in the doorway while her father hurried up the stairs. Narone returned her smile, and then felt obliged to say something as well. And he was surprised at how strangely comfortable he was with that idea.

'Hello there, *mademoiselle.* And how are you?'

'I am very well, *monsieur.*'

'Valérie Versanne is a lovely-sounding name ...'

'Thank you. And what is yours?'

Ah, thought Narone, very fast. He had not planned on holding so intimate and extended a conversation. And now he had dug himself a hole and jumped straight into it. He had better not reveal his real name, especially since he was hopefully about to part with a lot of stolen banknotes. But apart from that, he was *still* feeling very comfortable with the situation. And anyway he could already hear the others coming downstairs.

'My name is Roland.'

'And I think that is a very manly-sounding name.'

'Ha-ha-ha! Thank *you*, Valérie.'

The owner of the shop appeared in the doorway, ahead of her son. And she was dressed just as smartly.

'*Bonjour, monsieur.* I can hear you and Valérie are already well acquainted! My name is Yvette Versanne, and Giles tells me you are interested in the provenance of our beautiful agate ring ...'

'I am indeed, *madame.*'

She was already settling herself into the high chair behind the till.

'Yes, it was late November 1959, the week of the bank robbery. This little *gamine* comes bustling into the shop after dark, just as we're about to close up! She's carrying a big book under her arm, and she plonks it down on the counter and asks me if I want to buy it.'

Narone could not stop himself interrupting.

'Can you describe her more fully?'

'Not really. Nineteen or twenty. Small and slim and quite pretty. But she had not learned how to cut or dye her own hair!'

'Yes, that sounds like her! Please continue, *madame.*'

'Well, I told her at once that unfortunately we did not deal in books, and she looked very frustrated. But then I said I could probably recommend someone who would be interested, and asked if I might take a closer look. It turned out to be a large, leather-bound family bible, well over a hundred years old, with several faded inscriptions and other notes on the inside cover pages. And in very good condition for its age, I'd say.

'So I suggested she should show it to Quentin Dargon. He's the antiquarian bookseller in Rue de la Préfecture. If you live in Nice you must know his beautiful little shop.'

'Yes, I've walked past it a hundred times – including yesterday!'

'*Bien.* So you may want to visit him yourself.'

'I shall indeed. But what about the ring, *madame*?'

'Well, she was clearly very disappointed about the bible, but also quite reluctant to leave. Then she seemed to make a big decision, and stamped her little foot – she was obviously very unhappy, too – and held out her hand to show me the ring on her finger. I'd already noticed it, of course, but now she was asking me if I would take that instead. Not on deposit, mind, but as an outright purchase.

'There's little room for sentiment in my trade, *monsieur*. But when I made her an opening offer, and she agreed to it at once, I could not bring myself to buy it from her at that price. I told her I felt her lovely ring was worth considerably more, and that she should exercise greater caution when selling or pawning her precious possessions. So she asked if I was willing to increase my offer, and I suggested something I felt was very fair. We concluded the deal there and then, and the minute she had the cash in her hand she gave me only the briefest of thank-yous and hurried away with her lovely bible tucked back under her arm. And that, *monsieur*, was that.'

'You never saw her again?'

'No. But I worried for her. Was she a friend of yours?'

'Yes, she was. And now I'm trying to find her again.'

'Then I wish you well. And do have a word with Quentin. You never know ...'

'Indeed,' said Narone, taking out his wallet and pointedly removing ten of his 5000 Old Franc notes. 'So, how many of these do I need to buy the ring?'

Yvette and Giles exchanged glances and nodded to each other. They were clearly not at all uncomfortable about accepting and redistributing significant quantities of those particular bills, if the price was right.

'I regret that it is worth a good deal more than you have there, *monsieur*,' said Yvette. 'I will accept 1250 New Francs.'

'And since I trust that you are again proposing a fair price,' smiled Narone, 'I will agree to pay that without further debate.'

He handed over a total of twenty-five ill-gotten banknotes, and Emilie's desperately forsaken treasure was suddenly his.

'Thank you – all of you. And ... well, I must be going now.'

But Valérie was not willing to let him off so lightly.

'Oh, I wanted to have a proper talk with Roland, *mémé*! Can't we invite him to dinner tonight?'

Yvette laughed and apologised for her granddaughter's precociousness. 'I think not, *ma petite*. But if the gentleman would care to come back another day, when things are again quiet in the shop, I'm certain we should all enjoy hearing of any progress he has made in his search for his beloved young lady.'

'And perhaps I will, *madame*. So, *au revoir à tous!*'

It was not yet four o'clock. The sun was shining brightly again, and there was plenty of time to stroll down to the Old City and see if he could learn anything from the obviously celebrated old bookseller.

The front area of the shop itself was even smaller than he had imagined, but through the little gap in a pair of rich velvet curtains he could see a larger work-cum-storage section at the rear. The owner – who looked a lot younger than, illogically, he had expected an antiquarian to be – was busy back there with a customer, so Narone amused himself for several minutes by browsing, but never touching, the many beautiful old volumes on display in every nook and cranny of the tiny room.

But in the middle of that exploration he suddenly realised he was being watched. Two small eyes were silently observing him from one side of the gap in the curtains. Buoyed up by his merry little discourse with young Valérie only thirty minutes earlier, Narone decided to have a bit of harmless fun. He walked slowly all the way around the shop again, passed nonchalantly by the gap in the curtains, took two more short steps, then turned suddenly and loudly whispered 'Boo!' But there was no young child waiting there to be surprised after all. Two seconds later, however, he received a solid little kick in the backside, and an unrestrained "Boo to you too, blind man!" He turned to find a nine-year-old boy laughing his socks off right behind him.

'Bravo!' was all Narone could say. And he meant it. This must have been the first time he had been second-guessed by a pursuer in ... well, in a very long time.

'It was nothing,' was the immodest reply. 'It works every time. And *papa* won't be long now.' The boy lowered his voice to a whisper. 'I can always tell when he's about to lose another sale. But you look like a much better mark.'

Narone had not often felt truly out of his depth either, but this little kid was now running rings around him on every front. He was thankfully saved from any further humiliation by the histrionic, curtain-parting entrance of Quentin Dargon and the immediate and well-predicted departure of the unsatisfied customer. And now at last the bookseller was free to talk about Narone's '... long-lost old friend who may perhaps have come here, *monsieur*, to sell you a family bible back in 1959 ...'

Oh yes, he remembered that flustered young lady very well. And he had been happy to buy the bible from her on the spot. She had rejected his initial offer, of course, and had held out for a final price that was still a little on the low side but certainly not at all unfair to her.

Narone smiled to himself. Emilie always had been a quick learner.

'And I'm guessing you sold it on soon afterwards, Monsieur Dargon?'

'*Mais non!* Such delicate creatures need time and space to breathe and grow! I know the true worth of every item I purchase – give or take a little bit – so I must always be patient and wait for the right buyer to come along. That's why I need such a large stock and am always so poor! In fact, I don't think I'll ever be able to afford the luxury of dying. There will forever be so much still to be sold!'

Narone roared with laughter. He already really liked this eccentric character – *and* his impish son.

'I understand! Now, I don't suppose my friend told you where she was off to next, by any chance?'

'Oh, no. Good thing too, I'd say. She was a very pretty little lovebird. I might have shut up shop and chased straight after her!'

Narone guffawed again, but also cast an unmistakable little raise of the eyebrow in the direction of the young boy who was clearly taking in every word of their conversation.

'Oh, don't worry about Henri, old chap! His mother ran off with an insurance salesman when he was three years old. He knows I'm still hunting for the right woman! Trouble is, there's no time for that in this job!'

Narone chuckled once more, and decided to give up. He had obviously shifted accidentally into a very different universe and it was clearly time to leave, even though a part of him was actually having a hugely enjoyable time.

'Well, I hope you finally made a good profit on my friend's bible, anyway!'

'Not yet. But it *has* only been seven or eight years.'

'What? You mean you still haven't sold it?'

'I told you – I wait for the right buyer and the right price.'

'Oh! Then may I please have a good look at it?'

'But of course!'

Five minutes later, Emilie's beautiful old family bible had found its buyer at a high but mutually agreeable price, and Narone was on his way to the door with an almost empty wallet. But he suddenly stopped short and pulled out his handkerchief. 'Look, there's a big moth up on that bookcase, Monsieur Dargon! Last thing you want in here!' He reached up to swat it, then turned on his heels and gave the little scamp creeping up behind him a gentle but satisfying flick on the arm.

'Touché!'

'And bravo to you!' the boy exclaimed, with a big grin on his face. 'So, will you be back to fight another day, *mon ami*?'

'Maybe, Henri,' said Narone. 'Maybe.'

* * *

He shared the news of his triumphs with Pureza as soon as he returned to *her* bookshop. She did not conceal her delight.

'Oh, but they're both so beautiful, Arthur! Poor Emilie must have been really desperate to give them up for some quick cash!'

'Yes. Well at least it proves she did stay in Nice for a few days, and from what the pawnbroker told me I'm certain she *was* the girl who was spotted going into Rue de la Croix. But I'm not sure how much further it gets me ...'

'Well, we'll need to sleep on that, won't we? And maybe there will be a clue or two in these notes at the front of the bible. Mind you, it's going to take a while to decipher them ... some of this writing is very ornate, look, and a lot of the ink is badly faded.'

'Would you please keep the ring and the bible safe for me here?'

'Of course I will, *amigo*! Now, go and wash your hands for dinner.'

When dinner was over, Pureza moved back to the subject that had obviously been on her mind since the beginning of March.

'Arthur – do you want to tell me anything more about Thérèse?'

'No. I'm sorry, but I just can't.'

'All right. But have you ever ... oh, this is so difficult ... look, have you ever tried to somehow make amends for whatever it was you did?'

'No.'

'Are you still feeling guilty about all of that?'

'Yes, I think so.'

'And does she perhaps *deserve* some sort of apology, or whatever else might be appropriate – even after all this time?'

'I don't know. Yes, probably. But I'd really rather not talk about it.'

She sighed in exasperation. 'Very well, Arthur. But for Thérèse's sake, will you promise at least to *think* a little more about it?'

'OK, Pureza. I will do that.'

* * *

Narone woke early the following morning in a mood of deep sadness, and it took him several dozy minutes to pin down the cause.

He could not go back and visit the lovely Versanne family, even if he did one day make some headway in his search for Emilie. Apart from the fact that he'd bought the ring with stolen money, he had lied to the trusting daughter about his name and he could never face having to admit that to her, even if it were ever safe for him to do so. And he would hit the same problems of conscience if he went back to Quentin Dargon and his son.

No, he must never see any of them again. But he had been inexplicably delighted by his brief encounters with both Valérie and Henri. He'd had no idea he was capable of enjoying the company of young children in that way, and for the first time in his life he vaguely imagined some day having charming little kids of his own.

And then his thoughts turned elsewhere, in the direction Pureza had recommended the previous evening, and his sadness turned to shame once again.

He dragged himself out of bed and got ready as quickly as he could. He finished his breakfast while his ever-tolerant landlady was still in the bathroom, and called a brief goodbye up the stairs. He did not know why he was doing it, but Pureza had clearly worked some sort of black magic that he was unable to resist, and he was going in search of Thérèse.

He left the bookshop, crossed the Esplanade, and walked slowly and uncertainly down the backbone of the Old City and into Rue Barillerie. He reached the door of No. 1 and forced himself to look yet again at its tiny bronze knocker, beautifully moulded into an elegant little wrist and hand. And then, since he had nothing else to work with but spirit of place, he decided this would be as good a place as any to begin, and perhaps the bravest way to do it too. He glanced across the square towards the dilapidated old Senate building – his cold adopted home for all those years – and then, grimacing and shuddering, he reached up, lifted the slim fingers of the knocker as delicately as he could, and tapped them gently against the ancient wooden door.

It was eventually opened by an elderly lady whom he vaguely remembered seeing around here in the old days. She looked him up and down with suspicion, which seemed quickly to turn to dismay. But he had left this corner of the city when he was sixteen. Surely she did not recognise him now?

'Good morning, *madame*. I am an old acquaintance of the Vonier family, but I cannot recall which building they lived in. Can you help me?'

'An old acquaintance? Pah! Come to pay your dues, more like.'

'Please just tell me where to find them, *madame*.'

'I don't know where they are. They all moved away many years ago.'

'Oh. Well, perhaps you will remind me of their old address anyway, and then I can ask the people who are living there now.'

'You promise to behave?'

'Of course, *madame*.'

She looked him up and down again for several seconds more.

'Over there on Rue du Saint-Suaire. Third door, first floor, number eight.'

'Thank you.'

She closed the door without further ceremony.

The family at number eight knew nothing about their apartment's previous occupants. But they encouraged Narone to try the room directly opposite. The man in there, they told him, had been living in the building for years.

Narone knocked, the door was opened, and he posed his question yet again.

'Ah, yes,' said the doddery old boy, after scratching his head and working hard to recall what he could. 'Yes, it all happened quite suddenly, didn't it? Around 1960, I think it was. Madame Vonier had been sickening for many years, and then Thérèse became ill too. So neither of them could look after each other, or the little girl. And Jean-David was married by then, of course, and no longer living there, and anyhow he was away at sea most of the time ...'

'There was a young girl with them too?'

'Yes. Anyway, poor Thérèse went to stay with her sister-in-law Muriel – I think that was her name – and *Madame* ended up in the paupers' hospital. Very sad.'

'And after that?'

'No idea.'

'Do you have Muriel's address?'

'No. But we've probably only had two different postmen in the past ten years. One of them just might remember where they forwarded J-D's mail.'

'When did he move out of this building?'

'Pah! Let's see ... It must have been in '56, or maybe '57 ...'
'OK. *Et merci bien, monsieur.*'
'Et bonne chance à vous!'

Narone's earlier resolve was already diminishing, but he made the effort to keep on with his mission and found the postman an hour later in Rue Saint-Gaétan. No, said the young guy, he had *not* been doing this particular round in 1956! But there were records, of course. For a small private consideration, he would check them later this afternoon back at the Post Office.

They met up again the following morning, and Narone came away, in considerable private discomfort, with the address he had been seeking.

Jean-David Vonier. Hmmm. He was not looking forward to encountering *him* again. And there was no real rush to find *any* of them, was there? But perhaps, if he was lucky, the sailor might still be away at sea ...

He would sleep on this too, over the coming weekend. And maybe for a lot longer.

* * *

It was May Day morning. Time to take Luc's next call and try and goad him still harder.

'I hope you've got somewhere at last, Arthur ...'

'Yes, I have! I identified the renovation company that's been buying up the Fiat spares ...'

'The one in Imperia?'

'No. That turned out to be bad information, so I had to spend a lot longer in Italy than I'd intended. But I did eventually discover the outfit we're actually after. It's a completely different business.'

'Where are they?'

'Further to the east, in ... oh, hang on, Luc – you've always said you never wanted to know where the cash was hidden.'

'I don't care what I said nearly a year ago! Tell me where they're based!'

'Look, I really don't think I should. You'd probably regret asking me as soon as I did. You know you don't want to be tempted to go after it yourself, or to run the risk of singing about to anyone if you're ever ... well, pressurised, right?'

'Are you trying to tell me what I want?'

'Yes, because I'm trying to protect you.'

'Look, do you actually *know* exactly where the money is, right now?'

'Oh, no. I only said I'd definitely identified the operation that's been buying up spare parts. But there's every chance they did acquire those particular boxes and now have them stored somewhere in their big building. I did quite a bit of careful asking and snooping around last week, but I haven't managed to confirm it for you yet. And now I've had to come all the way back here just to receive this call!'

'So what are you proposing to do next?'

'I'm going straight back to Italy to find your money, of course! Isn't that exactly what you want me to do?'

'Yeah. OK, I'll call you again on the first of June, at the following phone box ...'

* * *

Narone had absolutely no plans to return to Italy, of course, to waste his time pretending to hunt for the cash that was still cunningly stored in those boxes of old books under Pureza's stairs. And he had effectively given up trying to track down either Luc or Xérus directly himself, for now at least, while he was pursuing his latest little leads on Emilie and finally beginning his reluctant search for the other girl from his past.

So with nothing much else he could usefully be doing on most of those fronts, he went back to working almost full-time in the bookshop, and the days of May drifted by without incident while he considered whether or not to continue looking for poor Thérèse.

And his expenses had been remarkably high since he had reclaimed the first of the four stolen wads stored in the anonymous rucksack that he had been carefully moving around the region's many left-luggage offices. Every note in *that* bundle was now gone. So he soon took time out to retrieve his weary traveller's belongings from their latest temporary resting place, extracted another lot of one hundred 5000 Old Franc bills, and re-deposited the rucksack, now reduced to safeguarding just two remaining wads, at the left-luggage office of Nice Bus Station.

* * *

On the fifteenth of May, Narone called Inspector Hardy from his room at Pureza's.

'Still nothing new for you, I'm afraid.'

'I'm getting very impatient now, Arthur!'

'I'm not at all surprised. Have you considered therapy? I have, repeatedly, but I simply can't afford it ...'

'Just tell me what you're doing, man!'

'All I can. Which amounts to nothing very much. But right now I'm following the Micawber school of thought ...'

'Pray enlighten me.'

'Something is sure to turn up. So, I'll call you on the fifth of June, unless that "something" happens before then. *Ciao!*'

Narone went downstairs to begin another unremarkable week's work in the bookshop.

* * *

He had promised to signal Xérus one day in May, to initiate their next checkpoint call. And since he obviously had very little to report, he decided to get it out of the way sooner rather than later.

So the following Friday he took a long morning coffee break and returned with a new bunch of flowers for his boss. 'Lovely red roses, this time, *chica*!' She shook her uncomprehending head. So he arranged them in a vase himself, and placed them prominently in the front window.

He went to the pre-agreed telephone box at nine that evening.

'Hello, X.'

'Have you found the man who was spending big old money in Sanremo?'

'No. False alarm, I'm afraid. But then they always are, aren't they? I need something more from you about Paul Ruford, for heaven's sake! Something much better than the stuff you sent me off to Marseilles with ...'

'Too bad. Anything else would be far too risky.'

'For whom?'

'I've told you before. Both of us. All of you. So just keep on it, Narone. I'll call again on the last day of June. Here's the location ...'

Irresistible Objects

Early on the evening of the twenty-fifth of May, after four weeks of deliberation and vacillation, Narone finally decided he must take the plunge and visit the home of Jean-David Vonier and his wife. But if someone had grabbed his arm at that moment and asked him to state clearly the reasons for his decision, he would not have known what to say.

He found their unassuming apartment block at the eastern end of Rue Barberis, not very far from where he had been living and working at the time of the bank robbery. And the door was answered at once by a rather tired-looking woman of about his own age.

'You are Madame Muriel Vonier?'

'Mais oui, monsieur.'

'*Bonsoir, madame.* My name is Arthur Narone ...'

He paused, looking closely for any change in the woman's countenance and noticing none. Maybe she had never known his name, or had long forgotten it. So far, so good.

'Oui, monsieur ...?'

'Well, when I was a young boy I lived quite near to Jean-David and his sister Thérèse, and I recently decided it might be nice to make contact again. And I have managed to discover your present address after talking to the people still living on Rue du Saint-Suaire ...'

'Oh! Well, how very nice to meet you, Arthur! Have you travelled far?'

Before Narone could reply, another door opened and a pretty, dark-haired teenager wearing a white T-shirt, blue jeans and bright red socks appeared behind Muriel. His jaw dropped in shock.

'Thérèse!! But – no, it can't be ...'

Muriel touched his arm sympathetically.

'No, not Thérèse, of course. This is her daughter, Julia Rochemont. But please do not worry. Many people have reacted as you have, over the years!'

'I am not surprised, *madame*. The resemblance is remarkable! *Bonsoir, Mademoiselle Rochemont.*'

'*Enchantée, monsieur ...*' the young woman replied in a velvet-smooth voice, clearly at a disadvantage but looking rather intrigued by their visitor.

Her aunt had spotted this too. 'Julia, this is Arthur. He is an old friend of Jean-David ...'

'Ah, I see.' She was smiling warmly now, and Narone sensed it was in more than just understanding.

'But I am forgetting all my manners!' exclaimed Muriel. 'Please come in, Monsieur Narone ... Arthur.'

He followed her into the living room and she sat down on the sofa, encouraging him to join her. Julia said nothing more, but padded slowly across the room and leant up against a bookcase with the two of them directly in front of her.

Narone decided to bite the bullet without further ado.

'Is Jean-David here, *madame*?'

'Hah! No, he's been in the Navy ever since we met, and he's away on yet another long tour of duty.'

Narone's nervous tension evaporated at a stroke. 'Ah. So when are you expecting him to return?'

'Your guess is as good as mine, Arthur. We don't have any children of our own, and I think he's always resented Julia living here with us ...'

Narone glanced across at the girl, and she lowered her eyes. He could not tell if the gesture was some sort of apology or a simple confirmation of what Muriel was saying.

'... and his service commitment will be ending soon, but I won't be at all surprised if he chooses to extend it forever, or just jumps ship in some faraway port once he gets his discharge, and never comes back.'

'Oh, I am sorry, *madame*. I don't know what to say ...'

'Do not worry, Arthur. *C'est la vie.* And you are so polite, but *please* do call me Muriel.'

'Very well,' he smiled. He was relaxing properly at last, and there was still a lot more he wanted to ask this kindly woman, especially about Thérèse. But his eyes were being drawn across to Julia's, and he now realised she was looking straight into *his*. And despite the heat of that intense spotlight, conversation came surprisingly easily and naturally.

'You have some fine books there, *mademoiselle*.'

'Oh, you must call me Julia, please! And yes, I am very fortunate. I adore reading. And writing ...'

'Me too.'

'Which?'

'Both. I've read a lot of wonderful books over the years, and I've had a couple of little stories published in magazines ...'

'You're an author? A real author?'

'Oh, I think that's a gross exaggeration! But I'm trying to become one.'

'Wow! What are you working on at the moment?'

'Ah. Well, let's just say I'm in the middle of a big research project. For a novel, or something of the sort ...'

'So is your visit here a part of that?'

'In a way. But then everything we do, or experience, or feel gives us material for our work, doesn't it?'

'Yes, of course. That's just what I have always felt myself. Oh, this is so exciting! We have a real writer in our home, *tantine*! Arthur the Author!'

Narone laughed out loud. 'And you're already a poetess! Julia the Eulogist!'

It was Muriel's turn to chuckle now, and Narone sensed she was very pleased at how well he and her niece already seemed to be getting on. But it was surely time to move back to his reason for being there in the first place.

'And where is Thérèse?'

It was Muriel's turn to be surprised. 'But you do not know?'

'No. The man in their old apartment block just told me she had come to live here with you when she and her mother became unwell ...'

'Ah. Well, Arthur, I'm afraid to say Thérèse died quite soon after that ...'

'Oh, I'm so sorry! But when was this?'

'In September 1962. Poor Julia was only eleven at the time ...'

Narone looked across at his new friend and saw long-established resignation in her sad little nod and her puckered-up lips.

'How awful for you, Julia. What happened?'

She shrugged her shoulders. 'It was cancer, Arthur. Nothing they could do. And she was only twenty-eight! But I've come to terms with it now, I think. It's been nearly five years, and I have a life to live ...'

'You sound very brave. And your father ...?'

Julia fell silent again, and Muriel came to her rescue.

'Denis and Thérèse were married in January 1950, and he came to live at her place. Julia was born that December. Denis put up with being a husband and a father for another twelve months, and then he just walked out. Thérèse and baby Julia stayed there with her mother and brother, of course. And I met Jean-David a few years later. We got married in '57 and came to live here. It took *him* a little longer to get bored with the idea of family life ...'

Narone the writer was fast running out of words to express his increasing sympathy towards them both. So he looked sadly back at Julia and steered a little to one side.

'And you've lived with Muriel ever since you first came here?'

'Of course. My grandmother had to abandon the apartment when she went into hospital. And anyway she died only a few months after I lost my mother.'

So he had in fact steered directly into another family tragedy. He gave up trying to outwit himself.

'I just don't know what to say.'

'Well, Arthur, we're both feeling very sorry for you too,' said Muriel. 'You've come all this way to find your long-lost friends, and all we've given you is lots of bad news.'

On hearing Thérèse and Jean-David described in those terms, Narone bit his tongue and reddened and broke into a sweat. But he said nothing.

Julia noticed his discomfort and added her own thoughts. 'And we *all* have lives to be getting on with, don't we, Arthur? So let us move forward now!'

He smiled wryly. 'You are a very positive thinker, Julia. And I shall happily take your advice.'

Muriel spotted her moment and stood up. 'I think it's time to make us all some coffee.'

Narone jumped to his own feet at once. 'Thank you, Muriel. That would be really nice. But please let me come and help ...'

'No, no, no,' she insisted. 'You must stay here and keep Julia company. I shan't be long ...'

He walked over to stand beside the still-smiling girl, and for the next ten minutes they looked together at many of the books on the shelves, sharing their thoughts on those they had both read, and giving their personal recommendations – and often otherwise – on several of the others.

Then Julia told him she had actually devoured every book in the place, good and bad, and many of them twice or more. And she was still at school, of course, so she couldn't buy any for herself. She went to the libraries whenever she had time, but right now she was far too busy revising for her major summer examinations to do that ...

Even before Muriel had come back in with the coffee, Narone had suggested to her niece that they should meet up at his friend Pureza's bookshop after school the following afternoon, and he would do his best to arrange the loan, over the days and weeks to come, of many other great works of literature.

Her eyes gleamed with joy. And when she told Muriel about Arthur's kind offer, her devoted aunt was clearly delighted too.

* * *

Narone broke the news to his landlady and employer over dinner that evening.

'I've finally done it, Pureza.'

'Done what?'

'Been to look for Thérèse.'

'Ah, that's very brave of you, Arthur. And ...?'

'And I've discovered she died almost five years ago.'

'Oh, how awful. She can only have been ... what, still in her twenties?'

'Yes.'

'So do you want to tell me anything more, *enfin*?'

'Not about *her*, no. But I met her daughter Julia today! She's living with her aunt these days ...'

'Poor child. She must still be quite young!'

'Actually, she's in her teens. And she looks just like her mother did! She's really cute.'

'Well, I'm very pleased you made the effort to do whatever you felt was needed, even though you were not able to apologise to Thérèse in the end.'

'Yes, I'm glad I tried, too. And now I'd like to ask another little favour.'

'Go ahead ....'

'Julia is very keen on reading. So may she come and borrow a second-hand book or two from the shop occasionally? I think allowing her to do that might go some way towards ... well, towards making the reparations I have not been able to make with Thérèse.'

'That sounds like a very noble idea, Arthur. Yes, of course she may!'

'Wonderful. She'll be here straight after school tomorrow afternoon.'

'Oh!'

'What?'

'Oh, nothing, Arthur,' Pureza sighed. 'Nothing at all. Now, while we're on the subject of literature, do you remember I said there was another writers' convention coming up soon?'

'Yes, of course.'

'Well, it will be taking place at the Negresco Hotel in the middle of June. I've just seen the advance list of delegates and guest speakers, and since your visit to Sergio clearly paid off, I thought you might like to try for some more ideas. I'm quite well acquainted with two or three of the novelists who will be attending. Maybe you could kill *several* birds with one stone this time?'

Narone was not convinced his search for Emilie's ring had actually done any more than cost him a whole lot of money – although it was admittedly somebody else's money. Maybe something would eventually come of his finding the bible, though. In fact, he probably should have made the effort to study those notes at the front of it, just in case. But Emilie really was not at the forefront of his mind right now.

'Well, I suppose there's no harm in trying. You never know.'

'Precisely, Arthur. You never know. So ...?

'OK. Yes, please try to arrange meetings for me with as many authors as you can.'

'And ...?'

'And ... thank you continuing to care, Pureza.'

She smiled wryly and went to make the coffee.

Julia Rochemont, sixteen coming on seventeen, walked into the bookshop the following afternoon looking more like an off-duty fashion model than a schoolgirl bookworm, and Pureza seemed completely taken by surprise when Narone jumped up to make the introductions.

'Oh, I *am* sorry, my dear,' she smiled politely – and a little strangely, he thought – 'but I didn't realise it was you. I was expecting someone a lot younger ...'

* * *

Arthur Narone and his latest girlfriend then spent that Friday evening and the whole of the weekend getting to know each other better. He would have been perfectly content to just lie on the beach the entire time, chatting about nothing in particular and admiring Julia's lovely face and everything that went with it. She, on the other hand, although quite happy to spend a couple of hours doing exactly that on both of the sunny afternoons, also insisted on lots of strolling round the town, and plenty of window shopping – 'Even though I can't even think about buying any of it!' – and the occasional stop for a tiny cup of coffee or a glass of water. Arthur went along with all of that, of course. Girls obviously enjoyed torturing themselves, and he was not going to rock this particular boat in any way.

He treated Julia to dinner in a New Town restaurant on the Sunday evening, and once they had placed their order she became quite serious, for the first time since they had met.

'Will you tell me a bit about your childhood days with my mother and her brother, Arthur?'

'Oh, there's not very much to tell. I only really met them once or twice. We were living near each other but in quite different worlds ...'

'But you specifically came hunting for Jean-David this week!'

'Well, I wanted to start making some new friends again, and so I thought I could try following up some old ones, even if I'd hardly known them.'

'That sounds a bit strange ...'

'Hmmm. Well, I did say I was in the middle of a writing project. Maybe I'll tell you more as my ideas get clearer.'

'OK, then. But I really would like to get to know absolutely everything about you, Arthur Narone ...'

'I'm not sure you really would, Julia!'

'Oh, I'm already quite certain of it, *chéri*!'

And she leant across and kissed him for the very first time.

* * *

The next morning, Arthur secured Pureza's rather grumpy agreement to his only working half-time at the bookshop until further notice. He would now be starting at ten o'clock each day, he told her, and taking a long early lunch break to meet Julia outside her nearby school, and then clocking off soon after three when she arrived to pick him up. They would be spending the rest of every day on the beach or in a coffee bar or whatever, so there would be no need for Pureza to prepare any more evening meals for him, thank you.

On their first evening together that week, Julia finally went back to her apartment at seven o'clock to get on with some revision for her upcoming examinations. On the second evening she delayed her departure until eight. And on the Wednesday she declared to Arthur that she was utterly fed up with revision, would not be bothering to do any more, and would be staying out with him until very late that evening.

Privately, Arthur felt that this was not necessarily in her best interests at all, but he was happy to go with the flow and enjoy her delightful company for as many hours a day as she could supply it. He was also well aware that the quality, as well as the quantity, of his own contributions at the bookshop had also sharply declined. But this was still May, after all – though only just – and in May you do as you please.

* * *

The following lunchtime Arthur left the bookshop even earlier than usual. Before he could make his rendezvous with Julia, he must take another start-of-the-month call from Luc. And he would need to stall him yet again. *Something's Gotta Give.*

'It's me.'

'Have you got the money now?

'No. I went back to ... well, somewhere in Italy – I know you don't want to know where – and I discovered that the company buying up the spare parts was actually *another* wholesale distributor. And then I found they *had* actually sold the boxes we're after to that repair operation in Imperia, after all – apparently only a few weeks ago! So I've been back there for a while. But it's even harder to keep sticking my nose in now, of course. I'm still on the case ...'

'This is getting ridiculous!'

'I kind of agree, Luc. But am I trying, or am I trying? I'll ask you again – do you want me to give up? Or do you want to come and help me? Well?'

'You know exactly what I want. But I'm not convinced the money really is in those boxes ...'

'Nor am I. We just have to *hope* it still is!'

'Stop hoping and just get in there and collect it, Arthur. Your five-wad bonus offer runs out at the end of this month, remember. And I've a good mind to phone the *flics* anonymously and suggest you're hiding the cash at that bookshop of yours. They'll give the place a full going-over, and that nice lady owner won't want to be your best friend for very much longer ...'

'Please don't do that, Luc. And I'll do all I can for you. Next contact on the first of July?'

'Yeah. Here's the call box you should use ...'

This was serious. With Luc heartlessly threatening to tip off the police – at any time – about the one place in the world the money actually *was* stored, Arthur needed to act fast. And quite separately, he really did wish he had somewhere more private to go with Julia in the evenings ... and maybe even the nights.

There was no doubt about it. He needed to move home yet again, and fast. There would be no time to meet up with Julia for their lunchtime walk today. She would worry a bit, maybe even a lot, but he would soon be able to explain.

So over the next two hours he checked out several property agencies, found a vacant place in Rue Edouard Beri – with double bed – that would do very nicely, and paid a month's rent in advance. And he was back at the bookshop well before three, explaining to Pureza that he would be discreetly moving out during the night, and would need to be away from work on the Friday and the Monday. But he would be back in on the Tuesday, although still part-time of course, and taking other time off whenever he needed to. As long as that was all right with her ...

She shrugged her shoulders, now completely resigned to the man's unpredictability.

Julia walked through the door a few minutes later, only mildly concerned that Arthur had missed their regular lunchtime date. He put a finger to his lips, mumbled their goodbyes to Pureza, and hurried Julia along to the nearest coffee bar to tell her the news of his imminent move. She was over the moon, and they stayed out for a celebration dinner on the town.

Later that evening Arthur packed his large suitcase once again. And while Pureza was otherwise occupied in the bathroom, he hurriedly extracted all seventy wads of stolen banknotes from the boxes of books still gathering dust under the stairs, stashed them at the bottom of the case, and sat on it until it could be closed.

The next morning he left the bookshop at four and walked in the darkness to a remote early-opening café for a long drawn-out breakfast, absolutely certain that nobody had been watching him leave or following him there. Later he moved on, to wait innocently at the Bus Station for another couple of hours. But once the shops were open he went into the town centre and purchased a small, high-quality travel case with very good locks. Now he was finally ready to move into his new apartment. And as soon as the door was closed behind him, he transferred the entire cache of hot money to his new makeshift strongbox and stored it under a spare blanket at the bottom of the wardrobe.

He met up with Julia again straight after school, and they went off to toast the future over some extravagant drinks in a nearby bar. But they fairly soon decided they would much prefer to continue their latest celebrations with a very private viewing of Arthur's exciting new home.

* * *

They spent the next day on the beach, aggressively sunbathing and vigorously swimming, happily chatting and kissing and cuddling and looking forward to being alone together again back in the apartment, and thinking about everything and nothing.

Arthur was thinking over and over again about how lovely Julia looked, and how closely she resembled her mother. And about her wonderful interest in literature, and how she seemed – ridiculously, unbelievably – to have transferred that interest to him! And about how incredibly fresh and straightforward she seemed, in everything she said and did! Unhampered by the past. Modern and forward-looking. Respectful of his experience and skills, of course, but at the same time somehow treating him as her equal, despite the big difference in their ages.

And suddenly it occurred to him to wonder what Julia might be thinking about him. So without ceremony he turned to her and asked exactly that.

'Me? Oh, those are girls' secrets, Arthur! We never tell a boy how polite he has always been, or how wonderful his first, long anticipated kiss was, or how much we'd love to be asked one day to go dancing! And I shall never mention how intrigued I am about my own still-so-mysterious man! My *writer*, no less! Or how we might sit and read together in the days to come, and how much I might be able to learn from him, and how he might help me with my writing ambitions. Or about the walks we might one day take, or the music we might listen to, or the beds we might test together.

'And of course I'll never say a word to him about his eyes. His beautiful bright grey eyes!'

On their way back to the apartment, Julia casually mentioned that she had told Muriel she might well be staying at Arthur's place overnight. And if it was all right with him, she would really like to cook something for them that evening, rather than go out for a meal.

So they stopped off to buy a few simple provisions, and the paella she placed on the table two hours later was beautifully presented and very tasty indeed.

After dinner they relaxed together on the sofa, and Arthur was almost ready for a little nap. But that was not what Julia had in mind.

'So, you know nearly all there is to know about me already, *chéri*,' she murmured. 'And I did tell you last weekend I wanted to know everything about *you*. Well, here's your opportunity to enlighten me. Why not start at the very beginning ...?'

This was an uncomfortably familiar situation, but Julia really was asking so nicely, and after consuming the lovely dinner she had made, Arthur was clearly at a disadvantage. So he shook himself from his post-prandial languor, and related once again the sorry story of his childhood that he had told Pureza almost a whole year earlier.

But when he reached the episode he had started to describe to her in March, he stopped short, as before, very uncertain whether to continue.

'Do go on, Arthur,' said Julia, tenderly stroking his hair. 'It's been really absorbing so far, and I've been feeling so sorry for you, but I didn't want to interrupt. Carry on, please ...'

Arthur sighed deeply. He had been dreading this moment for over a week.

'All right, then. One summer – I was only nine at the time – well, there was this girl. She must have been at least four years older than me. I used to watch her through the window when she was hanging around in the street with the older boys. And I became really jealous of them. And maybe I decided, without realising it, to get my own back one day ...'

'But what had any of those boys ever done to you, Arthur?'

'Not a thing. And *she* had done nothing worse than ignore me. Well, she did once make a horrible face across at me for my impertinent interest in her! But that was all. I suppose I just felt ... well, frustrated. Maybe I was a very early developer, or whatever!'

'Hah!'

'And then, on Bastille Day in 1948 ...'

'Bastille Day??'

'Yes ... well, that evening they let all the kids out of the orphanage to enjoy the celebrations, with the strict instructions that we must not move beyond the little square outside. And it was amazing! So different from usual! I was so happy to be out there among all the other ordinary people, running around and laughing at the drunks and watching all the comings and goings ...

'And then, suddenly, there she was again! Flirting with the older boys on the corner – again. And something inside me cracked ...'

Julia sat bolt upright.

'Were there fireworks in the street that night, Arthur?'

'Yes, there were. And I think you've worked it out now, haven't you? Someone must have tossed a large banger out of the crowd, and it landed at my feet. Don't ask me why, but I picked it up and walked towards the girl, and waved, and shouted 'Catch!!' Of course, it could have gone off in my own hand at any moment. But I tossed it gently over, as if it were a harmless tennis ball or a precious jewel, and she instinctively stuck out both hands and caught it. And *then* it went off!'

Julia was already shaking her head and weeping. 'That's exactly how my mother said it had happened, Arthur ...'

'Yes. It was Thérèse, of course. I didn't even learn her name until much later. But I'll never forget her screams at that moment, or the sight of her left hand with two fingers completely blown away ...'

He suddenly drew in a huge gulp of air and then burst into violent sobs which went on unabated for two long minutes. All Julia could do was to take his quavering head in her hands, hold it to her breast and stare into space as she tried to glimpse, through the mist of her own tears, just what her true reaction to this stunning news would turn out to be.

Eventually Arthur began to calm down, and he was soon breathing almost normally. She wiped the tears from his eyes and let him be, and finally he was ready to talk again.

'What happened to Thérèse after that, Julia? I never saw her again, and no-one ever told me ...'

Julia sighed, brushing away her own sad tears.

'Well, she said they took her off to hospital, of course, and although she'd lost those fingers there were no further complications, thank God. But what about you?'

'Only a couple of the lads had actually seen what had happened. But I took a good beating from all of them before the police rescued me. And because there was no real evidence against me, and I was only nine, they just dumped me back in the orphanage. The people there gave me a really hard time for months on end, of course. And years later, when they finally started allowing me out on my own once I was in my teens, I took another good backstreet beating from Jean-David himself.'

'You poor thing!'

'Me? Me?? I deserved everything I got! But poor Thérèse! To think I could ever have done something like that to someone so beautiful! To your own mother, Julia! Can you ever forgive me?'

'There is nothing to forgive, *chéri*. It was the stupid, reckless act of a little boy who had received very little love or moral guidance in his life. And you have paid for what you did many times over, in different ways, especially with the guilt that has been haunting you ever since ...'

'How did you know?'

'It's obvious, Arthur. Do you want to tell me more about it?'

'Well, ever since that day I've regularly seen "visions" of Thérèse's hand and fingers – in cloud formations and palm trees, and on door-knockers and ... oh, everywhere. It's been awful. But that's nothing compared to what she must have gone through ...'

'You poor boy! Listen, I *really* respect you for being brave enough to tell me all about it today. Me, of all people! That must have been very hard for you ...'

'Oh, you are so understanding, Julia ...'

'Maybe. Or maybe I just want to give you all the love you've been missing for so long.'

She gave him a huge and tender hug.

'And now it's my turn to tell *you* something very special. Because it's actually not a question of forgiving you, *chéri*. Almost the opposite, in fact ...'

'What??'

'My mother told me that "accident" got her a lot of sympathy but a lot less amorous interest from the boys. In fact, over the following year only one lad – it was Denis Rochemont – seemed able to completely ignore her disfigured hand, and she fell in love with him for that reason above all. They dated for a few months and married in January 1950, a few weeks after her sixteenth birthday. And I was born in December of the same year. So you see, Arthur, I reckon I owe my very existence to you and that awful childish prank.'

It was Arthur Narone's turn to weep now, in bitter-sweet joy at Julia's exquisite humanity.

They held each other tight and slept fully clothed on the sofa that night.

After waking stiff and unrefreshed on a dull Sunday morning, they decided to stay inside and take things very easy for the rest of the day. And there was still a lot more that Julia wanted to know.

'You said you were a car mechanic for a while, Arthur. Did you come to work at Pureza's shop straight after that?'

So over the next couple of hours, with Julia's continued gentle persuasion, Arthur steadily told her about the rest of his life. About Emilie, and the robbery, and the money, and his capture. A little about his life in prison. And almost everything that had happened since his release, including the secret of the stolen cash he had finally recovered and stored in a safe new hiding place.

The only thing of significance that he failed to mention was that the money was *now* languishing only a few metres away at the bottom of his bedroom wardrobe.

'So I guess that's that, as far as you and I are concerned, Julia ...'

'Were you going to tell me eventually?'

'I expect so. It *has* only been ten days, hasn't it? And it's not exactly something you blurt out on your first date, is it?'

'No, it isn't. And you must have been agonising over it since the day we met ...'

'On and off. Mostly on.'

'So, I accept it. It's you, isn't it? ... and I love you, Arthur. I just hope it will all be sorted out very soon.'

'That's amazing, Julia. Thank you. It will be good to have someone to share things with at last. But you'll need to let me play it my way ... and I really can't say how quickly it *will* be over. OK?'

'OK. And maybe I'll start looking for ways to spend even more time with you. 'Cos this weekend didn't go quite the way I had hoped ...'

* * *

Nine o'clock on the fifth of June had come along very fast.

'Hello, Arthur. So, has your little "something" turned up yet?'

'No, Simon. But it still might. On the other hand, of course, we may just have to wait for Luc and your mastermind to reveal themselves – either intentionally or through sheer carelessness. Time is running out, as I'm sure I don't need to remind you.'

'Have you been reading books on military strategy now?'

'No. Just more good works of fiction. Life's a pack of lies, after all.'

'Who said that?'

'I did. Surely you recognise my voice after all this time? And anyway this phone box isn't big enough for ...'

'What's making you so bloody cheerful today?'

'I think I'm in love, Simon! So, I'll call you again on the twenty-sixth. Unless, of course, something ...'

'Don't say it, Arthur. Just don't say it.'

A different something was bugging Arthur as he wandered back to his latest new home. But he could not put a finger on it for several minutes. And then it came to him. It was what he had jokingly just said to Hardy: 'Surely you recognise my voice after all this time?' But why was that particular question nagging at him? Why??

He had not come up with an answer by the time he unlocked his door and went back to bed.

* * *

For the next two weeks, Arthur continued to work part-time in the shop, and meet Julia outside school for lunch, and disappear off with her in the late afternoon, and spend long happy evenings with her in his new apartment. He had quickly spotted the existence of this newly established pattern, of course, but this time he was delighted about it. And the young lady was still doing no revision for her imminent exams, but he had long ago stopped thinking about that.

On the evening of Friday the sixteenth of June, Julia told him she had something very important to do the following morning – and that it was a secret for now. But when they met up in an Old City bar for lunch the next day, she spilled the beans.

'I've made a big decision, Arthur.'

'You're going to buy green socks rather than blue ones next?'

'No, stupid. I'm leaving home. And I told Muriel I would be meeting a man from the motor trade. But she didn't get it at first!'

'Neither do I.'

'Then you need to listen to The Beatles' latest album. It was only released this month, but it's all over Radio Luxembourg already, and it's the greatest pop music there ever has been! We've just bought our own copy. I'll bring it with me when I move in tomorrow.'

'You'll need to bring your record player too.'

'Yes. Muriel's not very happy about that. But I'll buy us one of our own soon.'

'Using what for money, exactly?'

'That's what I've been busy sorting out this morning! I've just got myself a little daytime job as a waitress ...'

'Starting once the school year has finished?'

'No. I'm dropping out right now, and I start work on Monday.'

'You know, I'm really not sure if that will the best thing for you in the long term, Julia ...'

'I don't care about the long term, Arthur. Life's too short, and this is the Summer of Love, in case you hadn't noticed. I only want to be with you.'

'But I'll be busy at the bookshop a lot of the time. And waitresses' hours are often quite long, aren't they?'

'Well, yes. And it's actually a six-day-week job. But I don't care about that either. Each afternoon once my shift is over, and every Sunday, we'll both be completely free to do as we please. To catch up on what we missed in May!!'

'OK, I give in! And I truly *am* delighted you want to come and live with me! But there *is* just one other little thing ...'

'What's that?'

'The stolen money is actually in my new apartment now.'

'What? You told me it was hidden somewhere really safe!'

'And so it is! Nobody knows I'm living there.'

'Until someone discovers you are ...'

'True. But no-one ever raided Pureza's shop, and everybody knew I was living there for months on end. So why should they suddenly decide to look for the money in my new place? No, I reckon it's just

as safe as it could be right now. Nobody would ever believe I could
be so stupid as to keep it there!'

'You sound like some of the poker-playing kids at school ...'

'Precisely, Julia. But now you're going to have to decide whether
you can handle this particular *ménage-à-trois* ...'

'Oh, I can handle it, Clyde.'

'What does that mean?'

'You need to do some other sorts of reading, *chéri*. Particularly on
twentieth century American criminal history, and on Hollywood
movies planned for release in the coming weeks. But just don't start
calling me "Bonnie" in public, right?'

'I'll get back to you when I've worked all that out, Julia.'

'OK. You go straight off to the reference library, and I'll go home
and start packing. My taxi will arrive at ten in the morning, and I
shall expect the answer at once! Well, maybe not *quite* at once ...'

Summer of Love

The following Tuesday, Arthur discovered for the first time the sumptuous splendour of the interior of the Negresco Hotel. And as he waited humbly for Claude Marasin to meet him in reception, he marvelled at the glory of the circular, columned Salon Royal blossoming before his eyes, and he wondered how long the entire haul from the bank robbery would last anybody in such a land of luxury.

The celebrated French author made his promised appearance and conducted his guest to the red-curtained bar for coffee.

'*Et alors?*'

'Well, I'm busy writing a novel, Monsieur Marasin. And I've reached the part where the hero needs to try and smoke a criminal out of his hole, but he has no firm idea where that hole is, even though the two of them are talking regularly on the phone using public call boxes. And, well, I've run out of ideas ...'

'Are the police involved?'

'Only on the side.'

'They're not trying to trace the calls, then?'

'No. Well, probably not ... or not yet, at least ...'

'But presumably your criminal phones from a different box each time, anyway?'

'Apparently. Often from different cities, it seems.'

'So by the time any call was traced, he'd be long gone from that spot ...'

'Precisely.'

'So, the resolution is obvious, is it not?'

'Not to me, *monsieur*.'

'Your hero must establish the location of the criminal's hidey-hole by other means.'

'Well, exactly. That's where I began just now. But how?'

'By alchemy, of course!'

'By alchemy? This is not a fantasy novel!'

'I am not speaking literally, young man. But your hero must take every piece of base material available to him, and work with it over and over again until he comes up with the nugget of gold he is seeking. Even if that should entail calling upon the explicit services of the devil himself.'

'You mean bringing the police fully into it?'

'Exactly.'

'And if that is undesirable?'

'Then pure magic probably *is* required.'

'I see. OK, I shall take it from there. Thank you. And ...'

'There is another little problem?'

'Well, yes.'

And although Arthur's interest in rediscovering Emilie had now dropped to an all-time low, it would make Pureza happy to hear he had made the effort. So he explained a little about his old friend's disappearance and his attempts to establish what had become of her.

'So – how might you have handled *that* sort of challenge in your own work, sir?'

'I do not know. I have never considered the topic. But I have recently read John Fowles' little novel *The Collector*. It was published in England in 1963, but a French version under the title *L'Obsédé* came out a few months later. I recommend the translation, even if your English is good, because Fowles' own style of writing in that particular work is very effective but rather unconventional.'

'Hmmm. I have actually heard of it. Didn't they also make it into a movie?'

'Yes, and it was quite successful at the Cannes Film Festival two years ago. Anyway, the novel has a very interesting structure – two separate accounts of the same awful events – but more importantly, the subject matter seems quite pertinent ...'

'What is it about?'

'A kidnapping ... and the aftermath.'

'Oh ...'

'But whether or not that was what happened to your friend – and I pray that it was not – the story gives some fascinating insights into the mentality of a kidnapper, and shows how hard it can be for anyone to locate him and his victim.'

'Which also suggests it may not give me much inspiration for my own search ...'

'But you never know. My advice is worth little more than what you have paid for it. The application of alchemy is again required!'

'Indeed. Very well, I shall buy a copy of *L'Obsédé* at once, and glean whatever I can from it. My thanks, again, *monsieur*.'

'*De rien.*'

Arthur spent the rest of the day reading Fowles' novel from cover to cover. It left him shocked and very disconcerted, and he tucked it away in his bedside drawer and said nothing about it to Julia when she came in exhausted from her second hard day's waitressing.

* * *

The next morning he went over to a somewhat lower class hotel on Boulevard Victor Hugo for his meeting with Pureza's Spanish novelist friend. Arriving with time to spare, he bumped into a junior porter polishing the brass rail of the front steps, and they began to chat. It turned out the young man's name was Alain Revaur, and he was a high-school student who had just finished his final exams and started a summer vacation job.

But within two minutes the head porter came blustering out, ordering Revaur to get on with his work and scowling disrespectfully at Arthur, who hurried inside for his nine-thirty appointment.

Oliver de Blanes emerged from the elevator five minutes late and still unshaven. But as they sat down on the chairs of the front lobby he was pleasant enough, passing fine compliments on their mutual friend and congratulating Arthur on his early publishing success.

But Blanes could come up with no good ideas about how to continue the hunt for the unnamed man whose profile and actions, as described briefly by Arthur, bore many similarities to those of Luc Comet, alias Paul Ruford.

'OK,' said Arthur, politely hiding his frustration. 'I realise how tricky it must be to try and jump straight into a "plot" like this, especially so early in the morning!'

'One always has one's own plots at the forefront of one's mind, no? It can be a rather unsociable existence ...'

'Oh, I agree. Luckily I was in a rather unsociable situation when I wrote my first little stories! Anyway, may we please try just one other plot line – about a very different character?'

'Why not? You never know ...'

So Arthur bit the bullet, mentioned Emilie by her first name only, talked about her apparent flight from Nice, and then asked 'How would *you* have then made such a character act, in that particular situation?'

Blanes seemed more inspired by this latest little challenge, and pondered for quite some time.

'Hmmm,' he said finally. 'Have you read *Don Quixote*?'

'Of course!'

'*Muy bien*. Then tell me what you know about Dulcinea ...'

'Well ... she was a humble peasant girl who lived not far away from Quixote ... and when he went quite mad and decided to become a Knight Errant, he built her up in his mind to be his Lady, someone much finer than she really was ... but she never knew that he had idolised her in that way, and she never learned anything of all the crazy knightly deeds he then did in her name. And of course throughout the story she is only ever *talked about* by the main characters – she never actually makes an appearance herself.'

'Very good. So how much did the real Dulcinea change, while Quixote was off doing all those things in her name?'

'We don't know, do we? We never meet her. But my guess is – not at all.'

'OK. And how similar are Dulcinea and your Emilie?'

'Not very! Not at all!'

'So since Dulcinea didn't change, *maybe Emilie did*. Maybe she's a completely different person now – not just in looks, but in name and place and lifestyle and everything ...'

'And ...'

'Well, that's all. You can develop it from there, no?'

'OK, Señor de Blanes. That has all been very helpful, and I shall think carefully about it.'

'*De nada, Arturo. ¡Y buena suerte con todo!*'

As Arthur left the hotel, Alain Revaur was still hard at work on the front steps. Keeping their eyes peeled for the domineering head porter, they hurriedly agreed to meet up for a beer in the Old City the following Sunday evening.

On his return to the bookshop, Arthur consulted large chunks of a second-hand translation of *Don Quixote* during every slack period, interrupting his reading only for the habitual lunchtime walk with Julia. He was once again hugely entertained by Cervantes' great story, but in reality he gained no further inspiration on how to proceed with his now extremely half-hearted search for his own fine lady.

Before leaving work that afternoon he gave Pureza a summary of the ideas on Emilie's disappearance that he had been given by her novelist friends.

'Well,' she said, clearly very disappointed, 'I don't find Claude's suggestion of a kidnapping very feasible, for lots of reasons.'

'Have you read *L'Obsédé* yourself, Pureza?'

'But of course. In the original English, actually. And I've seen the film. It just doesn't fit the situation, in my view, and I think you'd need an awful lot of "alchemy" to pick up a real clue from it. And as for Oliver's theory – well, it's far more generalised, and it's almost a truism, isn't it? You and I have probably already come to the same broad conclusions. So I really can't see how that helps you much either.'

'Well, I didn't want to tell you my own reactions until I'd heard your views, and I *am* very grateful to you for setting up the meetings, but I do have to say I completely agree with you. And yet, as everyone keeps telling me, you never know ...'

'So you'll be putting your own thinking cap straight back on?'

'I'm not so sure. Of course I'll do what I can, whenever the mood takes me. But I'm afraid I'm far more interested right now in getting to know Julia even better and spending a wonderful long summer with her.'

Pureza gave him one of her sad enigmatic smiles, and went back to counting the day's takings.

* * *

After spending the whole of the following Sunday relaxing on the beach with Julia, Arthur apologised for having to leave her on her own for the rest of the evening – and on her first day off from her tiring new job! She smiled, shrugged her shoulders, gave him a little kiss, told him to enjoy himself with his new pal – 'After all, you don't have many of them, do you, *chéri*?' – and firmly encouraged him to be back well before she went to sleep.

He then met up with Alain Revaur for their promised drink, and after ordering the third round of beers he somehow ended up telling him all about his long-lost friend Emilie, saying nothing however about the circumstances that had stimulated her disappearance. The young student was honestly interested and very sympathetic, especially when Arthur shook his head in frustration at the end of his sorry story, declaring that he still had no idea what might have happened to her after she apparently abandoned her apartment all those years before.

It was Alain's turn to order the drinks, and as the waiter moved away from their table he suddenly perked up.

'Hey, Arthur, I've had an idea! We should go and see Billy. He knows everything! I bet he even knows what I had for breakfast today!'

'Who the hell is Billy?'

'Oh, sorry. He's the head porter at the hotel. He's been there since the dawn of time. His name's Guillaume Fallier, but a lot of people call him Billy the Kid! He seems to like that! And some of them call him Billy Fury behind his back. I expect you can work out why ...'

'Yes. I don't like the look of him. And he didn't seem to think very much of *me* last Wednesday!'

'Oh, he's all right really. I've got to know him a bit better over the past week. He *is* very dismissive of what he calls "privileged" young people like me. But I reckon he has a soft side too. Somewhere ...'

'Well, I suppose I have nothing to lose by talking to him.'

'OK. He's on duty tonight. Wanna go and see him later?'

'After four long beers each?'

'Why not?'

The hotel lobby was quiet that evening, and Guillaume Fallier was standing upright and sober and proud behind his desk, browsing the

Sunday paper that was spread out neatly upon it. He did not seem at all pleased at the disturbance.

After a rapid introduction from his now rather wary new friend, Arthur asked his question abut Emilie as briefly as he could. Fallier just shrugged his shoulders, said nothing, and went back to his newspaper. Arthur took that, however, as suggesting the man *did* have some information but was in no way motivated to share it with him.

'So *can* you help me at all, Monsieur Fallier?'

'It's Billy.'

'OK, Billy,' said Arthur, getting increasingly frustrated. 'So, can you ...'

'No.'

Alain Revaur placed his hand on Arthur's arm and started to say something. But it was falling on deaf ears.

'If you do know anything about this, *monsieur*, may I please appeal to your basic humanity and ...'

The already aggravated head porter suddenly became extremely riled and began throwing insults at the "lazy, good-for-nothing, tipsy visitor" who was really testing his patience. That, plus the four large beers, finally did it for Arthur.

'No-one speaks to me like that, no matter how old they are!' he shouted. 'Come out from behind that desk and say it again to my face!'

The gambit worked. With a little more respect now showing on his own face, the ageing bully remained well within his fortress and held out his palms in a gesture of conciliation.

'All right, all right, man. Calm down, and I'll tell you what I can. But then you both get straight out of here, or I call the *flics*, OK?'

'OK.'

Alain Revaur was now looking very concerned, and Arthur did not blame him. It was clear who would need to be buying the next few rounds of beer.

'All I know,' sighed Fallier, patently keen to get this over with as quickly as possible, 'is that very soon after the robbery, the famous little singer spent one night at a cheap hotel up on Rue Hancy. She apparently knew the receptionist quite well and tipped him handsomely in exchange for a promise not to formally register her stay.'

Arthur had never mentioned the robbery, let alone his own involvement in it, nor even his own surname to either Alain or Billy. So the head porter was clearly on the ball, and might even have recognised him already. Almost certainly had, in fact. But Arthur decided to continue to keep his mouth firmly shut about all of that.

'That was really helpful, Monsieur Fallier ...'

'Billy.'

'OK, Billy. So if you can ...'

'And before you get all excited again, matey, there's no point in trying to follow it up. That hotel has changed hands twice since 1959, and it's had seven or eight receptionists in that time. Just forget it!'

Arthur nodded in reluctant acceptance, thought for a moment, and held out his hand in a gesture of final reconciliation. But Fallier would not reciprocate. 'Don't push your luck, pal. Just get out of here, now.' Then he turned to Alain Revaur. 'And that's the last time you pull a stunt like this on me, kiddo. Got it?'

The student nodded obediently, and the two of them left the place without another word.

After apologising to his friend for giving him a potentially serious problem with his new lord and master, and definitely promising to buy all the beers at their next meeting, Arthur hurried home, well aware that his piecemeal hunt for Emilie had led him into yet another cul-de-sac. And when he got back to the apartment he found the lights were all out and Julia was already fast asleep.

* * *

Arthur called Inspector Hardy, as promised, on Monday the twenty-sixth.

'I've been taking some independent advice on detection procedures, Simon – very discreetly, of course – and I've realised I need to go back to square one and have another very thorough look at everything I know about Luc and how he was behaving when I last saw him. That might just generate another little lead or two.'

'But you should have been doing that sort of thing all along!'

'And believe me, I have been! I'm just saying I plan to try even harder, yet again. Mainly – but don't tell everybody this – because I like you so much ...'

'Are you still staying with Pureza Seles?'

'You tell me.'

'You said you were using a phone box in your last call.'

'What a memory!'

'And you've hardly been seen at the bookshop since the start of the month.'

'Maybe you should have tried looking ...'

'Will you give me your new address?'

'Sorry, but no.'

'So we'll need to do it the hard way. Points off for that, Arthur. Now get back to work, and call me again on the seventeenth.'

* * *

On the last day of June, Arthur went to the latest phone box nominated by Xérus and told him bluntly that he had made no further progress in his hunt for Paul Ruford. And that he expected to make no more at all until Xérus was willing to give him a little of the extra information about the man that he was obviously still holding close to his chest.

Xérus categorically refused to do so, and repeated his broad threats against Pureza and her precious bookshop.

Arthur was no longer giving those threats any real credibility. But he feigned new humility and promised to keep up his search, fruitless though he insisted it was. And they agreed a time and place for their next checkpoint call at the very end of July.

* * *

Arthur had indeed been doing a little re-thinking about Luc, as he had promised the Inspector. But not quite along the lines he had implied.

First, Luc could not possibly know where Arthur was now living. So all things considered, he was quite safe and secure.

Second, the big cache of stolen banknotes was no longer at the bookshop for the police to find if Luc ever did carry out his crazy, inspired threat to give them that "fictitious" tip-off. So it too was quite safe and secure.

Third, he had absolutely no evidence from Luc that the guy knew anything about where Emilie had ever been living. So he really should stop worrying about any possible risk to her. Wherever she was, she must also be quite safe and secure.

And his own search for her had proved fruitless anyway. He was expecting to drop it completely, soon. So the need to continue humouring Luc, in the vain hope of picking up a scrap or two of information about her, had basically evaporated.

So, he had concluded, he no longer had anything to fear from Luc. He would at last call the man's bluff in their next upcoming game of telephone poker, and take the calculated risk of threatening to end his apparent co-operation with the increasingly desperate man.

And, of course, you never knew what might just turn up.

'Ready to claim your five-wad bonus, Arthur?'

'No, I'm afraid not. I can't make any breakthrough in the Fiat repair operations after all, and I'm going to have to drop the whole crazy business.'

'You can't do that!'

'Oh yes I can. I'm no longer scared of you, Luc.'

'Then you're being very reckless. Think again about your pretty little friend in the bookshop ...'

'I don't care about her any more. So, this has to be the end of the line for us ...'

'No, it is not! And don't hang up, for god's sake! Listen, I'm willing to keep the special bonus going – but it will reduce by one wad for every month that you fail to deliver. How's that?'

'Not interested.'

'Arthur, please agree to keep trying.'

'Why should I?'

'OK, the full bonus stands for as long as it takes, but I must have the cash by the end of September. There's only six month's currency left after that ...'

'I'm really still not interested, Luc. And I think I'll say *"Adieu"* now.'

'Wait! Let me at least give you the next call box details for the first of August ...'

'I really don't give ... Oh, very well, then. Just in case I happen to change my mind.'

'Please *do* be there, for everyone's sake, Arthur – whatever you have or haven't achieved by then!'

'I'm listening, Luc ...'

* * *

The next day was a Sunday, and that meant the beach again, of course. But while Arthur was off swimming, or talking to Julia about the books he had most enjoyed, and sometimes reading out loud to her, she spent most of the long hot day simply lying in the sun and recovering her strength. She was now working from ten till eight, six days a week, to earn as much money as she could while the going was good, but she was coming home exhausted every evening. It was most definitely not, thus far, the idyllic summer she had been hoping for when she dropped out of school.

* * *

Late one afternoon the following week, when the shop was briefly empty, Pureza came up to Arthur while he was shelving some newly delivered books.

'So have you done any more thinking about Emilie?'

'A little, yes. And I've even picked up an extra morsel of information. But it all still peters out before she leaves Nice ... assuming she *did* eventually leave here, of course.'

'I think I we *can* safely assume that, Arthur.'

'Fair enough. Now, as soon as I've finished this little job I'd like to get away, if that's ...'

'Hang on, my friend! I've been carefully studying those notes in Emilie's family bible, and I think I may have come up with something you could pursue. It's only a long shot, but ...'

'Look, Pureza, it's ever so kind of you to be doing this for me –
even though I'm not at all sure why you're still sticking at it – but I
really do want to concentrate on my relationship with Julia now.
OK?'

For only the second time since he had met her, Arthur saw a look
of real annoyance on his dear friend's normally tranquil face.

'Very well, Arthur. I shall put the bible aside and think little more
of it. May Emilie be happy in whatever she is now doing, and may
she not be in any way concerned about you or your own fate.'

Reeling at the unaccustomed harshness of Pureza's words, Arthur
said no more and went back to his shelving before making matters
any worse than they obviously already were.

* * *

On Saturday the eighth of July, Julia told Arthur she had another
little mission of her own to accomplish after work that evening. And
as they relaxed on the beach the next day, she reported that it had
been a complete success.

'I'm fed up with the long hours and the low pay at the restaurant,
Arthur ...'

'I'm not surprised. So am I, if you know what I mean.'

'Yes, I do. So I've fixed it. I've found a fabulous new job – only
six hours each evening, with Tuesdays and Wednesdays completely
free. The take-home pay is more than I'm getting now, even though
I'll only be working about half the hours! And the girls say the tips
are very good!'

'That's fantastic! So where is it?'

'At a gentlemen's club on Place Garibaldi.'

'A gentlemen's club?'

'Yes. It's private membership, very smooth, and that's why the
pay rates are so high.'

'So what do you have to do?'

'Just serve drinks. Topless.'

'Topless?'

'Losing your hearing, Arthur? Yes, that's right. Just like I am right
now! And that's all. It's hardly worse than some of the things you've
been getting up to over the last few years, is it?'

'No, it's not. And I'm glad you're so happy about it. I just hope you'll enjoy it and come home far less exhausted!'

'And richer!'

'Yes. But it probably means we'll see even less of each other for a while. Quite ironical, actually ...'

'Well, that's life, isn't it? Now, if I could sing like an angel and play the clarinet, maybe ...'

'Point taken, *chérie*. So when's it happening?'

'Trial run for a couple of hours tomorrow evening, then I start on Thursday.'

* * *

It was nine in the morning on the seventeenth of July, and Inspector Hardy's fingers were no doubt poised immediately above the telephone handset. But Arthur would still keep his powder dry on the subject of his long-running secret dialogue with Luc, let alone his recent pretended stand-off with the man.

'And where the hell have *you* been for the past three weeks?'

'Out and about, Simon. Mostly in intensive training for the American Moon landing programme. But I haven't left Nice, if that's what you're asking.'

'So what do you have to show for all your latest superhuman efforts?'

'Nothing more. I've actually been digging quite deep again, after my big re-think, and I've been asking about Luc and his situation in lots of different places. But still no joy, I'm afraid.'

'This really is not good enough!'

'But I seriously can't think of any other ways to jog people's memories.'

'Huh! That's just what you're out there to do! I've always assumed you've been giving them a rather better physical description than we've ever been able to ...'

'No, I haven't. I never saw his face on the day he press-ganged me. I told you that when you arrested me! And he was wearing that heavy disguise right up to the time he left the getaway car. I told you that too! Didn't *you* get some sort of description out of the other robbers – Irvoise and Aignant?'

'No. Both of them also swore they had never set eyes on him before that evening.'

'OK. So I'll just have to get back to my very vague enquiries, then. I'll call you again in three weeks' time, on the seventh of August. Unless of course I'm away on holiday with Julia.'

'But ...'

As he walked away from the phone box, Arthur had a minor brainwave. Simon Hardy might have absolutely no idea what Luc looked like, but there was someone else who quite probably *did*, and that certain someone was still being very protective of his information about the man.

'Good morning, *chérie* ...'

'Oh ... Hi, Arthur. What's the time?'

'Half-past nine. I'm off to the bookshop soon.'

'OK ...'

'Still enjoying your new job?'

'Oh yes! It's so easy, and everyone's so friendly, and the customers really *are* gentlemen!'

'Not like me, you mean?'

'Idiot!'

'Energy levels improving, then?'

'Try me ...'

* * *

On the last day of July, Arthur was for once ready to assume the driving seat in the upcoming phone call from Xérus.

'Found him for me yet?'

'No, X. But I *have* had a very good idea.'

'That makes a change! Go on ...'

'Well, you must know what Paul Ruford looks like, right?'

'Maybe, vaguely ...'

'But of course you do. Although I guess you don't have a photograph you can lend me, or you would already ...'

'Are you crazy, Narone?'

'No. And I didn't really expect it, but you never know, do you? Anyway, my bright idea is that maybe you could draw a little sketch of his face, and send it off to me or leave it somewhere for me to collect ...'

'Very funny. What makes you think I'm suddenly a portrait artist?'

'Nothing. It's just an idea ...'

'Even if I could draw – and I can't – I would not do it anyway.'

'Why not? I can't see what we'd have to lose ...'

'Because it's too risky for me to do anything of the sort! For any number of reasons. And that's my decision, and I'm not budging from it, OK?'

'OK, OK! I wasn't trying to aggravate you. Just trying to help us both ...'

'All right. So is that all you have to say?'

'No, it's not. If I can't have a sketch of Ruford – or whatever his real name might be – then I think I'm going to have to finally give up the hunt for him. I have absolutely no idea what to do next. I'm certain you know more about him than you've ever been willing to tell me – and I really don't understand why you're being so shy about it – but if you still can't bring yourself to share information that might be crucial to getting the result you want ... well, it's your funeral as much as mine, isn't it? I've had enough, X. So I think I'll quit, here and now.'

'You know what will happen if you *do* stop co-operating, Narone ...'

'I'm willing to take the risk. So if you really have nothing more to tell me, I'm going to put the phone down, OK?'

'Wait a minute! All right, there is something. You didn't get anywhere when you went across to Marseilles, so it's not likely to be of any use, but it may be worth trying ...'

'Go on ...'

'I know where Ruford was living in the months before the robbery. I really didn't want you sniffing around there and opening up any old sores or exposing yourself, but time is running out fast now. So maybe you can pick up something useful from the people still living in his old apartment block. But you'd better go there in some sort of disguise, as you did in February ...'

'OK. I'm willing to give that a try, sometime over the next month. What's the address?'

'130, Rue Marengo.'

'Very well. I'll go back to Marseilles as soon as I can, and I'll follow up anything I manage to discover. Are you planning to call me on the last day of August, as usual?'

'Yes. Here are the details ...'

Arthur put down the phone and punched the air. "Rue Marengo" matched what Vic in the Island Bar had told him back in February about Ruford's lodgings! He'd been very unwilling at the time to go asking after the man at every front door on that very long street. But now it should be easy to pick up any information that was still to be had there. Well, relatively easy, anyway ...

* * *

As Arthur waited, at noon on the first of August, for the call that Luc had so desperately wanted him to receive, he was feeling both supremely proud of his bluffing gambit in their last conversation and mildly concerned that this next call might never come and that Luc would later prove to have been plotting something dastardly against him – or any of his lovely ladies – after all.

But the phone rang right on time, and Arthur smiled broadly to himself and even began to chuckle. Then he pulled himself together and answered it as coolly as he could.

'Would that perhaps be you, Monsieur Comet?'

'I'm very glad you decided to take this call, Arthur. For everybody's sake.'

'Yeah, yeah, yeah. So, get on with it ...'

'What do you mean? I'm phoning to see if you've found the money yet!'

'I told you last month I'd already given up on that, Luc. But as it happens, I've just come across a most promising new lead ...'

'Seriously??'

'Yes. And of course I'm still very interested in collecting those five bonus wads if I can manage to locate the cash with a minimum of effort on my part. But it *is* going to take me back into Italy, which is a real drag ...'

'You're sounding far too cocky for my liking now, Narone.'

'Not calling me Arthur any more, Luc? You know, that really hurts. Perhaps I shouldn't bother wasting my time in Italy after all ...'

'No! You have to go back there and find the money!'

'Do I really?'

'Look, I'm sorry, OK? Please keep at it. For everybody's sake.'

'I've heard that line from you too often, Luc. I'll do it for my own sake, and maybe for yours as an afterthought. And if you really do want all that money back, you'll promise to keep the ladies completely out of this, as of now. OK?'

'OK.'

'Right. I'll take your next call, at noon as usual, on Friday the first of September. Tell me which phone box you want me to use ...'

* * *

On Thursday the third of August, Arthur woke Julia up with a gentle kiss and told her he would be away "on business" for the rest of the day.

She smiled and nodded without opening her eyes. 'I'll see you tomorrow morning then, *chéri* ...'

'Still love me, Julia?'

'Of course I do.' She had opened her eyes now. 'But do you still love *me*, with all those rich kids ogling my body every evening?'

'Well, I'd rather they didn't! But it's a good job, and you enjoy it, and you're not exhausted at the end of every shift, and it's not very different from hanging around the bars down on the beach these days, is it? Anyway, I don't own you, Miss Liberty 1967. So how can I complain?'

'It's a means to an end, Arthur. Just like all the crazy stuff *you're* still doing and I'm still placidly accepting. So let's just keep moving towards that end, eh?'

He chuckled and gave her another little kiss.

'Yes, I still love you, Julia. Madly.'

He took the mid-morning train to Marseilles. In the toilet compartment he donned a pair of heavy black plastic glasses with their lenses removed, a woollen bobble hat and a very droopy false moustache. He hardly recognised himself in the mirror, let alone saw any sign of the twenty-one-year-old teddy boy whose photograph had probably adorned a few newspapers for a day or two way back in 1959 and 1960.

Emerging from Saint-Charles railway station in bright sunshine, he headed south on Cours Lieutaud, and fifteen minutes later he was strolling along Rue Marengo.

Number 130 turned out to be a large apartment block at the very end of the street. Large enough to have its own live-in concierge, Arthur discovered at once. All well and good. That might save pestering a lot of other people ...

A withered old woman wearing a hearing aid finally answered his increasingly heavy knocks at her door.

'Ah, good afternoon, *madame*. I'm trying to help my father get back in touch with one of his old friends. His name was Paul Ruford. We have a letter from him written from this address in 1959, and I ...'

She raised her hands, shaking her tired head and stopping him in mid-speech.

'*Attendez, m'sieur. Norbert! Norbert!!*'

'*Ouai?*'

'*Viens-là!!*'

'*J'arrive, j'arrive ...*'

The elderly Norbert eventually shuffled up to the door and gave his visitor a long, hard look. Then he appeared to relax, and Arthur was able to start again and pose his question in full this time.

'Yeah,' nodded Norbert pensively. 'Paul was living here from '50, I think – or was it '51? No matter. Your father met him after that, did he?'

'Yes ...'

'In Marseilles?'

'Yes ... but we moved away in 1956.'

'OK. Well, Paul left here suddenly in late '59. Around the time of that big bank robbery in Nice! Everyone reckoned he must have done it!'

'Seriously??'

'Nah! On the other hand, he *was* a short little beggar, like the guy they talked about in the papers – the one that got away ...'

'So, do you have any idea where he went, *monsieur*?'

'He told me he was going back to his old home. Some sort of family crisis, I think.'

'I see. Trouble is, my father says he never knew where Paul was
originally from ...'

'Well, I dunno where he actually went. But it's funny – I had
family in Toulon, in the old days, and by the sound of his accent
when he first arrived here, I'd say Paul was from there too ...'

'Ah, that's very useful, sir. Perhaps we will be able to locate him
down there. And I don't suppose you have any other information that
might help us?'

'Don't think so. Let me think ....

'Nah. He paid ahead for his room when he went away, so we left it
well alone – for two whole months, if I remember rightly. But he
never came back, as far as I know, and we let it again from the first
of December. And that really is all I can tell you.'

'Very well. Many thanks, *monsieur. Et adieu.*'

'*Pas d'quoi.* And good luck, young man.'

As he walked back towards the station, Arthur was feeling delighted
with his own acuity in having long ago identified the city of Toulon
as a good possibility for Luc's hidey-hole. And now there were some
real facts to support his theory!

He still had no sketch of the man, of course, and he was never
going to get one without opening up far too many potholes. But
maybe he now had enough "evidence" to think about finally sharing
his burden and coming clean with the Inspector. Or partially clean, at
least.

Well, he had four whole days to think about that before their next
scheduled call. Meanwhile, he was relatively far from home, and still
in something of a disguise. So perhaps he would delay his departure
for a couple of hours and take a little time out to "exchange" a few
more of his hot old bills for some nice cool new ones in the
undiscriminating shops of Marseilles ...

* * *

It was approaching nine o'clock on Monday the seventh of August,
and Narone had made his decision.

He remained almost completely unafraid of Luc – he still thought
of him as "Luc" and not as "Paul Ruford" – and had concluded that it

would be safest and wisest to stake a claim for the substantial police reward for his capture, rather than accept the man's promised five-wad bonus of very hot money. And if by some miracle of detection Luc actually *was* apprehended ... well, Arthur could choose later whether to hand in the full haul of stolen cash for the additional bank reward, or deliver it to Xérus to satisfy him – in part. Or whatever.

But most of all, despite his new and quite convincing bravado in his recent conversations with Luc, he now wanted to get the man off his own back for good, and remove those nagging background "threats" to everybody else as well. Just in case.

He entered the call box, picked up the phone, and dialled Inspector Hardy's number once again.

'Good morning, Simon.'

'Hello, Arthur. Is it that time again?'

'It is.'

'So, still nothing for us, I suppose?'

'On the contrary. I have quite a lot to tell you. And I suggest you sit down first. Now, where shall I begin ...?'

'Just get on with it, eh?'

'All right, then. Well, Luc *did* actually leave the cash with me after the robbery.'

'What??'

'Please just listen carefully, Simon. And I hid it here in Nice the very same night. But when I went back to collect it last August, the "item" I had stashed it in had been moved away. Since then I've spent a whole year trying to find it for you – *and* for Luc – and I'm still trying.'

'You mean "Luc" *has* been in contact with you??'

'Yes.'

'Since when??'

'That doesn't matter, Simon. Please don't get all worked up about it, because you *really* need to concentrate now. I've only ever spoken to him in telephone calls that he has made to me, but I think you may at last be able to try and identify him from some stuff I've only *just* managed to pick up.'

'All right. But it had better be very good ...'

'I guess that depends on what you can do with it. OK, here goes. Luc was actually known as Paul Ruford – that's R-U-F-O-R-D ... although I understand that may *also* have been a false name – and he was definitely living in Marseilles shortly before the robbery. But it's quite likely that he'd moved there several years earlier – from Toulon! I've tried to get a photo or even a little sketch of him, but I haven't succeeded. But if he has any sort of police record anywhere, then maybe ...'

'But this is amazing! How on earth did you suddenly come by such information?'

'Oh, I finally struck lucky and found someone who was associated with the robbery in the planning stages but dropped out later.'

'Who?'

'I can't say, Simon ... and please don't make things even harder for me by pressing me about it! But I can guarantee that Paul Ruford is your man. All *you* have to do is find him. Detect him, Inspector.'

'But wait a minute, Arthur. Even if you're right, and we *did* identify him and then discovered where he was living, we'd still have no proof he was ever involved in the robbery. We have no fingerprints, no photographs, and no usable witness statements with that heavy disguise he was wearing. The forensic evidence from the bullet he fired at Orceau is probably useless – he's hardly likely to have kept that gun under his pillow, is he? – and the bank notes were all used and unmarked. And I doubt he's held on to the clothes matching the fibres left in those stolen cars. No, if we *did* locate him, Arthur, we'd have to set a trap. And you would need to be part of it.'

'Hmmm ...'

'No option there, I'm afraid. But don't forget all those possible carrots. Now, I assume you have some way of contacting your old friend again?'

'He's due to call me at the very start of next month. I've told him I finally have a strong lead on where the money might now be stored, and I'm busy working on it.'

'OK, I need to think hard about this. But at least we have over three weeks to work on it. Phone me back again, same time tomorrow.'

Arthur did just that.

'Right, young man, we have the beginnings of a plan.

'We've received a low-quality photograph of Paul Ruford from the Crime Prevention Team in Marseilles. Apparently it was taken secretly on the street in about 1954, when that team consisted of one man, part-time. The photo was one of dozens in a very early briefing package – vintage 1955! – produced for the security staff of the city's banks, to help them spot any of the suspicious characters the police thought might one day fancy doing a recce for a robbery. Very sophisticated – pah!

'And it now turns out that in their own private thoughts, Ruford *had* later been one of many vaguely possible suspects for the Nice bank robbery. But they'd never even arrested him on suspicion for any of the jobs they thought he might have done in Marseilles in all those years, and they had no knowledge of his whereabouts at the end of 1959, and they were not even sure if "Paul Ruford" was his real name.'

'But why didn't they discuss all of this with you and your colleagues at the time??'

'I think I'll choose to ignore that little question, Arthur, in the interests of equality and fraternity at least. Now, I'm about to start some *very* low-profile, off-the-record enquiries with our closest friends in the Toulon police, to avoid the possibility of any leaks. And I'm telling you all this because I trust you, despite what you may still think, but I want you to promise me you won't say a word about it to anybody else.'

'That sounds a lot like a test, or even a trap for *me*, Simon. But fair enough.'

'I hope you mean that last bit, Arthur. Your freedom and your fortune could well be hingeing on it ...'

'I get the message. And yes, I promise – of course. You know I want to see Luc behind bars as much as you do. Probably even more.'

'OK. Call me again at nine o'clock on the twenty-fourth. And in the meantime ... well, I suggest you forget all about this, and get out and have some fun with your new girlfriend!'

'Funnily enough, that's exactly what has been on my own mind. Permission to visit Italy again soon, sir? That's where Luc believes I'm going to try and find his banknotes ...'

'Don't you think that's pushing it a bit, in the circumstances?'

'No more than usual.'

'So where's the money coming from, Arthur?'

'Pureza is still a fine benefactor of the arts, my friend. And Julia's been making a bomb as a ... high-class waitress.'

'Should I enquire about her uniform?'

'It wouldn't take long to give you the answer.'

'Hah! OK, buster. Permission granted.'

Arthur left the call box and set off for the bookshop, pausing at a florist's to buy a small bunch of red and gold freesias. He would be early, for once. But not for work.

'These really are for you this time, Pureza. You can display them wherever you wish!'

'Oh, they're lovely, Arthur! Thank you!'

'But I'm afraid I have to quit.'

'But why?? I still love having you around here every day ...'

'Yes, I know you do. And I really enjoy it too, believe me – as much as anybody can enjoy work! But there are ... well, there are some developments with the police and all that unfinished business, so I may well be needing a lot more "flexibility" again. I'm certainly likely to be out of the country for a while, quite soon, for one reason or another. And so on ...'

'Well, you know you'll always be welcome back when things calm down again.'

'Thank you! Now, how much of my debt do I still owe, after deducting all my commission since I started in March?'

'None, Arthur. You cleared it two or three weeks ago. In fact I now owe you quite a few francs ...'

'Hah! Well, I'm certainly not going to accept them, *ma bonne amie*! And thank you for everything you have done for me over the past year!'

He opened his arms wide, gave his kindly benefactor a big hug, and kissed her fully on the lips for the very first time. And as far as he could judge, she was quite overwhelmed by it all. But he knew he had always been a poor judge of many things.

As he walked back to his apartment, with little else to do but wake Julia from her well-deserved slumbers and ask her to walk out of her own lucrative job on the spot and come fly, come fly away with him – well, take a low-cost bus ride just across the border, anyway – he was busy working on his latest cash flow challenge. Yes, he would need to go back to "exchanging" his hot bills in the shops of Nice as soon as they returned from their holiday. And if and when his latest wad started to run out, well, he would simply have to break into another one.

"Bonnie" took all of ten seconds to consider his carefully delivered proposal.

'Of course I'd love to go off on holiday with you tomorrow, Arthur! I want you, babe, and I'm still waiting for that long Summer of Love to happen. And of course I'll quit my fabulous well-paid job at once, if the management is not sufficiently charitable to let me take a two-week break, with absolutely no notice, after I've barely been working there a month ...'

'Julia, that was all very funny, and that's one of the reasons I love you so much, but can we please cut the sarcasm and be serious for a minute? I really do have a lot on my plate right now ...'

'I know that, babe, and I promise you I was only joking. Really. I can't wait! But please don't think I'm some sort of old-fashioned pushover! This is 1967, after all, and I'm a modern girl ...'

'Hah! So you'll take over the organisation of the whole trip, then?'

'Oh, no, Arthur! That's what *men* are for!'

* * *

'You know, I get the feeling you've been here before ...'

'You're very astute, Julia. Yes, this is where I came with Emilie on our little summer vacation in 1959.'

'Ah, I see. So you still have a lot to learn about women, then, Clyde ...'

* * *

'Isn't this just beautiful, Arthur?'

'It's glorious! And such lovely, soft, enveloping sands – especially after we've both been used to that stony old beach in Nice! You know, I was almost falling asleep ...'

'Did you come *here* with Emilie?'
'No.'
'Promise?'
'Yes.'

'I'm thinking of writing a novel.'
'That's very brave of you, Julia. A short story might actually be a much better way to start.'
'No, I think I have a novel inside me.'
'I do hope that's all ...'
'Shut up, Arthur. So, since you're a published author ...'
'Rubbish! I told you – two silly little stories in pulp magazines!'
'... then I'd like to ask for your advice on how to proceed.'
'Wow! That really *is* the quickest way to a writer's heart! Mere flattery comes a very poor second!'
'So ...?'
'OK, then. Well, I have this theory. I must admit I haven't tried it out myself, yet ... but I will, one day.'
'Go on ...'
'I reckon you should start with the very first paragraphs, and then write the *final* paragraphs, and then fill in the bit in the middle.'
'So that you know exactly where you're headed, you mean?'
'By George, she's got it!'
'Arthur, please don't ...'
'Only joking, *chérie*. Yes, for just that reason. But of course the actual text of those final sentences could later change a little or a lot, depending on how the story then develops.'
'OK. Thanks ...'
'And ...?'
'No, please don't disturb me – I'm too busy thinking. You may go off to sleep now ...'
'Hah!'

'I've done it, Arthur!'
'Huh? Oh, it's *you*! What have you done?'
'Written the final paragraphs of my novel. Before writing anything else!'
'What? Even before writing the *first* paragraphs?'

'Oh yes. I'm not at all sure how I'm going to start it, yet. But I know this is exactly how it will end!'

'That's not quite what I was suggesting, Julia ...'

'Wasn't it? Well, never mind – I really took your advice on board. You know, about needing a pretty clear idea about where the story was headed, before actually trying to create it ...'

'Well, that's fairly close to what *you* said ...'

'Good. So are you ready to hear my ending?'

'All right, *chérie*. I'm all ears.'

'OK. Here goes, then ...'

I unlocked the door of my apartment, pushed it open, and flicked on the light.

And then I saw him, standing in the kitchen doorway once again, in all his naked glory and grinning – no, leering – at me from cheek to cheek.

'No! I've had enough!' I screamed, seizing the broom that was leaning against the wall. 'You've trapped me in your selfish life for far too long! I should have changed the bloody lock! Today's the day it has to end!'

But he just laughed.

'And I'm going to make sure you'll never ever hurt me again!' I insisted. 'I'm taking back my life, Lawrence, even if it means taking yours away!'

I threw down the broom, reached deep into my handbag and pulled out my tiny gun, which I always kept loaded and ready for moments like this. Lawrence's expression turned from mockery to mild fear, and he instantly developed a medium-strength erection.

'Oh God, it's now or never,' I thought, and I cocked the gun, already shaking far more than he was. I walked stoically towards him, aimed at his forehead, pulled the trigger, and took off the tip of his penis. He screamed in pain, then recovered his presence of mind, lunged forward, grabbed the gun from my still-shuddering hand, and shot me through the heart.

'And ...?'

'That's it, Arthur.'

'That's *it*??'

'Yes. *FIN*. The desperate heroine is murdered by her cruel ex-boyfriend, proving there's still no justice in this man's world. It's a sort of ironically derivative postmodernist statement, right? At least that's what my university friends would have called it, I think.'

'Your narrator is dead, Julia. Stone dead. But in the brief instant between the bullet's penetrating her heart and the expiration of life, she found the strength to write what is presumably planned to be at least a sixty thousand word account of her life ...'

'Well ... yes ...'

'... which will probably be just as excruciating, throughout its entire length, as those few concluding paragraphs.'

'Oh, I hate you, Arthur!'

'I love you, Arthur!'

'Well, that obviously can't be due to my suggestion about the likely quality of the entire length of your proposed novel ...'

'You're certainly right about that, *chéri*. No, it's mainly due to the actual quality of your own entire length. But I do think I'm going to give up any idea of becoming a writer.'

'Just like that?'

'Yes. I'd much rather spend my life doing things that generate compliments rather than disdain.'

'You want to go back to working at the topless bar, then?'

'Of course I do! My public adores me! So I adore them. What could be more perfect? In fact I'd say that's pretty close to a recipe for eternal peace on Earth.'

'Steady on, Julia! Your tits aren't *that* good!'

'Oh, I hate you, Arthur!!'

A Better Rat Trap

The rest of Arthur's holiday with Julia had gone smoothly and very sweetly, and they had arrived back in Nice very late on the evening of the twenty-third. So he was seriously wishing his "Welcome Home" appointment with the Inspector had not been set for the usual nine o'clock the following morning. But the alarm clock did its job to perfection, and he hurried obediently out and found an empty call box with two minutes to spare.

'It's me again, Simon.'

'And did you enjoy your little vacation?'

'We certainly did. Both long sunny weeks of it. Especially whenever we thought about how hard you must be working back at the ranch. So, have you had any success?'

'More than we could possibly have hoped for, my friend.'

'Really?'

'Yes, really. I took the photograph of "Paul Ruford" over to Toulon myself, and an old pal from my training days helped me walk it round the central police station. Nobody on the morning crew recognised it, but they all said I should keep my fingers crossed for the afternoon shift. And when *they* came on duty, I met their oldest sergeant. He's due for retirement in eighteen months, and he's been keeping his relief in shape there for over twenty-five years!

'As soon as he saw the photo, he nodded his head in recognition, and then we simply couldn't stop him talking. "That's Paul-Philippe Carne," he declared, almost proudly. "Sharp little bugger. Made a huge nuisance of himself on the streets of Toulon from the age of seventeen. Summer of 1945, that was, soon as the peace had broken out. His mother couldn't control him any more, see. And his father was long gone – but it was the war, *non*? I pulled the kid in for a lecture at least four times a year till he was twenty-one or more, and then he suddenly disappeared. I was convinced he'd done a lot of petty shop robberies here during those years, but he was very, very clever – he never left a trace, he could bluff his way out of an elephant pit, and he was never formally arrested or charged with anything. So what's he been up to in Nice, Inspector?"

'How about that, Arthur? With your information, we came up trumps!'

'It sounds brilliant, Simon! Well done. Seriously. And ...?'

'Well, I'm going to make sure that old-school sergeant eventually receives some sort of commendation. Because he even remembered the address of the Carne family back in the Forties, and we quickly established that the mother, Anne-Gertrude, is still living there!'

'No!'

'Yes. So I stayed on in Toulon and called my own *brigadier* down to help me – yes, he's Brigadier Louis Furneau now, Arthur, and a very good one! – and the two of us mounted a discreet little observation. We soon discovered that Paul-Philippe is living there too! So a few carefully selected officers of the Toulon force now have him firmly in their sights, and believe me, they will not lose him. The old sergeant has even demanded to be part of the action, with his silence guaranteed!'

'Bravo!'

'They've already mounted a twenty-four hour surveillance on the Carnes' apartment block, and they know "Luc" – yes, I'm still calling him that too! – and his mother are still going in and out as normal. She's a good match to our own observations and your recent description of his "lady friend" in those first few days after your release. And the lads are following each of them whenever they leave the place, just in case they're on their way to another distant town in preparation for placing the next call to you.'

'I am truly impressed, Simon. I never knew you had it in you.'

'So now, Arthur, we are ready to plan the grabs. And if I remember rightly, "Luc" believes you are still searching for the cache of stolen money ...'

'Correct.'

'And he will definitely be phoning you on the first of September?'

'Right. At twelve noon, as always.'

'At which call box?'

'Corner of Rue Assalit and Rue Miron.'

'OK. Now, you're going to listen to me properly, for the first time in your life. From here on in, you will play this my way, with absolutely no arguments or disruptions. Right?'

'Right.'

'And you will be pretending to "Luc" that you have *actually found the stolen money*.'

'OK ...'

'Good. So this is what we are all going to do ....'

And Arthur and Simon eventually ended their remarkably affable planning session with an agreement to a final checkpoint call on the last day of the month.

* * *

Now that he was back in Nice, Arthur began, as he had intended, to launder some more of his stolen cash to cover the following month's advance rent and living costs. He could see clearly that, at this rate, his present wad of notes would be almost gone by the end of September. And there were only two more remaining intact in the rucksack languishing in its latest left-luggage home ...

Julia, meanwhile, had walked straight back into her job at the gentlemen's club. Arthur did not ask any further questions about this, concluding at once that both the management and her adoring public shared his own *actual* opinions about her fine endowments, and that one should not look a gift horse in the mouth when there were very good viewing alternatives.

* * *

Arthur dialled Hardy's number at nine o'clock on the thirty-first of August.

'It's me, Simon.'

'Hello, Arthur. OK, everything is in place for tomorrow. And ... well, are you quite sure you can handle this?'

'You bet! I can't wait!'

'Fine. Good luck, then. And I'll talk to you ... well, as soon as I can, right?'

'Right. Just get them for us, will you?'

'I will.'

Arthur was wishing that was the only telephone conversation he needed to hold that day. But at noon he would have to be in place for Xérus' regular month-end call.

* * *

'Talk to me, Narone. And it had better be good ...'

'Well, I didn't pick up anything about Paul Ruford in Marseilles. Another wild goose chase.'

'Really?'

'Yes, really. So I guess we're back where we started. Unless you have something else to tell me about him. Otherwise I think I'll just go out and get myself some more nice sunshine ...'

'I don't think you're being completely honest with me, Narone.'

'Whatever makes you say that?'

'Something in your voice.'

'I think it's just the biscuit I was eating. Swallowed it too fast when the phone rang. It's given me quite a rough throat ...'

'Very funny. So what exactly will you be doing next?'

'No idea. Whatever you suggest ...'

'I need to think again about all of this, Narone. And I want to keep more on top of it from now on, with only seven months' currency left on the money. Don't hang up ....'

'OK ...'

'Right, I'm going to call you exactly *five days* from now, at noon on Tuesday the fifth of September.'

'But that's my birthday!'

'Tough. Be there.'

'Where is "there" exactly, X?'

'Ah. Yes, I forgot to mention that. OK, write this down ...'

As he replaced the receiver, Arthur was already frowning and scratching his head. He had presumably revealed, in the tone of his voice, something of his own real nervousness about tomorrow's little task – although he really didn't believe he had. No great surprise, however, and no great problem either.

But that had set him wondering about Xérus. There had been a very different tone to *his* voice too ... and his attitude had also changed. There was more distrust around, and suddenly a new sense of urgency and a strong need for greater control. And the guy was clearly also rather distracted. But why? Did he know something new?

Arthur became ever more intrigued about this as he walked back to the apartment. Yes, once tomorrow's crucial little job was off his plate, he would start to think hard again about the mysterious Monsieur Xérus.

* * *

Arthur commandeered the call box on Rue Miron thirty minutes ahead of time, and five minutes later the phone rang. He picked up the receiver, listened for a few moments, and simply said 'Yes, fine.' After listening briefly once more, he hung up.

At exactly twelve noon the phone rang again.

'Well, Arthur?'

'I've found the boxes and the money at last, Luc!'

'Ah, that's wonderful news!'

'And it's all there!'

'How do you know that?'

'I hid seventy-two wads from your bag, back in 1959, and I've counted seventy-two again.'

'That sounds about right. So, you can keep five of them, as I promised, and hand over the rest.'

'OK.'

'Now, I've been waiting to hear this for over a year – nearly eight years! – but I obviously need to put a few finishing touches to the plan for how you're going to get the money to me. You still haven't involved the police in any way, have you?'

'No, Luc.'

'Well, if you want all of this to end without any further nastiness, you'll continue to keep them out of it. And I don't really care if you've been lying to me and they *have* been monitoring my calls. Or trying to trace them. Even if they've succeeded, they'll know I've travelled all over the South of France to make them.'

'No-one knew a thing about any of the calls you made to me, Luc.'

'Good. Anyhow, there's no way they'll be able to trap me when you do come to deliver the money. And listen carefully ... if they *were* to even try and do that, I have an associate who would know about it at once, and she would quickly make sure that Emilie and your bookshop girl would both despise *you* for the rest of their lives. Got that?'

'Yes, Luc.'

'So, I'll call you exactly forty-eight hours from now, at the box at the southern end of Rue Grimaldi in Nice. Backup is the box two blocks up, at Rue du Maréchal Joffre. Bring the money with you in a holdall, and make sure you have plenty of small change and notes of your own ready to travel with. And I repeat, do not contact the police. You know it makes sense.'

'OK.'

Arthur put down the receiver, walked shakily over to the kerb, sat down on the pavement, and waited.

Six minutes later the phone rang yet again.

'*Allô!*'

'It's Hardy. We've got them, Arthur.'

'Seriously?'

'Yes. Carne left his mother's place less than an hour before the time set for your call. We followed him for thirty minutes until he came to a phone box in the south of Toulon. He went in and stayed put until twelve o'clock, and then he rang you.

'We listened in to a radio relay of the entire conversation as it was being double-recorded, and we surrounded him as soon as it was over. Then we radioed the team waiting outside the apartment, and they went in and picked up his "associate". And our Control Room has just confirmed that both tape recordings are excellent. We got all the admissions, and all the threats, and even his implication of his own mother! We also have a documented trace on his call box, which will be perfect corroborative evidence. Madame Carne is in big trouble, and her son will be going down for a long time.'

'That's fantastic! So, can I go home now?'

'Yes. And I'll be bending a lot of rules to ensure we won't be needing to talk to you officially for a while – and I trust you'll be very grateful for that – but I do have a few ideas on how you might later continue to help us ...'

'Oh, wonderful ...'

'... so I suggest you keep your head firmly down for the time being. But you must call me first thing on Monday morning, OK?'

'OK. And listen, Simon ... will you please try very hard to find out if Carne really does know anything about what happened to Emilie?'

'I'll do my best, Arthur. And in exchange, we really would love to confirm precisely where *you're* living these days. Just so that we can send you a birthday card on Tuesday, of course. So my dear friend Inspector Lebrun should be pulling up beside you in another unmarked car, just about now. Am I right?'

'Yes, *Inspector* Hardy. Your intuition never fails to impress me.'

'Ah, the magic of radio waves. So, Ricard will be delighted to drive you straight home and see you safely through your front door. And then he'll leave you in peace. But please don't give him any problems, Arthur. Because we can happily accommodate you in a police cell for the rest of the month, on a mountain of viable charges, if you'd really prefer not to go home at once ...'

* * *

Lebrun escorted Arthur up to his apartment, grinned as he handed him a jangling paper bag, and watched him unlock the door and disappear inside.

Julia was out shopping. But as soon as she returned, with only an hour to spare before going back off to work, Arthur told her the good news about the capture of the gang leader.

'Oh, that's wonderful, *chéri*! So is it all over now? Can we start to live a normal life together at last?'

'Not quite yet. There are several loose ends to tie up. Some a lot looser than others, I fear. You'll still need to let me get on with whatever is necessary, day by day, for the time being. So bear with me, please, OK?'

'Of course I will. I know it's complicated, and I know you'll sort it out as fast as you can. But do be careful ...'

'I shall.'

'Good. Hey, what's in the bag?'

'Presents from the Inspectors. Two small bottles of beer. One has a label saying "As Promised" and the other one says "Happy Birthday".'

'How very thoughtful of them. But I don't like beer.'

'Yeah. They have absolutely no sensitivity. So, time for a quick little something else before you go off to work?'

'Definitely. I'm having water biscuits and cheese. How about you?'

Early the following morning, Arthur told Julia he had some important jobs to do in town straight away, but perhaps after that they could spend the rest of the day on the beach? And she was very happy with his plan – she had plenty of chores of her own to be getting on with.

He then spent a few hours "exchanging" the last of the 5000 Old Franc bills he had been hiding in his drawer. He had paid his month's rent in advance, as usual, and the good lump of completely clean cash in his possession would definitely last them through to the end of September and probably a bit beyond.

So now, as he had "pretended" the day before to Luc – or Ruford, or Carne, or whatever! – and to everybody else listening in, he was indeed holding precisely seventy-two wads of stolen money: the two presently nestling quietly in a locker at the Gare du Sud left-luggage office, and no less than seventy stored safely away in the locked suitcase in his own wardrobe.

And now he and Julia could go down to the beach for the whole afternoon, before she went off to work again soon after six o'clock.

* * *

They got up late on Sunday morning and discussed their plans for the day over an early lunch. Arthur said he needed to do some quiet, careful thinking and then maybe go out for a while, but Julia was keen to get back to the beach for a few hours while the weather was still good and the rain was holding off. So that was easily agreed.

'And can I borrow that book in your bedside drawer?'

'Which one?'

'The Fowles novel about a kidnapping.'

'Sure. It is a bit depressing, though. Not a very pleasant read for a lovely summer's afternoon ...'

'Are you trying to protect me, *chéri*? Or even play the censor?'

'Me? You must be joking! Go ahead, take it. It's very well constructed. But don't complain when you start crying at the way the kidnapper treats ...'

'Stop, Arthur! Now you're giving the damned plot and everything away too!'

'OK, OK! Just get out and enjoy it!'

'Thanks. I'll be back around five. Big kiss, please ...'

An hour later, Arthur sat back in his chair and stretched his tight shoulder muscles.

He had been working hard on re-applying a bit of Claude Marasin's "alchemy" to everything he felt he knew about the mastermind who was still on his back, and he had now filled three large sheets of paper with many scribbled notes and complicated attempts at reorganising and analysing his facts.

The man he had been talking to on the phone for over a year was well spoken, clearly intelligent, and usually rational. He had chosen to call himself "Xérus" – a rather "educated" name. And Arthur had guessed long ago that the combination of his cultured tone and his "southern" accent suggested that he was originally from the Ile de France, but moved away – probably quite some time ago – to come and live down here in the Midi.

But of course the man who telephoned Giuseppe Hauvert was seemingly a French-speaking Sicilian. Either a completely different person, therefore, or a rather convincing mimic ...

He had probably always been well off, and was now based here in Nice, quite possibly working in *that* bank. Because Inspector Hardy was still convinced the mastermind must have been an insider.

He had presumably always made his calls from different phone boxes, but they were always scheduled for twelve noon on the very last day of the month – whenever *Xérus* had dictated the date. Otherwise it was always at nine in the evening, if Arthur had left him an *ad hoc* afternoon "flowers" signal at the bookshop. That sounded like the work pattern of someone who could take early lunch breaks but was maybe not free again until quite late in the evening. So, a job with both flexibility and end-of-day responsibilities?

Xérus had always been extremely reluctant to reveal any specific information about the "Paul Ruford" whom he had almost certainly recruited over in Marseilles. And he had actually complained that Arthur might have "done harm" with his sniffing around in that city, and said it could have "opened old sores" to supply any kind of sketch of his partner in crime. So Xérus may well have lived and worked in Marseilles himself at some time between 1950 and 1959, when Ruford was "operating" there.

And Xérus had told Arthur he had the feeling that "Paul Ruford" was a false name. What was the source of that idea? The underworld, quite possibly. But maybe the police. Perhaps even the Marseilles Crime Prevention Unit, vintage 1955? And if that *was* where he got the idea, it almost certainly meant that Xérus had been working in the banking industry there at that time. With specific responsibility for security?

And last but maybe not least, Xérus was probably slightly deaf in both ears.

Arthur made himself a cup of coffee, then took a clean sheet of paper, wrote down a few key words, and produced his unified theory.

> "The mastermind is probably a well-educated Parisian bank employee who moved down to Marseilles and then transferred to Nice in the late Fifties. He is now a widely experienced professional here, possibly a senior manager, but he is starting to go deaf. He may also have a natural talent for languages. And for some peculiar reason he wanted to rob a bank nearly eight years ago – using his specialist knowledge of security procedures and the Marseilles underworld!"

But if it really *had* been an inside job, and if he ruled out all the younger or totally improbable members of the Banque Artisanale's staff back in 1959, that left only two possibilities: Raoul Tillier, previously Manager but now presumably retired and ultra-flexible, and Charles-Pierre Orceau, previously Deputy Manager but now almost certainly the new man in charge.

And Arthur knew very little about either of them. But he did know a man who knew a little more, and he could phone him whenever he liked.

First, however, he needed to get out and ask somebody else for another special favour.

A little after two-thirty he turned into Boulevard Victor Hugo, walked along to the hotel where young Alain Revaur was hopefully still in gainful employment – either just about to finish his shift or start a new one – and found him once again polishing the ever-gleaming brass stair-rail.

Mindful of the potential for the fury of the presently invisible Billy to erupt at any moment, he spoke to Alain for no more than twenty seconds, arranging to meet up with him for a quick beer as soon as his shift ended at three. And later, over that beer, he secured his friend's agreement to lend him a helping hand for a couple of hours before his afternoon shift on the coming Tuesday ...

On his way home, Arthur tried to call Giuseppe Hauvert at his grandparents' house in Genoa. But they were sorry to say he would be away for the rest of the weekend and then at work the next day. 'So perhaps you could phone back tomorrow evening, *signore* ...?'

He was lying on the bed, deep in thought once again, when Julia hurried in from the beach just after five-thirty, with less than half an hour to spare before going out to work. After gracing him with just a quick peck on the cheek, she tipped the contents of her handbag straight out onto the bed.

'It was full of grit and little stones!'

'That's a real exaggeration, Julia. There's only a bit, and it's all over the covers now. Thanks a lot!'

'I don't know how it could have happened!'

'Calm down. Someone must have kicked it up accidentally as they were walking past ...'

'I suppose so. Last thing I needed today! I'm late enough as ...'

Then she stopped short.

'Where's it gone?'

'What?'

'The sheet of paper with my final paragraphs.'

'That stuff you wrote on holiday?'

'Yes. You've taken it, haven't you? You've taken it and thrown it away because you hated it so much!'

'Of course I haven't.'

'Yes, you have!'

'No I have not!! You must calm down, *chérie*. Now, where was it when you last saw it?'

'Right at the bottom. I've been keeping it there in case I ever decide to try again. And now it's gone!'

'Let's just have a proper look for it, eh? Rather than ...'

'Ah, *here* it is!'

'I told you so ...'

'But it's inside the pages of your novel.'

'So you used it as a bookmark ...'

'No. I never do that. I fold the pages down – see, this is where I got to this afternoon. And I haven't touched that piece of paper since I stuck it at the bottom of the bag over two weeks ago.'

'Well, I suppose someone *could* have gone through your bag while you were swimming ...'

'But there's nothing missing. Even my money's all still there ...'

'Did you see anyone hanging around near where you'd left your towel and stuff?'

'No. But I wasn't looking while I was in the water. And there was nothing different when I walked back up the beach. Just the families and kids who'd been lounging around there before ...'

'Well, I suggest you forget all about it now and get a move on, or you're going to be very late for work!'

'You're right. And ... well, I'm sorry, Arthur.'

'I'll need another kiss to seal it.'

'No time!'

* * *

The next morning, Arthur left Julia fast asleep after her latest long evening's work and hurried out for his nine o'clock telephone rendezvous with Inspector Simon Hardy.

'Well, Arthur, it looks as though I may be able to get some of that reward money winging its way to you, sooner or later. But don't hold your breath.'

'That's great!'

'Yes. And I think you can safely assume that Carne knows absolutely nothing more about Emilie. I'm convinced he would have responded to my very gentle enquiries if he did ...'

'Hah! OK, thank you for doing that. Really.'

'Meanwhile ...'

'How did I guess ...?'

'Meanwhile, we still want you to sit tight and see what happens next. I've cleared it with the powers-that-be, and we're ignoring all your little "obstructions" for the time being. If our mastermind does exist – and you know I'm still convinced of that – he may pick up the news of Carne's arrest and start to get fidgety. Especially if the underworld grapevine starts wagging its tongue, if you'll excuse the mixed metaphor. He may even decide you really do have the money. But of course you don't, do you ...?'

'Of course not, Simon.'

'So, carry on as normal, *Gardien Narone*. But call me anytime you need to, OK?'

'OK.'

'And watch your back.'

The rain had come in now, so Julia and Arthur spent the rest of the day tucked up in bed at home. He did a lot more thinking, while she continued reading *L'Obsédé*. And when she finally sighed deeply and put the book down with the predicted tears in her eyes, she agreed out loud with him about how chilling an experience it had been.

At six o'clock she went back out to the club as usual, glad that this was the end of her working week and the next two evenings would be all theirs. And a little later, Arthur popped out himself and tried again to call Giuseppe Hauvert. But by that time the guy had already come in from work and gone straight back out for the night.

'Perhaps a little earlier tomorrow evening, *signore*?'

* * *

Julia helped Arthur celebrate the start of his twenty-ninth birthday in dazzling style for much of Tuesday morning. But he had already warned her that he would have to disappear well before twelve o'clock and could then be very busy all afternoon. Since it was still raining, she had simply warned him in return that it was the first of her lovely days off, that she would be doing no housework whatsoever, and that she might well still be in bed when he returned. 'And later on, we're going out for the evening, *chéri*. The restaurant's booked. My treat!'

At noon, Arthur was ready and waiting for Xérus' next call. But it did not go quite as he had expected.

'This is Narone.'

'The word on the street is that Ruford has been arrested!'

'What?'

'You haven't heard about it?'

'No. So how did *you*?'

'There must have been another police leak. And so much for *your* famous network of contacts! I'm not at all happy about this, Narone. You know I wanted some time on my own with Ruford before the *flics* got their hands on him!'

'It's not my fault if they suddenly get smart for once, is it?'

'I'm not so sure about that. But there's something else ...'

'What?'

'I've also heard he's been insisting that *you* took the cash when he left the second getaway car. And that he's been talking to you ever since you left prison, dammit! And that you have now found the money again ...'

'Your sources are *very* well informed, aren't they?'

'Just tell me if they're right, Narone!'

'They are wrong. I never had that money, X, and I have no idea where it is.'

'I don't believe you.'

'But it's true.'

'I know where you're living now.'

'How?'

'That's irrelevant.'

'Well, I don't care. I have nothing of value there.'

'Are you sure?'

'Yes.'

'All right then. Tomorrow night Pureza Seles' bookshop goes up in flames ...'

'No!'

'... and soon after that your precious Emilie Courbier will have her pretty little face permanently readjusted.'

'No!!'

'You're the only one who can stop it happening, Narone.'

'Do you really know where Emilie is?'

'You'd better believe it. But if you'll admit to knowing where the money is, and you hand it over to me, maybe I'll then tell you what you want to know about her – rather than paying her a little visit myself.'

'All right, X. I give in. Yes, I do know where it's hidden.'

'At last!'

'But listen – it's not stored in Nice, and it will take me some time to travel to ... well, to wherever I'm keeping it. And ... well, I'd better take a holdall full of old newspapers with me, so it will look as if I'm going off on holiday. Then I'll need to wait for the opportunity to go in and collect the cash, and then hole up with it and bring it back in the bag at the end of my "break" and stash it somewhere safe ready for you to collect or whatever ...'

'So how long will you need?'

'Four days at least. But we'd better allow a week, in case I hit difficulties. I can guarantee to have it back here by the twelfth. Want to call me again at noon that day?'

'Probably ...'

'But look, I really don't feel it's fair to make me give the whole lot up to you, after all the work I've had to do. I reckon we should split it fifty-fifty, OK?'

'Don't even think about it, Narone. You will hand over every single note that was in that bag when you received it.'

'No, I definitely want my fair share, X. If you won't agree to that, I'll leave Nice this afternoon, and collect the cash, and disappear off the face of the earth and keep it all for myself. Remember, I could have done that at any time in the past year, but I've stuck with you – to try and help you find Ruford, and in the hope that you would help me find Emilie. But all you're doing is continuing to threaten her.

Pah! And if you *do* decide to torch Pureza's shop, you'll certainly never see me or the money again, either. And where will that leave you, eh? So, do we have a deal?'

'Not yet. But you go and get the money, and I'll think about it in the meantime. We'll work something out in the call on the twelfth. Honour among thieves. Satisfied?'

'And you'll do nothing nasty to Pureza or Emilie in the meantime?'

'Right.'

'OK. What phone box shall I use ...?'

Arthur was reeling from the effort of playing so much by ear in so short a space of time. So he now stood quietly in the phone box for a couple of minutes, breathing deeply and recovering most of his usual sang-froid.

Then he tried to think properly again. And the first thing that struck him was, once more, the high quality of Xérus' information. That was still very hard to fathom ...

But then he found he could not concentrate on any of the details of the *real* new action plan he would quickly need to develop. Because something else was bugging him – again. Just like after his call with Simon at the beginning of June. He had never worked out what that was all about. And what was going on inside his head now?

Aha! Xérus' accent had been different during this latest call! Far more natural, rather than his usual, vaguely artificial half-and-half dialect. More natural – under stress. Now what did that remind him of? What, dammit?

Yes, that was it! That little joke he had made to Simon! 'Surely you recognise my voice after all this time?' But was he really recognising Xérus' voice from some time in the past? Long before the man had made contact last year?

How could that be possible? And why was that voice only showing itself now, in this relatively stressful phone call?

Stressful situations. Arthur had been in plenty of those over the years. But then it wasn't his own stress he should be thinking about, was it? It was Xérus'.

But he'd never met the man! Or had he?

Stressful situations ....

None of the people he'd come into contact with since leaving jail fitted the bill at all. Particularly those he'd met in "difficult" situations.

And he'd been in very few such situations during his two short stints in the Nice Maison d'Arrêt. So it wasn't anything to do with that place.

What about all the times those stressed-out young teds in Marseilles Prison had tried to drag information out of him? No, it was none of those petty criminals either. Xérus was far too old and "cultured" for that. And anyway, he had never gone to jail for the robbery! Hah!

And before that? There was the trial in the Palais de Justice in Nice, of course. With all those bank employees and customers staring daggers at him and the other robbers, and then going one by one into the witness box to give their own personal accounts of what had happened that day ....

Him! Could it really be him? Surely not? But yes, that was undoubtedly the angry, emotional voice he had suddenly been hearing once again!

It was still very hard to believe. But the information he was hopefully about to pick up might just clinch it ...

* * *

He met Alain Revaur at their usual watering hole, half an hour before the student was due to start his three o'clock shift at the hotel.

'Well, Arthur, I went into the bank for a few minutes at eleven-fifteen today, just as you suggested, and I did my best to identify the various members of staff, as distinct from the customers. Then I came back out and went for a coffee at one of the pavement tables at the café on the corner. I could see the bank's entrance very clearly from there.

'And just after eleven-thirty, the guy who had been working in the biggest back office came out of the front door.'

'Seriously? OK, tell me exactly what he looked like ...'

'Tall, mid-fifties probably, very conservatively dressed. And while I was inside I'd spotted he was wearing a hearing aid.'

'Yes! OK, Alain, carry on ...'

'Well, I stood up very calmly, and I was all ready to follow him on foot, as we'd agreed, but he walked a few paces to a smart car sitting in the only parking space beside the building, and he roared off up to the junction and down Rue Pastorelli.'

'Yes!! But what make and model was it, Alain?'

'No idea! I know nothing about cars! But it was light blue, and in very good condition.'

'OK. I can check it out myself soon. Hmmm, I don't suppose ...'

'Yes, I wrote down the registration number for you. Here ...'

And he handed Arthur a small piece of paper.

'That's brilliant, Alain! And then ...?'

'Well, twenty minutes later I went back into the bank, as you said I should if none of the staff had actually emerged, and I started browsing the leaflets and other stuff. And just before twelve noon, I made sure I was watching all the other employees as discreetly as I could. And *nobody* stopped what they were doing to make a phone call. I waited two or three minutes, and then I got out fast again.

'I strolled back up to the café, and this time I had a beer. And at twelve-thirty precisely that manager guy pulled into his parking space and went back inside.'

'Perfect! Exactly what I needed to know!'

'But what does it all mean, Arthur?'

'Don't ask, pal. Just look forward to that whole evening out, on me, one of these days! But right now I really have to rush! And take it easy with bully-boy Billy, eh!'

Well, this was further, strong circumstantial evidence that Charles-Pierre Orceau actually was Xérus, thought Arthur as he hurried away, but it was by no means good enough. He needed something far more definitive – maybe several things – before he could consider either confronting the man himself or involving the police as he had with Luc. Perhaps Giuseppe Hauvert could supply something later today, if he finally managed to get hold of him! Meantime, he must check out Orceau's car, and then try to establish some more basic information about the man.

He soon reached Rue Alberti and walked very cautiously up it until he could just see the vehicle parked in the space beside the bank, still some way further along on the other side of the street.

Light blue, Alain had said. And so it was. A five-door Renault 16 hatchback. No more than two years old, of course. Arthur was fully back up to speed on his car marques now.

He turned on his heels and hurried back down to Rue de l'Hôtel des Postes and along to the imposing Post Office building. He found a copy of the local telephone directory and studied the residential listings carefully. But there was no mention of *any* Orceau in the entire Nice area, let alone a Charles-Pierre.

Oh, well. If Arthur did not yet know the man's present address or phone number, it was at least quite likely that his family was not from this city. For what that was worth!

* * *

'Giuseppe! Ah, I've got hold of you at last! This is Arthur Narone. Remember me?'

'Could I ever forget you, Arthur? How are you?'

'I'm well, thank you. And I'm very sorry to disturb you again. But may I possibly have another quick word about the people who might have been behind the bank robbery ...?'

'For sure. It makes no difference to me any more ...'

'But maybe it actually could, one day, Giuseppe. So ... well, I don't know quite how to put this, but I really am beginning to think that either Raoul Tillier or Charles-Pierre Orceau was involved in organising the whole affair.'

'Oh, I'm certain you're completely wrong about both of them, Arthur.'

'And maybe I am, my friend. But if that *is* the case, then you will have helped me rule them out, right?'

'OK ...'

'So, what more can you tell me about Tillier, please?'

'Well, I was only working at the bank for four years, and I was quite junior, so I didn't know a lot about him. He was always very remote. Very superior. Old guard. And when I came back to work after the robbery, he sacked me on the spot. Just to avoid embarrassment. They had no evidence against me, you know ...'

'Yes, I did know all that, Giuseppe, and I'm truly very sorry for the part I played in it. But I do need to know more about *him* rather than you, right now ...'

'OK. All I can really tell you is that when our old Branch Manager retired in the spring of 1958, we all expected Charles-Pierre would get the job. But he didn't, and that was a real pity, 'cos he was very well liked. No, Sire Raoul Tillier was promoted in from the Cannes branch. No-one in our branch had ever heard of him! And he turned out to be a really dull boss, if you know what I mean.'

'Well, not really, Giuseppe, but I do get the message. And ...?'

'There's nothing more to say. I never really got to know him over the next eighteen months. I heard he was away at the Head Office in Marseilles on the day of the robbery, but that was perfectly normal. And I think he would have been due for retirement in about 1965.'

'Yes, I think that's probably when Charles-Pierre Orceau was promoted to Manager.'

'Great! At long last! And I knew *him* much better, of course. He helped me a lot throughout my training. Even took me out to lunch two or three times, and he was really interested in my ...'

'Just tell me about *him* please, Giuseppe!'

'OK. Well, he was a linguist by education. But he had a very good head for figures too. And he was always very kind, you know? Actually, he was almost a father figure to me. Maybe 'cos of what happened to his family ...'

'Go on ...'

'He told me he'd lost his wife and child in the war. There was a huge air-raid on Boulogne-Billancourt, just outside Paris, in 1942. An Allied air-raid! They'd only been married for about five years, and his son was just three.

'He never remarried, and he later moved south to try to forget and start a new life down here. He worked in our central Marseilles branch for many years, until 1956, when he was transferred to Nice and promoted to Deputy Manager. I'd started working there just four months earlier.'

'Hey, that was all *really* useful background, Giuseppe. And what about the man while he was actually there with you in Nice ...?'

'I think he kept out of the social scene most of the time. He was still quite a solitary character. But he did belong to the Rotary Club. I think they used to meet once a week on Friday evenings, and I know that on the very last day of every month they had a civic lunch with all the local bigwigs ...'

'Wow! I mean ... OK, so do you know where he lived? 'Cos you told me, when we met up in April, that all of you had access to everyone else's contact details, right ...?'

'Sure I did, Arthur. But I never actually looked at any of them. They were strictly for use inside the bank and only in emergencies. But I *can* tell you that in late '58, Charles-Pierre had a nice house up in Cimiez. He invited us all to a little Christmas drinks party that year.'

'Do you remember the address?'

'Oh, come on, man! That was nine years ago!'

'Well, the street name, at least?'

'No. But I remember it was quite a *long* street ... directly off the main Boulevard de Cimiez coming out of the city.'

'Was it Avenue Colonel Evans?'

'No.'

'Boulevard Edouard VII?'

'No.'

'Boulevard Prince de Galles?'

'Yes! That was it! And the house was very close to the main boulevard junction.'

'Thank you, Giuseppe. I think that's all I need.'

'I really do hope ...'

'Hmmm. Don't keep your hopes up too much as far as Orceau is concerned, my friend. But maybe keep hoping that one day your own reputation can be completely restored. *Allora, grazie mille, e arrivederci!*'

* * *

'I haven't received a birthday card from Pureza.'

'That's quite possibly because you decided not to tell her your new address.'

'*Merde!*'

'And she must be feeling really sad about it ...'

'OK, OK, Julia. So I'd better phone her on the way to the restaurant, right?'

'Right. And maybe try to find a few minutes to pop in and see her tomorrow?'

'That may not be too easy. I think I'll just have to say it with flowers again.'

* * *

The following morning, Julia Rochemont and Arthur Narone squeezed together into an Old City telephone box and she dialled the number of the Banque Artisanale. If she managed to get through to anybody of significance, she would simply pretend to be seeking holiday employment. And Arthur would be silently listening in, just in case they were lucky enough to reach Orceau himself and he was able to pick up a good feel for the man's natural accent. But they would anyway be able to double-check some of Arthur's other unconfirmed information in passing ...

'*Banque Artisanale à votre service!*'

'*Ah, bonjour, madame.* I wish to speak to Monsieur Raoul Tillier.'

'I am very sorry, but Monsieur Tillier retired from the bank almost two years ago!'

'Oh! So he's living a life of leisure in Nice now?'

'Not at the moment, *mademoiselle*. He has been touring Africa for the past year. We've received lots of lovely postcards from him!'

'How nice! So who is the manager now, please?'

'Monsieur Charles-Pierre Orceau.'

'Then may I kindly speak to him?'

'I regret not. Monsieur Orceau has just begun his summer vacation, *enfin*. If you would care to give me your name and the purpose of your call, I will consider arranging an appointment with Madame Padroux ...'

Arthur was shaking his head and making an unmistakable "Cut it!" sign with his hand.

'No, that will not be necessary, *madame*. I am happy to wait for Monsieur Orceau to return. *Merci, au revoir.*'

Julia was equally happy to return to their apartment for another lazy day off while Arthur carried on with his own grubby business. 'But the sooner this is all over, *chéri* ....'

And he certainly still had plenty to be thinking about. He would need to "leave" Nice very soon on his fictional money-recovery mission, just in case the now-vacationing Orceau was floating around the city and watching for him to keep appearing here when he was supposed to be far away for several days. And of course Arthur would indeed have to go away, for appearances sake, for a short while at least ...

But first he wanted to try and level the playing field a little and establish Orceau's home address if he possibly could. What did he have so far? Very little, really. No joy from the phone book. Information from Hauvert that the man had a house on a particular road in Cimiez nearly nine years ago. And a light blue Renault 16.

He did not want to "go public" in the area where Orceau might still be living. So breezing up to the postman on his rounds and pretending to be a courier with a "parcel for a Monsieur Orceau, but it has the wrong house number, see ..." would be pushing it too far, especially if that should end up happening right outside the man's front door. No, he would rely on a bit of discreet observation, for today at least ...

So he took a bus up towards Cimiez. He got off at Avenue Colonel Evans and walked the long way round to the far end of Boulevard Prince de Galles. Nobody had followed him. Then he came most of the way down that road and stationed himself behind a parked car not far from the junction with the main boulevard. And he watched and waited and prayed that nobody would report him to the police. And then it began to rain again, and he wondered why he was so very, very crazy.

But ninety minutes later he suddenly got his answer. The garage door of a large house only fifty metres further down began to open of its own accord, a light blue Renault 16 emerged onto the road and moved away towards the Boulevard de Cimiez, and the remotely operated door closed smoothly behind it.

* * *

Early that afternoon, Arthur told Julia that things were definitely hotting up. He needed time and space, at once, and might well be going away from Nice for quite a while – very soon. So it would be

much easier and safer for them both if she went to stay with her aunt
Muriel for the next few days. He would come and find her once he
was back in the city and happy for her to start living in the apartment
again.

She nodded rather sadly, but did not argue. 'Almost over, do you
think, *chéri*?'

'I hope so, Julia. I really hope so.'

Once she had packed a few essentials, given him a brave kiss and
departed for her aunt's house, Arthur sat quietly and completed his
plan for the week. Then he strolled down to the corner store and
came back with a dozen large newspapers. A little later he went out
again in the opposite direction, purchased his holiday holdall, came
home again, stuffed the papers into it and walked in clear view to
Nice-Ville station.

He took a westbound train, but got off at Cannes only forty
minutes later. No-one followed him over the next hour. So after
buying a week's worth of simple provisions and storing them in his
bag along with the papers, he hung around the backstreets until it was
dark. Then he took the train back to Nice and followed a roundabout
route home again.

He was confident that Orceau had been nowhere near him all day.
And now his self-imposed, five-day siege in his own little Fort Knox
could begin.

Fair Exchange

At eleven-thirty on Tuesday the twelfth of September, Arthur finally broke his own siege and headed off for his noon telephone appointment with Xérus. And he had his negotiating strategy all figured out.

But once again the call did not go at all the way he had planned.

'Do you have the money now?'

'That depends on whether you agree to a fifty-fifty split.'

'No such deal, Narone. I told you I would think about it, and I have. I want every last centime of that cash. And you're going to do exactly what I say. Because I'm holding Julia Rochemont.'

'What! You ...'

'So I'll ask you again. Do you have the money now?'

'Why should I believe you have Julia?'

'When did you last see her?'

'That's irrelevant.'

'She tells me the first meal she cooked for you was paella.'

'Ah.'

'So, for the third time – do you have the money now?'

'Yes.'

'*Enfin!* So, where is it?'

'Somewhere safe, under my control ... but ...'

'You will not talk to the police or anyone else. And at five o'clock this afternoon you will take it to the call box at the bottom of Avenue Pauliani and await further instructions. The backup is the box at the top of the avenue.'

'But the police might be watching me anyway.'

'That won't matter. I'm going to make sure they'll have lost you by the time you hand over the money.'

'And you will then release Julia unharmed?'

'Yes. But if you don't answer that phone ...'

'OK, OK. But hang on ... let me think about the timings of this ...'

Arthur was not actually wondering about any such timings, but was thinking very fast about something completely different. If Xérus really *was* Charles-Pierre Orceau, the situation might not be completely hopeless. A possible rescue plan was already forming in his mind. But if his hunch proved wrong, he'd need some breathing space, for Julia's sake – and then he simply *would* have to comply with this man's demands, or call for reinforcements ...

'Are you still there, Narone?'

'Yes. I'm just working it all out ...'

'Well get on with it!'

'Look, the thing is, X ... I need to travel some way to pick up the cash from its new hiding place. I never expected you'd insist on having it delivered within a few hours, you see. And ... well, if I leave straight away, I'll probably be back in Nice in time – but I can't be certain. And anyway I might get unavoidably delayed. So I definitely *will* try to be at that call box with the money at five, but can we also agree that if I don't answer the phone at that time, you will call again at seven o'clock? I can certainly be there by then ...'

'All right. That's sensible thinking. And if you're still not there at seven, I'll give you the benefit of the doubt and phone again at nine – but that's it. After that, you can regard Julia Rochemont as history, OK?'

'OK.'

Arthur put the phone down and took a deep breath. Everything had changed now.

Should he tell Muriel that Julia had been kidnapped? Because she surely did not even suspect her niece was missing, or she would have come knocking at his door! She was probably just assuming he had picked Julia up from work or wherever once he was back in town, and that she was now living at his apartment again. So, should he tell her, dammit??

No. Not for now. That would waste far too much time, and bring understandable but unaffordable panic and worry into the equation.

Maybe he should tell the Inspector? And say he was convinced Orceau was their man, and let the police take it from there?

No. Or at least not yet. *That* would add too much extra risk and complexity, and he would completely lose the small amount of control he still had. No, he would play it just the way he had imagined during the phone call. The perfect twist in the plot! And if that came to nothing, he'd then still have two ... no, *four* hours of grace to involve the police, if he finally decided to do so.

Yes, for now he would concentrate on rescuing Julia himself. And if his theory was right, then maybe something else would also come of it ...

* * *

It had been raining again for over an hour when Arthur boarded the bus heading north out of town at three-thirty. He was dressed in a long hippy coat with large pockets, a big floppy hat and sunglasses. A large umbrella helpfully completed his disguise.

This time he got off at the stop just before the junction with Boulevard Prince de Galles, and crossed at once to the other side of the main road. Then he wandered a little way up the gentle hill and turned around. Peeping out from behind the protection of his umbrella, he at once saw Orceau's car sitting in the front drive of the house. Fairly confident now that the man was still at home, more than an hour before their five o'clock phone appointment, he strolled back down to the bus stop on his side of the road and pretended to be waiting there for the return trip.

He was wondering why that car was out in the pouring rain when it could be inside that nice dry garage. Why Orceau had chosen to get rather wet, if and when he did emerge from the house to drive, presumably, to yet another suitably remote telephone box. Maybe the garage door was broken. Or maybe there was something else taking up space in there. Or *somebody* else ...

That was all wishful thinking, but there was nothing else to do right now, and at least it had given a little more focus to his planned search for Julia – assuming he was able to get inside the house at all!

He continued to wait. Four-thirty passed. Then four-thirty-five. He recalculated for the hundredth time. If Orceau were to leave the house at four-forty, he would be driving for no more than ten minutes or so, to allow time to move on to another call box if the first was occupied, and maybe even to a third. And when he got no reply, he would surely return home at once, and be back here by ten past five at the latest.

Four-forty came and went, and Arthur was beginning to think he had got it all wrong after all. Either Orceau was going to telephone from home – but surely not! – or he was already out and about without his car, or Xérus was actually someone completely different and Arthur would soon be rushing back down to the city to pick up the stolen money and do the awful man's bidding after all. Or whatever.

And the more the minutes passed, the shorter the window of opportunity for rescuing Julia was getting.

At precisely a quarter to five, Arthur's heart jumped as he saw, out of the corner of his eye, the light blue Renault pulling out of the drive. It approached the junction, turned left onto Boulevard de Cimiez, and headed off downtown. Orceau was at the wheel.

The moment the car was out of sight, Arthur threw all caution to the wind. He now had just twenty minutes to do this job, twenty-five at the very most. He strode across the road and along to the house. There was no handle on the automatic garage door. So he went straight up to the solid front door, knocked hard and rang the electric chimes, and waited thirty seconds while he assessed the lock.

No reply. And not much chance of breaking neatly into this high quality system in a hurry. So he would have to do it the other way. He reached into his deep coat pocket, extracted a heavy-duty wrench, and spent several precious minutes trying to find a way to open the door. But it would not succumb.

Plan B, then. He hurried to the other side of the house. There was a two-metre-high wall halfway back, attached to the neighbouring property and separating the front garden from the rear. He ditched the umbrella and his sunglasses and went for it at once, leaping up to gain a hold with both hands and then dragging himself over the top and dropping down onto the back patio.

Around the corner of the house there was a living room with tall glass doors. Then a kitchen. And then a length of wall with no windows. That must be the rear of the garage.

If he went through the small kitchen window and over the sink, he would have a hard time getting Julia out that way if none of the doors could be easily opened from the inside. No, it would have to be the living room. And the time for subtlety, or even using the wrench, had long gone. He would deal with any inquisitive neighbours if and when they confronted him ...

There were several large rocks decorating the flower beds. He hoisted up the heaviest of them and flung it at the right-hand door. The glass broke, leaving a large jagged hole in the centre but many sections still attached all round the frame. It took him another two minutes and several more rocks to smash out enough chunks to make a gap big enough to squeeze safely through.

He went straight into the kitchen. Nothing unusual. But he was looking for a way into the garage, and there was the door, with a key in the lock! He tried the handle. Solid. He turned the key and tried again.

The door opened outwards into the unlit garage, and there was Julia – at the back end, her wrists and legs tied to a wooden armchair which was itself tied to metal brackets on the wall. There was a thick pillow case over her head, but she was making some muffled sounds, so at least she was still alive.

'It's me, Julia. Close your eyes, *cherie*. I'm taking off the hood ...'

Her mouth was gagged and she looked and smelt awful, but when she opened her eyes her terror was mixed with a hint of hope. He worked on the gag first, with trembling fingers, and finally got it off.

'Oh, Arthur ...'

'Sshhhh! Don't try and talk. Let me concentrate on getting you untied. We've got to get out of here very fast!'

He threw off his cumbersome coat and hat, and found the light switch. Julia was breathing deeply and groaning as he worked on the rope securing her left hand to the arm of the chair. It was tied tightly, but it was slowly coming loose. If only he'd brought a knife! He looked up briefly at the workbench to his left, but there was no sign of one. He went back to undoing the knot, and it finally came loose. Julia moaned in some sort of relief, lifted her arm a little and feebly started to shake some life back into her wrist. Arthur forced a tiny smile, took a quick deep breath of his own, and then transferred all his attention to her right hand.

This knot was proving even harder to loosen.

'No!!' Julia suddenly shrieked. He looked up and saw new terror in her eyes. And as he began to turn round, she screamed and threw up her newly-freed hand ...

* * *

'Carry on whenever you're ready, Arthur ...'
  'I'm sorry, Inspector. It all got too much for me just then ...'
  'Of course. Take it easy. Want another glass of water ...?'
  'No, I'm OK. Just give me another few moments, eh?'
  'Sure.'

'So, I'd managed to undo the rope tying Julia's left hand to the arm of the chair. But as I was working on the one holding her right hand, she must have seen Orceau coming up behind me. I started to turn round, then she screamed and threw up her hand, and Orceau hit it with a kitchen knife and chopped two of her fingertips clean off! Some of the blood went in my eyes, and my vision was blurred, and I thought it would definitely be my turn next ...

'But it had all gone very quiet. Julia was just staring in shock at her mutilated hand, and Orceau had frozen too. Then he started moaning something like: "Oh, my treasure, my poor little butterfly, you made me hurt you, why did you make me hurt you ...?" and I realised he'd forgotten all about me for a moment. I didn't mess around. I grabbed the nearest heavy thing I could see – it was a small fire extinguisher sitting on the bench right next to me – and I smashed it into his face. He went down and he stayed down ...'

'You made a nasty mess of his nose, Arthur. And he won't be seeing very well for some time, either.'

'Too bad. Anyway, now I didn't know what to do first! I wanted to get Julia properly sorted out, but Orceau could have come round at any time. Too risky to ignore him completely. So I just got a towel from the kitchen and wrapped her hand in it as tightly as I could, to slow down the blood loss. She was still in shock, saying nothing and shaking her head in disbelief.

'Then I looked around for some way of keeping Orceau at bay. And there was a lot more rope coiled up under the bench! So I wrapped it round and round him until it ran out and then I tied it off as tightly as I could. And I stuck the pillow case on *his* head!'

'You did a nice job of that as well. Turned him into quite a chrysalis.'

'Then I finally recovered Julia's fingertips from the floor and went back into the kitchen, and rinsed them in milk, and put them in a glass and covered them with some more milk. I'd heard that was a good thing to do if you lost a tooth, just in case ...

'And then I heard Julia sobbing loudly, and I rushed back into the garage ...'

'Can you hear me, Julia? Julia??'

'What? Yes, I can! And stop shaking me!'

'All right. But *you* must stop that shrieking, and sit still, OK? Good – now I can try and do something better for your hand. I'll use the rope to make a tourniquet ...'

'Oh Arthur, it really hurts! And I'm so scared!'

'It's OK, Julia. He's not getting up again.'

'No, about my fingers ...'

'I've put them in some milk. Maybe they'll be able to rescue them. Try not to worry too much ...'

'What!!'

'Calm down, Julia. Right, that's a tourniquet of sorts. Bend your elbow and hold your arm up. Good. Now I'll finish untying your other wrist and we can use *that* bit of rope to improve it .... Nearly there .... Right, that's got it .... Hold still .... Almost done now ....'

'Oh, hell, Arthur, I'm sorry I shouted at you. You're doing wonders for me.'

'I haven't finished yet. Is there a phone in the house?'

'Yes. I've heard it ring a couple of times. It must be in the kitchen.'

'OK, I'll call for the police and two ambulances now. Don't try to stand up – your legs are still tied. Just try to relax. I'll make you a quick cup of tea while I'm out there – that's good for shock. And keep your eye on that bastard, just in case ...'

'Those were all good moves too, Arthur. And apparently there's a fair chance the surgeons can successfully re-attach at least one of the fingertips.'

'I hope you're right. Anyway, five minutes later the ambulances were well on their way, and Julia was drinking her tea and I was finally untying her legs. And then the first police car arrived ...'

'OK, we'll leave it there for now. I'll need to hear what she has to say after the operation.'

'Can I be with her, Simon?'

'Only if you sit directly behind her and say nothing. One single word and you're out of the door.'

* * *

'So exactly what happened next, Julia?'

'The guy must have realised what was happening as soon as he got back to the house, and gone straight into the kitchen and picked up that meat knife. Arthur had just finished undoing the first rope from my wrist when he came through the garage door with a crazy look on his face, and I saw him lift the knife and come towards us. Arthur started to turn around, but the bastard was already swinging the knife down towards his back. Oh, God ....'

'Easy does it, young lady! Take a few good deep breaths.'

'OK ....'

'Better?'

'Yes, Inspector.'

'And then ...?'

'I screamed and just threw my arm up to try and protect Arthur ... and the knife sliced through two of my fingers! I remember staring at my poor hand in utter shock – and then I saw the guy was still hovering right over us with the knife in his hand ... and that's when Arthur hit him with something, and the bastard went down. And then I must have fainted, or whatever ...'

'OK, Julia, we'll stop there. That's enough for the time being. More than enough. I'll leave the two of you together now.'

'Arthur, you really are a very resourceful man!'

'Me? I'd say you win that prize, with your left-arm swing. And look at the price you've paid for it!'

'It's a very small price, Arthur. A fine deal. I've been thinking clearly again. You took my mother's fingers, all those years ago, but in return she got her husband, and *that* gave me my life, no less! And now you've brought me back again from the hell that bastard had put me in. And maybe I saved *you* from a much more serious injury, or even let you hold on to the life you might have lost.'

'Wow. That's some thinking ...'

'Actually, I reckon it's far too much. Writers! Probably better to just say "Thank you, *chéri*," and try to get back to living my own life. And let you get on with living yours ...'

'Your life? My life? Oh, come on! I'd say we've gone a bit beyond that now, wouldn't you? Why don't we start talking about *our* life?'

'Did I really just hear you right ...?'

'I hope so. He didn't manage to cut off your ear as well, did he?'

'Oh, Arthur ...'

'Want to talk about how it all happened?'

'Not yet.'

'OK.'

Cooling Off

'I think you deserve a bit of an explanation, Arthur.'

'I think you deserve a gold medal for understatement, Simon.'

'Be gentle with me, pal. You and I are locked together in a pretty tight survival dance right now ...'

'OK ...'

'It was the bank's idea to get you out of jail early. Now, I always assumed it was Tillier who had instigated that, and I still suspected he was the insider, keen to get his hands on the money at last. But he was due to retire soon – which was another hint that he might be our man, ready to go into action with no other demands on his time – so all my actual dealings on your "liberation" were with Orceau, from the start.

'Of course I now know that *he* actually suggested the scheme to Tillier. But the guy had been shot by the gang leader, for heaven's sake! So nobody ever really suspected him. And we probably all denied or ignored the tiny hints that later came our way. Which *you* did not, of course ...'

'Didn't you know that Orceau had previously worked in the Marseilles branch for several years??'

'Yes, I did.'

'Huh! I only learnt that myself a few days ago, from Giuseppe Hauvert, but *you've* always been going on about an insider! Why didn't you put two and two together as soon as you heard about that Crime Prevention briefing material?'

'Because I'm not as smart as you, Arthur. And you're not the first person to have asked me that question this week. I told you we're both under a lot of scrutiny ...'

'Pah! So why do you think the bastard *was* shot?'

'I've already asked him that myself. He says he thinks he overplayed his role as the aggrieved bank manager, and Carne just lost his cool at the last minute. Of course, Carne had no idea he was shooting his own *Gruppenführer* ...'

'Hah!'

'Yes. So, once you were finally released, Charles-Pierre and I were in regular communication. But all I was able to report for over a year was that you were "doing your best" for us. I had no idea that "Luc" had got to you even before I made contact, let alone that your "Xérus" then started to throw his weight around behind my back as well. Thanks a lot for nothing, Arthur!'

'You want me to say sorry?'

'No, not really. And so I kept giving Orceau simple little progress reports, as agreed. And that just fuelled his fire, of course.'

'I feel so proud of our wonderful police force, Simon.'

'Cut it out, Arthur. I keep telling you we're both in this together. Half the people who matter out there think the two of us are national heroes. The rest of them want us both in jail for the next few years. And I'm the one having to manage that, while you ...'

'OK, OK.'

'Anyway ... nothing much of what I ever said to Orceau really mattered, until I told him you'd moved away from the bookshop. But of course I did not know where you'd gone, at the time.

'Then, once we'd built a sound plan for catching Carne and his mother, I told Orceau – naturally! – that there was a fair chance we might get them soon. And I also said you were part of the trap, as we'd always half-expected. But it must have annoyed him a lot to discover you'd been talking to "Luc" all this time ...'

'Yes, I sort of spotted that in his next phone call.'

'Hmmm. Well, after we'd arrested the pair of them, I phoned him at the bank that afternoon with the news. And I told him you *had* made off with the money that night, and discovered it was lost when you finally went to retrieve it, but you pretended to "Luc" that you had recovered it. And I also told him you were now living on Rue Edouard Beri.'

'Thanks a lot for that too, Simon.'

'It was just information, Arthur. Just an update. I had no idea, remember ...'

* * *

'I encouraged Orceau to make a much fuller statement this morning, Arthur. Well, you know the drill yourself, don't you? The more you tell me, the more I might ...'

'Yes, yes ...'

'So, do you want to hear how he worked the kidnap?'

'I certainly do, Ollie.'

Hardy consulted his typewritten sheets.

'After finishing work on the Friday, soon after I'd phoned to tell him about Carne's capture and your new address, he watched your street from a discreet distance, and eventually spotted you coming up it and going off for a drink. And when you returned, he saw you go into your apartment building itself.

'He hung around there again the next day, and this time he saw you *and* Julia coming and going. He followed you both down to the beach. And that evening he tracked Julia when she went off to work.

'The next day, while you stayed at home, he followed her again when she went to the beach on her own. And while she was having a long swim, he took a good look at the contents of her handbag, to try and find out as much about her as he could. Then he saw her swimming back towards the beach, and he hurriedly put everything back. But he *had* taken a quick look at that novel she was reading ...

'That Sunday evening he tracked Julia to the gentlemen's club again. But this time he waited in a nearby café until she finished work, well after one o'clock. He watched her walking back towards your apartment, then he broke off and went home.

'The following day he was at work at the bank, as usual. But in the evening he was back near the club again to watch her arrive around seven. He returned before midnight and saw her leave at the same time as before. So he had now established a solid pattern, and he knew she worked there on Saturday, Sunday and Monday at least.

'He was aware that we had taped and traced your final call with Paul-Philippe Carne, of course, so the next day he drove off to a phone box well away from work for his call to you on your birthday. He was very angry that he'd lost the chance of getting his own hands on the man ...'

'I know he was!'

'And then you "admitted" you really did have the money hidden away. But you raised the stakes by asking for a fifty-fifty share of it, and after that he had a long think and decided he needed more direct leverage to counter your fight-back and obtain *all* the cash.

'So then he made a plan to force you to concede. A plan to kidnap Julia on the night before your next phone call.

'He finished work early that afternoon, to start the holiday he'd been delaying ever since he'd heard that we might be on to Carne. And he drove straight to a bookshop he'd never visited before, and bought a copy of *L'Obsédé*.

'And over the next few days, while you were apparently somewhere far off collecting the loot – but actually holed up in your apartment, guarding it! – he was watching the club each evening. He soon discovered Julia was staying at her aunt's place while you were "away" for a while. So he finalised his plans. As she walked back there after work, late on the Monday night, he grabbed her in a dimly-lit side street, held a wad of chloroform over her mouth till she passed out, bundled her into his hatchback, and drove straight home and into his windowless garage.'

* * *

'Julia's ready to talk about it herself now, Arthur. Want to be there?'
    'Of course.'
    'Same rules, then. Don't go and spoil it all, OK?'
    'OK, Simon.'

'I was only five minutes away from Muriel's. It was pretty dark. He must have been hiding in a doorway, or maybe he came up very quietly from behind, because I was suddenly just grabbed. His left arm was tight across my chest and his right hand was holding a pad to my mouth. I never got a chance to make a sound. I struggled for a while but he just kept holding me tight ... and that's all I remember.

'I woke up tied to that chair. My mouth tasted awful, and the gag was hurting, and I started to panic because I couldn't see a thing. But then I realised there was just some sort of hood over my head. Of course I tried to make a lot of noise, but I soon gave up.

'He spoke to me soon after that. He asked me if I wanted a drink of water. I just ignored him. Then it went quiet for hours. But later I started hearing the occasional noise. It was probably early morning traffic in the street outside. And then he was there, asking me again if I wanted a drink. I was desperately thirsty, so this time I nodded. He said if I made the slightest sound when he took off the gag it would go straight back on and there would be no water for me after all. Then he lifted that pillowcase a little bit, from behind, and undid the gag, and let me drink from a plastic cup. Then the gag went back on at once, and the hood came down again.

'Then he said he wanted me to tell him something that only Arthur would know about the two of us. Something simple. And that it was essential for my survival that it was true. And that I should make no other sound, of course, or else. I nodded underneath the hood. So he lifted it a little again, and loosened the gag. And I just said the first meal I cooked for us was paella, and he was satisfied.

'I had a little more water a few hours later. And then I heard his car start up outside, and he drove away. He gave me more water when he came back. Then some time later he went off again, just as before.

'And then Arthur came! And then ....'

'Good girl, Julia. That was very brave of you. Sit back now and have another nice rest. Can I leave her in your capable hands again, Saint George?'

'Oh, yes.'

'Oh, Arthur ...'

* * *

'Do you want the good news or the bad news?'

'Why don't you just tell me one of them and let me guess which it is?'

'There are several pieces, actually. First, you do appreciate I can't let you out on bail for some time, if at all ...'

'Always full of surprises, Simon.'

'Just carry on trusting I'm doing all I can for you, eh? Behind the scenes, stage left, stage right, up in the fly loft, and ...'

'Yeah, I believe you.'

'Really?'

'Really.'

'So, later today you'll be transferred up to the Maison d'Arrêt on remand. But you know your way around there very well, of course. Might even bump into some old friends ...'

'I can't wait. So that was the good news, right?'

'Hah! Secondly, one of Julia's reattached fingertips is apparently doing very well indeed. But the other one is not looking so good.'

'OK.'

'Thirdly, we picked up the case from your wardrobe and the rucksack from the left luggage office, of course. Seventy-two wads in all – just as you said to Carne. And I'm told you may well have a valid claim to the bank's reward for the recovery of the money, when all the relevant facts and influences upon you are taken into account. They might reduce it a bit, because they only got back about ninety percent of what they lost, but it should still be a very tidy sum. I'm doing all I can to protect your claim from those who would like to prevent you getting it.'

'Thank you.'

'And there's more. I told you last week that the police reward for the arrest of Carne is looking promising for you, and that is still the case. But many of the movers and shakers of Nice have also been very uncomfortable, ever since the day of the robbery, about the possibility of a rogue element deep within their precious world of commerce. It turns out they've had a secret bounty on the head of the insider for years – if he could ever be unmasked. And now that he has not only been proved to exist, but has actually been captured and found to be a greater beast by far, many of them are apparently saying it would be immoral to refuse you the bounty just because you were part of the original gang. All those mitigating circumstances again, Arthur. So there may be even more pennies from heaven raining down on you soon. Funny old world, isn't it?'

'Why do you think a man as successful as Orceau changed into such a monster, Simon?'

'Well, I do have some of the answers now. In 1959 he was still trying to break out of the depression he'd been suffering in silence since his wife and child were killed in the war. You know the dream, Arthur – gamble a big lump of cash on those hefty advances to the gang, make a quick and easy fortune out of it, and start a new life abroad after quitting work on grounds of ill-health or the shock of it all.

'He's also admitted to me, off the record, that he used to have a vague "common justice" mentality about the desirability of the redistribution of wealth. A sort of fifth-column Robin Hood, if you like. But over the years those ideals steadily turned from altruism to self-interest. And he was really offended when he was passed over for promotion in 1958. Tillier would now be in situ for six long years. So the desire for revenge against the bank completed the circle.

'He says he even pretended to himself, at that time, that if the gang did end up double-crossing him and never delivered his two-thirds share of the loot, he'd have lost nothing anyway and would have won a moral victory against capitalism!

'But after Carne shot him, and the money was not forthcoming, he actually got very angry instead, and eventually built the cunning plan that we all then fell for. After your release his frustration just continued to grow, of course. And when he lost the chance to punish "Luc" in person, and discovered *you'd* been stringing him along all this time as well, he finally flipped, and poor Julia took all his crossfire.'

'Unbelieveable.'

'Or all too believeable.'

'Yeah. So do you reckon *he* knows anything about what became of Emilie?'

'I thought you'd never ask. No, I gave him even more encouragement than I gave Carne on that particular subject, and you can be quite certain he's never known a thing about her. It was a huge bluff from them both, all along.'

* * *

'So how are your fingertips, under those bandages?'

'One of them is doing really well, *chéri*.'

'Great! And ...'

'Don't ask.'

'But of course I have to ask! Have you lost the other one?'

'Yes.'

'Oh, no ...'

'Come on, Arthur! Please don't dig yourself even deeper. For *my* sake, if nothing else!'

'OK. Yes, I understand, *chérie*. So when do you think you'll be going back to work?'

'I quit.'

'But surely nobody ever looked at your fingers?'

'That's more like it, you awful man! No, I decided that if *you* are going to be off the face of the earth again for the foreseeable future, I could do a lot worse than go back to school. I want to repeat the whole of my last year, if they'll let me. And I know I was actually in very good shape for those summer exams, so I reckon it should be easy!'

'You'll be going back to live with Muriel, then ...'

'I've been there since I left hospital.'

'I bet she really hates me now.'

'No, she doesn't. She's distressed and confused, but I'll have plenty of time to explain things properly and bring her round while you're away. And I'll be keeping my eye out for another nice little apartment for us when you finally get out of here ...'

'There won't necessarily be any money for that, Julia, especially if you're going straight back to school ...'

'Ah, you ought to stay a lot closer to your good friend Simon Hardy. He's just told me that all three rewards have already gone into the approval process!'

'Wow! Well, that's *something* for me to look forward to, at least ...'

'And that's all, is it?'

* * *

'Another fine mess, Arthur ...'

'Please don't rub it in, Pureza.'

'So how long do you think you'll be back in here?'

'Hardy now says it'll be many weeks. Probably months. There's a lot to do, to prepare for another big trial, and he reckons I'll need to be kept on remand the whole time. For all sorts of reasons. But he seems confident I'll be free again once the show is finally over. "Dues paid" and all that ...'

'Well, you take it easy, *chico*. Watch your back. And do a lot more thinking, eh? Maybe some *better* thinking this time.'

'Yeah ...'

'What do you want me to do about Emilie? I did pick up a clue or two from her bible, several months ago, if you remember ...'

'Not now, please, Pureza. Some other time, eh?'

'As you wish, Arthur. And I still have those boxes of awful paperback books. Want a little light reading while you're inside?'

'Hah! Thanks, but you can dump them now. No reading for me, this time around. I have a novel to write ...'

Book III

LOST IN ACTION

Foreword: *Que sera, sera*

Soon after I met my soul mate Arthur Narone, he gave me some very good advice on how to go about writing a piece of fiction.

But I still made an utter mess of my first attempt!

Maybe this little story has greater merit. I'm dedicating it, of course, to Arthur and Emilie, and to what might have been.

But of course ... *Que sera, sera.*

Julia Rochemont
Nice, September 1968

Unfinished Business

During the long winter months of 1967-68, while my heroic boyfriend Arthur Narone was being held on remand in Nice Prison, his old friend Pureza Seles and I met up regularly for a drink and a chat, and we soon became quite good pals.

I think.

But I did steadily come to sense that her interest in Arthur had always been far greater than the merely charitable. So although he had never indicated to me that he considered her anything other than a very faithful friend, I became ever more determined to do all I could to hold onto him when he finally came back fully into my life.

And I hinted as much to him whenever I visited him in prison and we talked about our future plans! Maybe Pureza did so too, on her own occasional visits. I'll certainly never ask either of them about that!

But it came quite naturally to the two of us to agree, on Christmas Eve, to wait happily together outside the front gate of the jail on the day our dear friend was eventually delivered back into our world, whenever that turned out to be.

Several months later, soon after the "Orceau & Carne" trial was finally over, Chief Inspector Simon Hardy contacted us individually to inform us of the actual date of Arthur's planned release. Hardy was proposing to meet him personally outside the prison and drive him safely to wherever he was intending to live. And to remove any understandable suspicions on our part, and prevent any exposure to Hardy himself, he asked if we would both care to accompany him on the day.

Pureza and I met up not long after that, to consider his suggestion and adjust our rendezvous plans as necessary. And of course we were then obliged to discuss a previously unmentioned subject. To my

great relief, she made no complaint when I told her firmly that Arthur
would be moving into the apartment I had selected and had now
rented in his name for the foreseeable future. But she *was* a little
inquisitive.

'How *did* you manage to pull together the advance payment, my
dear? I thought you were still back in school ...'

'I didn't, Pureza. Two of the three rewards that Arthur was looking
forward to have already been paid. He now has a bank account for
the first time in his life, and he signed the cheque and the rental
agreement yesterday. And you'll never guess which bank he's
using ...'

'You're kidding!'

'No. It was their only condition for paying him their reward! And
before the Old Franc notes finally went out of circulation this month,
they even let me cash in the small number he was still holding when
he went back to jail. I'll swear Madame Padroux winked at me when
she said they had no way of telling if they had been stolen!'

I called Simon Hardy to confirm we agreed with his plan, and he then
offered to pick each of us up on his way to the prison. So when the
glorious Monday the twenty-second of April 1968 finally arrived,
Arthur received a tripartite welcome and an incident-free lift home!

And when the two of us were finally alone together, I opened a
surprise bottle of Champagne and we celebrated in style! All of the
day and all of the night!

* * *

'Wasn't it kind of the Chief Inspector to ferry us all around
yesterday, Arthur!'

'*Chief* Inspector?'

'Yes. He mentioned it when he contacted me to arrange it. And he
said that taking us to meet you like that was a kind of thank-you
present.'

'He could have told me that to my face!'

'Maybe he's waiting for a moment when you're not surrounded by
all your other devotees. Or maybe he wasn't sure quite how delighted
you would be ...'

'You'll be telling me his latest *gardien* has been promoted next!'

'Well guessed!'

'Oh, boy.'

'So, did you finish the novel?'

'Your turn to guess now.'

'Well, I've always assumed that having little personal deadlines such as getting out of jail were probably good for concentrating a writer's mind ...'

'Quite right. Yes, it's all done.'

'Bravo! So can I read it, please?'

'What, now?'

'Well, maybe we should have some breakfast first ...'

* * *

'I've finished it, Arthur!'

'Already?'

'Yes. I'm a very fast reader!'

'But are you a careful one?'

'I like to think so. Anyway, I reckon you're very brave to put it all down in black and white like that. Are you actually planning to try and get it published? Because ...'

'I'm not sure, Julia. But I probably won't. For the very reasons you're hinting at. I'd rather go back to a simple life with no more complications and pressures.'

'I'd say that's a very good idea. So why did you write it, *enfin*?'

'Because it needed to be written.'

'Yeah. That makes sense. And I haven't given up on my ambition either, you know. Despite what you said about my first effort! But I shall definitely wait until there's something that really does need to be written.'

* * *

After three days of blissful relaxation with Arthur, I was confident that all was still well between us. So I then pointed out that he had made absolutely no effort to contact his dear old friend Pureza since the police had dropped the two of us off at his apartment on Monday morning and taken *her* back, uncomplaining, to the solitude of her bookshop.

He agreed at once, and he was chivalrous enough to say that he had not wanted to do *anything* to upset me. So I threw him back onto the bed and told him what an idiot he was, and thirty minutes later I sent him straight out to the nearest phone box.

He was home again before I'd even finished my shower. Pureza had invited us to dinner the following Sunday. And she apparently had some very special news to share.

* * *

The meal Pureza cooked for us was wonderful, and Arthur's compliments were even more exuberant than mine! So I knew within minutes that I must still maintain my guard! I would never be able to compete with her in the kitchen, so I would need to make sure I kept Arthur happy in the only other important department!

And then he mentioned his novel.

'I finished it ten days ago, Pureza!'

Her face was a picture of admiration.

'*¡Bravo, amigo!*'

'And Julia has read it already. So would *you* like to look at it now?'

I was still watching her carefully, and I saw exactly the change I was expecting.

'But is it really intended for public consumption, Arthur? I had the firm impression it was going to be an extremely personal, not to say privileged account of things. You certainly promised me you would fully respect my own family's privacy in it ...'

'Yes, I promised you that, Pureza, and of course I kept my promise! And no, I don't have any plans to try and publish it. So, do you want to read it, or not?'

'I think not, Arthur. Let's just say I was probably too close to it all to be able to appreciate or judge it properly, OK?'

'OK.'

I admired the woman absolutely. And I feared her. Absolutely.

As Pureza was pouring the coffee, I prompted her to tell us her very special news. She gave me a mildly disdainful look, and I realized my timing had been atrocious. And then she once again took centre-stage, and looked me straight in the eyes.

'Tell me, Julia: as a young woman of roughly Emilie's age when she disappeared, where might *you* have considered going, if you had been in *her* shoes in those awful days immediately after the bank robbery?'

I was stunned. She had never raised this subject in all the time we had been meeting up in Arthur's absence!

'Well,' I mumbled, 'I suppose I would have thought about a naturally safe place to escape to. And quickly – so by train, of course. And I'd probably have wanted to maintain my anonymity.'

'OK ...'

'And ... well, maybe I'd have been thinking about a complete change.'

'Yes, that's something Arthur contemplated briefly himself last year, wasn't it, *mon ami* ...?'

Arthur nodded silently, and I could tell he too was not at all comfortable with what was going on.

'And what else might you have considered, Julia?'

'Well ... good opportunities for work, I guess. Low-paid jobs *and* my ... I mean Emilie's own speciality.'

'Exactly. So where would you naturally go for both of those?'

'The big city, of course. Certainly not the country.'

'In France, or abroad?'

'Oh, in France, I think. Surely you can only go so far in such a perilous frame of mind?'

'Indeed. So, would Marseilles have fitted the bill, in the circumstances?'

'Oh no. Too close to home.'

'*Bien.* So ... Toulouse, maybe? Or perhaps Lyons? Or even Paris?'

'If it had been me, Pureza, I would have gone to Paris. But only because I've never been there before!'

'Precisely, my dear. And please do not think I am being unkind. I have only been trying to make you think hard about this for just a few moments, in the way I myself have been doing, on our mutual friend's behalf, for the past two years!'

I looked across at Arthur. His face clearly said he was still intending to keep well out of this, at least for now.

'Very well, Pureza,' I countered politely, feeling nonetheless that this continued pressure on me was both undeserved and quite unreasonable, 'I will accept all of that, if you will please, *enfin*, tell us your very special news.'

And then she turned her inscrutable gaze upon Arthur, and revealed her latest hand.

'As you are well aware, *mon bon ami*, I began to study the notes in Emilie's family bible a full year ago. And I recently made the decision to try and contact her grandparents. Their address was written, you see, in one of the entries on the inside cover – as I attempted to tell you last summer, but your interest lay elsewhere at that time, did it not? – and although the ink was badly faded, I managed eventually to decipher it. The telephone company was then happy to give me their number ...

'And when I called the elderly couple – yes, they are both alive and well – and told them simply that I was an old friend of the family, they at once gave me the address and the telephone number of their daughter and son-in-law – Emilie's delightful, self-righteous parents.

'Even better ... when I rang that number, those awful parents were not at home, and the phone was answered by her little sister, whose name turned out to be Béatrice. How very saintly! And she is not so little any more, of course.

'I told *her* I was an old school-friend of Emilie's and was keen to try and make contact with her again. And she told me, without further prompting, that she had only spoken to her "pathetic drop-out sister" twice in the past ten years ... first, when Emilie had "deigned" to call her from Nice to wish her a happy sixteenth birthday, and then precisely two years later, when Emilie had phoned on her eighteenth. I asked her the date of that second call, and she told me. It was the twelfth of October 1960.'

'Long after she probably left Nice!!' Arthur exclaimed.

'Exactly! So of course I then asked Béatrice if she knew where Emilie had telephoned from. And she told me her sister had confided in her that she was living in Paris – yes, Paris, Julia! – and was now playing the guitar rather than the clarinet. And that she had changed her name ...'

'To what?'

'That's exactly what I asked her, of course. But Béatrice said Emilie had refused to tell her.'

'Why?'

'I think I understand why, Arthur. It was clear to me from the way Béatrice was speaking that they were both still extremely unsympathetic to each other's way of life. Béatrice was obviously following in the footsteps of her devout Catholic parents rather than rebelling in the way her big sister had chosen to do. So Emilie was obviously keeping her new door pretty firmly barred.'

'This is amazing, Pureza,' said Arthur, looking at her altogether too admiringly. 'But I suppose that's all you were able to discover ...'

'From that short phone call, yes. But it was the spark that lit the fire. Since then I've done a lot more work on it ...'

'And ...?'

'Well, I've been talking to people in the music business, both here and in Paris, and I've consulted a lot of reference sources, and I've come up with two long lists of female singers who have been active there over the past eight years.'

'That's even more amazing!'

I did not want to admit it, but of course I secretly agreed. And then this remarkable woman pulled four closely-typed, double-column sheets of paper out of her metaphorical hat.

'I believe the first list can effectively be discounted. Everybody on it is either very well known, or completely the wrong age, or their photograph does not match what you have told me about Emilie's looks. But please take a quick peek at all the photos anyway, just in case I'm wrong ...'

She discarded two of the sheets of paper and handed Arthur a folder containing a sheaf of newspaper clippings and photocopied pictures. He leafed through them rapidly and agreed at once with her conclusions.

'So these two other sheets are what you will need to work with. It is a list of Parisian singers who are apparently not at all well known outside their immediate sphere of work. I have been unable to obtain a photograph of any of them. And it goes without saying that the name "Emilie Courbier" does not figure on it.'

Arthur was scanning the long list of names and suddenly looking puzzled.

'Why are you doing this for me, Pureza?'

She smiled benevolently. 'I told you from the start, my friend, that I would do everything I could to help you with your attempts at "reparations" ... and it seems to me that this particular labour is still outstanding.'

'Yes,' he said. 'And if you *were* to read my novel, you'd see that I have often felt rather guilty about not trying harder to find Emilie.'

He turned to me. 'Wouldn't you agree, Julia?'

I was obviously going to have to get involved again.

'I suppose so. You clearly went up and down in your apparent ardour for her. It seemed to have become almost nonexistent after ... after we met. But I don't *really* know how you're feeling about her right now, after all that time back in prison.'

'Well, frankly, neither do I. So I'd like to sleep on all of this for a while. And even if I decide not to pursue it, Pureza, I'm extremely grateful for everything you've done.'

'It was my pleasure, as always, Arthur. And my own view, for what it's worth, is that you need to decide who, if anybody, would benefit from any follow-up work. Emilie's family is clearly still not at all interested in her. And it will not be too difficult for you to make a judgement as far as the three of *us* are individually concerned. The only person you cannot consult on it, of course, is Emilie herself.'

I took that as the conclusion of Pureza's clever little cabaret act, and moved the conversation on to something far less emotive.

* * *

'So what are you proposing to do?'

It was two days later, and I had already grown very weary of Arthur's strange new state of distraction.

'I just don't know, Julia.'

'But that's not good enough, babe! Everything was wonderful again until we went to dinner with that woman. And now ...'

'What do *you* think I should do?'

'You really want to know?'

'Yes.'

'Right. I think you need to get Emilie out of your hair once and for all. Or the opposite.'

'Meaning ...?'

'Meaning you should go to Paris and try to find her. If you do, and you wake her from her poisoned slumber with a magic kiss, and you both then want to live happily ever after, so be it. But if you discover you're not in love with each other any more, or you fail to find her after a reasonable effort, I want you to completely forget about her and come back here and be with me. For good.'

'That's very close to what I've been feeling I should do.'

'Well you'd better get on with it, then.'

'And I've also been wondering if I should ask Pureza to accompany me. She's so good at researching things and making clever deductions and ...'

'No! That's *not* what I suggested, Arthur! And do you seriously think she can afford to shut down her business for goodness knows how long while she breezes off with you to Paris in the springtime ...?'

'OK. And you're probably right. She never hinted at wanting to spend any more time on this herself, did she?'

'No.'

'But I don't want to go on my own, Julia. Will you come with me?'

'Hah!! To help you find your old girlfriend and maybe propose marriage to her?'

'Well ... yes.'

'Now it's my turn to need to sleep on it.'

* * *

'We're going to need a photograph.'

'Yes. But she never gave me one, and I've never had a camera of my own.'

'OK, how's your sketching?'

'Awful.'

'Then put your thinking cap on.'

'Hey Arthur, I've just remembered something! You said in your novel that when you went looking for information about Emilie at the

Casa della Musica – well, the Happy Halliday now, right? – there was an old picture of her stuck high up on the back wall.'

'Of course! You're brilliant! As good as Pureza any day!'

'That's what I like to hear, *chéri*. So you'd better cross your fingers and hope it's still there. And be willing to spend some good reward money on it.'

Arthur was back from the club within the hour, the proud owner of another little treasure: a framed black and white photo of Emilie Courbier in 1958, aged eighteen, complete with clarinet and *gamine* haircut.

'They didn't even want any money for it. Nobody remembers her, Julia.'

'*C'est la vie*. And the good thing is that her name's not written anywhere on it. So we can respect her wish to leave her old life completely behind her, can't we?'

'Yes. And I think we must make that one of our golden rules.'

'Agreed.'

'So, it's May Day and the sun is shining. *En mai fais ce qu'il te plaît!* Want to spend the rest of the day having a bit of fun outdoors and planning our little trip?'

'Yes!'

* * *

'OK, *chéri*, let's take stock of what we know for certain. Emilie was living in Paris in October 1960. She was playing the guitar, and presumably still singing, but under a different name, which just *might* be one of those on Pureza's second list.'

'Exactly, Julia. But that's *all* we know.'

'And we also have a ten-year-old photograph of a teenage girl who had already made a hurried effort to change the way she looked even before she left Nice.'

'It's not going to be easy, is it?'

'No. But if we assume she went by train, we should do the same. That will take us to the Gare de Lyon, and if we find ourselves a cheap hotel nearby, as she might well have done for her first night or two in Paris, we may get a sense of how she was feeling and what she might have done next.'

'Excellent thinking, Julia. I knew it was a good idea to invite you along.'

'Be careful, Arthur. Be very careful ....'

* * *

On the Thursday morning, we resolved to depart for Paris on Sunday the fifth of May, and we spent the rest of the day gently getting ourselves organised.

That evening a radio news bulletin made brief mention of the re-closure of the University buildings at Nanterre, out to the west of Paris, after what they called "further incidents" there following the student occupations of the previous weeks. But we thought little of it at the time.

The following evening, however, brought the news that the Sorbonne itself, in the heart of the Latin Quarter, had been declared closed and unceremoniously evacuated by the police. The university authorities were apparently determined to avoid, within their walls, a serious escalation of overnight clashes between certain extremist groups. But the Sorbonne students appeared to be in a very angry and unstable mood as a result, and later that evening we heard the first reports of violence and arrests on the streets of the Latin Quarter ...

On Saturday the fourth of May we learnt the full news of the awful riots that had taken place overnight, with nearly six hundred arrests and many injured. It did not take us long to put the next day's travel plans on hold! And on the Monday evening we heard about the latest terrible battles between the students and the police, with reports of many hundreds of further injuries and arrests. We were very glad we had decided to stay in Nice.

Throughout that week, the radio and the papers were full of discussions of the still-volatile situation in the heart of Paris. The major trades union groups were becoming more and more vociferous, and the taxi drivers were already all on strike. And on Friday the tenth, the situation came to a head once again with another enormous afternoon demonstration around the Left Bank, followed by a huge stand-off with the police. We listened all through the evening to the live radio reports of the construction of dozens of barricades and the huge tensions that were building as the night wore on. And we awoke in the morning to news of an even greater toll of serious injuries and arrests!

No-one in their right mind would be visiting Paris voluntarily at this time, let alone venturing out onto any of its streets without very good reason.

That same Saturday, the students here in Nice came out in their thousands to support their comrades in Paris. And on Monday the thirteenth, a General Strike was called by the combined trades unions of France. We at once wondered if and when it would affect the railways. And sure enough, later in the week the SNCF workers walked out and the trains stopped running.

The following Monday, since there had been no reports of rioting that weekend, Arthur wondered out loud whether we should try to hitch-hike to Paris. But I laughed and said that could take us days and days, if we were unlucky, and anyway the city was still at a virtual standstill: the metro and bus workers had now come out on strike as well, and the rubbish was piling up and rotting in the streets.

And at the end of that week, just when we were hoping things might perhaps start to calm down and get back to normal, there were further ghastly riots on the night of the twenty-fourth, with more burning barricades and another huge toll of injuries and arrests.

So we stayed safely here, of course, as the strikes continued and even intensified. There was stalemate in the rail and bus sectors in particular. On the twenty-ninth there were further huge demonstrations throughout the country. Ten thousand people even came out onto the streets of genteel Nice!

And then President de Gaulle at last made his long-heralded appeal to the patriotism of the people, and the government was reshuffled, and negotiations with the unions immediately began to get moving again.

So as June began, the intensity of the nationwide strikes was finally starting to reduce. But the rail transport unions in particular were still not at all satisfied, and Paris was still in a real mess. Arthur and I agreed to wait a little longer.

On Tuesday the fourth, after hearing that agreements had finally been reached between the Ministry of Transport and the various trades unions, we were told by the Tourist Office that the national railways and the Paris metro and buses should be functioning again by the following Thursday, but probably not providing a very predictable service. So we made our decision. We would depart that day – and if there *was* no train service, *enfin*, we would definitely hitch-hike. It would be an extra little adventure for us, after all!!

Arthur had only telephoned Pureza twice during our month's enforced wait in Nice, and had dropped in on her just once for a little chat. I don't think she put him under any further pressure in those conversations.

He called her again now, of course, to tell her of our latest plans. And she, of course, wished us *bon courage*.

Combing Through the Rubble

There were, after all, no serious problems with our trains that Thursday – just some understandable delays – and after making a very early start we arrived at the Gare de Lyon soon after five in the afternoon. The sky was remarkably clear and the sun was still shining brightly. We went straight to the Accueil de Paris at the station and they found us a cheap room only fifteen minutes' walk away. So we strolled up to Place de la Bastille and on into Rue de la Roquette, and checked in at the Hôtel Bastille.

That evening we allowed ourselves a night out in the Latin Quarter, but we were tired from our long journey and dismayed at the devastation still obvious in many of its streets, so it was hard to relax and enjoy ourselves. Our dinner in a lovely little restaurant on Rue de la Harpe was delightful, but we were back at the hotel by ten o'clock, in no mood for further entertainment of any sort.

* * *

The next day we started our hunt for Emilie up in Montmartre, figuring it might be a good place to find a performer who had probably wanted to stay out of the central Paris limelight – at least when she first arrived here. So we visited all the music shops and clubs we could find in the streets and little squares of the famous old artists' quarter.

In every one of them we showed people the ten-year-old photograph of Emilie and asked if they recognised her. Then we ran through Pureza's list of names and asked if people had heard of any of them, and if so how long they had been performing in Paris, and whether they were still active, and where they had typically worked, and what they looked like, and if there was any chance of finding a photo of them in a magazine or a publicity poster or whatever ...

But no joy. Just two names to be definitely crossed off our list.

By early afternoon we were pretty sure we'd exhausted all the places that were open during the day. So we called a halt, had a late lunch, and went to enjoy the splendour of the Sacré-Coeur.

When we emerged from the basilisk into the bright spring sunshine, Arthur gazed across the vast panorama of Paris spread out before us, and said quietly 'I wonder if she really is down there somewhere?'

And I said 'I feel she is, Arthur. But God knows where ...'

'We'll find her,' he declared, and we began our descent back towards the great northern boulevard.

We stayed in Montmartre all evening, drinking in the rather sleazy atmosphere, enjoying the food, and asking after Emilie in a dozen or more clubs and music bars that were now open for the night. But all we achieved was the removal of three further names from our very long list.

* * *

On Saturday the eighth of June we visited some of the music shops and clubs we'd spotted on the Left Bank on our first evening in the city.

We once again got a very meagre set of comments on our list from the first six or seven places we tried, but at least they helped us rule out one more name. And still nobody recognised the old photo of Emilie. But in two separate shops we were told: 'Ah, you need to visit old Hubert. He's been in the business here since 1950. There's nothing he doesn't know about the Paris music scene!'

We found Hubert in his little shop in Rue de Lanneau. And he half-recognised the face in the old photo, but could not put a name to it. But as soon as we showed him the list, it all added up for him.

'Ah, of course! That's Rosie Renart! Same little face, but she must be ... what? ... ten years older now?'

'Yes!'

'And her hair is completely different. These days it's long and straight, very American folkie style. And look at those Fifties clothes! Today she usually performs in a man's lumberjack shirt and a pair of blue jeans. Hah! You know, all the students here will finally be getting round to wearing jeans now, after their little social revolution last month!'

'Oh, this is wonderful!' Arthur exclaimed. 'So, do you have any up-to-date publicity photos or press cuttings?'

'I'm afraid not. But I *can* tell you where she's been performing recently ...'

And he wrote down the addresses of two music clubs – both of them back in the Saint-Antoine district, very close to our own little hotel!

Early that afternoon we found the first place, in Passage Thiéré just off Rue de Charonne. There were many tatty publicity posters on the grubby old front doors, but none of them featured anyone looking like Emilie. And when the owner heard why we were there, he was not at all happy.

'Yes,' he told us rather angrily, 'Rosie played here quite often over the past year or so. But she hasn't turned up for work since her show on Friday the third of May. And everything in the city's gone to pot since then! She's probably been wasting her time on sit-ins with those lazy students. How are we supposed to make a living when bloody baby intellectuals go and screw it all up for us?'

I was stunned. 'So you don't support what they're trying to achieve?'

'Of course I don't!'

'But you employ lots of beat musicians and protest singers here! Look at all these posters!'

'That's business, girl, not my politics! This is Saint-Antoine, dammit, not the Champs-Elysées! And I've got better things to do than talk to you about someone who let me down. She won't be working here again, I can tell you!'

'One moment, please, *monsieur*. Do you happen to have a poster of Rosie that we could take with us?'

'No, I don't! I tore it down and threw it in the bin. I told you – she's history now.'

'OK. But do you perhaps know where she lived?'

'Non! Foutez-moi le camp, hein!'

And he slammed the door in our faces. We walked back to Rue de Charonne with an unspoken sense of growing concern.

We moved on to the second address we had been given: a slightly smarter-looking club called the Cheval à Bascule, just one block further down on Rue de Lappe. There were even more posters on the outside wall of this place, but none of them featured Rosie Renart either, and not one of the few female singers looked the slightest bit like Emilie.

And there was no reply to our repeated knocking on the door.

So we found a nearby bar, and we bought some more expensive drinks and we talked, both voicing our obvious concerns, but both also agreeing that we still had absolutely no firm evidence that Rosie was our girl. Just one "celebrated" man's possibly over-confident guess, based on a ten-year-old photo ...

The club was still closed when we tried again an hour later. So we decided to go back to the hotel – it was literally around the corner! – and change into some smarter clothes and have another nice evening meal together. Then we could hit the night-time scene at the end of the evening, But not, sadly, for the music or the dancing ...

The place was open when we finally arrived back at around ten o'clock, and there was already quite a queue to get in. But as we slowly shuffled forwards, I spotted some more posters inside, on the far wall of the lobby. One of them showed a guitar-girl looking just as Hubert had described Rosie Renart *and* a lot like the old Emilie too – and probably not a lot older than her, either. From where we were, I still couldn't read the rather small and over-groovy handwriting at the bottom of the poster. But I knew I had to get someone else's opinion on this first, without any special prompting ...

'Arthur, look at all the pictures on the wall ahead of us! Can you see a face you recognise?'

'Yes!' he hissed in my ear. 'It's her, Julia! It's her!!'

'So, shall we start asking the people in the queue ...?'

'No. Not yet, anyway. Let's go straight to the top first.'

We eventually extracted the manager, whose name was Oscar, from a back room and persuaded him to talk to us in the far corner of the lobby.

'Yeah, man, Rosie played here every Sunday and Thursday night for the past three years or more. Very popular ... but she's an acquired taste, you know.'

'Yes, I do ...' Arthur began. I gave him a look that said 'Shut up and listen!' and he got the message.

'So when is she playing next?' I prompted the very cool cat.

'No idea, sugar. She hasn't been in since ... hmmm, it must be about four weeks now. Hold on ... yeah, she played here on the ninth of May, as usual, and she sat down afterwards at the end of the bar, as usual, and she had a little chat with her friend Sophie, as usual, and then she went home. As usual. But she never turned up for her spot the following Sunday, or the next Thursday. I was a bit sad, you know, sort of disappointed, but nobody seemed to care, 'cos they were all talking about the riots on the Left Bank. Have been ever since ...'

'Is Sophie here tonight?' I asked.

'Nah. She only ever comes in on Sundays and Thursdays. Must have liked Rosie's style.'

'So she'll be here tomorrow?'

'Maybe. Haven't seen much of her recently, either. So maybe not. Anything's possible in Paris this spring, man!'

'OK. We'll be back tomorrow, then. Meanwhile ... do you know Rosie's address? Or Sophie's?'

'Are you kidding? Most of the time I can't even remember my own!'

'OK. But can you possibly let us borrow that poster?'

'Sure. I've got a couple more of them in the office, and it's no good to me up there ... till she comes back down to earth. Yeah, help yourself – and you can keep it!'

'Thanks!'

'So, are you guys coming in now? We have a couple of great acts on tonight!'

Arthur and I exchanged glances and decided firmly against it. This was no time to be letting our hair down.

We spent an uneasy Sunday back on the Left Bank, showing the poster of Rosie Renart to hundreds of people on the damaged streets, but failing to find anyone who recognised her name or her face, let alone remembered seeing her recently.

We wondered at lunchtime about whether we should now go to the police, but then decided we actually had very little to report, and that it might be best to leave it at least until the next day, just in case we managed to meet up with Sophie and pick up any more information from her.

So we went back to the Cheval à Bascule as soon as it opened that evening, and we waited. And finally Sophie arrived! Oscar pointed her out to us as she walked past, and once she was settled at the end of the bar we approached her very politely and asked if we could join her. And after accepting another large glass of wine to rapidly follow her first one, she was happy to talk.

'Yeah, I first met Rosie here a couple of years ago, and one evening she told me a little bit about herself.

'She'd come up to Paris from the south a few years earlier. I think she said she'd been working in a hotel in Aix-en-Provence, and hadn't been singing for a while. Anyway, she found some digs here in a poor area south of the Gare de Lyon, and picked up another cleaning job in a cheap hotel. I got the feeling she'd chosen the sorts of places that don't worry too much about identity cards, but I didn't ask, of course ...

'Apparently her hair was a lot shorter at that time, but she then let it grow very long. She was trying to get a kind of "French Joan Baez" look, and I think she succeeded!'

Arthur showed her Emilie's old photograph.

'Wow, was that her? Really pretty, wasn't she?'

'Yes ...'

'So, after a few weeks she managed to get a better job, as a waitress in a side street café up near Place de la Bastille. Told me she borrowed a cheap Spanish guitar from one of the waiters and tried it and enjoyed it. So she sold an old clarinet she'd brought along with her, and got herself a good quality steel-string folk guitar.

'Over the next few months she learnt to play some simple chords and developed her own new style. And eventually she felt confident enough to enquire about playing in the local music bars and folk clubs, and she got work quite easily. Her first little spot was in late

1960, I think she said – at a beatnik club in a rather unsavoury stretch of Rue Oberkampf. She was determined to stay firmly out of the central Paris limelight. I didn't ask why.

'And she's been playing on and off in this area ever since.'

Arthur had been getting fidgety.

'OK, that was all very useful, Sophie. Thank you! But what about last month? Oscar says you were with her here on Thursday the ninth ...'

'Yeah. She normally just sits right here after her show and I do most of the talking. Sometimes I think she gets a bit bored with that. But it's nice to talk to talented people, isn't it? Well I think so, anyway. But that night she was in a funny mood, and *she* did most of the talking. Basically she was getting all het up about the students and the workers, and saying she was going to join their demo the next day ...'

'What??'

'That's just what I said. And I told her she wasn't getting any younger or any prettier, and how stupid I thought she was to be playing Joan of Arc instead of getting some milk in her tits. That's when she walked out.'

I didn't know whether to laugh or cry, and I dared not look at Arthur to see his reaction.

'So have you seen her since then?'

'No. I didn't come in the following Sunday. The next Thursday I turned up late, and I was rather preoccupied with other things, especially the riots. So I didn't ask anyone about her. And I also missed the next Sunday. So it was two weeks before I actually wondered where she had got to. I mentioned it to Oscar, and he said she hadn't been in since the ninth – the evening I last spoke to her.'

Arthur was still really quiet, so I moved rapidly on.

'Do you know where she lives, Sophie?'

'Somewhere on Passage Josset, I think.'

'Where is that, please?'

'Five minutes' walk from here. Up Rue de Charonne, on the right just before you reach Avenue Ledru-Rollin.'

'OK. Is there anything more you can tell us?'

'No.'

'Did you ever think of going to the police about this?'

'Hah! Those crazy students injured nearly a thousand of their officers in the last few weeks. Do you really think they have the time or the will to care about some missing little leftie folk singer?'

'Well, they ought to!'

'So you'd better talk to them yourselves.'

'Don't worry, we're going to. And thanks for ... well, thanks for all your information, at least.'

She shrugged and drained her glass. 'It was given for free. Well, almost. *Bonne chance.*'

The Long Day Closes

On the Monday morning we got up early and went straight to the central police station on the Ile de la Cité, just across the square from Notre-Dame Cathedral. And we had decided to continue to respect Emilie's wish to keep her real name a secret, at least for now.

We showed the two pictures of "Rosie Renart" to the officer at the front desk. He mumbled something like 'Not another one ...' and made a brief phone call, then told us to sit down in the busy waiting area.

Over thirty minutes later a uniformed *brigadier* came up to us and took a look at the photos for himself.

'No,' he said, 'I don't recognise her, and her name doesn't figure in our arrest records. But you told my colleague she went missing during the last few weeks, right?'

'Yes,' said Arthur, 'possibly on the evening of Friday the tenth of May.'

'Well, we weren't very heavily involved *here* in what happened across the river that night. The authorities had ordered all the bridges between the Ile and the Left Bank to be blocked off for most of the time. So almost everyone arrested down there was originally taken to the police stations of the fifth and sixth *arrondissements*. Some of them *were* brought up here for processing whenever it was considered safe to open a passage for our vehicles. But definitely not this woman. Sorry.'

'Do you have access to the records of the other stations?'

'You must be joking!'

'OK. So where are they located, please?'

'The *commissariat* of the Fifth is in the Mairie on Place du Panthéon. And the Sixth's is on Rue Bonaparte, at Place Saint-Sulpice.'

'And that's it?'
'What else would you have me do?'
'I don't know.'
'Et voilà. Adieu, mademoiselle, monsieur.'

We consulted our map. Each of the buildings was about fifteen minutes' walk away, in opposite directions. We decided to start out to the west and then work our way back to the Latin Quarter, so we set off across Pont Saint-Michel and then along Boulevard Saint-Germain and Rue Saint-Sulpice.

We received a similarly polite but cool reception at the front office of the police station in the Mairie of the sixth district. But the desk sergeant who later came out to see us was a little more receptive, once he had looked at the photo of Rosie Renart.

'Well, we processed a large number of arrests that night. And a lot more two weeks later. I handled some of them myself, but not all. Pretty girl, memorable name. Don't think I'd have forgotten her. But stay here, and I'll show it to the others ...'

He was back five minutes later.

'No-one's ever spotted her in here, and her name doesn't appear in any of our own arrest records.' He pointed at the Cheval à Bascule poster as he handed it back to Arthur. 'But one of the guys has actually seen her performing at this club.'

'Recently?'

'No – he said it was several months ago.'

'OK. So, should we try over at Place du Panthéon now?'

'Yes. They handled a lot of arrests there too, on each night of rioting – once the barricades had been dealt with.'

'But you don't have access to ...?'

He was already giving us a very mocking grin. We knew it was time to leave.

We decided to combine a little more light sightseeing with our much weightier aim. So we made our way back to *Boul' Mich'* and wandered around the newly defaced streets north of the Sorbonne until we reached Place Maubert. Under darkening skies we climbed the hill to Saint-Etienne church, and then strolled past the imposing bulk of the Panthéon and around to the magnificent twin buildings housing the University's Faculty of Law and the Town Hall of the fifth district.

Here we encountered a far more sympathetic police officer at the front desk. But he did not recognise the name of Rosie Renart or her photos, and a quick call through to the custody sergeant confirmed that she was not known at that station either.

'And you say you have already been to see our colleagues in the Sixth?'

'Yes,' said Arthur impatiently.

'So now, of course,' the officer continued, 'it is time for you to start checking the hospitals.'

'But should we not file a Missing Person Report while we are here?' I asked.

'On a twenty-eight-year-old woman, in Paris in June 1968, without contacting the hospitals first?'

The kindly man was clearly offering us some good advice on the most effective way to negotiate the famous bureaucracy of the capital, particularly in these difficult days. We took the hint.

'Of course. So which of them received the injured on the night of the tenth, please?'

'Three, mainly. The closest is Cochin, at the top of Boulevard Saint-Michel at Port Royal. Then there's La Pitié-Salpêtrière, up the river behind Austerlitz station. And Saint-Antoine is over to the east, beyond Bastille and the Gare de Lyon.'

We thanked him with as much warmth as we could muster.

We had an early lunch on Rue Soufflot, in a mood more pessimistic than optimistic. Then, with the Eiffel Tower rising proudly above the horizon directly ahead of us, we chose to avoid the devastation around Rue Le Goff, turned south on Rue Saint-Jacques, passed the military hospital of Val de Grace, crossed the busy boulevard at Port Royal, and found the entrance to the Cochin Public Hospital.

As is the custom in Paris in the afternoon, it had just begun to rain.

We asked about Rosie Renart at the reception desk, mentioning specifically the night of the tenth of May. They checked and could find no record of her name at all. But then the Almoner was called out to talk to us.

She explained without further ado that, during the nights of the riots, many of the young people admitted were not carrying any papers. But most of those had identified themselves verbally, as soon as they were able to, and many had quickly departed as walking wounded. Only a few of the original "unknowns" were still not well enough to leave the hospital, but all of them had been identified long ago.

Then we showed her the club's poster of Rosie Renart, and she recognised her at once.

'Ah, yes. *Enfin*. This young lady was brought in at about four-thirty on the morning of Saturday the eleventh of May. Like many of the others, the poor thing had probably been lying injured in a huge fog of tear gas for some time before the Red Cross were able to get her out. On admission she was semi-conscious and had a bruised head, but there was no visible bleeding. She was not carrying anything to identify her, just wearing a shoulder bag across her body containing a few bits and pieces, including a well-worn notebook with no owner's name on it.'

I was holding Arthur's hand very tightly and trying desperately not to cry – nor to try and guess what might be coming next. *He* was just hanging poker-faced on the woman's every word.

'Her condition was poor – in and out of consciousness, but never talking, as far as I know. With no external injuries to be handled by the overwhelmed emergency operating theatres, she was prepared for a high-priority examination by a neurologist as soon as one became available, and then placed in a temporary holding area nearby. But at five-fifteen, one of the overburdened ward nurses discovered she had disappeared.'

'What?' exclaimed Arthur.

'Yes. And they had already got her changed for the examination, into a light cotton hospital gown and nothing more. Her clothes and her bag with its few possessions were all still hanging off the end of the trolley-bed. But, you know, there were many other sets of clothes lying on and around many other beds on that awful night. In her confused state of mind, as she made her way out, she could have suddenly realised just what she was wearing and walked straight into another hectic ward, or even back into the emergency area, and borrowed the first women's clothes she came across ...'

'So she was never seen here again?'

'No. The police were routinely informed of her disappearance, of course – but they were as overwhelmed as we were during those tempestuous days, and nobody ever came to follow it up. I can just imagine some harassed junior officer glancing briefly at our seemingly insignificant report the next day and concluding that, in the regrettable absence of a nurse or a doctor who might possibly have discouraged it, an unidentified adult female Caucasian – who was suffering from what had obviously been only mild concussion, no doubt incurred after tripping up and falling on the scandalously vandalised pavements, and who was just one among hundreds of far more seriously injured citizens and policemen admitted to the hospitals of Paris that night – had simply taken the decision to discharge herself.'

She lowered her voice.

'I would also suspect that there has been a general ... how shall I put it? ... a general keenness, throughout the organs of authority in the city and the nation at large, to do nothing to disturb the remarkable statistic that despite the thousands of injuries on the streets during those days in May, not one single person is known to have died.'

Arthur was getting impatient again.

'Have you kept her clothes and her bag?'

That brought the Almoner straight back into official mode. 'But of course, *monsieur*. We await the eventual arrival of the responsible authorities with admirable patience.'

'But they don't seem to know anything about it! Which police station did you report it to? The Préfecture on the Ile de la Cité? Or the fifth district? Or the sixth? Because we have already visited each of them today ...'

'Oh, none of those, of course. This hospital is located in the fourteenth *arrondissement*!'

'What!'

Arthur's frustration with the ways of Paris was clearly about to cause a real problem. So I thrust my arm out in front of him and took command.

'So, *madame*, since the police do not seem at all interested, may we please take the items ourselves? Then we can return them directly to poor Rosie when we eventually find her.'

'I regret that would be completely out of order, *mademoiselle*.'

'Very well. But may we at least take a look at her notebook? In case it can give us some hint as to where she may have gone ...'

'We have already done that ourselves, of course, to no avail. But I cannot think of a good reason to refuse your request. Please wait here.'

As soon as she was gone, I warned Arthur to leave it to me until further notice. He obviously recognised that made sense, and he gritted his teeth and nodded his agreement.

The Almoner returned a few minutes later with a slim, stapled notebook in her hand, passing it to me with a very sympathetic look on her face.

The word "Paris" was written on the plain vanilla cover. I opened it at the first page, as Arthur watched over my shoulder. The paper was unlined, and the neat writing was clearly a woman's.

'This is her handwriting, Julia!'

'Oh, Arthur, we have some real proof at last! And it's a sort of journal, isn't it? Beginning on the twenty-second of March this year ...'

'Yes,' the Almoner cut in delicately, 'and there is quite a lot of it! I'm afraid I don't have the time to stand here while you study it all.'

'In that case,' I began, as plaintively as I could, 'would you kindly trust us with it while I transcribe it into my own notebook?'

'That would take you rather a long time too, my dear. Hmmm ... I think we had better avail ourselves of one of our more useful items of modern technology.'

She led us across the foyer to her office and through to a huge photocopier in the room beyond. She showed us how to operate the machine, then put a discreet finger to her lips and retreated into her own office, closing the door firmly behind her ....

We had reached the last page of handwriting. While Arthur was removing the copies from the hopper and checking they were all legible, I carefully ran through the rest of the notebook to ensure there was nothing written on any later pages. And as I reached the back, I discovered there was indeed some more – but it was upside down!

'Arthur!' I whispered, turning it over. 'There are some extra entries here, starting from the other end of the book. But the handwriting is younger. Yes, *mon Dieu*, it starts in Nice, with the first of her phone calls to her sister Béatrice! And very soon she's talking about meeting *you*!'

He grabbed the notebook from my hands and took a quick look for himself.

'Right, we'll copy these pages too, Julia. But I don't want either of us to read them yet. OK?'

'OK ....'

As soon as the job was done, Arthur quickly checked the second set of pages, folded them up and stuffed them straight into his jacket pocket. Then we went back into the Almoner's office, and as I returned the notebook I thought of one more question.

'You said there were a few other bits and pieces in Rosie's bag ...'

'Nothing of any significance, *mademoiselle*. A comb, a mirror, lipstick, cigarettes and a lighter, a ball-point pen, and the usual ... well, you know. Far less than most women carry in their bag!'

I smiled wryly. Then we thanked her for her forbearance and her obvious bending of the rules, and made our way back to the main entrance area. Sitting down on the first two adjacent chairs we could find, we were about to begin our study of the journal when I had another sudden thought.

'Hang on, Arthur. Before we start reading this, maybe you *should* look at those earlier notes straight away. Emilie might just have written something about coming to Paris in 1959 or 1960 ...'

He agreed. Pulling the other sheets from his pocket, he quickly browsed the final page without letting me see it.

'No,' he said after a few moments. 'The last entries *were* written in the days following the robbery, but there's no mention of Paris, only the places where she was staying after she left her apartment on the Tuesday. It corresponds with what I discovered last year. And her final words are "I'm leaving this goddamned town for ever!" That was on the twenty-sixth of November – just two days later.'

'OK,' I nodded. 'So now we *can* focus on what she wrote in the past few weeks.'

And we began to read together the first entry in the recently restarted, anonymous journal of Emilie Courbier, also known as Rosie Renart.

<u>22 March 1968</u>

I haven't written a word in this notebook since I left that goddamned rich man's town behind me more than eight years ago.

Huh! Maybe I only feel the need to write when I'm *really* angry.

All the time I've been here, I've been working in a much lower-class club scene than before, and I've started to identify more and more with the ordinary workers of Paris. Since January this year, there have been several violent strikes and student protests demanding reforms in education and wages and freedoms and just about everything. And now the administration tower of the university over at Nanterre has been occupied by hundreds of so-called "anarchists"!

I'm beginning to sympathize strongly with what is happening in the factories and universities and streets of this archaic nation.

Something's got to give, soon.

Hah! I actually have no idea if I'm talking about society, or me! But then I never had a university education.

Maybe I *am* talking about me. I must be the world's greatest failure. I've only ever had one proper relationship in my whole life. And look what happened to that!

I'm certain Arthur was the reason I never attempted to build any significant new relationships here. Men always seem to bring me nothing but trouble. Maybe I should have stuck with those randy convent girls after all!

Something's got to give.

'Well,' I said, 'what she has written there about you is not very ...'

'Let's move on, shall we?' said Arthur impatiently. 'Look, it jumps straight forward to May ...'

Saturday 4 May, morning

Oh, this is quite appalling! The newspapers say a hundred people were injured and nearly six hundred protestors were arrested in demonstrations in the Latin Quarter last night, after they locked the students out of the Sorbonne!

I'd like to be able to participate in some way. But I have to perform at one or more of the clubs every evening, and I can't be late. The show must always go on.

Damn! I am not in contact. I'm still a part of the old machine. I am not in contact.

Monday 6 May, midnight

Glorious and abhorrent!

I went down to the Left Bank this afternoon and saw the build-up of another huge demonstration at Place Saint-Germain des Prés and along Rue de Rennes.

And then, from a mercifully safe onlooker's distance, I watched in horror as tear gas was repeatedly fired and the police, armed with shields and batons, charged over and over again upon the crowds, ferociously clubbing not only the protesting students – brave young girls as well as brash young boys – and their teachers, but innocent bystanders too, many of them carried off by the Red Cross, their heads streaming with blood.

And then I walked safely home. Too safely.

The Vietnam peace talks are due to start here in just a few days' time.

Yes, *à la fois* glorious and abhorrent!

I did not go to work this evening. I did not sing my songs. They will be very angry with me.

'Wow!' Arthur exclaimed. 'She really *was* getting worked up about it, just as Sophie said.'

Tuesday 7 May, morning

Nearly one thousand citizens have been injured this time, including hundreds of policemen – and they are also workers, anyway! ... those men and their families are also the unwilling victims of the damnable conservatives! – and the students' and teachers' unions have called for an unlimited national strike to secure the release of all those arrested last weekend ... and hundreds more arrested last night.

I am convinced that this is still only the beginning of a Necessary Civic Action in the cause of the liberty of the French people.

I cannot just continue to sing my pretty little protest songs and remain on the cowardly sidelines.

Thursday 9 May, midnight

After my little show at the Cheval à Bascule, I sat down at the end of the bar, as usual. And Sophie came and sat next to me, as usual. She never takes the hint.

But for once I spoke out properly to her, instead of just playing along with all her pathetic girl talk.

I told her that I intend to join tomorrow's big demonstration.

She had already had several glasses of wine, and she said she saw absolutely no point in my doing that. 'Why don't you just concentrate on finding yourself a man after all these years, and having a couple of babies and an easy life? 'Cos that's exactly what I'll be working on again tomorrow evening, while you're out across the river pretending to be Joan of Arc with those bloody bourgeois students! Weekend hippies! I despise 'em! So, the best of luck to you, Rosie Renart. And if *I'm* lucky, while you're away I'll pick up the man you could have found ...'

Yeah, that's almost exactly what she said. Well, it was worse, actually. The little fascist.

'That ties up well with what Sophie told us, Arthur.'
'Yes ...'

Friday 10 May, 6 p.m.

The schoolkids joined forces late this afternoon at Gobelins and marched down Boulevard Arago into Place Denfert-Rochereau, where I've been waiting for the university students to convene at six-thirty. They filled the entire boulevard! I could see there were lots of young girls among them! *And* a few teachers!

It's a really relaxed atmosphere, the weather's beautiful, and they're being very well managed by their leaders, who are now making sensible speeches from up on the Lion of Belfort monument.

7 p.m.

The university students and professors have arrived at the square *en masse*, and their union leaders are making their speeches. But I can often hardly hear a word they're saying ....

They now seem to be arguing about the route the demonstration should follow. Some want to go to the Saint-Antoine Hospital to find out if there have been any deaths among the protestors in the earlier confrontations. Others want to go to the Radio and TV building. Others want to go and fire up the people in the working-class districts. This seems to be turning into a bit of a mess.

7:30 p.m.

They've finally decided to go along Boulevard Arago past the Santé Prison. And they're saying there are about twenty thousand people here!

We're moving off now.

8:45 p.m.

The police would not allow us to stop and protest at the prison. So we marched on to Gobelins, and down Rue Monge, and along Saint-Germain, and then they forced us to turn away from the river and go up *Boul' Mich'*. I'm not far from Place Edmond Rostand, and everything's come to a halt now. It's all been very peaceful and disciplined on both sides. So far ....

Ah, I spoke too soon. People all around me have started pulling up fence posts and are using them to lever up the paving stones. But others are shouting at them to stop, and to keep the demo peaceful.

9:30 p.m.

People are listening to speeches and discussions of the situation on their transistor radios, and the word is that barricades are now going up all over the Latin Quarter.

10:30 p.m.

A lot of people have drifted away, either because they're fearful of what might happen or because they've now had their evening's fun. But it's obvious that a lot of others have only just begun, and the barricades are known to be multiplying fast. There's been a lot of police movement in the distance, and the atmosphere is electric now. And it feels as glorious as I expected it would.

I'm no weekend hippy!

<u>12:30 a.m.</u>

There was an incident just now, with police buses being stoned as they drove into Rue Soufflot. Things seem to be calm again, but a lot more paving stones are being dug up.

<u>2:20 a.m.</u>

Something else is happening now ...

I can see hundreds of CRS troops coming down *Boul' Mich'* towards us. It looks as if we'll be forced back down to the square. I must find a side passage or a lobby and get out of their way!

<u>2:40 a.m.</u>

They've been firing tear gas! I've managed to move around and keep out of it so far. The students are throwing everything they can back at them! And one of the barricades has just fallen. This is getting really serious ...

And now the police look as if they're about to charge, and there's a lot more tear gas coming in. It's not safe to stay where I am. I must stop writing and run ... somewhere ....

'And that's it. Oh my God, Arthur ...'

'Are you certain there was nothing more?'

'Yes, I am. I checked all the pages right up to the notes at the other end.'

We sat in silence for several minutes, obviously both pondering what we should do now.

* * *

It was half-past two. With plenty of the day remaining, we agreed to carry on. But we decided at once that there was little point in visiting the clearly uninterested *commissariat* of the fourteenth district. We already knew far more than they did about Emilie's disappearance. No, we would return to that very helpful *agent* in the Fifth.

The walk back down to the Mairie under our shared umbrella was a ponderous one. And the friendly officer was no longer at the front desk. But his replacement phoned the custody sergeant again, and this time the senior man came out to see us himself.

We asked him straight away if he was aware of any reports of a woman found wandering the nearby streets during the weekend of the eleventh and twelfth of May, maybe wearing only a simple hospital gown ...

No, he told us. He had heard of nothing like that throughout the month.

'But I do remember someone mentioning a young woman had been found, a few weeks ago, in a run-down building in the Saint-Antoine area.'

'What condition was she in?' I asked at once.

'No idea. That's all I heard.'

Arthur had learnt the drill by now ... and the need for diplomacy.

'So which *arrondissement* is that, please? For the police station, you know ...?'

'Depends which side of the Rue du Faubourg Saint-Antoine she was found on. It's the Eleventh to the north, and the Twelfth to the south.'

I gave Arthur a warning look, and he acknowledged it and took another deep breath.

'And so ...?'

'Well, if I were you I'd start at the Eleventh. Place Léon Blum. Voltaire metro station.'

'Thank you.'

The rain had slackened to a light drizzle but the sky was still dark. I looked for a sign of a break in the clouds, but there was none.

'We'd better take the metro as he suggested, Arthur. It's rather a roundabout route, but if we try and walk it will take us quite a while, and it might start to really pour soon.'

He didn't argue. In fact he said nothing at all, and he stayed silent throughout the convoluted journey.

At the *commissariat* in the Mairie on Boulevard Voltaire, we told yet another policeman our story – still referring only to Rosie Renart, and without mentioning our own copy of Emilie's notebook – and we showed him our photographs.

He shook his head and said he knew nothing about her. We pressed him to ask his colleagues, and he got us to wait while he dealt with the people behind us. Finally he made a call, and a sergeant soon appeared.

He took one look at Rosie's publicity poster and nodded.

'Well, I can give you a little help. First of all, I recognised her before even seeing her name at the bottom here. She's been singing in the clubs just down the street for some years.'

'Yes,' said Arthur. 'That's where we picked this up.'

'Right. And the other thing I can tell you is that the woman you've heard about was found somewhere down near Bercy railway station. But that's all I know. Just through the grapevine, you see ...'

'Let me guess,' said Arthur wearily. 'Another *arrondissement*?'

'I'm afraid so. You need to visit the Mairie of the Twelfth on Rue Bignon. Take the metro to Dugommier. Change at Nation.'

It was just after four o'clock. Arthur and I looked at each other, nodded, and pressed on.

Half an hour later we walked into yet another police station, and we re-told our partial story and showed our photographs once again.

This time the man at the front desk nodded sadly in obvious recognition, and asked us to sit down in the waiting area. Arthur was just staring at the wall ahead. I didn't try to talk to him.

Two minutes later a plain-clothes officer emerged, carrying a slim manilla folder. He identified himself as Detective Sergeant Brazon, and he ushered us into an interview room.

'*Monsieur, mademoiselle,* I regret to tell you that on Wednesday the fifteenth of May, in a backstreet near Place Lachambeaudie, an itinerant maintenance janitor discovered a woman matching your photograph. She was apparently sleeping peacefully under a couple of large sheets of cardboard on the concrete floor of a small, disused commercial building. But when she could not be woken, he called an ambulance. She was found to be wearing only a thin, grubby dress and a pair of old sandals. Death was confirmed on arrival at the nearby Saint-Antoine Hospital, and we were then informed. In the reported circumstances, and pending the results of an autopsy, no investigation into foul play was commenced.'

Arthur's face had gone grey.

'Do either of you wish to see a photograph of her face before I continue? Just in case of any possible ...'

'No,' Arthur interrupted.

'Very well ... but we shall need to do that soon,' Brazon replied gently, opening his folder and consulting his notes. 'So, the post-mortem examination was conducted two days later. The pathologist concluded that the unidentified female had suffered, at some time during the week prior to her death, a medium-to-severe untreated head trauma, which was probably incurred after a heavy fall directly onto or against some relatively smooth and obtundent object or surface such as a thin wooden stair rail, and was aggravated by extended hypothermia. No inquest was deemed necessary, and a certificate was issued with name and age unknown and death declared as "Accidental (in the absence of other information)".

'Five days later, on Wednesday the twenty-second of May, she was buried at public expense in a pauper's grave in the Cimetière de Bagneux.'

He put down his papers and asked us if we were now willing to look at the photograph. This time, Arthur agreed.

And then he cried.

Brazon turned to me. 'A glass of water or some coffee, perhaps?'

I nodded. And as soon as the detective had left the room I gave Arthur the biggest hug I could manage.

After we had composed ourselves and drunk our coffee, the questioning began. But we stuck to our plan. Once all the formalities were completed, I said nothing apart from stating that I had never met the woman myself and was simply here supporting my friend Arthur in his search for her. And *he* played things very cautiously ...

'So, Monsieur Narone, can you tell me where Mademoiselle Renart was living in Paris?'

'No, I have not been able to discover that,' Arthur replied, quite truthfully.

'Do you have any information about her family?'

'Not here and now. I believe she had been out of contact with them for very many years. But I should be able to locate some. I'll need to work on that when I'm feeling a little stronger, and get back to you later – or ensure someone else does. OK?'

'But we are the detectives, *monsieur* ...'

'I'm certain it will be easier for everybody if I establish what I can, and then let all of you take it from there.'

'Very well.' He scribbled on a piece of paper and handed it over. 'Here is my full name and direct telephone number. Be assured we will liaise with our colleagues in the Nice police if we do not hear from you before you leave Paris. And we shall of course learn at once of your departure, from your hotelier.'

'I have no doubt of any of that, officer. But may we please go now? I'm really not feeling up to any more questions, you know ...'

I chipped in. 'I think Arthur's right. He's in quite a state of shock. You surely couldn't rely on anything else he might tell you today, could you?'

'I agree. And I would have recommended, in the circumstances, that you take a cab direct to your hotel. But I regret the taxi drivers of Paris are still on strike, and it is the height of the rush hour now. So perhaps a gentle walk in the fresh air this afternoon, rather than the pressures of the metro? It is not far up to Place de la Bastille, and it has stopped raining at last.'

'Yes, I think we'll take your advice, Sergeant Brazon. And ... well, thank you for your understanding, too.'

'*Merci à vous également, mademoiselle, monsieur. Et bon courage.*'

We had actually been walking the streets of Paris for four very long days, and as soon as we arrived back in our room our bodies gave in to the exhaustion and the pain of the latest news. We fell onto the bed and held each other close, and within minutes we were both fast asleep.

Love Hurts

In the morning I was up early and already dressed by the time Arthur awoke. And now he was angry – but not with me or anybody else.

'I could have come to Paris months ago, Julia, if I'd worked straight away on deciphering the bible notes with Pureza! And then I'd have found Emilie long before she started showing an interest in all of this ...'

'Maybe, Arthur. And maybe not. But if you *had* found her, you might never have gone looking for Thérèse. And then you and I would never have met.'

'That's true. And that would have been awful! But ... well, if you and I had come to Paris as soon as we got Pureza's information at the end of April, or even stuck with our decision to leave Nice on the fifth of May, we would probably have found Emilie within a couple of days, or at least on the Thursday evening when she was talking to Sophie for the last time ...'

'Or maybe we would have been caught up in that Monday's riots ourselves! Or simply *not* have had the lucky breaks that gave us the clues about where to look for her this week. *Que sera sera*, Arthur. Stop blaming yourself for other people's decisions and actions – good or bad.'

'But we sat around enjoying ourselves in Nice all the time she was ...'

'Yes, we did. And we played no part in her tragic death – whatever the cause. Anyway, what makes you think we could have made any difference, even if we *had* found her that week? Let's face it – she didn't want anything more to do with you. In fact I suspect she actually *hated* you for what you did in Nice and the effect it had on her life! And as for me: can you imagine what she would have said? "Excuse me?? Who the hell are *you*, baby Julia? Some sort of reactionary Sister of Mercy come to redeem me? Just piss off, will you!" Hah! No thanks, Arthur.'

He had given up and was just staring at the blankets. I knew there was no point in any more talk, for now.

'OK, I'm going out on my own for a while. I suggest you have a good think about how you plan to move on from here.'

As I opened the door, Arthur looked up at me with tears in his eyes.

'Thank you for all you have done to help me find her, Julia.'

I nodded sadly, and went for my walk.

I had planned to be out for quite a while, but I soon began to regret what I had said to my poor grieving man, and after a single turn around Place de la Bastille in the dull morning light I was back in our room only thirty minutes later.

Arthur was sitting on the edge of the bed with our copy of Emilie's journal hanging loosely in his hand.

'I'm so sorry, *chéri*,' I whispered. I went over to him, knelt down, and gave him a hug and a long, tender kiss.

'It's OK, Julia,' he murmured. 'You were right in everything you said. You need to take a look at this ...'

And he handed me the first few sheets of paper. They were the entries Emilie had made back in 1958.

'Are you sure you want me to?'

'Yes.'

'Really sure?'

'Yes.'

'OK.'

I sat down beside him on the bed, drew him close, and started to read.

<u>Sunday 12 October 1958</u>

It was Béatrice's sixteenth birthday today, and something made me want to speak to her again after all these months – no, years. So I phoned her at a time when I guessed mother and father would be out of the house.

But the two of us were still distant, still at odds on every front. Still both angry with each other for our stubbornness. Nothing in common.

She will never change. Why did I bother to call her?

I had to buy a notebook and write this down. Don't ask me why.

'That ties up with what Pureza told us, doesn't it?'

25 October

There was a really cute boy at the club this evening. I fell in love with his eyes in an instant, and I sang him a special song on the spot. He could have carried me off to Wonderland if he'd wanted to!

But although he smiled like a Cheshire cat all the way through my song, *and* the rest of my performance, he completely ignored me when I came back out for a drink with the gang at the end of the show. And then he just walked out.

Why are men so useless? And why do I get so angry, so easily?

2 January 1959

Arthur and I have been seeing each other for two whole months, but my birthday and Christmas Day and New Year's Day all passed with nothing special to mark them. Maybe he really doesn't know how to celebrate. He's very unwilling to talk about himself, even though I've told him *my* whole life story already ...

<u>10 January</u>

He walked me home, at last. After more than ten weeks! It was a lovely starry night. Could have been perfect. Then he just left me at my door!

I'm still not going to push him into anything. I want a bit of true romance in my life for once.

But how long do I have to wait?

<u>11 February</u>

I finally got tired of waiting. When he walked me home at two in the morning, after more Carnival craziness, I persuaded him to stay the night.

It was OK.

I still love his eyes.

'And that all matches quite well with what you told me about meeting Emilie.'
　'Yes.'

<u>22 May</u>

He was so reserved and undemanding at the start. But now he expects me to be there whenever it suits him. And he just ... well, he just takes me whenever he wants to. He seems to think I'm happy about all of that.

Maybe I should complain. But I still ....

'But *that* doesn't sound at all like you!'
　'Keep reading, Julia.'
　'I'm not sure I ...'
　'Please keep reading.'

<u>6 July</u>

He's been pestering me to go off on holiday with him. But he doesn't recognise how hard it would be for me to be away from the club in the high season. I told him to try asking his own boss for time off when the garage was at its busiest, and see what *he* said. That shut him up.

<u>9 September</u>

I finally gave in, and we've just spent a week in a tacky corner of the so-called Italian Riviera. The little rabbit couldn't keep his hands off me the whole time! And he was keen enough to celebrate his *own* birthday in a "very special" way. No prizes for guessing how.

I *still* love his eyes. And I *still* want my first true love to be my last. But it really isn't working. What shall I do??

'I've never seen you behave like that, Arthur!'
    'Huh! I was twenty-one that week, Julia, but I might as well have been fourteen. Nobody ever gave me any advice on how to live in the real world ...'

<u>30 October</u>

We had a row at the club tonight. I'd told him I had a headache after the show and wanted to go straight home. He said he didn't believe me.

I didn't have a headache.

<u>12 November</u>

I can't understand why he's suddenly become so secretive about what he's been doing recently. And he seems to be really preoccupied with something.

I reckon he's got another girlfriend. What shall I do??

<u>20 November</u>

He has aggravated me so much this month! So I didn't bother to show up for our last date, and I've stopped visiting him at the garage and his apartment.

And he hasn't reacted at all! Or rather, he's stopped coming to the club, and he hasn't tried to phone me there or leave a message anywhere.

Thank goodness I can't phone *him*. And if he thinks *I'm* going to start leaving messages ...

Oh, it's over, dammit! I was wrong to think I'd found my ideal mate. Well, good riddance to him. Maybe I'll agree to a date with one of the smoothies who've been showing so much interest in me at the club ...

<u>Tuesday 24 November, late evening</u>

I didn't get to bed till three last night. That guy was something else! So I wasn't up till nearly noon today!

I was due to play an early spot this evening, so after a quick bite to eat I picked up my clarinet case and a good book and went down to the beach for a few hours' relaxation in the calm autumn sunshine.

I hadn't seen any of the morning papers, of course, but I did notice the headlines about a bank robbery as I walked past a news stand. And just before six, after I'd left the beach and was doing a spot of last-minute shopping in the New Town, I saw the "LATEST DRAMATIC NEWS" being trumpeted on the final edition. Don't ask me why, but I bought a copy, and I was then shocked to see the report about *him* and a reference to *me* (though mercifully I was not named)!!

Actually, I was not just shocked. I was really angry with him and very frightened for myself.

But – stupid girl!! – I then agonised for ages over whether to visit him at the police station and "get involved" or just leave him to stew in his own juice. And I finally decided I'd already had enough, and now this! I don't need it. I have a life to live.

So I made my way towards the club. The show must go on. I was planning to get changed a little earlier than usual, and then try to shake off my anger by having a quick drink with Max and anyone else who might be around that early in the evening.

But as I approached the place I saw two youths lounging around outside. As soon as they saw me they started to walk slowly towards me! Seeing that newspaper report had given me the advantage over them! I ran straight back up the busy little backstreet and out onto the boulevard, and dived into a taxi.

The old boy whose apartment overlooks our street saw me arrive, and as I walked down the corridor he came out and told me there had been people knocking on my door on and off all day!

I knew at once that I must get away. I was packed and ready to leave by eight. My neighbour opened his door again as I passed by. I had worked out what I was going to say, if questioned, and I told him I was going straight to Marseilles. Which is the last place I'd ever want to go!

I hurried out into the darkness, and once I was at least three blocks away I took another taxi to the New Town. I found a hotel where I knew the receptionist quite well, and for a very good tip he let me have a room for one short night with no questions asked.

At half-past nine that evening I phoned the club and quit. Max was not at all happy! So now I have another "enemy" ... and it's ALL ARTHUR'S FAULT! Oh, how I despise him for having done this to me. It's the last straw, and I will never forgive him. But I will not waste my time trying to tell him that, or anything else.

Thank goodness he'll probably be going to prison for many years!

I *must* try to get some sleep now.

<u>Wednesday 25 November</u>

I left the hotel as agreed at six o'clock this morning. As soon as the shops opened I bought some hair dye, went straight to the Bus Station, and cut and coloured my hair in the washrooms. Then I found this awful apartment in the Old City and paid a week's rent in advance. That took almost all the money I had left in the world. So, late this afternoon, I hurried out and sold Grandmother's ring and her beautiful bible. I cannot even begin to say how much pain that has caused me ...

Then I bought a few simple provisions and came back well after dark.

<u>Thursday 26 November</u>

I stayed in this horrible little apartment all day. But after only thirty-six hours here, I already feel people are watching or following me. In particular, there was a young man on the street outside who seemed to recognise me as I came back from the shops again this evening.

I can't cope with this. And I can never go back to my parents or Béatrice.

Tomorrow I'm leaving this goddamned town for ever!

'I don't know what to say, Arthur.'
  'I knew that's exactly what you'd say.'
  'Do you want to talk about any of this?'
  'I'd rather put it all behind me.'

'Are you going to treat *me* like that in the future?'

'No. I promise.'

'OK. So let's talk about what we need to do now.'

We did not actually do much talking that morning. Just a lot of private thinking. And then we agreed to get something to eat nearby, and make a proper plan.

Paris was still a very unhappy city. The taxi drivers were out on the streets *en masse*, demanding further negotiations on pay and conditions, and there were rumours all around of worse to come that evening. And our lunch was a very sombre affair.

I suggested to Arthur that he might like to visit the cemetery. At first he said 'No!' without appearing to even consider the idea. I gave him a quizzical look.

'I've been thinking about that all morning, Julia. I'm not ready for it yet – if ever. Still too much guilt. Do *you* want to go there?'

'No. But then I don't feel the need to close anything off ...'

'All right. I'll make a final decision on it before we leave the city. But I *do* know what I want to do this afternoon ...'

We left the restaurant and walked down Rue de Lappe, past the Cheval à Bascule music club and then along to the narrow, unassuming Passage Josset. We knocked on a lot of doors and showed our poster photo to everyone who answered. And finally somebody pointed us at the apartment of the landlord of the block where they knew "Rosie Renart" had been living.

The old man shook his head sadly as soon as we mentioned we were friends of hers.

'Ah! Where has she gone, *la grisette*? I have not seen her since the Saturday after the night of the barricades! She was wearing a dirty old dress and she looked very different from usual, very tired and distant, you know, and she did not even acknowledge me when I asked her how she was. She just walked straight out of the front door of the building ...'

We broke the news of her death to the poor man as gently as we could, and he was clearly distraught.

'*Ah, bon Dieu!* I adored our little Rosie! *Mais quelle tragédie!*'

And then he beckoned us inside and showed us her room. And he agreed without argument to hand over all her possessions, since – he whispered – she really should not have been living there without ever showing him any identification. He had been planning to sell it all soon, anyway ...

We packed up Emile's clothes and her other bits and pieces, and gave the landlord a little cash in compensation for his help. Then we set out again along Rue de Charonne and followed an indirect route back to our hotel, avoiding all the streets where we knew she had worked. We were carrying two old suitcases and a steel-string guitar.

* * *

'What are you going to do about telling Emilie's family, Arthur?'

'Hmmm. I certainly don't think we should try to contact them out of the blue from here, especially since we haven't yet digested the news properly ourselves. There's hardly any big rush, is there? And I somehow feel Pureza should be involved ... if she wants to be.'

'I agree. So what else do you think we need to do in Paris?'

'Well, maybe we should let a few other people know what we've learnt about "Rosie". Old Hubert, for example? Or Oscar and Sophie, and perhaps even that other club owner? And what about the Cochin Hospital?'

'Or we *could* just leave her landlord and the grapevine to do the job for us.'

'How about keeping our options open? Let's get hold of a telephone directory and note down a few numbers. Then we can contact anyone we choose, if and when we decide to.'

'Good idea. And then ...?'

'Well, we've come all this way and we've been focused on Emilie almost the whole time. Maybe we should try and enjoy a bit of Paris together before we go home to tidy things up – and for you to sit your exams, of course!'

'I think I'll find it rather hard to be as carefree as I've always imagined I would be on my first trip here, Arthur. And it must be even harder for you ...'

'Yeah. OK, how about giving it twenty-four hours? If we can shake off the mood by then, maybe we'll stay a little longer. But if not, we'll hit the road on Thursday.'

'Sold.'

We had a special dinner at Le Bastille early that evening, and toasted the memory of Emilie as bravely as we could. Then we went wearily to bed. The mood had certainly not yet been shaken off.

And at breakfast the following morning we learnt there had been yet more violent demonstrations during the night, with barricades once again raised across the city from the Latin Quarter to the Gare du Nord. The students were now protesting against police action during a strike at a car factory the previous day. It had resulted in serious injuries and the death of one of the workers.

We decided, rather uncertainly, to stick with our plan to visit some of the wonders of the Right Bank, and we spent the morning in the Louvre, shutting out the madness for a few hours and revelling in the glory of the fine arts.

But when we stopped at a café for a quick drink and a bite to eat, we heard on the radio that another of those striking car workers had died from his injuries. And then came the news that a one-hour nationwide protest stoppage had been called for three o'clock that very afternoon.

And there were still students barricaded inside the Sorbonne.

'We've gotta get out of this place, Arthur. First thing tomorrow, please ...'

'Of course. We can do it all properly another time, right?'

'Right. But what about the rest of the day? How about the Bagneux Cemetery, *enfin*?'

'No, I still can't face that, Julia. But let's go across to the Père Lachaise Cemetery instead, before the buses grind to a halt. We should be safe enough there, and we can honour our artistic heroes and remember Emilie as one of them at the same time.'

'Nice idea, *chéri*. Let's do it. Now.'

* * *

Early the following morning, at the Gare de Lyon just twenty minutes before our train was due to depart, Arthur called Detective Sergeant Brazon to thank him again for all his help, and to say that he regrettably had nothing yet to report, but that he soon would have. And to save the good officer any wasted time or personal embarrassment in the immediate future, he casually dropped the name and phone number of Chief Inspector Simon Hardy as his personal point of reference among his many friends in the Nice police force.

Home Truths

I was stunned at Arthur's insistence on taking a taxi direct from Nice-Ville station to the police headquarters on Rue Gioffredo. I had not seen him act so decisively since leaving prison! But although I was feeling drained by the long day's journey and the sadness of my reflections on everything we had seen and discussed at the Père Lachaise Cemetery, I did not argue with my man. He was surely close to the end of his long drawn-out crisis, and the sooner it was resolved, the better for us both ...

The *agent* at the front desk at once recognised "Narone" and was quite short with him. Arthur ignored this put-down with admirable style, and simply said we wished to see Simon Hardy at once, *s'il vous plaît, monsieur*. The young officer remained unmoved. Arthur then remarked that he would *not* want to be in that man's shoes if he were now obliged to wander back out to the nearest phone box and call his good friend Simon on his direct extension number 312 to report that ....

The guy suddenly got the message.

'Welcome back from Paris in the spring, young lovers!'

I was stunned for the second time in thirty minutes! While Arthur and Hardy were shaking hands like old football team-mates, I could not stop myself from blurting out 'You knew we were there??'

Hardy gave Arthur a gently raised eyebrow.

'But of course, Julia,' smiled Arthur. 'Simon was my insurance policy ...'

I shut my mouth while the going was still half-good. And then Arthur told the Chief Inspector all about Emilie. The man was clearly *very* sad to hear the news. And no, he had not yet been contacted by the Paris police.

'Good,' said Arthur, 'because that's why I've come here straight from the railway station. I had to ... well, let's just say I needed to limit the completeness of some of my statements to Detective Sergeant Brazon. But he really is one of the good guys, Simon. So perhaps you ...'

And the Chief Inspector promised Arthur he would square everything with Paris, as and when it became necessary.

* * *

We visited Pureza the following day. She put up her "Closed" sign as soon as she saw the looks on our faces, and Arthur then gave her a full account of all that had happened in Paris over the previous week.

She was looking at him with pity in her eyes when he finally fell silent.

'I don't need to tell you how sorry I am, do I?'

'No, Pureza, you don't. I always said you were a saint – although I guess I never said it to your face! – and I would expect nothing less.'

'I'm very glad you said that with your ironic smile, Arthur, or we'd already be in a fight to the death.'

'Hah! So now I need to decide how to break it to Emilie's parents. Simon Hardy is content with leaving it to me – he doesn't think he needs to get involved in that particular side of things ...'

'Are you happy to dive headfirst into that quagmire yourself?'

'Definitely not! I just feel I have to. But if you'd like to help in any way ...'

'What do you think they really need to know, Arthur?'

'Simply that the daughter they rejected all those years ago is now lying dead in an unmarked grave. That all her worldly goods are presently gathering dust in a hospital in Paris and some wardrobes in Nice. And that a very understanding police sergeant is looking forward to hearing from them as soon as possible. They can take it from there, if they care to.'

'Do you also think they need to know that it was your actions in 1959 that sent Emilie to that fate?'

'They'll find that out soon enough anyway, if and when they recover her journal from the hospital. But what do *you* think about that, Pureza?'

'I think we need to respect the life decisions of an adult woman, and leave it at that.'

'OK. So who's going to make the call ...?'

Saint Pureza telephoned the saintly Béatrice the very next day, and broke the news to her as gently as she could.

She told us soon afterwards that she had been surprised at how badly the young woman had taken it, considering the strength of her antipathy towards her sister in Pureza's original call. And so she had no doubt that the whole family, under Béatrice's persuasion, would follow things up with the kindly Sergeant Brazon and perhaps, in time, find a way to bring the soul of their errant daughter back into their hearts.

Arthur, bless him, then suggested with absolutely no prompting that he would collect Emilie's family bible and her grandmother's ring from Pureza's place at the earliest opportunity, and would arrange for them, and all the items we had retrieved from Rosie Renart's humble Paris apartment, to be delivered anonymously by courier to her parents' luxurious Cimiez home.

* * *

Late this afternoon, Arthur took me down to the Old City, to Rue Droite and the apartment where he had eventually found the pink sofa and its cache of stolen money. He said he was confident the elderly couple would be at home – if they were still alive.

He was right, of course.

The old man opened his door warily at first, then more widely once he'd taken a good look at the pair of us. But he said nothing. His wife was hovering nervously in the kitchen.

Arthur extended his hand. He was holding a sheaf of modern banknotes.

'One thousand New Francs, *monsieur*. For you and *madame*.'

The old boy did not move a muscle.

Arthur smiled, reached forward, tucked the notes into the man's shirt pocket, and said *'Et merci.'* Then he took my hand and led me back down the corridor.

We reached the stairs and I glanced back over my shoulder. The old man was still standing in the doorway, watching us disappear, with a very bemused look on his very tired face.

One block further down Rue Rossetti, just fifty metres from the Happy Halliday piped music bar, Arthur stopped and pulled out his penknife. He knelt down, quickly gouged out a single cobblestone, and stuffed it in his pocket. I started to protest, but he just said 'Sshhhh, Julia. This is *my* ending.'

We strolled arm-in-arm down to the Place du Palais, and he slowly walked me round and round the square until he spotted a young policeman heading away from us into Rue du Marché. We followed him till we reached the corner, then Arthur took a quick look around, satisfied himself that no-one was watching, pulled the cobblestone from his pocket, and launched it underarm towards the retreating *flic*. While it was still high in the air, he took my arm again and guided me smartly off to the left, and we continued our promenade along the north side of the square. We never looked back, and I'll never know if Arthur aimed to hit or to miss.

As we crossed the Esplanade, he chuckled. 'I can think of a few real writers who would have enjoyed all of that!'

I told him I did not understand.

He said 'You will soon. Gratuitous acts, Julia.'

And when we got home, he gave me some more stories to read.